GETTING A LITTLE RESPECT

"Turn around." Cold, empty voice.

I did so, slowly and carefully.

Wakefield's Luger was gone. "So," he said, "you're not as dumb as you look, huh?"

"It's a struggle, sometimes," I said.

I kicked him. I let him have it with the steel-reinforced toe of my high-topped LeHigh safety shoe, smack dab where it hurts.

Vince Wakefield was strong, but was caught totally by surprise. He jackknifed forward with a strangled grunt. I caught him, hoisted him back up on his rubbery legs, grabbed the open collar of his denim shirt with one hand, and with my other fist gave him several short, sharp blows to the face. I'm short on boxing skills but plenty long on mean. I spun him around and shoved him against the wall. He hit hard and slid abruptly to the floor.

You never want a guy to think that roughing him up was hard work, so I kept my breathing under control as I said flatly, "Get up."

He coughed and snuffled. His fingers roamed his face, assessing the damage. He said, "Ohh, man."

"Vince, old buddy, I was only warming up."

Bantam Crime Line Books offers the finest in classic and modern American mysteries. Ask your bookseller for the books you have missed

Rex Stout

Broken Vase
Death of a Dude
Death Times Three
Fer-de-Lance
The Final Deduction
Gambit
The Rubber Band
Too Many Cooks
The Black Mountain
Plot It Yourself
Three for the Chair

Max Allan Collins

The Dark City
Bullet Proof

A. E. Maxwell

Just Another Day in Paradise
Gatsby's Vineyard
The Frog and the Scorpion
Just Enough Light to Kill

Joseph Louis

Madelaine
The Trouble with Stephanie

P. M. Carlson

Murder Unrenovated
Rehearsal for Murder

Dick Lupoff

The Comic Book Killer

Margaret Maron

The Right Jack
Baby Doll Games
One Coffee With
coming soon: Corpus Christmas

Randy Russell

Hot Wire

Marilyn Wallace

Primary Target

William Murray

When the Fat Man Sings
coming soon: The King of the
   Nightcap

Robert Goldsborough

Murder in E Minor
Death on Deadline
The Bloodied Ivy
coming soon: The Last
   Coincidence

Sue Grafton

"A" Is for Alibi
"B" Is for Burglar
"C" Is for Corpse
"D" Is for Deadbeat
"E" Is for Evidence

Joseph Telushkin

The Unorthodox Murder of
   Rabbi Wahl
The Final Analysis of Doctor
   Stark

Richard Hilary

Snake in the Grasses
Pieces of Cream
Pillow of the Community
Behind the Fact

Carolyn G. Hart

Design for Murder
Death on Demand
Something Wicked
Honeymoon With Murder
coming soon: A Little Class on
   Murder

Annette Meyers

The Big Killing

Rob Kantner

Dirty Work
The Back-Door Man
coming soon: Hell's Only Half
   Full

Robert Crais

The Monkey's Raincoat
coming soon: Fallen Scarecrow

Keith Peterson

The Trapdoor
There Fell a Shadow
The Rain
coming soon: Rough Justice

David Handler

The Man Who Died
   Laughing
The Man Who Lived by
   Night

Jeffery Deaver

Manhattan Is My Beat

THE
BACK-DOOR
MAN

Rob Kantner

BANTAM BOOKS
NEW YORK · TORONTO · LONDON · SYDNEY · AUCKLAND

THE BACK-DOOR MAN

A Bantam Book / published October 1986
3rd printing through September 1989

All rights reserved.
Copyright © 1986 by Rob Kantner.
Cover art copyright © 1989 by Steve Assel and Will Cormier.
No part of this book may be reproduced or transmitted
in any form or by any means, electronic or mechanical,
including photocopying, recording, or by any information
storage and retrieval system, without permission in
writing from the publisher.

ISBN 0-553-25717-X

Published simultaneously in the United States and Canada

Bantam Books are published by Bantam Books, a division of Bantam Doubleday Dell Publishing Group, Inc. Its trademark, consisting of the words "Bantam Books" and the portrayal of a rooster is Registered in U.S. Patent and Trademark Office and in other countries. Marca Registrada. Bantam Books, 666 Fifth Avenue, New York, New York 10103.

PRINTED IN THE UNITED STATES OF AMERICA

O   12 11 10 9 8 7 6 5 4 3

for
my six parents,
my three children,
and my wife Valerie
with love

CHAPTER 1

"Sure, I'm sorry the bastard's dead. He got killed before I could get back the money he stole from me."

When it comes to cash, the milk of human kindness is nowhere to be found in Joann Sturtevant. That isn't how she got to be filthy rich, but it's one of the reasons she's stayed that way.

I leaned back in the comfortable, upholstered patio chair and lighted a short cork-tipped cigar. The sunroom of Mrs. Sturtevant's Bloomfield Hills mansion was ablaze with midday light, and glowed with exquisite taste in furniture, paintings, and other appointments. There are prettier places in the world. There are prettier places in Michigan. There may even be prettier places around Detroit. Or so I've heard.

Through my fresh, fragrant (at least to me) cigar smoke, I watched her stew. Mrs. Sturtevant is the classic specimen of Bloomfield Hills widowed wealth: well fed yet thin, well dressed yet understated, well coiffed yet simple; angular, taut, blond, smooth; who is very picky about spelling "Joann" with no "e" at the end; a very damn good-looking sixtyish; a tough old broad who pays well.

When she didn't enlighten me further, I prompted, "Papers said it was some kind of commodities flimflam?"

"That's right, Ben." She pulled her elbows against her sleek flanks and gazed out a broad expanse of sunlit glass toward the golf course. This wasn't hers, she had informed me once. Though it had been offered to her, and she certainly could afford it, but,

1

after all, she'd added innocently, she already owned a country club in Palm Springs, Florida, and one golf course was enough for the average person.

Right.

As her gaze faded into the past, I saw the coarse uncaring sunlight revealing all her little facial lines, but she was rich enough and tough enough not to care. "Arthur Barton was a top rep for Trans-Ocean Commodities out of Cincinnati. Really knew his stuff. I invested heavily with him, made a lot of money. Then about seven years ago he simply vanished. Along with about a hundred and fifty thousand dollars of my money. Plus, so I learned, huge sums that belonged to other people."

"Didn't Trans-Ocean make good?" I asked.

Her voice went hard, gaze clicking back to the present. "Didn't have to. Turned out Barton was in business for himself, on the side. He'd set up my investments, and a lot of others, through a paper company that he controlled. When he disappeared, the company's money disappeared with him. Trans-Ocean, 'regretfully,'" she added sarcastically, "had no obligation to us since our business wasn't placed through them."

"Seems to me a good lawyer could—"

"A good lawyer tried, Mr. Perkins!" she flared. "I sued his estate, I sued Trans-Ocean, everybody else we could get our hands on. We turned them upside-down trying to shake money out, and came up empty."

Poor old Joann. 'Course, I didn't say this, I only thought it. Insulting clients can be bad for business. "So then he turned up again."

"Yes." Her voice had the quiet of impending disappointment. Of course I knew part of the story, at least what had been in the papers, but you let Mrs. Sturtevant tell things her own way. "Couple weeks ago. Turned himself in to the FBI in Cincinnati. Apparently he'd undergone some kind of religious awakening. Came from nowhere to do penance for his crimes. And, so I'm told, turn a lot of the money back over to the people he stole from."

She went silent as a maid came in and gave her a large chunk of cylindrical crystal filled to the brim with sparkling something and ice and shavings of lime peel. Of course the maid brought me nothing. I was as much a hired hand as she was. And, the way things were shaping up, this time Mrs. Sturtevant would be hiring me for more than driver and body-guard and stuff. Good. I could use the excitement and the money, not necessarily in that order.

Mrs. Sturtevant sipped her drink, ice clinking, and, uncharacteristically, didn't continue with the story. Not that she really needed to. According to the papers, Barton refused to tell the FBI where he'd been hiding during the seven years he'd been away. But he did tell them he'd hidden a lot of the money around the Detroit area, and offered to lead them to it.

So the FBI chartered a plane, and Barton boarded it in Cincinnati along with four special agents. Just east of Detroit City Airport, the plane went down, killing all aboard. An accident, they called it.

"What struck me as ironic," I mused, "was that Barton's wife in Cincinnati had just had him de-clared legally dead when he turned up out of nowhere."

"So she was put to some inconvenience," Mrs. Sturtevant said acidly. "Too goddamned bad." She set her drink down on the glass table between us, fixed me with a piercing gray stare, and said with great precision: "Now, Ben. I want you to go out and find my money and bring it back here to me. You want the job?"

I shifted, gnawed on my cigar, rubbed the back of my neck, squinted. Yes, I wanted the job. Business was slow. But, as sometimes happens, my insatiable desire to maintain a regular eating schedule went into hand-to-hand combat with an inbred compul-sion to level with my client. It shouldn't come as a great shock to learn that this has been known to cost me business.

"Seven years," I said. "And nobody knows where he was all that time. Long cold trail."

"You're a professional," she replied evenly.

"And, as far as you know, there's not a hint of where he might have hidden the money."

"I know you thrive on challenge," she said with uncharacteristic patience, figuratively leaning back in the fighting chair with her rod bending double. "It's in Detroit somewhere, that's all anybody knows."

I sighed, took a reinforcing toke on my cigar, and tapped off the gray ash in the heavy glass ashtray in front of me. Into the breach, as the fella said. "Case you haven't heard, Mrs. Sturtevant, you're world-class rich. A hundred fifty G's is chump change to you. You probably spent that on living expenses alone—"

"More," she interrupted, not bragging, just giving information. Given a choice, which she always is, believe me, Joann Sturtevant prefers that people get their facts straight, right down to that damn "e" that isn't on the end of her name.

"Okay," I said, waving my hand. "You probably dropped a chunk on your lawyer already. Now you want to hire me to work on it, and to be honest with you, there's not a lot to go on. How much more money do you want to pour into this thing?"

I was setting the stage in the event of failure. She can buy anything she wants, but she wasn't buying this. "It's not the money, it's the principle."

"With me," I said with a grin, "it's never the principle, it's the money."

Her first smile. "Don't try to con me, Perkins. I know you better than that."

"Then for God's sake keep it to yourself. I got a reputation to maintain." I took a deep drag on my cigar, pretending to consider. "Okay, I'll look into it. Have to do some traveling, I'll need an advance on expenses."

"Naturally," she said coolly. Her elegant hands went out and opened a plain manila file folder before her. She picked up a shiny piece of gold plastic and tossed it over to me. I fielded it, and stared.

It was an American Express Gold Card with BEN PERKINS embossed in black in the lower left-hand corner. Maybe I could do TV commercials now. If I played my cards right, heh heh. "Do you know me? Well, I unplug toilets and track down runaways and fix broken windows and collect overdue bills...." Well, no sense in dreaming; watching commercials is about as close as guys like me ever get to cards like this, usually.

Mrs. Sturtevant was talking. "It's in your name, but the account is billed directly to me."

I was still staring at the card. "What's the credit line on it?" I asked faintly.

"Adequate."

"Yup. Well fine then." I breathed deeply.

Mrs. Sturtevant went on, "I've also arranged a cover for you." Her hands went back into the file folder and came out with a couple of typed letters on heavy bond letterhead: personalized "To Whom It May Concern" letters from the editor and publisher of a major national news magazine, informing the reader that I was on assignment to do a feature story on Arthur Barton, and requesting the reader to render me all the courtesy and cooperation due to a member of the press. Very impressive and official.

I said to her, "Won't cut any ice with the FBI. I've tangled with them before, they know me, they won't buy this. I'll just have to steer clear of them."

She closed the now-empty file folder and sat back. "As my husband would have said, don't bring me problems, bring me solutions."

A man of many qualities, her late husband: top executive, former Secretary of Defense and also, apparently, phrase-coiner. I crushed out the red-hot stub of my cigar in the ashtray. "Can I ask you something?"

Her face said our business was concluded, but Mrs. Sturtevant is nothing if not civil. "By all means."

"Why me?"

"Why *not* you?" she returned.

"Hey, let's face it." I spread my hands, palms up. "I'm small potatoes. I maintain an apartment complex to put food on the table and do this stuff for walking-around money. You could hire a platoon of the best detectives. So why me?"

For the first time since my arrival—and probably the first time in the years I'd known her—Mrs. Sturtevant's imperious, businesslike demeanor slipped just a notch. "I'll tell you why." She leaned forward on her arms, folding her fingers together, eyes direct. "Because you're about the only man I know whom I can trust to bring me a hundred and fifty thousand in cash money without helping yourself to the goodies. And because you've done other jobs for me and I like the way you work. You're street-smart; you use the rules when you can and break them when you have to. You're not a pretty face or a smooth talker; you're a back-door man, like in the old jazz song."

"Never heard it. Musta been before my time."

"Not before mine." She straightened and stood, and what for her was a sentimental moment evaporated. "Good luck."

I know an invitation to leave when I hear one. I stood up, slipped the Gold Card into my shirt pocket, folded the reference letters into thirds, and put them in the inner pocket of my one-and-only suit jacket. The maid appeared to show me out, and Mrs. Sturtevant shook my hand firmly. "Get it back for me, Ben."

"Do my best." It was the only thing I could promise her. I turned and followed the maid toward the foyer.

When we reached the door, Mrs. Sturtevant

called me and I walked back. "Did you hear that Emilio Mascara is back in Detroit?"

"No, ma'am. The union doesn't brief me on prison releases anymore."

She laughed. I went out to my car, a blue '71 Ford Mustang convertible parked in the sweeping horseshoe driveway, fired it up, and drove away.

Telegraph Road ran white-summer hot, jammed with rolling stock in both directions. I drove absently, thinking not about Joann Sturtevant, or hundreds of thousands of dollars lying around loose, or even about the American Express Gold Card whispering seductively in my pocket. Instead I thought about Emilio Mascara.

In a way, you can make a case that I got into all that trouble with Mascara because of my typically Detroit raising. Like a lot of people in these parts, I was raised by emigrants from the South—Georgia hill people, Mother and Daddy—who were lured here by the promise of five-dollars-per-day jobs in Mr. Ford's car factory. They married real young and started having kids late. By the time I came along, Daddy had long quit Ford's over some unspecified union trouble. He was a sour little scrapper with a sarcastic mouth and a lethal temper and, being right handy with tools and best suited for employment at a place where he wouldn't have to deal with people, he found his niche at last as a trim carpenter for the old Kerns Casket Company in Detroit.

Despite that, I was aimed from day one at the assembly line. My Uncle Dan worked for Ford's, my older brother Bill started there before I even got into high school, and that's where I was headed, too. That was the ultimate, the goal to strive for. There was plenty of overtime, the union protected you, the benefits got better all the time, the calendar was packed with holidays and vacation days and personal days, and once you made seniority the bread was good enough so you could get you a nice place to live, and a snazzy (Ford, naturally; we drive what we build) car, and a boat or a cottage up north, and every three years or so you even got to go out on strike, which was especially nice if it coincided with hunting season.

Man, I could hardly wait. Only catch was, my folks insisted that I finish high school. I did, too. I was the first and, to this day, am the only member of my family to do it. It was considered a monumental achievement at the time; I couldn't tell who was more impressed—the folks or the teachers. But along with that, in my junior year, when Ford's was working three shifts six days and hiring extra heavy, I signed up and put in two years on the graveyard shift till I graduated and came blinking like a mole into the sunlight of a day-shift job at Ford's River Rouge plant in Dearborn.

Hanging doors. Eight hours a day of hanging doors on Comets and Fairlanes and Falcons and T-birds, red, green, black and white ones, a never-ending stream of them, shiny and clean and stinking of rubber and leather and paint. Sounds boring, but it had its good points. Money, like I said, plus lifting all those thousands of doors gave me the shoulders and arms I still have twenty years later; and I really enjoyed the post-shift boozing and carousing at Miss Penny McNasty's saloon.

Which was where I got hooked up with Emilio Mascara, when I busted up an attempt by two beered-up chain-wielders to mug and roll him in the alley behind the place.

I had no idea who he was at the time, of course, and his name wouldn't have meant anything to me if I had. He was, at the time, a vice president and organizer for the union, but there was a shakeup going on at the top level and Mascara, like Nikita Khrushchev, shouldered his way out of anonymity and took over as head man of the union a couple months later. Nobody was more surprised than me when he looked me up and hired me as "liaison man" (a real scream, when you think about it), ending forever my five-year career on the assembly line.

I was too young and cocky and arrogant to see the thing going sour. All I knew was that I was wearing a suit to work, and riding in air-conditioned, chauffeured limousines, and eating in nice places with serious, important men, and regularly doing discreet, sensitive, and occasionally violent little chores for them. I was an efficient, dedicated, and valued employee. So valued that, when the feds came for Mascara, they came for me, too. It took three long years—1968 to 1971 are like blurs in my mind—for the investigation and trials to be over, and by the time they were, Emilio Mascara was on his way to Lewisburg and I was on the street, down and out.

Now, I thought as I cruised up to the stoplight at Tel-Twelve Mall, they've finally let old Mascara out.

I felt like it had been three or four lifetimes ago that I'd worked for him, instead of a mere fifteen years. I'm not one of these whining, pampered, self-indulgent introspective kind of guys. I never give a second thought to what I'm like. I've never worried about "finding myself"; I may not be any intellectual giant, but I know where I am: right here, see?

But hearing the news about Mascara's release made me think about what I was like back in the old days. The Ben Perkins who did strong-arm, security, and bodyguard work for that ex-titan of the labor union was a callow, hot-tempered, easily led, chip-on-the-shoulder jerk.

As opposed to the wonderful guy I am now, naturally.

I found myself wishing I could meet Mascara once more, to see how the Ben Perkins of today would react to him. Not that it was likely to happen. I was yesterday's news in Mascara's world, just as he was yesterday's news in mine. After all those years in the slammer he wasn't going to bother tracking me down, I thought.

Fifteen minutes later, he did.

CHAPTER 2

Norwegian Wood is a three-hundred-unit apartment complex on Ford Lake in Belleville. It's fully equipped with golf course, marina, indoor and outdoor pools, tennis and racquetball courts, sauna, Jacuzzis, and all the other absolute necessities of life.

I live there, not because I can afford it, but because I'm chief of maintenance for the place, and part of my compensation is a free apartment. In return for living quarters and a modest (believe it) salary, I supervise a small crew of custodians, lawn men, and security people.

Like most things in life, I more or less fell into the Norwegian Wood gig. After the trials ended and Emilio Mascara was carted off to jail, I found myself *persona non grata* with the union. Ford's, of course, wouldn't hire me back either. I inventoried my skills and interests and found none that matched the classified employment ads in the papers. So, like innumerable other young men in this situation before me, I pulled up my stakes, sold most of what I had, borrowed what I could get, and headed west. I hitchhiked, took buses, rode in boxcars a time or two, worked odd jobs on muddy construction sites and cheesy restaurants and bat-infested warehouses and smoky factories, and never stayed any one place very long. I had no money, but I also had no bills and obligations. When a town or a situation turned boring, all I had to do was punch my ticket, pick up my check and split. There was always a highway headed to somewhere I hadn't been. I had my youth and strength and independence, and I had it made, and boy oh boy, was I impressed.

I was also lonely. Though sour and bitter about the collapse of my union "career," after eighteen months of drifting I missed Detroit. You don't realize how much the old gal gets to you till you leave her. So, without promising myself anything, I made some "hi, how are ya" calls to cronies back in the Motor City. Come to find out that, while Mascara and his gang had been replaced by a high-minded group espousing reforms, ideals, and ethics (funny, though, how most of them still looked like Mascara and Frank Fitzsimmons and Jackie Presser and Chuckie O'Brien; meet the new boss, same as the old boss), there were still career men in the union who remembered me, liked me, and felt like they owed me, not for what I had done on the job but for the way I handled myself during the investigation and trials.

They couldn't give me a job in the union, of course. But they did line up a job as maintenance man at Norwegian Wood, which was, at the time, brand new. I came back to Detroit and took the job, telling myself it was temporary, a stepping stone to better things; I'd be there three months max.

Twelve years later, I'm still there.

Part of the reason is because they haven't fired me, which means that they think I do a pretty good job. And they kept giving me more responsibility. I started out there doing strictly inside stuff—carpentry, electrical, plumbing, drywall, appliance repair, and the like. Guess all those years of Daddy putting man-sized tools into my boy-sized hands, and then screaming at me till I got it right, paid off after all. Then a few years later they let me hire a couple of assistants to help. In '78 they assigned me responsibility for outside maintenance as well, plus a larger crew to supervise. Then last year I took charge of security, too.

Another reason I've stayed is that I'm lazy. The job is ridiculously easy, no one makes me punch a time clock, I get a free place to live, and I get a degree of populist satisfaction out of being an old ex–Ford Motor factory rat living alongside people who drive Mercedes and BMW's and Porsches.

Another reason I've stayed is that I like it. Daddy found his niche building caskets; I found mine in maintenance. Cleaning up. Fixing. Putting things back the way they were. Life in the gray zone between construction and destruction, including some of both.

Though, because I have a staff, I don't routinely get involved in the day-to-day work, I enjoy it when I do. In fact, I look forward to it. When a tenant calls or comes up to me, disturbed about a problem, I am of course sympathetic and professionally calm, but inside I smile. Other people's problems make me happy because I can't wait to get in there and find out what's wrong and fix it.

Yeah, Norwegian Wood's all right. I get respect and dough and freedom and satisfaction—in short, everything my little heart desires except the thing I really want: an apartment facing the goddamn lake.

Security is pretty tight at Norwegian Wood, not because it's necessary, but because it's part of the image the advertising people created for the place. Our residents fall pretty evenly into three groups: people who genuinely have money, people who wish they had money, and people who absolutely don't have money but get by somehow.

I rolled up to the guard shack at the entrance. Arn Vogel, the elderly security guard who worked days, sure as hell knew my car by then and usually opened the gate, allowing me to roll through without stopping, but this time the gate stayed down. Wondering if the miserable thing was busted again—the gate, not Arn, although there was always that possibility, too—I stopped the car, engine rumbling ominously in front of me.

Arn leaned his thin hatchet face out of the guard shack's window. His policeman's cap was askew, showing shocks of bristly white hair. Behind him his tinny radio—"eight transistor," he'd proudly told me a million times—crackled elevator music. He was about as scary and intimidating as old Mr. Whipple. "Hey, Ben," he squeaked, chin bobbing, wattles quivering.

"Arn," I greeted, grinning. Arn was my foreman during my day-shift time at Ford's, and one of the best the place had ever seen. He knew his job, he knew his way around and he stood up for his men. Foremen have about the toughest job in the car companies because they're not quite union and they're not quite management so they catch hell from both. Arn handled it well, plus he took me under his wing when I signed on. He hated it when I went to work for Mascara, and warned me against it, and as usual he was right. When he exercised his thirty-and-out retirement option, the least I could do was offer him the security job, which he took gladly. Arn was a lot older by then and had lost a lot of his edge, but what the hell, the security gate job was ninety percent cosmetics anyhow.

I gestured at the closed gate. "What gives?"

"Somebody looking for you, Ben." By God, he was excited, which didn't mean much, since in that kind of job a bird crapping on the roof gave Arn conversation grist for two weeks. "They're inside."

"Well, who are they?" Access to Norwegian Wood is limited to employees and tenants and people whose names are placed on the complex's "authorized visitors' list" by tenants.

"Didn't get no names, Ben. Man showed me a pass from the management company, asked if you was here, I said no, he said he'd wait. They're inside."

"More than one guy, huh?" I felt my jaw thoughtfully.

"How could I tell?" he bristled. "Windows were tinted damn near black. Could have been eight, ten guys in that thing."

"What, a van?"

"No!" Arn said impatiently. "A Lincoln limo."

"A *limo*?"

"A limo."

"I'll look for it," I promised, giving the gate a meaningful glance.

"Won't have to look for it. It's the biggest thing in there." As the wood gate rose, I shoved the Mustang into first and rolled through.

The parking lot was surrounded by the three big apartment buildings, and was laid out in parallel rows with those peculiar apartment-house entities we call "semienclosures." These were kind of half-assed roofs on stilts that our well-heeled residents could park their cars under and tell themselves they were doing a super job of protecting their wheels from the elements.

Arn was right: I didn't have to look for the limo. It was sitting in front of the unit my apartment was in: a block-long, sleek black execution of Ford Motor Company luxury that had never heard of down-sizing.

I'm cool by nature; I didn't stare at the limo for more than a couple of hours. Instead I parked the Mustang in my semienclosure, got out, and sauntered toward the entrance of my building. This put the limo directly in my path.

The driver's side back window sighed down and a heavy, jowly Neapolitan face peered out. "Ben," Emilio Mascara greeted hoarsely.

I stopped and stared at him, hands hooked in my pants pockets. "Hi," I said inanely.

He smiled wearily. Irrelevantly, I noticed that his teeth were still discolored and gapped; funny how you forget what people look like after a while, no matter how close you were to them once. As I studied him, I saw that he had certainly aged; there was hardly a vestige left of the scrappy street kid who'd come out of Detroit's tough Italian community. His dark face hung heavy as if it had been folded and refolded every day for the past sixty years; his hair, black as the limo, was thin now and smeared down on his big head.

He said cordially, yet in a voice to be obeyed, "Get in. I want to talk to you."

"No, sir," I said without hesitation. I'm funny about getting into black limos.

His lips pressed together with displeasure. The window sighed back up, the door opened with a well-engineered click, and he got out.

Emilio Mascara looked good for well past sixty after a lot of years in the can. He hadn't shrunk any, but still came up only to my shoulders, and I'm six feet period. His snappy dark blue suit was well tailored and right in style. Out here, in the bright summer sunlight, I noticed that his folded face was deeply tanned—none of that chalky prison pallor—and he looked fit and vigorous and radiated authority.

I'm not sure he was going to offer a handshake, but I kept my hand to my side and he did the same. He leaned against sixty thousand dollars of Lincoln iron as if it were a telephone pole. "So how's things?" he asked abruptly.

"Cooking," I answered. I remembered how much I looked up to him, back when I was a self-impressed kid enamored of my job and of the man who gave it to me. It embarrassed me to think about it. I said, "You look good. Prison agrees with you."

"Ben," he said in the fatherly tone I remembered so well, "when it's time for you to select a prison, make sure it's Lewisburg."

"I'll make a note of it." We looked at each other. I asked, "So how'd you track me down?"

"Blob informed me." Blob is a top union executive who managed to keep his job after the scandal put Mascara out of business. His real name is, of course, Bob, but he got the nickname hung on him for eternity after a flustered, tongue-tied local TV news reporter addressed him that way during an interview at the height of the scandal.

Mascara looked around the complex as if he owned it. Hell, for all I knew, he did. "Nice joint."

"*We* like it," I replied, proud of myself for daring to smart-mouth him.

"Ben," he said in a pliant tone, "I rode out here to see you personally. To thank you, man to man, for what you did for me during the trial."

"You mean, for what I *didn't* do." I fished a cigar out of my shirt pocket and lighted it with a kitchen match struck on my boot heel. Mascara reached out his right hand and tapped on the driver's window. It sighed down and the driver handed Mascara a long stogey and lighted it for him from the dashboard lighter. Mascara straightened to face me, the window hummed back up, and we puffed in silence.

He grinned briefly. "That's right. For what you didn't do. I know how the feds played it. They tried to sweet-talk you into ratting on me, but you wouldn't. Then they threatened to charge you, but you wouldn't talk. They gave you immunity from prosecution, and still you wouldn't sing. They cited you for contempt and you still played clam. You got balls, Ben. It wasn't your fault they got me anyways."

He spat out a scrap of tobacco, looked at me hot-eyed, and snarled, "Net worth! I *still* don't believe it! All those charges, all that smear they wrote about me in the papers, all those things they said I did, and the only thing they could nail me for was an accountant's double-cross called *net worth!*"

He'd conveniently forgotten his additional convictions for racketeering and jury tampering, which bought him the heavy end of his sentence, but I didn't mention it. All I said was, "Just doing my job. Forget it."

He looked at me. "I can't, Ben. I don't forget people who come through for me. I owe you, and I know it, and if I can ever help you, you let me know."

I said casually, "You been out of touch a long time. Hell, you clean missed the seventies, Mr. Mascara. Times have changed. I really can't think of a way you could help me."

Mascara smiled indulgently and gave the limo roof a proprietary pat. "I still got friends."

Anybody can rent a limo for a day, I thought.

Mascara was watching me closely. "Maybe you're one of them?"

I sure didn't like where this was headed. I said abruptly, "I got my own act now. What about you? You angling to get back into the union?"

Mascara made that sunny, gap-toothed, very Italian grin that—I'd learned during his trial, during the seemingly endless verbal jousts with the prosecutors— meant he was lying his ass off. "No, no, Ben. I'm an old man. I'm tired. All that's past, too much like work." He reached out and gave my biceps a brief, powerful squeeze. "Remember what I said. Something I can do for you, you just speak up."

I stood back very deliberately, breaking his grip. "Yeah, well, fine, thanks. Listen, I got a plane to catch." I gave him a half-salute and turned and headed up the walk toward my building. I got one last look at his face before turning my back on him. His expression was narrow-eyed, shrewd, almost cruel: a boxing promoter giving fresh meat the once-over.

I grabbed the door of my building, opened it, and paused to let old Mrs. Shaw pass me. She gave me that patented unfriendly smile bestowed on the help by paying tenants. Behind me, the limo door slammed and the big V-8 motor came alive with a purr. I let the apartment house door close and ran up the stairs.

Well, I thought, curiosity's more than satisfied. And Mascara could forget it. Guys like him grease wheels with guys like me.

When we let them.

CHAPTER 3

As I clonked open the bolt lock of my apartment door, I heard heavy footsteps mounting the stairs.

Dick Dennehy came into sight around the corner and walked toward me. "Enjoy your little reunion— heh heh—down there, Ben?"

I swung my door back. The afternoon was pushing ahead and I had to make tracks, but you don't put off an inspector from the Michigan State Police, even if he is also something of a pal. "Oh, you saw that?"

Dick puffed from the exertion of running up the stairs as he followed me into my apartment. Chaos reigned, of course: dirty clothes, newspapers, video and audio cassettes, general madness. Some people have the idea that lifelong bachelors are fundamentally neat. They haven't met me.

Dick swung the door shut behind him and said, "Sort of. I was waiting out there for you to show. Then this Lincoln stretch rolls up and stops. I says to myself, Dick, old boy, your buddy Ben's been holding out on you. He didn't say anything about being close personal friends with Mick Jagger."

"It wasn't Mick Jagger."

"No shit, Sherlock." He stared at me bleakly. "And, speaking of Sherlock..." he began portentously.

"*He* wasn't a licensed detective, either," I interrupted.

Dick Dennehy is a square-shouldered, square-faced man who's gone a bit pudgy around the edges. Gray streaks his short blond hair; gray stares skeptically out from behind his aviator glasses; gray is normally the color of his cheap suits. He could never pass for anything but a policeman, and he doesn't try.

Dick's eyes brightened with impatience, then he relaxed. "Got something to drink?"

"Yeah, but not now. I got a case, I got to roll."

"Okay, then I'll make it short and sweet," Dick said, voice brittle. "Over the past few months I've been hinting to you that the State of Michigan would be delighted to license you as a private detective.

And you've resisted our courting, which has become a real concern."

"Why?" I asked, starting to gather up the mess of video cassettes on the coffee table. "I'm small-time. I don't represent myself as licensed. I just help friends out from time to time."

"And take money for it," Dick reminded me unnecessarily. "In the eyes of the law that says you're acting as a private detective. But you're not licensed, which is an offense. And speaking of money—"

In the pause, I shoved the pile of cassettes onto the shelving unit next to the VCR, Marantz receiver, and tape deck. While there I glanced at my phone-answering machine. No red light. Good.

I turned to Dick. "What about money?"

"The penalty," he said, lighting one of his filthy-smelling Lucky straight ends, "is a thousand dollars a day. How much do you charge for your—how shall I phrase this—services?"

"Two fifty a day plus expenses."

"So if we nick you around one a day, you'll lose your financial fanny, to use a technical-type accounting term."

I stepped toward him, kicking old newspapers out of the way. "You busting me, Dick?"

"No." Dick stuck his weed in the corner of his mouth, went into his coat pocket and came out with a folded paper. "I'm here to get you to fill this out. Sit down."

Since I dislike taking orders from policemen posing as pals who are guests under my own roof, I felt like telling Dick to sit on it and rotate. But fortunately I realized that he was in a real position to help me with Joann Sturtevant's problem. And, after all, forms are only forms. Besides, to be honest, Dick was right—I *had* been acting as a private detective, for over ten years.

It began because I needed—what else?—money. When I returned to Michigan to start work at Norwegian Wood, I was broke; I had a job and a place to live and a couple bucks of feed money, but I was out of everything else. What I was most out of was a car. In Michigan, you've got to have a car. Besides, we build them here and, frankly, you're sort of expected to have one. Since people are known more by what they drive than who they are, without wheels you don't exist in these parts.

I was hoisting beers with an old pal of mine from the assembly-line days, exchanging moans. Mine was money, his was the wife. She'd disappeared. In my beered-up cockiness I volunteered to look for her. To my surprise, my pal agreed wholeheartedly, so wholeheartedly that he pressed two C's into my palm and promised me the same when I found her. Which I did. She'd gone off with a long-haul trucker out of a Woodhaven steel mill, riding shotgun (and probably something else, too) with him between Detroit and Youngstown, Ohio. My pal paid me the balance without question. Don't ask me if they ever got back together again.

But it didn't matter. Word got around. I started getting other track-down jobs, more marital stuff, runaway kids. Personal protection work, too, like the chores I do for Joann Sturtevant. Corporate security. Courier work. Credential verification. Process serving, witness protection, advance work for public events. And the occasional weirdo stuff, too, like the time my sister Libby hired me because she'd lost her luck and wanted me to find it. And the old guy who needed me to investigate a coffin company to get evidence for a lawsuit he was filing against them because, in the middle of his wife's funeral, the coffin bottom cracked open, dropping the departed onto the venerable tile floor in the narthex of the Cathedral of St. Peter and St. Paul.

Though I could never make it pay as a full-time job, the investigating work gives me bread for my increasing inventory of toys such as my ultralight airplane, my motorcycle, and my stereo and video gear. My appetite for such things soaks up more than just the investigating money, so the income doesn't get me ahead, it just makes my slide down the tubes take longer. The work dovetails nicely with the Norwegian Wood gig, which, thanks to my staff and my (ha!) management ability, never requires my full-time attention.

And, though I keep the Norwegian Wood work and the investigating work strictly separate, they do have something in common. Maintenance. Cleaning up. Fixing. Putting things back the way they were. Life in the gray zone between construction and destruction, including some of both.

Dick Dennehy and I stared at each other. Then I sat.

Dick parked his big butt on the leather chair facing me and slid the form on the coffee table before me along with a pen. "Fill out, and sign."

It bore a Michigan State Police heading, and was an application for a private-detective license. I read the requirements with interest. "U.S. citizen": check. "At least twenty-five years of age": yep. "High school education": right on. "Resident of Michigan": for sure. "Ever convicted of a felony or misdemeanor": negative, no convictions anyhow. "Ever dishonorably discharged from any branch of the military": no way, never in uniform.

Then the killer. "Ever lawfully employed as: A. employee of detective agency for three years; B. as a detective, special agent, or agent for the U.S. government for at least three years; or C. graduate in police administration from an accredited university."

I looked up at Dick Dennehy. He sat spread-legged, elbows on knees, fingers steepled before his face, cigarette puffing in his lips. I said, "This last one, I got none of those things."

Dick said distantly, "Don't sweat it, leave it blank."

"You want me to sign this thing and leave that part blank. Right."

Dick said even more distantly, "It'll be took care of. Any more questions?"

I rapidly checked the rest of the blocks, signed on the line, filled in my name and address, and shoved the form over to Dick. He picked it up and tucked it away and made to rise. I said, "Okay, now that I've come across for you here, maybe you can help me with something."

Dick said warily, "Well, I've always given you a hand when I can. What's up?"

I filled him in on the Joann Sturtevant problem without referring to her by name. Dick seemed to sink in the big chair, cigarette burning untended in his fingers. I finished by asking, "So I got to start at square one, with Barton's employer in Cincinnati, then back into it from there. My question is, what dope do you guys have on him? Any speculation on where he was hiding out? Or where he hid the money, or anything else?"

Dick Dennehy laughed. "By God, Ben, you sure get yourself in some situations."

"Meaning what?"

Dick finished laughing and stubbed out his cigarette. He said, grin broad, "Every free-lance hot dog in the city of Detroit is sniffing around looking for that money."

"I got a client. It's a job for me."

"Yeah, okay." Dick flapped a hand. "Sure." He took his pack of Luckies out of his coat pocket, located his lighter, flicked it, and puffed. "I'll just, you know, take your word for it that a big pile of hidden, untraceable cash money is only of theoretical interest to you. Fine." He clicked his lighter shut and stowed it. "You have to realize up front that the State Police isn't directly involved in this thing. Jurisdiction's with the Detroit police and the federals, mainly the FBI and the FAA, or rather, their Bureau of Air Safety."

He leaned forward, worrying the cigarette with his lips. "But you know how my section works. The Office of Special Investigations is copied on any weird shit that's going on. Nobody's turned us loose on it yet, but I've seen the reports."

"Okay, so," I said, settling back, "give over."

Dick Dennehy curled his lips as if he'd just tasted straight lemon. "With a dry mouth? Get real."

The afternoon was pushing on. The Gold Card was burning holes in my pocket. The thought of landing in Cincinnati on someone else's nickel was biting me, making me want to get up and roll. But I was on a case, and Dick Dennehy was a good straight source, and I had no way of knowing whether or not his input would be helpful. I stifled my impatience, got up, grabbed a couple of Stroh's beers from the fridge, handed him one, popped mine, drank, and sat down expectantly.

Dick Dennehy schlooked half his beer down without breathing, then took a heavy hit from his cigarette and said, "Arthur Barton disappeared seven years ago, as you probably know. A bunch of agencies looked into it—the FBI, the SEC, the IRS—and got nowhere. Whatever hole he dived into, it was a good one and no one heard a thing about him till he turned himself in to the FBI in Cincinnati a couple weeks ago.

"Like you heard, Barton told the feds he could lead them to the money here in Detroit. So they chartered a plane to fly him up here. It was a Beechcraft Baron. Pilot was an FBI employee with about nine zillion hours in the air. Aircraft seated six and was fully loaded: Barton and five agents from the Cincinnati office. Origin was Lunken Airport, Cincinnati, and destination was City Airport, Detroit. Aircraft was westbound, about eight miles from City Airport, when apparently it developed engine trouble. Pilot called in to control at Metro—they handle air traffic control for City—and reported trouble. Guess he didn't think it was serious, he sounded calm.

"Anyway," Dick Dennehy went on, "the aircraft lost a lot of altitude. Thinking is, maybe the pilot was attempting an emergency landing on Conner or Gratiot or one of the main drags. Whatever, he didn't make it. Witnesses reported hearing the engines running real rough, maybe missing on a few cylinders. She came in real low over Gratiot, plowed into a dirty book store, and exploded. Everyone on the plane was killed instantly; on the ground, three injuries, one serious."

I took a long cool sip of beer, fished out a cigar, and lighted it, grinding the cork tip with my teeth as I puffed. "Any idea of the cause of the crash?"

Dick drained his beer and eyed the empty expectantly. With a sigh, I went and got him another, which he inhaled with a long slurp, finishing with a belch. "Ben, you know how that works, it'll take months for an official report. Unofficially, the techies are calling it an engine malfunction caused by a vapor lock."

A swallow of beer stood in my throat for a moment before I flushed it down the rest of the way. "You're kidding."

Dick shrugged. "That's the word. I mean, pilot error has been ruled out. Witnesses reported the engines running rough, and the pilot said he was experiencing some kind of malfunction."

I took another long draw on my beer. "Vapor lock," I said distinctly, "is the old catchall diagnosis that automobile mechanics give when there's something wrong with the motor and they can't figure out what it is. Somebody's putting somebody on here."

Dick smiled tightly. "I don't know anything about engines, but the guys tearing into that plane do, and maybe even more than you, Mister Ex–Assembly-Line Worker."

I stared stonily at him.

Dick said bluntly, "So you think sabotage is involved."

"I didn't say that," I retorted. "I just walked into this story, remember? I never *think* anything, anyway. I don't bend the facts to fit my theories. I ask around, gather the pieces, see how they come together." I tapped the ash off my cigar. "Seems mighty convenient the plane went down, that's all. Barton's leading the FBI to a huge pile of money, and the plane goes down. I don't like coincidences."

"Well," Dick said with finality, "for now it's being filed as a coincidence, partly because there's no reason to think otherwise, and partly because it's easier that way." He drained his beer and asked casually, "So you got a line on the dough?"

"Nah."

"But you're going to work on it."

"Yep."

"Scare you any?"

I looked into that large flat cop face and made a laugh that had some nervousness in it. "Should I be scared?"

"Ben," Dick said soberly, which was quite an accomplishment considering the quantity of beer he'd put away inside just a few minutes, "this isn't one of your little missing-persons or marital-relations or bodyguard or fetch-and-carry cases. This is real bread, hundreds of thousands, maybe over a million, in cold cash, small untraceable bills. There's a certain element of asshole out there that gets seriously crazed in situations like this. We're not talking the old knock-on-the-head and penned up in a pantry with a dirty hankie stuffed in your mouth. We're talking wrists wired together, down on your knees, and your head blown clean off."

I leaned back and looked down at my lap. "Damn! And me clean out of Elvis-sized diapers."

"That's right, go ahead," Dick said, nodding, "be your usual tough, hard-nosed, wise-ass self." He stood, stowed his weeds and his lighter in his jacket pocket with quick economical movements, and went to the door. "Just don't forget what I said. My advice is to develop a real close personal relationship with that .45 automatic of yours. You're going to need it."

I rose, cigar smoking in one hand and beer bottle in the other. "Can't. I'm flying, it's tough to get through security toting a piece."

Dick smiled, winked, and pointed at me with one hand as he opened the door with the other. Carole Somers stood in the hall there, fist up, prepared to knock. Dick said, "Oh, hi, Carole. See you at the funeral, buddy," he bade me farewell, and swept out past her.

Carole stepped in silently, face closed and sober. I thought about another of life's many little ironies. I could keep my apartment spotlessly clean and sit around there alone for weeks and never get a phone call or a visitor. Now, today, the place was a pigpen, I was in a hurry to leave, and people were swarming around me like flies.

CHAPTER 4

I closed the door and turned to Carole, who had her back to me. "I came to return your apartment key," she said tonelessly.

Some greeting, after two weeks' silence. I was, frankly, surprised to see her at all, and I wondered what she wanted. Let's face it, the key thing was bull. She could have slid it under the door, or mailed it back, or tossed it into the Rouge River for all I cared. I said, "Fine, thanks," and went to the phone.

The lady at Delta Airlines was more than delighted to reserve a seat for me on the late-afternoon flight to Cincinnati. I hung up the phone and chanced a glance at Carole. She'd caught the name of my destination and that cold cloud was crossing her face again. Though it had never come out in the open, she knew what Cincinnati meant. It hadn't been the reason Carole and I split up—as usual there was no single reason, just advancing boredom, the waning of sexual interest, and finally the killer: We quit communicating.

I said briskly, "You know how I hate being a lousy host, but I've got to pack." I went into the kitchen, rescued another bottle of Stroh's from the fridge, popped the top, and went back to my bedroom. I had my overnight bag out on the bed and was stuffing underwear and shirts into it, thinking that Carole had probably left, when she entered the room.

She leaned against the doorframe, arms folded across her chest, watching me. I went out of my way to ignore her as I worked, but in real sleuth fashion picked up a few glimpses of her in the floor-length mirror on the other wall. Tall, blond, perfect Carole. The Princess Diana hair, the rich dark Mediterranean eyes, the youthful smooth face with good high cheekbones, the strong jaw, perfect teeth, and snub nose. It was, as well I knew from the two years of our unformalized relationship, an expressive face: at turns perky, passionate, furious or fun, seldom at rest even in sleep.

She wore what I sarcastically thought of as her trial lawyer disguise: dark blue two-piece suit over a white silk blouse with a small gold medallion at the throat, and low, conservative black shoes. She was on her way either to or from a court appearance, and had apparently taken a moment out of her busy day just to drop in on little old me. Question was: Why?

She asked, her husky voice bland, "How long will you be gone?"

"Couple of days, more or less." Good old Positive Perkins, they call me.

She nodded, face expressionless. "Business or personal?"

"Looking into something down there."

Only a woman who knows you well can make the weary, skeptical look she gave me then. "Since it's Cincinnati, I could make a rather lewd speculation on what you'll be looking into."

"No foul talk in my home, goddamn it," I said with a grin. I went to the big walk-in closet, kicked off my loafers and jammed my feet into my black dress LeHighs with their steel-reinforced toes.

From out in the bedroom she said, "Come on, Ben, you can level with me now. There's a woman down there."

My .45 automatic lay on the top shelf of the closet. I took it down, hefted it, worked the slide, and clicked down on the empty chamber. Dick's parting words ran through my mind, but I returned the piece to the shelf anyhow. Dick's a street-happy cop, I thought, with an overactive imagination and a case of high-octane paranoia. Besides, like I told him, packing a piece on airplanes is tough. You can check them through in baggage, but if they spotted mine on the X-ray, they'd brace me about it, discover it was unlicensed, and then get real upset. Hell of a note: The damn hijackers screwed things up for us good guys.

As I walked out of the closet, Carole said in an even voice, "In my own inarticulate way, I'm trying to clear the air here."

I finished packing the overnight bag and zipped it up, fighting every step of the way. I checked the I.D. tag—BEN PERKINS, DETROIT—and tore three or four old luggage tags—CVG (Cincinnati)—off.

To Carole I said, "I got no problem articulating when I want. If I got no comment on something, then I got no comment, end of sentence, period." I grabbed the overnight bag in one hand and my half-empty Stroh's in the other and walked to the bedroom door as Carole quit holding up the wall. She was a tall woman, able to stare levelly into my eyes. I added, "And if there is a woman there, theoretically I mean, you never had no call to bitch, not after you and Eddie Ames."

I walked up the hall, through the kitchen and into the living room. Carole followed me. I dropped the overnight bag on the floor, went to the phone-answering machine, and rewound the tape; then I retrieved the remote triggering device off the top shelf. Real convenient thing, being able to retrieve your phone messages from somewhere else.

I wasn't looking at Carole, but I had no trouble feeling the ten thousand BTU's—origin: anger or embarrassment, I couldn't tell which—she was putting out at the other side of the living room. She broke the silence: "Okay, so you know. I'm not denying it. Now tell me about yours."

Time pressure was really on me now. Even if it wasn't, all this was sour, stale cardboard talk, leading nowhere. There was no more Carole and me, it was dead, and now time to forget about it, get past it, go on to something else. I couldn't figure out why she didn't see it that way.

I looked at her, cocking an eyebrow. "Oh, yeah? What you lawyers call a *quid pro quo?*" I grinned humorlessly. "You learned your law in school, but I learned my law on the street, and I'll share one with you: It takes two to quid. And you can include me out." I picked up my blazer, slid into it, and held my hand out to her. "We're closed for the day. I got a plane to catch. The key, please."

Her fair skin flushed furiously dark. She picked her purse up off the table, reached inside, and flicked the key toward me with a snap of her thumb. Lousy shot: the key bounced off the shelving unit and landed silently on the dark blue carpet. I left it there as she marched past me to the door. There she stopped, turned, and fired furious words like bullets in staccato bursts, trial-lawyer style.

"I sure as hell was wrong about you, Ben. Apparently, for you, women are wind-up dolls made only for screwing. You have the same childish interest in them that you have in your other toys, like your car and your ultralight and your motorcycle. Buy 'em, use 'em, keep 'em working, then, when you're tired of them or they break, toss them and replace them without a look back. That's you, all right, and I hope you *choke* on it, you bastard!"

I raised my elbows, spread my hands and bowed

my head slightly, eyes still on her. "What—did I *do*? I *invite* you here for this shit? You an adult or what the *hell*? I pop your cherry and then brag to the guys? Nah, no way, we had a *thing*, see, and it was great, but, like everything else, things die, and that's what this did and that's *all*. It's time for us to take a walk, Carole. Past time."

She shook her head somberly. "There's no getting through to you, is there." She opened the door, walked slowly through it, and slammed it like the report of an .88.

I stared at the expressionless door. Anger froze me, warring with the adrenaline that ran hot in my blood and the remorse that sat heavy in my gut. I shook my head once, abruptly. Good thing I had a case to work on, I thought. Between Mascara, Dennehy and Carole, it was beginning to look like a good time to blow town.

I quickly completed my going-away arrangements. I checked over my luggage, cash supply, and the like; secured the apartment windows; turned off gas leads to the appliances; checked the operation of the telephone-answering machine; and then, finally, made a call to Marge, who runs the sales operation at Norwegian Wood—and is not my boss or my lover, no matter what she thinks—to tell her I was taking a few days off and that all the maintenance assignments were booked ahead with my staff.

As I headed out the door, overnight bag in hand, I thought about Carole one more time. She was an adult, had had "relationships" before and would have them again, and surely must know by now that when a relationship dies, you let go of it, quick and clean. I could not fathom why she kept trying to disinter ours.

But with the Barton case to work on, I was just plain booked up with mysteries for the moment. Plus I was going to Cincinnati, which had an attraction to it quite apart from the search for Arthur Barton's million bucks in small, untraceable bills.

* * *

The flight to Cincinnati was routine boredom, and I disembarked the aircraft with the usual mob of tired businessmen into the modern terminal. For once, I got a working pay phone without standing in line behind 9,560 aggressive salesmen.

It was the first thing that went right that day, and the last thing that did for several.

I dialed Terry Lowe's apartment number and a female voice—not Terry's—answered. I asked for Terry anyhow, and when after a long pause she came on the line, heard my voice, and learned I was at the airport, she made a bitter frustrated sound. "Oh, Christ, I'm in Paducah!"

I instinctively looked around the terminal as if to verify that I had in fact landed in Cincinnati. To Terry I said, mystified, "But I dialed your apartment number."

"Call forwarding, Ben," came the long-distance sigh. "I'm here visiting my brother and his wife. You should have told me you were coming."

"Didn't know myself till this noon or thereabouts." Paducah, eh? Damn it.

"Damn it. *Damn* it." Pause. "I'll be back tomorrow. I guess I hope you didn't come to Cincinnati just to see *me*."

"Well," I said easily, "you're the only girl friend I've got in Cincinnati, if that's what you're asking."

"Of course that's not what I'm asking."

But of course it was, and she'd been asking indirectly and in various ways for a year, since we'd met when our lines of duty had crossed in the course of a rather bloody case. I'd been hired by a Detroit woman to check out her daughter, who worked for a major Cincinnati advertising agency and who, according to my worried client, was acting "strangely." I went to Cincinnati but just missed meeting the daughter, who was found strangled on the elevator of the building in which she worked.

Terry Lowe, an officer with First District Homi-

cide of the Cincinnati police, was one of the investi-
gators on the case. We discovered that the daughter
had been working a rather nifty blackmail game on
her boss and, when we confronted him, Terry blew
him away in the process of saving my life.

Since then, I'd made several trips to Cincinnati
and points between there and Detroit to be with
Terry. It was the ideal male fantasy, a compartmen-
talized love life: Carole in Detroit, Terry in Cincinnati. Each sensed the presence of the other, but I
made no disclosures. I guess I thought I could carry
the thing on that way forever. I cared about them
both equally, was careful to make no promises to
either, and therefore felt that my dual attentions did
neither woman any harm.

Now, standing at the open airport phone booth,
Carole's comment about women as wind-up toys echoed
uncomfortably in my mind for a second. But I shut it
out. I was in Cincinnati now and Terry Lowe was still
in the picture, even if she happened to be in Paducah
for the moment.

I said to her, "I'm here on a case. Convenient,
huh?"

"I'll be back tomorrow morning," she answered.
"How long will you be in town?" Voice intimate, next
to my ear.

"Could be a couple days, could be a couple
weeks. Depends on how efficient my sleuthing is."

"I hope it's *real* inefficient. I hope it's the most
inefficient sleuthing you've ever done. I hope you
screw up left and right and have to stay days and *days*
and—"

"I get the idea," I said, grinning.

"Call me at the division tomorrow after lunch-
time." There was a long, comfortable silence, then
she hung up quietly.

It was past suppertime, getting toward sundown,
too late to do anything on the Barton case. Cincinnati suddenly became a very large place in which to
have nothing to do. I rented a car, did some quick

shopping, got myself a room at the Westin downtown, and crashed for the night.

CHAPTER 5

Seth Flint did nothing to disturb my long-held opinion that every corporate vice president is a horse's ass. Haven't met one yet that wasn't a coat-carrying grunt with delusions of grandeur. Now, I have nothing against coat-carrying grunts—I'm one myself, have been all my life; it's the grandeur bit that gripes me.

Over and above all that, I was nervous. After all, this was the kickoff of the Barton case: my "opening night" (early morning, actually) as a fake journalist. At least, for once, I looked respectable. I wore a light blue blazer and dark blue slacks, short-sleeved white shirt with a sharp maroon tie, and I carried an expensive leather briefcase and a portable cassette recorder, all acquired the previous evening at several Skywalk shops in downtown Cincinnati, courtesy of Joann Sturtevant's American Express Gold Card. I hadn't left home without it, and already the damn thing was beginning to spoil me.

Seth Flint was slim and natty, silver-haired and mature, tricked out in a three-piece black pin-striped suit with a starched white shirt. Considering how hot and humid Cincinnati is in late summer, it was a lot to wear, but then, Seth Flint looked like the kind of guy who spent his life cooled and refreshed by air conditioning with no need or desire to go outside. Must be nice.

Gold sparkled from his big cuff links, the watch chain draped across his vest, his tie tack, and big rings on both well-tended hands. Flint's office was wholly consistent with my grandeur theory: lots of deep dark carpet, original oils on the wall, new, heavily stuffed and expensive furniture, a huge walnut desk with a bare top (no work in sight), and a gorgeous view out the big, broad eighteenth-floor window: Riverfront Stadium, the Ohio River, and Newport, Kentucky, rolling in rows of houses up the bluffs away from the river.

Seth Flint silently studied my reference letters. I was encouraged to see that he didn't move his lips silently, run a finger under the words, or call someone in to read them to him. Bored, I studied his heavy engraved business card. SETH L. FLINT. EXECUTIVE VICE PRESIDENT FOR PUBLIC RELATIONS. TRANS-OCEAN COMMODITIES, CINCINNATI, OHIO, AND OTHER PRINCIPAL CITIES.

I wondered what the "L" stood for. I wondered what made an executive vice president better than a vice president and a senior vice president. And I was wondering if Flint was taking so long to read two one-paragraph letters because he was proofreading them, or merely a slow reader, when he set them down and spoke.

"It's odd that no one informed me that the magazine was working on this story."

Diplomacy isn't my strongest suit, but I made a brave attempt. "We don't make a habit of revealing the nature of upcoming articles. Lots of competition in this business, you know."

Flint responded in a light voice, "And, no offense, Mr., uh, Perkins, is it? But I've never heard of you. Never seen your by-line."

Old Joann sure slipped up there, I thought. I answered, "I'm free-lance. My main thing is aviation; my book on ultralight aircraft is coming out in the fall." This was pure impulse, but I liked it, and, with my personal experience with ultralights, knew I could make the story fly—heh heh—as long as Flint didn't ask me a lot of probing questions about the "book." I went on, "The magazine gave me this assignment because of the aviation angle and the crash."

Flint pursed his lips and tapped the letters casually with his fingers. "This is the first contact I've had on it from the national media. The local press wrote up the story, of course, when Barton showed up here, and when the plane went down in Detroit. They presented it very competently. It's my job to see that these matters are presented competently, and to protect our company from unauthorized inquiries and incompetently presented articles. It should come as no surprise to you that, with the large amounts of hidden money being discussed, there've been some queries made of this office by transparent adventurers."

He stared at me. I stared right back. I noticed that his face was puffy and lined, his eyes milky and indistinct. This was a guy who, in his time, had gone more than a few rounds with booze. I puckered my brow like a good nosy journalist and asked, "Like who?"

He waved his soft, fleshy, gold-bedecked hand. "A man was here yesterday. Claimed to be a private detective. Very cagey. He got as far as this office and no farther, I assure you. Now: Mr., uh, Perkins, is it?"

I've seen four-year-olds retain information better, but I kept my own counsel. Another p.i., huh? Hm. "Perkins," I confirmed. "Ben Perkins."

"Mr., uh, Perkins." Flint leaned back in his big high-backed executive chair and gazed to his left out the window. "You must understand that the Barton, uh, episode has been a great embarrassment to our company." He said the phrase "our company" with reverence, savoring it like fine wine. "May I say, uh, a long-term embarrassment. We're concerned that any additional public discussion of the events will only serve to, uh, increase the embarrassment."

"You're a professional, Mr. Flint," I said, carrying it off with acceptable sincerity. "I don't have to tell you about the public's right to know, and the obligation of people in my business to report the news."

He perceptibly stiffened in his chair and said in a hard voice, "Cut the bullshit. The public's right to know is a very fine idea, as long as what they know reflects favorably upon Trans-Ocean Commodities."

I made my most reasonable smile. "Well, I'm doing the story regardless, and it'll be in the magazine regardless. Might as well see to it your side is presented—competently—as well." I permitted myself a moment of sarcastic humility. "Even a pro like me can make mistakes. I'll undoubtedly make fewer of them if you talk to me."

The glossy surface of his desk fogged from the moisture on his hands. His mouth pursed, and then he nodded abruptly. I clumsily set up my cassette recorder and mike, switched it on, propped a steno pad on my knee and industriously doodled as he talked.

According to Seth Flint, Arthur Barton was one of Trans-Ocean's star reps. A good, quiet, extremely stable family man. Friendly, universally liked, a hell of a salesman. He'd been with Trans-Ocean for over ten years before his disappearance, and consistently booked more sales than any other Trans-Ocean rep in North America. He used direct mail to uncover prime investor prospects, then visited them, closed the deals, and booked the investments. He was on the road most of the time.

Then, abruptly and for no apparent reason, he vanished.

"That was distressing enough," Flint said slowly. "Then we began to get phone calls from his customers. They'd received no statements or income checks from their transactions for months." I noticed that Flint was getting more fluent and loquacious as he talked, most likely conscious that he was being taped.

"We investigated," Flint went on heavily, "and found that the investments were never made with us. Apparently Barton booked his orders through a shell company he owned and sent his customers documents falsely stating that the investments had been made on their behalf. Instead, he kept their money for himself, and then began playing what I believe is referred to in some circles as the pyramid game, paying 'dividends' to Investor B with money he got from Investor A, so to speak, to keep anyone from getting suspicious. In the meantime, he converted to his own use, and apparently concealed away, many hundreds of thousands of dollars in cash."

I stopped doodling and stared at him.

"Million or more, we think," Flint said mildly.

Lotta clams, I thought. "Big money," I said solicitously. "I understand some of the victims came after Trans-Ocean."

"Inquiries were made," Flint said, tapping his fingertips together. "Meetings were taken, discussions were had. Our insurance carrier was consulted and counsel retained. We explained the realities of the matter in great detail to the—uh—victims. Though most, being sophisticated, educated individuals with great depth of understanding of corporate practices, accepted our explanation gracefully, some who had received unwise legal counsel displayed a shocking amount of belligerence, and persisted to the point of litigation, in which our company"—that savor again—"prevailed, naturally."

I found myself wondering if this guy had ever heard himself talk. I actually started for the cassette recorder to arrange just that, but saw that the tape had run out some time before. Hoping Flint wouldn't notice, I gave the graffiti on my pad a professional examination, then asked, "You people try to track Barton down?"

"For years," Flint said, nodding, "for years." He almost sighed, and I thought maybe this experience explained his white hair. "He'd simply disappeared."

"Till a couple weeks ago."

"Ye-e-e-s. But then. Unfortunately."

Somehow, I didn't think Flint's mournful expression at the thought of Barton's demise was genuine, but I didn't call him on it. I asked, "Far as you know, when Barton came back did he say anything to anybody at all about where specifically the money was hidden?"

Flint looked back at me with his dull eyes. He looked like he needed a drink badly. "Only that it was in Detroit. Beyond that, the FBI would not let him say. A silly security precaution, it seems to me. That's off the record," he added.

I studied my specious notes. "Is there anyone here that knew Barton well? Maybe worked with him? Or for him?"

"Barton was on the road most of the time. He had little daily or intimate contact with employees in this office." Flint considered. "He did have a girl, of course. A secretary. Jeanette McGraw." He paused again and I waited silently, not giving in to his desire to be persuaded. "She is executive administrator now. I suppose you will want to speak with her?"

I pretended to consider his question. "Yes, I'd like to, very much. Perhaps work some human interest into the story." I really had my journalist shtick rolling now.

Flint nodded, distaste with the whole situation obvious on his face. He was cooperating nicely, but he was also making it clear that he was doing so only to get me out of his life as fast as possible.

His ringed hand reached behind him to an intercom set on his credenza. He pressed a button and said, without taking his dull eyes off me and without waiting for an answer, "Miss Blanton, please call Jeanette McGraw and inform her that I am on my way to her office with a visitor."

I have to admit, I felt pretty smug as I followed Flint's short, dapper frame down the hushed executive-suite hallway toward the elevator. The best you can expect to get out of a guy like Flint is a lead, and that's exactly what I'd gotten. Now, we'd just have to see.

I'll never know, because I didn't ask her and have no intention of doing so now, but I suspect that Jeanette McGraw was a third-grade teacher in some previous life. The expression permanently engraved on her face said it all. Weariness, skepticism, latent hostility, and willingness—hell, eagerness—to learn and believe the worst about everyone.

Flint introduced us glumly and left as fast as he could—by now it was nearly eleven in the morning, he probably needed his first snort of the day—leaving me alone with the woman in her tiny, windowless, cabinet-lined cubbyhole office.

Jeanette McGraw was in her late forties, a tall woman with the shoulders of a bull and a figure that had probably once been decent but had since gone the sags/veins/wrinkles route. She wore a dark purple one-piece dress that went to her knees, was cinched around her waist by a wide black patent-leather belt, and was tight enough to show the definite marks of a girdle underneath. I had the feeling that if she ever inhaled a full breath she'd explode.

She made a quit-picking-your-nose look. I made my best smile, which got about ten percent of the way toward making a dent on her. She scanned my journalist credentials with distaste. I kicked off with, "Mr. Flint tells me you were Arthur Barton's secretary."

"Many years ago," she said, her voice a raspy combination of whistles, hoarse grunts, and loose dentures.

Many years ago. Right. I began fishing, walking her through her background with Barton. She offered nothing substantive beyond what Flint had told me. She had no personal relationship with Barton and, I got the feeling, didn't care for him one way or the other. She barely concealed her distaste and impatience with the whole proceedings.

It was half an hour before I struck a nugget.

"By any chance, are any of Mr. Barton's files, business papers, or other effects still on premises?"

The temptation to evade was naked on her face. She said finally, "We have several boxes of his records which he left. Yes. The FBI had them for a long time. A very long time. They returned them to us after Mr. Barton . . . passed on."

"Uh-*huh*," I prompted, scribbling like a madman. "How about letting me take a look?"

She volleyed back, "I don't think that's permissible. Our attorneys are trying to determine what our obligation is with respect to retaining them—"

She was beginning to get on my nerves. I interrupted in a hard voice, "I just want to look. I won't take anything. You can watch me if you want."

She drew herself to her feet, and towered above me, palms flat on her cluttered desk. "Mr. Perkins, I am not authorized to—"

I retorted, "Maybe you should check it out with Mr. Flint. I think he would conclude that supervised access to the records would, overall, be in the firm's best interest." I stood, reached over to the phone, picked up the receiver, and held it out to her. "How about giving him a call?"

Long-Shot Perkins, they call me. McGraw glared at me, took the receiver, and slammed it back down in the cradle. "Very well. Come with me."

The sub-basement storage room was long and narrow, with racks and racks of dusty old boxes, and two bulbs of about eleven watts each for light. I marveled at the volume of junk they had squirreled away down there. Even in this halcyon age of computers and electronic filing, there exists, particularly in people of the accounting persuasion, the very human tendency to *keep* things, no matter how small the likelihood is that they'll ever need them, and no matter how difficult it would be to find anything in all that mess.

Jeanette McGraw tottered ahead of me as if her

legs hurt, guided me down to the end of the room, and pointed at a couple of medium-sized cartons on the floor under a shelf. I dragged them out. Printed on each was the interesting imperative BALL PERFECT MASON, along with the debatable felt-tipped plea, DO NOT DESTROY MCGRAW. The woman folded her arms and towered above me, glowering, as I knelt and opened the boxes.

I'd just thrust my hands into the mess when McGraw let go with a sneeze that went off like a howitzer. She gasped, snuffled, and, eyes watering, produced a handkerchief from somewhere and sneezed into it three or four times. When she straightened, her face was gaunt, eyes shining, mouth a slash of anger. "Filthy place!"

"Dust, huh?" I asked sympathetically, then went back into the boxes.

It was a lot of old moldy papers: bundles of blue credit-card slips, files of expense reports, old copies of airplane ticket vouchers, ream after ream of mind-numbing proposals, and the like. As McGraw sneezed practically every minute, I leafed through the junk. Boring, boring, boring.

I was almost through with the second box when McGraw said hoarsely, "Excuse me," and darted out of the room, probably to clear her lungs.

At the bottom of the second box was yet another bundle, this one of two-by-two cards with typewritten names and phone numbers on them, and no other identification. I glanced through them curiously, and when McGraw came back into the room after a minute, I asked, "What're these?"

She squinted down through watery, reddening eyes. "Oh. Those. Mr. Barton carried a personal phone directory. A looseleaf notebook with names and numbers of his contacts." She sneezed again. Had the M-16 possessed her muzzle velocity, we'd have won Vietnam. "Once he misplaced it. Actually he left it in a rental car in Los Angeles. When he got back here and realized it was gone, he nearly pan-

icked. Fortunately, someone found it and returned it
to him. But he had me type out the numbers on
Rolodex cards and maintain it in my desk for him,
just in case he ever lost the book again."

She sneezed with a shriek that made the hair
rise on the back of my neck. I looked back at the
cards, then up at her, and said, as bored as could be,
"Uh-huh, yeah." Making a disappointed shake of my
head, I closed the cartons up and slid them back
where they belonged. With a look of relieved triumph
Jeanette McGraw turned and practically ran out of
the room as I followed her.

The hall was dimly lit and smelled of rebreathed
air. We walked to the elevator, and I said, "Well, I
really appreciate your help, Ms. McGraw."

The doors sighed open, we entered, and she
savagely poked the lobby floor button with a freckled
finger. The calming of her respiratory system had
restored her icy, haughty control. "An unpleasant
duty, frankly."

The elevator hummed up. I took her upper arm
gently in my hand and said conspiratorially, "Don't
bother getting mushy with me. I'm spoken for."

She convulsively jerked herself loose and gave
me an evil look. I think she was about to say something real honest just then in a loud tone of voice,
but unfortunately for her the elevator door opened
into the lobby. As we stepped off, I asked offhandedly, "Know anything about a private detective here
yesterday asking about Barton?"

"Yes. I spoke with him," she said readily, and
added with pointed venom, "another pest."

I kept my face placid, but inside I was surprised,
since Flint had said with some smugness that the
detective didn't get past him. Somehow the fella,
whoever the hell he was, had gotten to McGraw
anyhow. Resourceful. Apparently more resourceful
than I am, as hard as that is to believe.

Jeanette McGraw walked me purposefully toward the big glass revolving doors across the lobby

and past the conservatively dressed salesmen sitting on expensive couches, cooling their heels, reading *The Wall Street Journal.* "What was his name?" I asked.

McGraw's diamond-hard eyes glinted. "I don't know. He wouldn't tell me. He was obnoxious, abrasive, and impertinent. Thought he could just walk in and ask me questions about Mr. Barton. I turned him away, I'll tell you *that.*"

We got to the doors and stopped. "I'll just bet you did," I said sympathetically, facing her. "Well, thanks—"

"The big jerk even thought he could make a long-distance phone call from my office," McGraw went on in high huff. "I told him, no sir, you don't make long-distance calls on Trans-Ocean money. He got all sweetly apologetic with me and made his call on his credit card." Her face was triumphant at the memory.

"Good for you." I grabbed her unwilling hand and pumped it. "You've been a big help. If I think of anything else, can I ask for you personally?"

"If you must." She spun on her heel and walked away. As I thumped through the revolving door, I heard her sneeze again.

CHAPTER 6

Big, plush downtown hotels are not my speed at all. They tend to be chrome-glass-polyester cages with lousy, impersonal service, indifferent food, and zero atmosphere. Plus, I can never afford them.

However, thanks to Mrs. Sturtevant's American Express Gold Card, I could afford the chrome-glass-polyester cage several hundred feet in the air in the Westin, and I walked back there through the stifling, muggy Cincinnati heat after my morning at Trans-Ocean.

The room was big, obscenely big, damn near as big as my own apartment in Norwegian Wood, which isn't what you'd call shabby itself. Two big double beds stood on raised platforms. A heavy dresser and desk and couch lined the walls. A TV as big as a freezer chest stood on a swivel pivot in the corner and was controlled by buttons in the nightstand between the beds. A patio door with half-open drapes gave a view of downtown, and you could just catch the blue ribbon of the Ohio River in the distance. My mother, a hard-nosed proponent of cash-and-carry, manifest destiny, and the Protestant work ethic, would have been aghast: All this just by flashing a hunk of plastic? I shrugged and grinned, breathed cool machine-produced air, and decided I could get used to this in a hurry.

I kicked off my heavy LeHigh shoes, hung up my blazer, stripped off my sincere tie, flopped back on one of the beds with my briefcase beside me, lighted a short cork-tipped cigar, and became myself. The draft from the air conditioner wafted the cigar smoke away as I watched absently. Time to prioritize, I thought.

Far as the case went at this point, I'd formulated a pretty slick little scam to run past Jeanette McGraw, but that had to wait till the next morning. I also had to call Terry. I had to see what I could learn about this mysterious private eye who'd paid a seemingly unproductive call on Trans-Ocean the previous day. And, finally, there was Barton's widow to check out.

But, being a man with an unerring sense of priorities, I first called room service and ordered up a fistful of Old Style, having determined that they didn't sell Stroh's. After that I called Division One and arranged a meet with Terry that evening. Finally, I sprawled back on the bed with the Cincinnati phone directory beside me, cigar smoldering in the big glass ashtray, and began working the phones.

It sure would make things easier for fellas in my line of work if everyone had different last names. I had to deal with the fact that there were dozens of Bartons in the Cincinnati telephone area—which includes parts of Kentucky and Indiana, for God's sake; Interstate Perkins, they call me—and, as for BARTON, CLAIRE, there were two, as well as a multitude of BARTON, C.'s. None of them was Barton's wife, I found after making a few calls. I toked the last hit off my cigar and stubbed it out, thinking hard.

If she had an unlisted number, I was in trouble. But then it dawned on me that maybe her phone was still listed in her husband's name. Back to the directory. Three listings for BARTON, ARTHUR. Located in Anderson, Indian Hill, and Norwood. The middle name rang a bell, probably from the newspaper articles I'd idly read about the case before Joann Sturtevant hired me. I squinted at the number and dialed.

A civilized male voice answered the phone. Hired help? I wondered, and asked for Mrs. Barton. Unavailable, he said politely, and hung up.

A guy in telephone sales once told me you hardly ever close a sale on the first call. I mashed the cradle button and dialed again. Same male voice answered. I began by naming the national news magazine I was "working" for, and asked for a moment with Mrs. Barton. He hung up again. Maybe he thought I was peddling subscriptions.

The sales guy had also said, "Many are called, but few are chosen." But I wasn't out of tricks yet. I leaned over to the nightstand, switched on the TV, and idly spun the dial, looking for just the right program.

I was interrupted by a tap on the door, which revealed a short Hispanic waiter in white, who wheeled in a cart the size of a gurney with three bottles of Old Style, already opened, nestled in ice in what looked like a big silver trophy. Wondering to what heights of splendor they went when serving champagne, I grabbed the bill and only after scribbling my name on it—this is how those credit cards spoil you—did I check the price. Four-fifty a pop. *Wowee.* The waiter smiled and nodded deeply, almost bowing, and wheeled his gurney out.

I locked the door behind him and, rubbing my hands together, returned to the bed and the TV controls. Best thing, I figured after checking all the stations, was a broadcast of the incomprehensible proceedings of some government body on one of those public-access cable stations. Nice authoritative male voices, no music. Perfect.

I turned the volume up, picked up the phone, and dialed Mrs. Barton's number again.

Same male voice answered. Busy day for him out there. I let the blather from the TV go on a few seconds, then, in a flat voice somewhat higher pitched than normal, said, "Claire Barton, please."

"I'm sorry, sir, but—"

"O'Gannon, Internal Revenue Service," I said with perfect bureaucratic boredom.

"Ah." A pause. The politicos yacked from across the room. "One moment, sir."

Thank God for the old IRS ploy. Like the income tax itself, the con probably goes back to 1862, but it mostly still works. Who says we've lost our traditions? I waited, my face stretched wide with a big grin, which vanished when a different male voice came on the line. "Mr. O'Gannon?"

"Who's this?" I asked impatiently. No IRS guy would put up with this shit.

"Kevin Kohls, sir. As you probably know from your files, I am Mrs. Barton's personal and business representative. How can I help you?"

"You can help me by getting Mrs. Barton to the phone, immediately if not sooner."

Kohls, whoever *he* was, was a smoothie. "Mrs. Barton is indisposed. The events of the past couple of weeks have been a severe shock. Frankly, Mr. O'Gannon—"

"*Agent* O'Gannon."

"*Agent* O'Gannon. Frankly, it disturbs me that you're, uh—well, no other way to put it—bothering Mrs. Barton so soon after she lost her husband."

The TV cut away from the government meeting, and a fat prissy guy in jammies woke up his wife and began whining that he couldn't sleep. Damn it anyhow, you can't count on anything anymore. I clamped the phone mouthpiece against my thigh, then reached over and shut down the volume. Back in the phone I said, "I would be skeptical of a significant display of ashes and sackcloth now, seeing as how the taxpayer in question disappeared seven years ago, Mrs. Barton had him legally declared dead, he surfaced a couple of weeks ago, and was then killed in a plane crash."

Kohls was getting hot, too. "While in *federal* custody."

I decided to let O'Gannon have a small sense of humor. "That was Justice Department. We're part of Treasury." Guess Kohls wasn't in a laughing mood. "Now let's get one thing straight. I'm responsible for researching Mr. and Mrs. Barton's personal income tax situation. You must appreciate that, under the circumstances, it's a complex matter. I have to start by interviewing Mrs. Barton and getting some background."

A pause. Then Kohls said, "Why don't you start by interviewing me? As you know, I am Mrs. Barton's personal and business representative. Moreover, I was Mr. Barton's personal accountant and, if it matters, best friend. I do not believe there's a question you could ask that I couldn't answer to your utmost satisfaction."

I paused, gnawing on my thumbnail. The politicos were jabbering silently—for once—and I brought the volume up again to a dull roar. Accountant and best friend, huh? Why not? I'm flexible. "Well," I said with heavy reluctance, "in view of Mrs. Barton's purported emotional state—"

"Would tomorrow morning be convenient?" Kohls pushed.

No way, not if I was going to run my con on Jeanette McGraw. Plus, I decided it would be out of character for Agent O'Gannon to knuckle under completely. "I return to Washington in the morning. It is essential that I speak with you or, preferably, Mrs. Barton, this afternoon."

"Jesus," Kohls breathed. I sensed that he was checking something, like a calendar or an appointment book. "All right," he said abruptly. "I've got a supper meeting with a client. Have to see you before that. Where are you staying?"

I told him, hung up, then got underneath a bottle of Old Style and made half the contents disappear. I shut the TV off and stared at my reflection in the mirror over the dresser on the other side of the room. The guy looked glum and a little jumpy, and I knew why.

I mean, as Barton's best friend, Kohls might have something helpful to tell me. But I'd overlooked one fundamental problem with the old IRS ploy. If you get carried away with it, it can turn around and bite you in the ass.

That's what had happened this time. Now I was stuck with—and as—O'Gannon, with no ID or anything else to back me up.

Well, like my daddy always said, "no guts, no glory."

Right.

An hour later—after sucking down the rest of the beer, showering, shaving, and climbing back into my suit—I was just on my way out the door when I remembered that private detective who'd poked around at Trans-Ocean. I stood uncertainly at my room door, then swung it back shut and went to the telephone. Kohls could just stew for a minute or two.

I dialed a Detroit-area number. After a few seconds of long-distance purring, Kenny Slingluff answered. I could hear kids yelling in the background, and pictured Kenny, lanky and blond-haired and mustached, leaning on the counter in his tiny house in Garden City. "Ben!" he said, surprised. "Been a long time. How's it going?"

Does anyone ever answer that question honestly? "Great, just great. I'm on a case and I got a question."

"Yeah?" Kenny's a regular client of mine; you do good work, you get repeat business. Especially from guys like Kenny, who regularly goes on substance-abuse binges, has flings with shady chicks, invests in broken-down nags, and, to finance this, stays up to his hips in hock to friendly fellas of Mediterranean extraction.

By various means—which include, I might add, regular assistance from yours truly—Kenny stays straight enough to hang on to his middle-management job and wife. There's nothing particularly unique about him. He's just your typical 1980s working stiff who clings to respectability with well-gnawed fingernails.

I asked, "What's involved in running down a telephone credit-card call?"

"You mean calling card. We call them calling cards now."

Some days you can do nothing right. "Pardon me, I'm sure."

"Huh. You got the card number?"

"That's the trouble, I don't, but I have the number where the call was made from, and when."

"Well, let's see. Um, better give them to me."

I gave the date of the call and the number on Jeanette McGraw's office phone. Memory's a wonderful thing.

"Five-one-three area code? That's Cincinnati," Kenny chided.

"So?"

"I work for Michigan Bell, remember? Different state, last time I checked."

"Michigan, schmichigan. Ma Bell sees all and knows all, right?"

"It's not that simple, but what do you want to know?"

"The name and address of the person who made that call."

"Oh, man. Different operating company and everything. I don't know."

"I know you'll come through for me, Kenny."

"I'll try, anyhow." Pause. "I suppose you want this yesterday?"

"Have I ever been demanding and unreasonable? Hell, no! By tomorrow morning would be perfectly okay."

"'By tomorrow morning would be perfectly okay,'" he mimicked. "I could get my whang in a wringer, you know."

"Kenny, if a wringer was all you ever put your whang in, you'd live a more peaceful life, pal. And like my daddy always said, 'no guts, no glory,'" I said, grinning. "Talk atcha tomorrow."

I hung up and left to meet with Kevin Kohls.

CHAPTER 7

For a downtown hotel saloon, Yeatman's in Cincinnati's Westin wasn't half bad. It was roomy, decorated with understated elegance, smelled of good seafood, and attended by conservatively dressed, brisk, efficient young men and women.

Kevin Kohls had given me his description and he was, as I'd expected, already there, seated in a corner booth by the bar. I went over and slid my briefcase onto the seat across from him as he rose. "Agent O'Gannon," he said with a pro forma smile.

"Right." We sat. The waitress came over and took drink orders: whiskey rocks with water back for Kohls, Diet Pepsi for me. Efrem Zimbalist never drank on the job, so by God neither would I.

Kevin Kohls was a balding, four-eyed butterball: average height, wearing a sky-blue business suit over a white shirt and dark blue tie. His wispy hair was startlingly blond but mostly gone on top except for a few puffy strands that arched wildly over the shiny spot. Horn-rimmed glasses sat smack in the middle of his pudgy face, and he had a small, thick-lipped mama's-boy mouth that was petulant when it wasn't smiling. Looked like the kind of guy who, as a child, had never been told he couldn't have a cookie.

O'Gannon, I decided, was a get-down-to-cases guy. For a figment of my warped imagination, he was okay. I said, "You claim to be Mr. and Mrs. Barton's personal financial counselor?"

His smile was well made, but there was steel in his eyes and a sneer looming behind them. "No claim, Agent O'Gannon; fact."

"Uh-huh," I said in perfect bureaucrat: no acceptance or agreement, just acknowledgment that the words had been received. "And you are—or were—Mr. Barton's best friend, as well?"

"Yes. We grew up together in Point Pleasant." The waitress brought our drinks. Neither of us touched them. Kohls had fat, soft, unworked fingers and they played absently with the edge of his cocktail napkin. "Agent O'Gannon, before we go any further, can I ask you something?"

I didn't like having the tables turned, and I especially didn't like the way he kept repeating my specious title. "What?" I asked impatiently.

"Well," Kohls said, "I hate to be stuffy and everything"—which was a lie; this man was an authority in the research and development of stuffiness—"but could I see your identification, please?"

To coin a phrase: whang in a wringer time. Once, while yacking with a real, licensed private detective, I asked him what quality was most essential to be a successful private eye. His answer: the ability to wing it.

So here went.

I think I handled it pretty well, considering. I pressed my lips with a resigned look and felt up to my blazer pocket. Changed my expression to bewilderment, then allowed myself just the touch of a deprecating smile. "Oh, hell," I said quite sincerely, "apparently I left my wallet somewhere."

Kohls nodded readily, which wasn't encouraging. He took a sip of his drink, set it down quite deliberately, and said, "In that case, I believe this interview is concluded."

He started to slide out of the booth. I said with unfeigned anger, "Hey, Kohls, you're making a great big mistake here."

He stood, peered down at me through his glasses, and asked with good humor, "Oh?"

"I've got a hectic schedule," I said heavily, "and if we can't get our business done here and now, why, I'll just have to have you hauled into the office where the appointments and the service aren't quite as nice as here, you follow?"

"Uh-huh," he said in perfect bureaucrat—no acceptance or agreement, just acknowledgment that the words had been received. "The office *where?*"

"Up the street," I said, gesturing at nowhere.

"Mm," he said. "Odd thing. Before I came down here I called the local IRS branch. Never heard of an O'Gannon. Then I called Washington. No O'Gannon in the IRS there either. Or in the Secret Service, or the Bureau of Alcohol, Tobacco, and Firearms, or in the Bureau of the Mint, or in the Customs Service. Would you believe it? A body the size of the Treasury Department, and *not one person* with a common name like O'Gannon employed there?"

My old employer of many years back, Henry

Deuce, has an expression which I value: "never complain, never explain." "Damn switchboard operators screwed up."

He nodded coldly. "Well, I don't know who you are, but I think I know what you want. I suppose every two-bit con man in the country has read the papers and knows that Arthur embezzled a lot of money and hid it somewhere. You came here thinking you could con a lead to it out of Claire or me. Well, you hit a dead end here, friend. My suggestion is that you pack your duffel and crawl back to sleaze alley where you came from."

He turned and walked out of Yeatman's without looking back.

What was worse, I also ended up paying for the bastard's drink.

If you stumbled on Rooney's Pub by accident, you'd automatically figure it for being the roughest bar in Cincinnati. It's a basement joint on a garbage-strewn alley near Third Street, close to the river, and within the shadows of the abutments of the Suspension Bridge. You trip over winos, panhandlers, reds freaks and other street types on your way there. You enter through a battered, barely lit, steel fire door. You're intercepted by the tallest, widest bouncer in the Midwest. When you get inside, you can't help but notice that the patrons are mostly male, and most wear jackets.

That's to conceal the artillery. Rooney's is the biggest cop hangout in town. You may get propositioned, mugged or knifed on your way there, but once inside you'll be guarded with your life.

The bouncer took one look at me and let me pass. I walked into the dark, noisy expanse of lounge. They don't go overboard on appointments there: Most of the tables were old, battered wood jobs with rickety vinyl straight chairs scattered around. A row of tall wood booths was barely visible at the back. When I got there, past suppertime by now, most of the tables and all of the booths were jammed with off-duty police officers in plain clothes.

The juke box did some good Juice, telling us about how hard love had been on her lately. I squinted through the smoke and stink and noise and spotted a long table toward the back. Terry Lowe sat at the center, surrounded by male officers, including her boss, Sgt. Neal Hall. I made my way over there when my eyes had adjusted to the light.

The policemen were rowdy, joking, guzzling beer out of big glass steins. At my approach they quieted. Eleven pairs of eyes gave me that hard sober cop appraisal. The twelfth pair—Terry's—brightened when she saw me. "This is a raid," I said, by way of humor.

Silence answered me. Terry said, "So you found the place!" and got clumsily to her feet. Now I saw that she was better than half-tanked—the first time I'd ever seen her so. She introduced me around the table. The policemen were overwhelmed with apathy. All except for Neal Hall, who bounded to his feet.

He's an enormous whale of a man, six-four vertically and, I expect, longitudinally. His spectacled baby face puckered into a big grin and he nearly tore my hand off shaking it. "Ben Perkins Detroit," he boomed, mimicking my normal self-introduction. "Welcome back to the Queen City. Hope you don't uncover any murders while you're here. We got enough on our hands right now."

I liberated my hand. "Just passing through."

Hall shouted, "We're having a little celebration here. Your friend Officer Lowe got a citation for heroism from the Mayor today."

All she'd told me on the phone was to meet her at Rooney's in the evening. Typically, she hadn't mentioned a citation or a celebration. I grinned at her. "Hey, good going."

Hall went on, "Turned out there was a Cincinnati version of Murder, Incorporated, in business here. Officer Lowe uncovered it, made the case, and wrapped it up with an old-fashioned shoot-out right across from Fountain Square. Iced two of the assholes."

Terry shrugged. "They wouldn't come quietly." She gave me a secretive, knowing smile, which I don't think a cop in the joint missed.

They snorted and booed, their mood relaxing now that my credentials as an enlightened civilian had been established. I gave Terry a raised eyebrow. "Talk somewhere?"

"Ohhhhh," came a knowing chorus from the cops.

"Shaddap, animals!" She snarled at them. "C'mon over here, Ben. Let's get away from the nickel seats."

I stumbled and tripped over wooden and human legs around to her side of the table. She took my arm, as much for support as from affection, and we made our way to a booth that had just emptied at the far end. She slumped into it with relief as I sat down across from her.

"Oh, good," she breathed, brushing some stray brunette strands off her forehead. "I was beginning to wonder when you'd get here. Those bastards have about drunk me under the table."

"Awful inconsiderate of them," I observed, "holding you down, jamming that I.V. tube in, and forcing all that booze into you."

"I have to keep up with them or it'll hurt my image."

"You just iced two assholes in a shoot-out," I said, grinning. "I think your image with those guys is safe."

She smiled back, and glanced over at her colleagues. "Boy, friend," she said in a low voice, "are *you* getting the once-over. I know what they're thinking. So *that's* the mystery man who got to prim little Terry Lowe. The traditional coarse, dark, raw-built out-of-town stranger." She looked very directly back into my eyes, clasped both her warm hands over mine, and said quietly, "Glad you're here."

Terry Lowe had just turned the corner around

thirty. Lot of guys I know go for the young stuff, twenty and under, and while there's certainly something appealing about dewy, untried youth of the female persuasion, I personally think women don't start to look interesting till they're thirty. Terry Lowe looked interesting, all right, every five feet six, freckled, fit inch of her.

She had thick brown hair swept back to just below her shoulders, thickish brows over pale blue eyes, a small, straight, perfect nose, prominent cheekbones over a straight, assertive jaw, a slightly cleft chin, and a good mouth that looked comfortable when expressionless but, when broadened in a smile, showed dimples and good straight teeth that were slightly gapped in the middle. She'd spent nine years as a Cincinnati police officer—five of them as an investigator with First District Homicide.

Inevitably, as I watched her in the dim smoky light of Rooney's, comparisons with Carole Somers came to mind. Whereas Carole was tall and seemingly all limbs, Terry was of average height and build. Carole was voluptuous and creamy-skinned; Terry, while not in the least unfeminine, was honed, angular, and freckled. Carole's hair was pure blond Princess Diana, pristine and golden; Terry's hair was shoulder-length layered brunette, thick and naturally obedient, with (chemically unassisted, she'd once assured me) streaks of blond strewn throughout.

Carole had taken her share of knocks, including a marriage to a guy who routinely beat the shit out of her. She'd paid plenty of dues, including putting herself through college and law school, and was now raising her little boy Will all by herself. But she'd been raised in comfortable middle-class circumstances in Birmingham, Michigan. Terry was a street rat like me, born and raised in the Lower Price Hill section of Cincinnati, and had been taking knocks, and paying dues, all her life.

Both women were professionals. Carole's tools were in her head and her briefcase, while Terry's were in her head and, more to the point, strapped to her hip.

Till recently, I'd felt very lucky to have both of them as friends. Now, sitting in Rooney's in the hot rowdy Cincinnati summer night with Terry happily half-drunk across from me, I felt equally lucky to have kept one of them. And, suddenly and quite out of nowhere, I felt a twinge of regret about Carole. Things die, I reminded myself. Things die.

Terry Lowe let go of my hand and leaned back. A well-endowed young barmaid wearing a flashy yellow T-shirt with the saloon's logo across the chest brought us a pair of icy beers: Hudepohl, local product; a tad light to my taste, but I didn't break all precedent and send it back. Terry took a long slug of hers and clumsily set the sloshing mug down. "So, old friend, what's the case?"

I told her the whole thing in some detail, starting with my conversation with Joann Sturtevant and winding up with my meeting with Kevin Kohls.

Terry's eyes sharpened when I finished telling about Kohls. "I wouldn't call that meeting an overwhelming success," she commented.

"You're too generous. I tripped on my dick, is what I did."

She drank some more beer and squinted blearily, the smoke and the booze and the long day finally getting to her. "Cheer up. Tripping on your dick has therapeutic value, you know."

"I know, kid. Like my Uncle Dan says, 'a man ought to try to make an ass of himself at least once a week.' Keeps you humble."

"That's not what I mean, stupid." She leaned closer to me. "Tripping on your dick makes it longer and harder."

I laughed, suddenly feeling much better.

"You want to get out of here?" she asked softly.

"Sure." I drained my beer, dropped a couple of bucks on the table, and stood. Terry rose, steadied herself on the table, then caught my elbow with both hands and held on as we headed toward the door. As we passed the cops' table, Neal Hall rose like an iceberg beside me and grabbed my other arm like a vise.

"This an arrest?" I growled.

"Naw!" Hall roared. "You prob'ly gotta take a piss, right? *Sure* you gotta take a piss. What a coincidence, so do I. And as it happens I know where it is. Be glad to show you. Happy to oblige."

"Meet you at the door, Ben," Terry called as I was hauled away.

The john was a tiny two-holer, dim and rancid, with the usual graffiti on the walls, most of it unimaginative. Sole exception was the exhortation, etched in the Formica over the gigantic urinal I used: KEEP THE POPE OFF THE MOON. Cincinnati, home of obscure political causes, I thought. When I turned to the sink, Hall was there, taking up most of the available space, wiping his hands, fleshy baby face adult and serious.

He said abruptly, "Looks like you and Lowe are pretty close."

"Yeah," I answered, running water over my hands.

"Well," he said, his large-man bonhomie gone, "you oughta be worried, then. *I* am."

" 'Bout what, Sergeant?"

He threw a basketball-sized wad of paper towels into the overflowing waste barrel, muttered "Two points," then looked back down at me. "She's a damn good cop," he said slowly. "Got that citation from the Mayor today, and that's good. But she's just a bit reckless, and that worries me."

I looked up at him, wiping my hands dry. "Hey, way it lays out to me is, she was just doing her job. Not her fault they opened fire on her."

"*I* know all that," Hall said testily. "It's the law of averages I'm talking about here. Take me. I've got twenty-one years in, and I've only fired my piece once in the line of duty, and that was a warning shot.

"Then take Lowe. Nine years in, two major

shoot-outs—including the one you were involved in, when she iced Wentworth. Then the one last month. Three guys dead. Point is, she's drawing lightning. Thinks she's Dirty Harry or somebody. Like she's got something to prove. And I think I know what."

Dirty Terry, I mused.

Hall said, with unaccustomed difficulty, "It's 'cause she's a woman. Now I know, I know. I didn't like it any better than any of the guys when they hired women in. I admit I gave 'em a hard time, Lowe included. I don't do that anymore. To me she's just another officer, period. But she's working extra hard at looking for trouble, and it's gonna get her killed."

"You're her boss," I said. "Talk to her about it."

"Can't," he snapped. "Again, 'cause she's a woman. She'd read it that I'm trying to cool her off because I want to protect her or something. That's not true, I'd say the same thing to a male officer. But she'd never believe it."

The tiny john was getting hotter than hell. I actually began to feel claustrophobic with the big man between me and the door. "Sergeant," I said, "I wish I could counsel you with your personnel problems, but—"

He stabbed a finger the size of a rolling pin into my chest. "Now *you*, on the other hand. I don't know what's going on between you and Lowe, and I don't want to know. But you're close to her, plus you're a civilian, and not just any dumb civilian. You know the streets, you know what I'm talking about here. Get her to cool it, huh?"

His words did rattle me a little. I pictured Terry alone in a darkened slum building, walking slowly and alertly, a .38 Special in her hand, while, unnoticed and behind her, a man in ragged denims tiptoed toward her, a pistol in both his hands pointed at her head—

Did I want that for her? No. But police work was her life. She was a trained professional and she'd do things her way. She'd no more accept a counseling effort from me than from anyone else. And I didn't want to be Hall's messenger boy.

I said, "Haven't you heard, Sergeant? Our days as protectors of the fair sex are long over."

He sighed grimly. "You haven't heard a word I said." His face went flat, dead, frustrated. "C'mon, let's get the hell out of this shithouse."

Terry met me at the door and we walked out into the hot dark alley. As we dodged garbage cans and prone bodies, she wrapped her left arm deeply around my right, her fingers intertwined with mine. Not surprisingly, I thought about sex, but I found myself thinking how it gets old with anybody, no matter who it is, after a while.

But it hadn't gotten old with Terry, and we'd been seeing each other over two years. Part of me, on that night that seemed almost magical at the time, wanted to believe that it was because she was, to use my daddy's highest superlative, special. A couple other parts of me intruded rudely to suggest that it was because she'd been, in the context of my life, the "other woman," and, let's face it, there's something extra tangy and spicy about the other woman. Also, with the entire length of the state of Ohio in between us, our opportunities to get together, which had included a couple of half-way meetings at the otherwise uninteresting town of Lima, Ohio, were very limited.

We were nearing the end of the alley when she butted in on my thoughts in a soft, light tone. "You carrying?"

The expression has two meanings, one referring to drugs, one to firearms. I made the correct interpretation, recalled my .45 sitting peacefully on the closet shelf back home in Belleville, and said, "No."

"Drop something."

Beer and fatigue had dulled me, I guess. "Huh?"

"Just do it. Drop something, so we can stop walking."

I fished out my keys and dropped them. Terry

said in a normal tone, "Clumsy!" and reached down and picked them up. At the same time, I saw her boost up the cuff of her blue slacks for a second. The oily black glint of her .38 showed briefly as she clasped it against her side and we continued walking. She said softly, "We're being tailed."

I laughed, partly from genuine amusement. "You're kidding."

"Ben," she whispered fiercely, "someone's following us. Let's turn around real casual, like we decided to go back to Rooney's. I want to run him down."

I slithered my hand down and wrapped it around hers and the butt of the .38. "Listen, Dirty Terry."

"Ben!" she hissed.

"Terry," I interrupted, feeling the warmth of her hand and the coldness of her piece, "my place or yours?"

After a second she exhaled. "Where you staying?"

"Westin."

"My place then."

The three-way switch of the shaded lamp was on the forty-watt setting, sending soft golden light up to the off-white ceiling of Terry's small apartment bedroom. She was half golden, half shadow, straight-spined atop me, impaled to the maximum on me. The light made her skin luminescent from her flat firm belly, across her firmed-up breasts whose dark nipples looked away from her in opposite directions, to her damp face which relaxed now, finally, jaw unclenching, as her eyes opened and gleamed with contentment. She smiled and relaxed and set her pelvis harder on me, leaning forward a bit with her hands on my chest, fingers toying with the coarse black hair. "Mm," she purred, "I could have sworn you came."

I took my first deep, calm breath in a half hour. "You made sure of that, ya tease ya."

She grinned and looked down over her breasts at

my waist, moving her hips back and forth experimentally. "Can't keep a good man down."

"Come here." We kissed, and her lips felt moist
and tender; I put my arms around her and held her
hard, sex not on my mind for once, but rather closeness
and her, wanting to be close to her. She pulled her
face back from mine finally and there was silence for a
time until I said, "About that bit in the alley."

"Mm-hm."

"What was with you? Who'd be following us?
Who cares?" My voice was languid, almost toneless,
but I couldn't shake the feel of that alley incident off
me, particularly after my talk with Neal Hall.

Terry's fingers stopped playing. "I'm a police
officer. I keep my eye open for things. It's my job."

"Not all the time."

She did her pelvis-play again, slowly, teasingly.
"Not here, Ben. Not in here. Not with this."

I shook my head, refusing to be distracted. "Try
to cool it out there, Terry. You could get yourself in
trouble."

Her eyes gleamed brightly and she smiled
crookedly. "I *want* to get in trouble." She inhaled
and her breasts swelled and she gently bit her lower
lip, head starting to arch back as her thrusts deepened
and lengthened.

From very far away I said, "I don't want . . . you
in trouble. . . ."

"Yes, Ohh, yes. Trouble, I want trouble. I want
real trouble. . . . Do you like this trouble, Ben? Can
you feel it? Can you feel it, Ben?"

CHAPTER 8

The guy in the Sixth Street office-supply store got a
little impatient with me when I insisted on seeing

every kind of Rolodex card he had. Grumbling, he opened a big steel drawer and let me leaf through the samples. I found the kind I wanted, bought a big box of them, and left for the Trans-Ocean Building in a practically invisible humid drizzle. Though it was just nine in the morning, it was already hot.

"Mr. Perkins, you are beginning to annoy me," Jeanette McGraw said when she appeared at the reception desk.

The feeling was mutual. The ugly old bat had kept me waiting in the lobby for over an hour. Fortunately, I had nothing better to do that morning than sit in air-conditioned discomfort, reading exciting things like *The Wall Street Journal, Business Week*, and Trans-Ocean's slick, self-serving, and basically incomprehensible annual report. But I kept my irritation to myself. I needed McGraw's cooperation.

For the next few minutes, anyway.

"You know how us toilers in the vineyard are," I said, entirely too cheerful for that early in the morning. "We always have loose ends to wrap up. I'd like another look at Barton's records, please."

McGraw stared coldly at me. While she was still possessed of a third-grade teacher's persona, today her dress was pure third grader: bright pink sleeveless blouse with an enormous bow at the throat, red skirt that reached to her big knees, plus honest-to-God penny loafers on her feet, and a tiny pink bow in her hair. It'd have been a tough decision whether to pat her on the head or kick her in the ass. Well, maybe not so tough.

She said finally, her voice rich with the pain of the put-upon, "If you must. But it'll have to be quick. I have many *important* matters to attend to today."

In cold, unfriendly silence we made the trip down the elevator to the sub-basement and into the storage room. The two eleven-watt bulbs glowed dimly in the dusty and stuffy air. I went down to the end where the boxes were stored. "Mind if I drag one of these over under the light? It's hard to see over here."

"Very well," she answered. I was pleased to note that her voice was already becoming strangled. "Please be quick."

"Oh, sure," I said lazily. I picked up the bigger of the two boxes and carried it down to the light. "Oooh, heavy," I lied, puffing. McGraw stepped closer, the better to watch me, I suppose. Instead of setting the box down, I dropped it with a crash. It bounced once, tipped over, burst open, and sent a cloud of dust balls boiling up from the dust-fluffy floor.

McGraw got one good snort of that, and let go like Hitler's opening salvo at the Polish border.

I can't explain how she managed to inhale between sneezes, they came so fast. She bent, cupping her face in both hands. I squatted and began shoving papers back into the box, saying comforting things like, "Gee, I'm sorry...God, it just got away from me...you all right, ma'am?" To reward me for my solicitude, she turned and stumbled awkwardly out of the room, her sneezes echoing violently off the cement walls, their volume exceeded only by the slam of the steel fire door as she lurched out into the hall in search of clean air.

The Rolodex cards were at the bottom of the box, still bundled together. I popped my briefcase open, grabbed my bundle of fresh unmarked cards, slathered them with dust for authenticity, and substituted them in the box for the originals, which I threw into the briefcase, snapping the lid tight.

I had the contents back in the box and was dragging it back to its home when McGraw returned, holding a handkerchief over her face like one of the Hole in the Wall Gang. She said in a muffled, moist voice, "You must leave. Finished or not."

I was tempted to resist, just for effect, but I'd gotten what I came for. That salesguy friend of mine once counseled me, "Once you close the deal, you get the hell out fast. You don't stand around jawing with the help." I stood, brushing off my hands, and said reluctantly, "Okay. I guess I've got what I need."

I wished I could be sure of that.

Back in my room at the Westin, I shed my blazer, hung it over the shower rod to dry (forgot my damn raincoat; have to put Mrs. Sturtevant's Gold Card to work again), loosened my tie, dumped the dirty Rolodex cards out on the newly made-up bed, and began flicking through them like a Vegas pit boss counting his markers.

The cards were a study in boredom. Each card was meticulously typed in all caps. Most had just three entries: a person's name, a phone number, and sometimes a company name. The area codes seemed pretty dispersed all around the country. Nothing was familiar about any of the names. There were no notes, memos, or, as far as I could see after one pass through the cards, clues.

For the hell of it, I called some of the numbers listed for the Tri-State (to use Cincinnatians' term) area. A couple of them made an unfamiliar, harsh, protesting whine—out of order or disconnected, I supposed. But I did get through to a bunch of the numbers.

Bringing my old friend O'Gannon back for a curtain call, I asked vague, fishing questions about Barton, and got what you usually get in expeditions like that: nothing. Several people had never heard of him. Some had done business with him. A couple mentioned the crash. But that instinctive ear most guys in my line of work have—and I think you're born with it—turned to tin listening to them. There was nothing there.

I paced the silent room, staring down at the bustling streets of Cincinnati. Time to prioritize, I thought. This meant, naturally, that I first opened a warm beer and guzzled half of it. Then I lighted a short, cork-tipped cigar, stuck it in my teeth and puffed, watching pigeons strut sullenly around the concrete ledge of a building across Vine Street from me. And I added up my options, such as they were.

I could take a crack at Kohls again. A part of me—the part that hates being licked—wanted to do just that, and the hell with the consequences. But he'd made me real good, and to work him I'd have to import some fresh talent. That was no problem, but I'd do it only as a last resort; I don't like working with other people.

I could also have a go at Claire Barton directly, but now that Kohls had made me she probably had her drawbridges up.

Or, I could...I stiffened straighter, the cigar sending smoke into my sightless eyes. I could call Kenny Slingluff and see what luck he'd had with that credit card—sorry, calling card—call. Should have done it an hour ago.

I only had his home number, though. Good old Prepared Perkins, they call me. I called there, got his wife to give me his work number, and raised him there.

"For this deal you owe me," he said upon hearing my name.

"Got my poopy?"

"I got your poopy all right, but it cost me. I had to give IOU's to a fella at Cincinnati Bell and another one at Canada Bell."

"Half of Detroit's holding your markers," I answered pleasantly. "You ought to be accustomed to *that* feeling." His last words registered. "Canada?"

A long silence on the phone, then Kenny said, "The name of the calling-card holder is Vincent Wakefield. The address is—get this—one-nineteen John Donne Close, Windsor, Ontario."

"John Donne, as in," I groped, "'Send not to know for whom the bell tolls...'"

"I'm with the phone company, not the University of Michigan English Department."

"Any record of his occupation?"

"I'm with the phone company, not the credit bureau."

I was thinking hard. "I thought I knew Windsor pretty well. Any idea where John Donne Close is?"

"I'm with the phone company, not Rand McNally."

"Okay okay *okay*." Wakefield, John Donne Close, Windsor, I thought. A private detective, at least that's what he'd told the Trans-Ocean people. It didn't surprise me that another player was in the act. In fact, considering the stakes, I'd have been surprised if he was the only one. I could butt into his action, see what he had, and maybe cut out a lot of intermediate steps. After all, I didn't have much to go on here. And, if I came up empty with Wakefield, Kevin Kohls would still be here, and so would Claire Barton, and so would those numbers on the Rolodex cards.

Slingluff had been talking. "—see what you can find out?"

"About what?" I asked impatiently.

He made a sound that was somewhere between a snort and a sigh. "You haven't even been listening! Mona. My wife. She's, uh—she's spending a lot of evenings out all of a sudden. Will you see what you can find out?"

"Yeah, in a few days, soon as I wrap this up," I said distractedly. "It'll keep till then. I mean, with your marital record, what's the big deal?"

His tone went haughty and superior. Having done what he considered a significant service for me, Kenny Slingluff now felt entitled to order me around. "Because it's betrayal. What else would you call it?"

"Poetic justice?"

"What?"

There I went again, smart-mouthing a paying client. I backed off. "Nothing. Talk to you in a few days."

I pressed the cradle button down before he could answer and, propping the receiver against my ear with my shoulder, rescued the phone book, located the Delta Airlines number, and punched. After reserving a seat back to Detroit, I dialed the First District number from memory and asked for Terry Lowe.

The saloon in the Delta terminal was half-jammed with salesmen, students, and advertising people watching the Bengals get mauled by somebody on the big TV mounted above the bar. The buzz of half-drunk conversation mixed with the bleating of the sportscasters and warred with the jukebox, which was doing some .38 Special when I got there. I ordered beer, and was half through with that when Terry Lowe swept in.

She looked sharp in an unbuttoned brown cotton corduroy blazer over an open-necked white-and-bronze-striped blouse and snug tan slacks. Her face was flushed with hurry, her eyes warm and alive. I managed to order her a vodka collins from the barmaid, and we didn't do anything but hold hands till her drink came.

Terry sipped, set the glass down, and made a pout which belied the sparkle in her eyes. "Back to Detroit so soon?"

"Duty calls."

"Tell me."

I lighted a cigar and told her. As I talked, the sparkle in her eyes faded away, replaced by the hard glint of the professional cop. When I was through she took another sip of her drink and said offhandedly, "Roundabout way to go at it, Ben."

"This guy Wakefield might be ahead of me. If I can catch up with him and find out what he knows, it'll save me a lot of running around."

"Hey," she countered, "you could stay here a few more days and work the leads on those Rolodex cards. There's no law says investigations have to be easy."

"There's no law says I got to reinvent the wheel,

either. If Wakefield's got a piece of the story and I can get it from him, I might be able to wrap up the job that much faster. Save me a lot of hassle." I drew on my cigar and signaled for another drink. "Besides, it's kind of my way, you know? Going at stuff from left field. Mrs. Sturtevant mentioned that. Called me the back-door man. Said it was out of some old jazz song."

"Before my time," Terry said dully. She let go of my hand, picked up her glass with both hands, and drank till the cubes clinked. She set it down and looked into my eyes. "I wish you weren't going so soon."

"Hey, sweetie," I said easily, "I'll be back, or we'll do Lima again, or maybe you'll actually break down and come all the way up to Detroit for once—"

Terry said, with great effort, "I'm tired of this."

I stopped an exhalation midway. The hot ember of my cigar glowed at my fingers and I stubbed it out without seeing. The barmaid sauntered by, placed a couple of drinks on our table, and collected the empties with the same motion. Terry's face was set in stone, lips pressed, her gaze fixed somewhere just beneath my chin. I cleared my throat and said, "You didn't seem so tired of it last night."

Her lips flattened farther into a grimace that had no humor in it. "I'm not tired of *you*," she said pointedly. "I'm tired of saying good-bye to you, Ben. You come here for an overnight or a weekend, then we say good-bye, and you're gone for months. Or we meet in Lima, of all the godforsaken places, and spend a night or a weekend, and then say good-bye, and I don't see you for months."

The man in the booth behind Terry was studying his newspaper but had his head cocked curiously. I bent forward toward her and said quietly, "I'll call you."

Her eyes found mine again. "Sometimes that makes it *worse*. It makes me realize how far apart we are. Frankly, you might as well not ever call me again. It depresses me for days. I mean, what kind of love affair *is* this, anyhow?"

"Let it be noted," I answered, "that this is the first time the word 'love' has been mentioned, and you were the one who used it."

For the very first time, I saw her composure, her self-possession, begin to go. She reined herself in but it left her eyes a little shiny, her cheeks flushed. At that point I wanted more than anything to grab her and pull her to me, and to hell with the table between us and the eavesdropper with his newspaper and the hillbilly barmaid and the whole bunch of half-stoned road-happy businessmen around us.

But I didn't. Not me, no sir. That sour hard-head who lives inside me and runs things occasionally took charge: arm's length, kid, arm's length; let 'em any closer and they'll take over.

After a moment, she nodded. "I suppose that's what we get for being so hip and with-it. We play long-distance boyfriend and girlfriend with lots of laughs and plenty of good sex and we never, *ever* let that evil word 'love' intrude, do we."

She unclasped her hands and raised them, leaning on her elbows. "I don't need more bullshit in my life. I can live with the rest as long as this doesn't go that way, too. I love you, Ben."

The massacre of the Bengals, the juiced mutterings of the drinkers, and the atonal announcements over the airport intercom faded back from me. I took her wrists in my hands and encountered zero resistance as I pulled her face to mine and kissed her. We held it as her hands caressed the sides of my face, slinking up into my hair. The kiss broke at the impersonal sound of the barmaid's voice: " 'Nother drink, sir?"

I kept hold of Terry's wrists and lowered them to the table as I looked up at the barmaid's stony face. "Can I get back to you on that?"

She stomped away. I looked back at Terry. Her face was bright with vast satisfaction, head slightly cocked, and her fingers insinuated their way under my shirtcuffs as I held her slim wrists. I said, and my voice could have been steadier, "That answer your questions?"

"Except for one," she answered. At my puzzled silence her eyes narrowed. "Who moves where, and when."

I decided to smoke another cigar. I told myself it was because I was about to board a plane and wouldn't be able to smoke for over an hour. But maybe it was an excuse to let go of her, I don't know.

When I had it going I said, "I got an idea. You move to Detroit, soon as you can."

She sighed. "My job's in Cincinnati, Ben. I was born and raised here. My mother still lives here, my brother in Kentucky. I can't pull up and start all over again."

I replied calmly, "My job's in Detroit. I was born and raised there. My Uncle Dan and my brother Bill and my sister Libby live there." I ignored the little voice that reminded me that, while I do see Uncle Dan frequently, my brother and I get together maybe twice a year and I hardly ever see Libby. "I can't pull up and start over again."

She leaned back and crossed her arms on the table in front of her. "Dilemma, huh?"

"Pretty solid one, at that."

"Well, okay," she said breezily, checking her watch. "Better get to the gate, what do you say?"

I flipped a five onto the table, grabbed my briefcase and overnight bag, and we headed down the wide concourse toward the crowded security checkpoint. Terry said casually, "I think I'll leave you here. I'm carrying, and it's too big a hassle getting through security. Besides, I'm not much for waving hankies at departing aircraft, if you don't mind."

I got in line and turned to her. "Next year in Lima?" I asked. It sounded crueler than I meant it.

Her smile was clench-jawed and fidgety. "Maybe. See you around, okay?"

The line shifted forward. I kept my hands full of handles, my cigar smoking in my teeth. Terry waited a minute, then turned to walk away. I blurted, "I'll call you."

She kept moving and sent back over her shoulder, "No, somehow I think I'll be the one calling you." She merged with a mass of departing passengers and was gone.

I stood there for a second, squinting, mouth dry. Well, old son, this one's probably going sour, too. Things die, they always die, so take it in stride and board the airplane. But the tried-and-true line of reasoning didn't work nearly as well this time. I was just about to turn and trot after her when—

The sweating fat bald man behind me snarled, "You want to move some ass, bud?" I turned, tossed my overnight bag onto the conveyor belt, and soundlessly submitted to another routine rape of my Fourth Amendment rights.

CHAPTER 9

The plane was jammed. For once I got a seat several rows from the flight's quota of screaming babies. We rolled away from the gate on time, the take-off was perfect, and when we reached cruising altitude, the aircraft hung droning, rock-steady. You could sleep through the whole thing, as a couple of businessmen, obviously veterans of millions of miles in the air, were doing.

I ordered a beer—on airplanes, you have a choice between two famous brands: Regular or Light— and flipped through the in-flight magazine and generally exhibited every outward sign of calm. But, inside, I was as jumpy as if they had sounded battle stations on the intercom. And I couldn't figure out why.

It wasn't because I couldn't smoke. I'm known as a fiercely disciplined ascetic; in fact, on several occasions I've done without a cigar for as much as an entire hour at a stretch.

It wasn't because I couldn't drink. On the flight attendant's first pass with the refreshment cart I ordered two beers (Regular, which, in case you're wondering, turned out to be the generic-tasting but fully acceptable Budweiser); and, with the resourcefulness instinctive in every good flight attendant, she gave me the second one wrapped in a barf bag with some chunks of ice to keep it cold till I needed it, which was, as it turned out, 32,000 feet above Lima.

It wasn't because of what had happened with Terry. That I had shut away to be dealt with when I didn't have more important issues on my agenda, like the Barton case.

But I was jumpy, all right, and I couldn't get to the bottom of it. At one point I got up and made an unnecessary trip to the bathroom, scanning the five-across rows of passengers as I walked the trembling deck. I didn't see anybody I knew.

By the time I got back to my seat, I'd made some decisions which cost me some extra time, and Mrs. Sturtevant's Gold Card a good chunk of coin.

Windsor, Ontario, sits directly across the river from Detroit. Thanks to a kink in the Detroit River, Windsor is actually south of Detroit—the only place where any part of Canada is south of any part of the United States. Ben Perkins, student of geography, they call me.

Many Detroiters tend to regard Windsor as a suburb of Detroit. They think of Windsor as a less-favored cousin, maybe an aspirant to U.S. citizenship. I suppose that's because it's so damned easy to get over there, thanks, since 1929, to the Ambassador Bridge and the Detroit-Windsor Tunnel, plus the liberal border-crossing policies employed by both sides.

Plus, they're so friendly. They smile at you, and talk in funny, folksy little accents, and you finish your big meal and take a big gulp of beer and look around at the sturdy people serving you and say, You know, these'd make right fine Americans, huh, Dave?

Forget that in the strictest sense they *are* Americans. They're the first to tell you that they are Canadians, and proud of it, and that Windsor, along with the rest of the nation of which it is the southernmost outpost, is not the United States but a foreign country, U.S. investments, encroachment, and proprietary attitude notwithstanding.

You shouldn't give the least damn about that unless you plan to go over there and operate, and then you'd better not forget it for one little second. I'd done enough business in Canada to know, and with what was at stake on this case, I didn't dare screw up now.

By the time I landed at Detroit Metro, I had my plan set. Without fanfare I hied me over to the international terminal and, thanks to my trusty Gold Card, booked an Air Canada hop to London, Ontario, which is a ways up the 401 east of Windsor. The flight over there was uneventful, and I went through Canada Customs at London's sleepy little airport, then turned around and caught the Air Canada shuttle to Windsor. I got there a little after five in the afternoon.

Now it could have been a lot easier. I could have retrieved my Mustang after arriving from Cincinnati at Detroit Metro, driven about twenty miles, crossed the Ambassador Bridge for a buck, fogged the mirror at the Canada Customs checkpoint on the other side, and ended up just as precisely in Windsor. That way, I'd have had my own car, a couple of hours to spare, and have avoided two extra take-offs and two landings.

But I still felt jumpy. I'd messed up bad with

Kevin Kohls, and had no desire to repeat that experience. I'd sensed Terry Lowe's unexplained nervousness in the alley near Rooney's. I'd felt my neck hair prickle on the flight up from Cincinnati, for no reason I could identify. I remembered Dick Dennehy telling me: "There's a certain element of asshole that gets seriously crazed in situations like this."

When the stomping of feet gets loud enough, a smart street rat becomes invisible. Being nothing if not a smart street rat, I knew the time for invisibility had come. I had to have a car with Ontario plates, and the best place to rent a car with Ontario plates is Windsor Airport. It might become essential later to disappear, and it's easier to disappear if no one knows where you're from in the first place; being from west of Windsor, I entered it from the east.

By the time I got to the Holiday Inn on Riverside East, I was, thanks to Mrs. Sturtevant's Gold Card, driving a Canadian car and carrying Canadian currency. The room faced the Detroit River, giving a panoramic view of Detroit from the squat, domed Joe Louis Arena on the left to the multi-towered, glass-and-steel Renaissance Center on the right. I studied the view with unusual intensity as I gobbled a roast beef sandwich and swigged a beer in the motel's Riverview Restaurant. As I left to track down Vincent Wakefield of John Donne Close, I reflected that I'd never been so near to home, and yet so far away from it, in my life.

"Close," it turned out, is a term of British origin meaning "dead end." John Donne Close is a square-ended stump of a street in Walkerville, now merely a part of Windsor but once a town in its own right, named after, and dominated by, the Hiram Walker Distillery whose massive brick plants dot the entire area.

John Donne Close and the surrounding neighborhood had the look of a factory-owned mill town gone seedier. Fully a third of the properties were abandoned and/or for sale. Scrubby little trees lined the narrow, car-lined streets. The houses were two-story chunky things that looked like they'd been stamped from cookie cutters, butted up together so close that, by reaching out your window, you could shake hands with your neighbor, or make it with his wife.

Wakefield's house, 119, cornered at Argyle, across from the Richmond Variety Store. It looked too big for one guy, but who asked me? I wedged my rented Chrysler Aries—hell of a thing: I'm a Perkins, and between me, my Uncle Dan, my brother Bill and my daddy, we've put in ninety-plus years working for Ford's; yet the best I could do today was a Chrysler with a tinny gutless little motor and, what was worse, only AM in the dash—into a spot a couple of doors down from Wakefield's place and took up watch.

Two hours had passed and the sun set to my right before I got any action. An enormous Ford pickup truck on gigantic oversized wheels with lots of chrome, tinted windows, and a rollbar rolled into the driveway of 119 John Donne Close and parked in the ramshackle shed in back. I squinted through the dimness and got a quick look at the man who emerged from the truck, slid the shed door shut, and trotted into the house.

He was a tall, spare, raw-boned man with tight curly hair. He wore dark slacks—could have been blue, could have been black—and a light nylon jack-et. He could have been thirty, he could have been fifty. He moved with a springy, athletic walk.

That's the best I can tell you because it was dark, I was tired, and he didn't come out again. I know that because I waited around another two hours with nothing to do except scout the AM dial for decent music and watch the lights on Vincent Wakefield's house switch off one by one till the place was completely dark.

                    *   *   *

The drapes on my motel room's window wall were pulled back, showing the bright lights of downtown Detroit reflecting on the glassy rushing surface of the Detroit River.

I wasn't sleepy. I wasn't hungry. I didn't even want something to drink. I wanted action and I couldn't wait till morning for it.

So I flipped impatiently through Arthur Barton's Rolodex cards, sorting out the ones with Detroit-area telephone numbers, and began calling. Two were disconnected. Two rang and rang and gave no answer. The next one I came to gave a loud, weird whining sound. I hung up on that and looked at the card. Wilbur Withrow, no company name, 558-6980, extension 9. Have to try it tomorrow or something.

I smoked a cigar in the silence, then picked up the phone again and called Norris Johnston, a private detective operating out of Dearborn. Norris doesn't like me and, probably for that reason, I don't like him; but we've done each other enough favors on an armed-truce basis that we keep talking.

He bristled like a wire brush at the mention of Wakefield's name. "Private *detective* my Aunt Angela's ass! For one thing, Canadian law's real strict about licensing private detectives. As opposed to these United States, where just about any warm breather with an IQ in excess of his neck size can get licensed. Except probably *you*."

"Like the fella said, Norris," I said, grinning, "your *mother*, man! Invective aside, what *is* the book on Wakefield then?"

"What Wakefield is, is a small-time hustler. Quick-buck artist. Wherever there's a little action, Wakefield's always there trying to scarf off a buck or two for himself."

"Dealt with him personally?"

"He keeps to his side of the river, I keep to mine."

"Got a sheet?"

"Don't know, but I doubt it. Word on him is, he's

a smart character, stays this side of the line. *Just* this
side."

Not much help.

By now it was past eleven o'clock. I stared at the
telephone for a long time, then picked it up resentfully
and dialed Carole's number. It rang for a long time
before I hung up.

CHAPTER 10

Partly due to my having been raised in a strict
schedule-oriented automobile manufacturing society—
in which six A.M. shift starts are not uncommon—
and partly due to my relatively light consumption of
alcohol the night before, I bounded briskly out of
bed before sunup the next morning.

As much as I'd like to claim that I began my day
with a blood-churning round of calisthenics, honesty
forces me to confess that I began it by scrubbing my
body briskly with Dial, and my teeth with Crest.
That's as much exertion as I voluntarily undergo
that early in the morning, and just about any other
non-horizontal time, as well.

By six A.M. I was parked in my rented Chrysler
just up the block from Vincent Wakefield's house in
Walkerville, finishing my first cigar of the day and
uncapping a hot cup of coffee I'd bought at a Donut
Hole shop on Ouellette.

At nine-fifteen the coffee was long gone and I
was stubbing out my fourth cigar when Vincent
Wakefield finally emerged from his shabby house. I
fired up the Chrysler and got on the tail of his
copper-colored souped-up Ford pickup truck as he
drove away.

I'd gotten a good look at him as he sauntered
from the side door of his house to the shed. In the

crisp sunny summer morning light, Vincent Wakefield looked closer to fifty than to thirty. He was very fit, a bony, hard-muscled man with long arms and long legs who moved with the trained grace and authority of an ex-athlete. His face was hard-planed and set-mouthed; his eyes were shrouded with deep black wrap-around sunglasses. He wore high-waisted, dark blue beltless slacks, a tailored short-sleeved maroon shirt worn halfway open, a heavy gold watch, and black ankle-high boots.

He looked tough. Whether he actually was or not remained to be seen, but I planned to spend the day watching him before I made any move.

Wakefield's first stop was McDougall Cartage, a trucking company on the Tenth Concession Road southeast of the airport. I followed his slick copper-colored pickup down a long gravel lane and saw him park by the grimy gray-brick terminal. I found myself a place to park amid a row of cars by the administration building and kept my eyes on him.

Vincent Wakefield climbed down from his truck and sauntered to the huge open garage doors of the terminal. Several burly men in work clothes—apparently drivers and mechanics—clustered around him. Though cut from the same tough bolt of cloth, they were as different from Wakefield as could be: short, burly, poorly dressed. The conversation went on a long time; the men did most of the talking and Wakefield did a lot of nodding.

After half an hour another man approached the group. He'd come out the front door of the administration building and trotted over there. He was older, balding, in shirt sleeves with his tie loose. The drivers and mechanics faded back at his approach, forming a rough semicircle around Wakefield. The older man shouted something at Wakefield—what I couldn't tell because of the roar of a Canadian Pacific train charging along in the distance—and Wakefield, hands on hips, shouted something back.

The older man said something to the drivers, and they walked sullenly away. Wakefield put his arm around the older man's shoulders and walked him back toward the administration building, talking urgently down at him. The older man kept his eyes on the ground, then looked back up at Wakefield and nodded grimly. Wakefield gave the man a friendly slap on the back, turned, sauntered jovially back to his pickup, and drove away.

I followed him back into Windsor. The summer day was pushing toward the noon hour now, the heat building rapidly. Wakefield drove fast and expertly and seemed to know Windsor's tangled streets very well, judging from the tortuous route we took. I began to sweat in the car and didn't dare turn on the air conditioning because I needed all of the Chrysler's feeble power to keep the Ford pickup's high tail in sight as we twisted and dodged toward the center of town.

I damn near lost him when he ducked up an alley off Ouellette and disappeared. The one-ways were against me, the traffic was heavy and slow as porridge, and I made a couple of wild turns on an interception course before I caught sight of the pickup as Wakefield parked in a public lot on Chatham across from the *Windsor Star* plant.

He'd gotten the last open space. I searched frantically, and finally grabbed a metered spot on the street, bounded out of the car without locking it and without feeding the meter, and trotted a full block behind him as he sauntered along the crowded sidewalk, his head and shoulders high above the other pedestrians as his truck had been above the other cars.

As he turned and entered L'Auberge de la Bastille, I saw that he'd put on a natty single-breasted jacket with gold buttons, and he now wore a dark tie over his maroon shirt. I was tieless, but wore my blue blazer and acceptable slacks. I didn't think even a class joint like L'Auberge would throw me out, not in these informal times. As I entered the restaurant, I thought grimly, whither thou goest, Vinny baby, I shall go.

Vincent Wakefield ate lunch with three elderly, paunchy, well-dressed businessmen types. L'Auberge is laid out in a dark, rambling series of rooms connected by arches, and I was seated nowhere near them, so I couldn't hear what they were talking about. I did notice that the men listened attentively to Wakefield, and that his demeanor with them was quiet, sober, authoritative, formal; quite different from his conduct out at the trucking company. Interesting.

After finishing my excellent roast beef platter washed down with a couple bottles of Molson—referred to across the river as "Canadian"—I paid my bill and chanced a glance at the Wakefield table. They'd finished eating and were leaning back casually in their chairs. The amiability on their faces told me that the business part of their lunch was done and that they were going to relax over the remains of their bottle of Burgundy. After glancing around to make sure that the only public entrance to the restaurant was the one in front, I stood, dropped my napkin on the table, and walked out to the pay phone in the foyer.

Considering that Kenny Slingluff worked for the phone company, it was very difficult getting a call through to him there. I was put on hold a couple of times, assured twice that he was being paged, and asked three times if I'd been helped yet, before Kenny finally came on the line.

"What the fuck you doing calling me here?" he greeted.

"Had to. Track doesn't open till later, your girl friend's phone's been disconnected, and you're never at home anymore."

"Jesus!" He covered his mouthpiece inexpertly

enough so I could hear him say to someone, "I gotta take this call, okay? I'll get back to you." After a pause he came back on. "What do you want, Perkins?"

I leaned against the open pay phone. "In general, a lot. But from you, just a little bitty piece of help, pal."

"You checked out Mona yet? She was out again last night till two or later."

"I said I'd get to that when I've taken care of this other."

He grunted. "What's the problem?"

"Any way to get the history of a phone number? Like who's had it, and all that?"

"Sure, it's available somewhere, I guess. What's up?"

I told him about the Wilbur Withrow Rolodex card and the weird whining sound I'd gotten when I dialed his number.

"Wait a minute, let me write that number down." I heard him breathing. "I don't know, could be anything. Call me back later. And for Chrissake get going on Mona."

I cupped the mouthpiece closer to my face. "I said I'd do it and I'll do it. Don't lean on me."

A harsh, bitter edge came into his voice. "I won't take shit from her, Perkins. You understand me? I won't take shit from any of 'em." He hung up with a slam.

Good old strung-out Kenny. Man's his own worst enemy, I thought with a grin. I was just replacing the receiver on the pay phone when the double doors to the restaurant opened and Vincent Wakefield came through. I turned, opened the street door, and stepped out as Wakefield went for the pay phone. I eased the street door shut behind me, and before it closed, Wakefield gave me an incurious glance as he picked up the pay phone receiver with one hand and probed the coin return slot with the other.

A parking ticket waved merrily on the Chrysler's windshield. I don't know why, but events like that bring out the ham in me. I pulled the citation out from under the wiper blade, made a show of reading it "Herein fail ye not on pain of fifty dollars," it concluded), bopped my forehead with the heel of my hand, and tucked it with considerable reverence in the inside pocket of my blazer, where, as it turned out, it stayed untouched for better than six months.

As Wakefield approached his truck, he shucked his jacket and loosened—but did not remove—his tie. He clambered aboard, fired it up, and I assumed the position about a half block behind him. His route was pretty direct this time. We tooled east on Wyandotte to Huron Church Road, in the shadow of the Ambassador Bridge, then headed south on the heavily truck-traveled four-lane strip till we left the city limits and entered Sandwich West Township.

Huron Church Road turned small and light as we entered the boondocks. Wakefield led me east on the Sixth Concession Road and we rolled into a fairly new subdivision of winding, tree-lined streets and wide lawns. It was the kind of place where the moneyed of Windsor had fled, just as the moneyed of Detroit had fled to places like Warren, West Bloomfield, Livonia, Farmington Hills, and Belleville.

We ended up on Elvis Street—no connection to the King, far as I know—and Wakefield pulled into the driveway of a long low ranch about halfway down. I cruised innocently past the house, made a U at the end, and came back slowly as Wakefield, tightening his tie, sauntered up to the front door, rang the bell, and was admitted.

I parked at the curb about a hundred yards from the house. The subdivision was a roomy cluster of ranches and colonials that looked custom-built till you examined them closely and realized that, exterior cosmetics and landscaping aside, there were basically only five different models.

I rolled down all the car windows in a fruitless effort to catch a wisp of breeze, and slid down, trying to get less uncomfortable on the hard seat. The neighborhood was silent on this hot midweek afternoon. Kids were in school, dads were at work, moms were inside doing whatever moms do, and Vincent Wakefield had come a'calling at the home of—I squinted at the mailbox at the curb—THE MASTERS, 1090 ELVIS STREET.

I was lighting a cigar fifteen minutes after arriving when the front door of the Masters home opened, disgorging two children: a girl about six years old and a boy about four. They wore shorts and T-shirts and were redheaded and noisy and violently active. They threw a Frisbee and yelled and tussled and ran around for better than an hour, when finally the front door opened again and a woman came out, calling to them softly.

She was quite short and, I figured, in her late thirties. Despite the heat, she wore a full short-sleeved blue blouse and white cotton slacks. She was full-figured yet agile, a woman who exercised, ate right, took good care of herself. Her hair was dark reddish—was probably the brighter red of her children when she was their age—and swept back on her head, ending just at her shoulders.

I saw that her children put up only token argument when she ordered them back inside. They picked up their toys without being told and scooted along ahead of her toward the door. I saw the casual pat of affection she gave each of them as they passed her. I watched her with appreciation as she followed them to the front door, and saw, behind the screen, the tall athletic form of Vincent Wakefield standing there, a glass of something in his hand. His tie was still knotted securely around his neck.

I saw no sign of any of them till the afternoon started to run out. Wakefield came out the front door, waved a farewell back at the woman, sauntered over to his truck, and drove away. After a moment, I followed. As we headed back into Windsor in the going-home rush-hour traffic, I added up what I had seen at the Masters home.

It seemed obvious to me that Wakefield's visit was, at least on the surface, innocent. No married woman meets her lover in her own home, in the middle of the day, with her children there and his truck parked on the driveway outside.

On the other hand, maybe she was unmarried; maybe she and Wakefield were dating. It still didn't add up. I remembered the neat exterior of the house and grounds, the modesty with which she dressed despite the heat of the day, the sturdy, happy young children, the affectionate pat she gave to each of them, and knew that she wasn't the type of woman to have a tryst at her house at midday with her children right there.

So if they weren't lovers, what was Wakefield doing there? I could easily come up with explanations for his visit to the trucking company and L'Auberge. But on the woman I was stumped. He'd spent more time with her than anyplace else that day. If he wasn't screwing her, he had to be doing something equally important.

We were heading east on the E. C. Row Expressway when I finally let Wakefield go. You didn't have to be a genius to figure he was heading for Walkerville and home; it was getting late; I had a lot to think about; and I was sick of playing tail, as well as sitting on it.

Back at the Holiday, I changed into jeans and a fresh sport shirt and walked down to the Riverview Restaurant. After standing uncertainly at the entrance and thinking about yet another motel restaurant meal, I said to hell with it. I left the motel on foot, crossed Riverside, and tracked down a little sleazehole that served up a pair of highly respectable and lethally spiced hot dogs, topped with a chili that kicked like a boot, sided with a greasy pile of onion rings, and washed down with several bottles of cold

Canadian. I topped off the feast with a fresh, leisurely cigar that I smoked while reading the day's *Detroit
Free Press*.

When I returned to my room, the sun was
setting behind the skyscrapers of Detroit, sending
shadows in long blocklike fingers across the rolling
sheen of the river. I shucked my LeHighs, opened
my briefcase, retrieved the Rolodex cards, sat on the
big double bed, and picked up the phone to call
Kenny Slingluff.

I'd dialed half the numbers when I froze, considered, and set the receiver back down on the hook.

It occurred to me that calls to Detroit from here
would be a matter of record at the front desk. I
remembered my vow to become invisible. To some
people, the term *paranoia* is a pejorative. It's just the
opposite to me. Paranoia has saved my neck more
than once in this business, and I have a world of
respect for it.

I laced myself back into my LeHighs, put the
Rolodex cards in my briefcase, walked down to the
lower hallway of the motel and used one of the pay
phones there.

"Home for once, huh?" I asked Kenny when he
answered.

"What choice do I have? Somebody's got to
watch the kids, and Mona's 'out' again." He sounded
sullen and tense.

"Man, that's tough. You got to actually hang
around the house and watch the kids and stuff."

Kenny went into shrill, fake bluster. "I don't
need that wise-ass tone, Perkins, particularly when
I've honest to God been busting my ass trying to help
you."

"Sorry."

"Save the apologies, just get done with what
you're doing and get over here and find out for me
what Mona's up to, okay?"

"I'll be done with what I'm doing a lot faster if

you'll cut the yap and give me an answer to my question about that phone number."

"Yeah?" Kenny laughed. "Well, try this. The number doesn't exist, Perkins. Never has. Exchange isn't even legal. The number is a total, one hundred percent fake."

I breathed long and deep in the silence, then thanked Kenny and hung up quickly. I picked up my briefcase, turned for the elevators, and ran smack into the tall, athletic Vincent Wakefield. He was grinning.

CHAPTER 11

Vincent Wakefield insisted on escorting me to the Fore 'n' Aft Lounge, the Holiday Inn's saloon. When I demurred, he discreetly showed me the butt of the 9mm Luger he had tucked in his waistband under his blue, gold-buttoned jacket.

Let's just say that I've been more terrified in my life. Unless Wakefield was some kind of dummy, which I doubted, he had to appreciate the risk involved in blowing me away in the middle of a crowded motel. But I think everybody's entitled to his little fantasies. I was planning to talk to him at some point anyway. I saw no harm in letting him think he was in control. I accompanied him to the lounge.

We got ourselves a table in the corner of the sparsely populated saloon. The long plate-glass windows gave us that terrific view of the Detroit skyline. The heavily stuffed, wraparound chair gripped my sides as I slipped my briefcase under the table and got comfortable. A waitress with the face of a teenager, the body of a grown woman, and the dress of a dancehall whore cheerfully took our beer orders—

Canadian for me, Old Vienna for Wakefield—and flounced away.

I got a cigar going and looked at Wakefield. This close, I saw that my estimate of age was pretty good; Wakefield had lived in that lined, leathery face for close to fifty years. His short brown hair was so densely curly I wondered if it was chemically permed, but after examination decided it probably wasn't. However, he obviously had more than his share of vanity about his looks: his teeth were conspicuously capped, the nails on his long hard fingers were manicured and buffed, and he smelled of several variations of Old Spice. His narrow eyes were shrewd and slate-gray, and he radiated pent-up, adrenaline-fueled power. I waited till he talked first; Patient Perkins, they call me.

"You been following me," he said, his voice a choppy rasp.

I paused while our waitress delivered two bowl-shaped mugs of beer, then hoisted mine in his direction with a grin, and asked, "So tell me. How did you like Cincinnati?"

Wakefield had been raising his beer to his mouth; at my question he hesitated, then raised it quickly and drank. "You and that wind-up-toy Chrysler. Thought you were being real slick. I made you ten minutes after we left my place this morning."

I puffed on my cigar. "You ought not to make credit-card calls. They can be traced. Bush-league, old son."

Wakefield leaned back in his chair and gave me a squinted stare. "What were you doing in Cincinnati?"

"I asked you about Cincinnati first," I answered.

Vincent Wakefield made a half-smile. "I enjoyed it. I didn't get much of anywhere, though. How about you?"

"I did better. I ate some great meals, I met some fine people, I got laid three times, and I found out about you."

Wakefield laughed. "Doesn't do you much good, now does it?"

I drained my beer, set the mug down, flicked a finger at the waitress, and answered casually, "Not unless I've got a clue to the money that you don't have." Those numbers, those damn phone numbers that did not exist and never had existed. They *had* to mean something. They were in Barton's directory for *some* reason.

"What money?" Wakefield asked, his mouth round. I mean to tell you, he was *good*.

Our fresh beers came. In an elaborate ritual, I propped my cigar in the ashtray, picked up the mug, took a sip from the icy surface, swallowed it, and set the mug down. Though I didn't look at Vincent Wakefield once during this process, I got the definite impression he was getting impatient. At just the right strategic moment I said, "I've got the numbers, Vinny."

"That so, Benny?" he squinted.

"Ben."

"Vince."

I was encouraged that he showed just the faintest interest in the numbers. I retrieved my cigar and puffed the air between us full of smoke and decided to move the conversation around to keep him off balance. "What do you do for a living, Vince?"

"Little of this, little of that. Whatever the market will bear."

His eyes had gone distant, yet stayed rock-steady on mine. I said, "You told the Trans-Ocean people you're a private detective."

Wakefield grinned, showing rows of even, white teeth. "Me? Oh, hell, *no*. I'm a consultant. Labor relations, business management, employee motivation, that kind of thing." He shrugged. "As for you, pal, clumsy though you may be, *you've* been operating like a p.i."

"Me? Oh, *hell*, no. I'm a maintenance guy. Fixing

busted stuff, cleaning up messes, putting things back the way they were, that kind of thing."

"Uh-huh. Uh-huh." He leaned forward on his big arms, his face elongating, his eyes going narrow. "And who just rung you in on the money, is what I want to know."

No doubt. Oh, well, to get something, you have to risk something. I laid my cigar back down in the ashtray and very deliberately drank a big swallow of beer. "Now that's a long story. Fact is, there's this woman. She got herself separated from a whole big pile of money, more'n I ever seen in one place at one time. She gave me a call and asked if I could do anything about getting it back. Now you."

Wakefield's lips tightened down over his teeth. "Okay. Fact is, there's this woman. She had a husband who went off and left her with two little kids to fend for herself, and got himself killed. He told her about some money. She gave me a call and asked if I could do anything about getting it back."

"Have any luck?"

"Got part of the story," he said cagily, "but no scratch, not yet anyway. You?"

"Pretty much the same. You didn't get anywhere with McGraw, I take it."

Vince Wakefield's leathery face widened in a derisive smile. "That ugly old bitch? Naw. Wasted trip, actually. I had what I've got before I ever went down there. You're not telling me she helped *you*, are you?"

"Inadvertently." I stubbed my cigar out. "Could be we each got part of the answer, Vince. Could be we could put it together, that way both our clients make out." I studied him closely. "What I got are the numbers, Vince."

"And what I got is the map."

We stared at each other for a long moment, grinning. The waitresses and bartender were making closing-up sounds. There were a million things I wanted to ask, a million more things I needed to know. But I felt it was time to disengage. Wakefield and I were, figuratively speaking, pacing around each other like wary alley cats, and a misstep or a poorly worded statement could bust things up and turn it ugly. If I could get what I wanted without tangling with him, that was fine with me. Just because my cases never got wrapped up nice and easy before didn't mean there couldn't be a first time.

I swirled the beer in my mug thoughtfully, then downed it with a long draft. "Where'd you get it?"

"My client. That's all I'm saying."

"Got the map with you?"

"Oh, no," he said, sounding like he'd expected the question. "How about the numbers? You got them?"

"You kidding?" I lied, thinking about the briefcase at my feet with the Rolodex cards.

"You got any suggestions?" Wakefield asked, leaning back in his chair and propping an elbow on its back.

"How about we meet here in the morning. In the dining room. Seven A.M. sharp. You with map, me with numbers. We got mutual interests, we'll talk about it then and see if there's any way we can do business."

"Seven A.M.," Wakefield repeated, "dining room. Right." He shoved back from the table and rose. I did likewise, retrieving my briefcase. Wakefield, who topped me by a couple of inches, grinned again. "Something tells me, Ben, that this whole thing could go down real smooth, pal."

He nonchalantly fished some bills out of his pocket, dropped them on the table without counting them, then turned and sauntered out of the Fore 'n' Aft Lounge without looking back.

Vince Wakefield's parting statement was proven very, very wrong less than five minutes later when I got back to my room.

The door was ajar. I knew I had closed it upon

leaving; that was second nature. I glanced up and down the empty hall, then backed up to the wall on the hinge side of the door and, using my steel-reinforced toe, silently pushed the door open. No sound.

Holding the briefcase across my chest with both hands, I sidled silently into the room. Every light was on, no one was there, and the place looked normal except for the fact that it had been brutally tossed.

Both double beds had been stripped, the sheets and spreads wadded and tossed across the room. Bits and pieces of my smashed cassette recorder lay sprinkled on the table by the window wall and glittered from the carpet. My overnight bag, which contained, by this time, mainly dirty laundry, was overturned on the floor, underwear and socks and T-shirts scattered around. Every drawer of the dresser was ajar and one had been removed completely and leaned cockeyed against the wall.

I took it all in, breathing slowly and silently, straining to hear even the slightest sound. A glance into the bright gleaming bathroom to my right showed nothing unusual except the medicine chest hung open and my shaving gear lay under the dripping faucet in one of the sinks. No one lurked in the shower stall, no one could hide under the bed (it was on a pedestal) or in the closet (it was a doorless alcove). I was alone.

After two full minutes I quietly set the briefcase down, shut the door, and bolted and chained it.

Oddly, it was only then that my heart started to pound. I walked aimlessly into the middle of the room. Could have been just a random B&E, I told myself. Not unusual, not by a long shot, in a midtown motel like this.

But I only had two things of real value with me. My money, which was tucked in the wallet in my back trouser pocket, and the Rolodex cards, which were in my briefcase. My only suspect, whom I immediately had to rule out, of course, was Vince Wakefield.

I didn't reason my way through to the decision. It just appeared, fully formed, in my head. I picked up my briefcase, left the room, went down to the reception desk and did some business—special business. Then I made a call to Kenny Slingluff from one of the lobby phones, and during our brief and not particularly friendly conversation my eyes suspiciously surveyed the few strangers hanging around the lobby. None of them paid me the slightest attention.

Back up in the room, I made up one of the beds, stripped, stretched out and tried to relax. It was hard, because I found myself wishing for the first time on this job that I'd brought my gun. It was also hard because, quite naturally, I began to second-guess the move I'd just made. Kenny Slingluff is not exactly the world's most trustworthy soul.

But there was no way he could hurt me; the worst he could do was not help me, and, though not the world's brightest man, Kenny Slingluff knew better than to screw me up. I switched off the light, feeling a little better. In this business, ignoring your instincts can get you killed. So, when paranoia talks, Perkins listens.

I'd just finished shaving when the phone rang. Face stinging from the aftershave, I padded in my underwear to the phone and answered it. "Yeah."

"Wakefield," came the rasping voice. "What room you in? They won't give out room numbers down here."

"Two-oh-eight, but don't come up here. I said we'd meet in the breakfast room, remember? Just cool your jets." I slammed the phone down, out of general peevishness.

I had exactly one pair of clean slacks left, and exactly zero clean shirts. I sorted through the mess, found a shirt that passed the smell test, shook out the wrinkles as best I could, and put it on.

Then I set about straightening up the room. Not that I'm a neat person—far from it; my apartment's looked worse even without the assistance of an intruder—but I wanted things in some semblance of order in case I had to leave in a hurry. And it didn't break my heart any to keep Wakefield waiting. While he couldn't have tossed my room personally, he could easily have arranged it, giving this case exactly the kind of complication I didn't need.

Finally, when I'd made sure I had wallet, keys, cigars, and matches on me, I unbolted the room door and opened it to go downstairs. There stood Vince Wakefield, a solid denim manifestation today from shirt to slacks, topped off by a denim baseball cap that said CAT DIESEL POWER. He carried an impressive-looking black map case in one hand. "Good morning," he said in a harsh, businesslike rasp.

I glanced around me. "This look like the breakfast room to you, Wakefield?"

"Better if we talk private," he answered. "Gonna invite me in?"

Call me lazy. "Sure, what the hell." I stood back to let him pass. I swung the door shut, turned, and found myself looking down the business end of Wakefield's Luger, which, like a pro, he held at navel height, tight against him, pointed steadily at me. His flat-planed face was impassive, except for maybe just a glint of satisfaction in his small hard eyes.

I sighed. "So what now?"

"The numbers."

"What about 'em?"

"I want 'em."

"They're not here."

"You said you had 'em."

"Watch my lips. I do have 'em. I just don't have them here." Which was God's own truth. I'd shipped them off to Kenny Slingluff, express delivery, the night before. At the request of paranoia. I was pretty glad now that I had.

"Somehow," he said in a measured voice, "I find it hard to believe you."

"Whether you believe me or not will have little effect on Western civilization as we know it, Wakefield."

His lips pressed together. "Smart ass. Turn around. Assume the position. You know the drill."

"Suit yourself," I retorted. I turned, leaned on flat palms against the wall, and spread my feet a bit. There are no sudden moves available to you from that position, if the guy with the gun is smart, and Wakefield was. He didn't do a full field search, just patted my sides, my groin, my pockets with one rough hand, maintaining the right distance from me, and found nothing interesting.

"Stay put," came his calm voice. I did so in helpless silence, and listened to the sounds of my room being tossed for the second time in twelve hours. At least this time I knew who was doing it; wondering who had done the same last night had me really bugged.

Wakefield was fast and thorough: sheets and mattresses, bureau drawers, medicine chest, luggage, clothes. Rip, crash, bang, slam. Then, for a long moment, silence.

"Turn around." Cold, empty voice.

I did so, slowly and carefully.

Wakefield's Luger was gone. He stood a yard from me, making a big man-to-man grin. "So," he said lightly, "you're not as dumb as you look, huh?"

"It's a struggle, sometimes," I said, matching his casual tone.

He chuckled, then turned earnest. "Here's how I see it. I got a map which is no help at all without some numbers. You got some numbers. Now, why in the world shouldn't we just partner up peacefully? We both got clients and there's plenty for all. What do you say, pal?"

"Hey, swell! Great idea, Vince! One thing first, though."

"What's that, pal?"

I kicked him. I didn't hold back a thing, just let him have it smack dab in the balls with the steel-reinforced toe of my high-topped LeHigh safety shoe.

Vince Wakefield was strong and in top shape, but was caught totally by surprise. He jackknifed forward with a strangled grunt, the CAT cap spinning off his head. I caught him by his shoulders just before he hit the floor—I didn't want him hurt, not accidentally anyhow—hoisted him back up on his rubbery legs, grabbed the open collar of his denim shirt with one hand, twisted it in a knot against his throat, and, with my other fist, gave him several short, sharp, economical blows to the face: eye, nose, mouth, eye again. I'm short on boxing skills but plenty long on mean, and I kept hitting him in the same spots till the blows brought blood. Then I spun him and shoved him against the wall where he'd braced me a moment before. He hit hard and slid abruptly to the floor with a thud, wheezing wetly.

You never want a guy to think that roughing him up was hard work, so I kept my breathing under control as best I could and said flatly, "Get up."

. He coughed and snuffled. His fingers roamed his face aimlessly, assessing the damage. He said, "Ohh, man."

"Vince old buddy, I was only warming up."

He pulled his long legs forward and made it to his knees. I took him by the elbows and, trying to make it look effortless, lifted him to his feet, turned him around, slammed him against the wall, and did a thorough field search. I've never been a policeman, but I've been on the receiving end enough times to know how it's done.

The Luger was tucked under the waistband of his jeans against his left hip. I retrieved it, hefted it, and tossed it onto the unmade bed, then stood back and let him go.

Vince Wakefield turned around slowly. He felt his face again and brought his hands away wet with blood. The eye I'd worked on was purpling up nicely but wasn't entirely closed; have to improve my quality control, I thought.

Wakefield coughed once, wiped his hands on his pants, and said, "You can't get the money without the map."

I smiled. "Meaning, the map case is empty."

"That's right. But I know where to get it. You got the numbers?"

"I had them, and I got rid of them, but I can still get at them, whenever I want."

Wakefield tried to grin, but his lips were too cracked and swollen for that. "So each of us still has something the other wants. Partners?"

Not hardly, I thought. This would have to be an arrangement of convenience, with the threat of violence on both sides keeping things in check.

"I play straight," I said quietly. "Long as I get done what I'm hired to do, I don't hurt or double-cross anybody else. Which is more'n I can say for you."

The cramping in Wakefield's midsection seemed to be easing already. That was impressive, considering the nut-shot he'd taken. He said, "Hey, pal, I made a play. It didn't work. Them's the breaks. No hard feelings."

I didn't buy it, but at least I knew how he worked, where he stood. A smarter and more ruthless man would probably have made plans then and there to cut him out of the play as soon as possible, but I don't work that way. Not anymore.

"Feelings got nothing to do with it," I said. "Just play it straight from here on out, or I'll purely stomp you into a little bitty puddle, and you'd best believe it."

Wakefield managed his grin. "Feel better now?"

"Yeah, lots."

"Good! Tell you what, let me clean up some, then we'll go pay us a little visit."

He didn't saunter into the bathroom, he sort of slunk there, good eye wary on me, giving me a wide berth. I liked it, even though the threat I'd just uttered tasted pretty silly in my mouth. Threats are, I've learned, worthless, and this one turned out to be no exception.

CHAPTER 12

Kids dressed in their high school uniforms—jeans and T-shirts—clumped the corners of Sandwich Township West, waiting for their buses, as we rounded the corner onto Elvis Street.

I have to admit, I felt pretty good. I had Wakefield under control, I had his Luger tucked under my jacket, the numbers were safe with Kenny Slingluff, except for the one I'd memorized, and I was on my way to meet his client—and see the map. Not bad for four days' work.

Except for giving me directions, Wakefield didn't talk to me on the way down there. He lounged, half slumping on the passenger side of the Chrysler's bench seat, his long arm reaching along the back of the seat toward me, fingers tapping. One eye was swollen nearly shut; one of his cheekbones was purpled; his nose glowed. But his good eye glinted bright and gray. I had no idea what he was thinking.

We parked on the driveway of the long low ranch house at 1090, walked to the door, and knocked. After a moment the door opened and Mrs. Masters looked up at us. Her warm, welcoming smile vanished when she saw Wakefield's damaged face. "Mr. *Wakefield?*" she asked, eyes narrow and concerned.

Vince Wakefield said, "This is Ben Perkins, Mary. He's involved now. We need to talk."

She studied me coolly, then looked anxiously at Wakefield. "Is it all right?" she asked softly.

"Yeah, no problem." Wakefield answered.

She looked doubtful, but she unlocked the screen door and pushed it open. "Make yourselves comfortable back on the deck, gentlemen. May I serve you coffee?"

I let Wakefield precede me into the foyer. She took our coffee orders and went into the kitchen on our right.

Wakefield knew his way around the house. He led me through a mirror-lined hall and down a couple of steps to the left into the plush family room. The two redheaded children lounged in their pajamas on the floor in front of a big color TV that was built into a massive entertainment center.

Mrs. Masters's boy jumped to his feet. "Hi, Mr. Wakefield," he said. Wakefield made totally insincere sounds of friendship. The little girl ignored us haughtily. Wakefield slid open the patio door wall and led me onto the deck.

It was twenty by twenty, and of genuine redwood, not stained construction-grade junk. To the left, steps led down to a brick patio which surrounded a gas grill. To the right, a mass of carefully tended foliage meandered around the corner of the house. Carpetlike dark green zoysia ran down the slight incline to the back of the lot, ending at heavy forest. From the looks of it, I wouldn't have been surprised if there was a creek back there.

There were expensive patio chairs and tables on the deck. We stayed standing, said nothing, and didn't look at each other as TV sounds floated out from the family room. Somewhere down Elvis Street a diesel-powered school bus puffed and roared.

Mrs. Masters came onto the deck, carrying a beaten-copper tray holding a stainless steel coffee decanter, three large white china mugs, a bowl of sugar cubes, a pitcher of cream, and several silver spoons. Wakefield darted over and closed the patio door behind her as she set the tray down on the large glass-topped patio table which dominated the deck. "Cream and sugar, Mr. Perkins?" she asked.

"Black is beautiful." Wakefield agreed. She served us and herself, and invited us to sit as she stirred a slug of cream into her coffee. I took a chair with my back facing the woods. Wakefield put his angular body in a chair to my right, and the woman sat down facing him and blew gently on the steaming surface of her coffee, hands cradling the mug.

In high heels, done up in one of those towering formal hairdos, Mary Masters would probably have reached five feet six. As she was today, she was probably just a shade over five even. Her dark reddish hair was smooth and absolutely straight, combed back on her head and bound at the nape into a short, loose pony tail. Since meeting us at the door, she'd changed into a white, floppy, open-necked shirt that disguised her figure which, I knew from having seen her before, was full and voluptuous. Below she wore stylish, white denim carpenter's pants and clunky, uncomfortable-looking wood sandals. Any male with standard-issue hormones would be hard-pressed to look at that body and not get ideas.

It was the face that changed it. No, no; she wasn't a hag. Hers was almost a model's face, a model a few years past her salad days, perhaps, but still earning a comfortable living in TV bit parts and commercials. It was a face with no discernible flaw: oval shaped, fine cheekbones, good strong teeth, generous mouth. Her skin was a silky white that probably would tan okay but hadn't seen a lot of sun.

It was also a face totally without guile. Her eyes were open and watchful, yet friendly and accepting. It was a face that had known a lot of pain, yet had fun, too, and had laughed, and still laughed, at good jokes. It was a face that loved and was loved in return. It was the face of a person equipped with the kind of strength that money can't buy. Or rent, even. Not even in America. Believe me, I've tried.

To Vince Wakefield she said in her contralto voice, "You've been hurt."

"Uh, yeah." He shifted uncomfortably in the

eminently comfortable chair. By God, he was nervous. I knew why because I was, too. This woman was not of our world. She was a civilian. Guys like me and Wakefield may work for them, but we sure as hell don't understand them.

She turned her gaze on me. "Did you hurt him, Mr. Perkins?"

I said, "Well, let's just say he kind of ran into my fist a bunch of times, ma'am."

"I don't understand."

Wakefield said, "Mary, Ben here got hired by somebody—I don't know who—to find the money that John stole."

There. That was the source of some of the pain she carried in her face. She covered it beautifully. She sipped some coffee and said to me, "Please tell me about it, Mr. Perkins."

I gave her the *Reader's Digest* condensed version: Mrs. Sturtevant, Cincinnati, Trans-Ocean, the Rolodex cards, the credit-card call, the trip to Windsor, my tail of Wakefield. For the most part I told the truth. All I left out was where the Rolodex cards were. I figured I'd made enough mistakes that morning.

The tall man listened attentively; I realized he hadn't really heard all of the details. But, as I got to the events of the morning, I saw him begin to fidget. The hell with him. I told how Wakefield held me up, and what had happened to him as a result. Mary Masters looked a little pale when I was done, yet, surprisingly, more resolved.

She faced Wakefield. "Do you still have the gun?"

Wakefield stared down at the table.

I said, "No, ma'am, I've got it."

"Give it to me."

I leaned forward in the chair, slipped the Luger from under my jacket, and handed it butt-first into her small, smooth white hands. She stared down at it, breathing through parted lips, then asked, "Is it loaded?"

"Yes, ma'am," I replied.

"How do you unload it?"

I showed her. When the clip sprang into her palm she jumped as if bitten. She stared for a minute at the dark oiled clip, then laid it and the weapon twelve inches apart on the glass table. Her glance found me, then Wakefield, and stayed there, and it was sharp, as was her voice. "No more of this, gentlemen. I mean it."

I don't know if Wakefield looked at her. I know I didn't, and I know that neither of us replied.

After a second she said in a lighter tone, "Mr. Wakefield, I know how Mr. Perkins found you. How did you find him?"

"Well," Wakefield said, looking past her shoulder, "I saw him following me, of course. Shoot, he followed me all day, here, even. I got his plate number and ran it through my buddy at Windsor police. That got me the fact that it was a rental car out of the airport, which led me to believe he was at one of the hotels. There aren't that many hotels in Windsor. I called around till I found him."

Mary Masters picked up her coffee mug with both hands and drank from it slowly, her eyes distant. Then she set it down and looked at me. "Your client—whoever she is—she was one of the people that John...stole from?"

John Masters. Arthur Barton's Windsor identity. Solved the question of where he'd been hiding out for seven years. Just a river's width from Detroit, yet in a foreign country. Cute. I replied, "That's right."

She said with feeling, "I do feel sorry for her. I wish I could apologize to her personally." *That* would have been a scene, Mary Masters apologizing to Joann Sturtevant. "I want her to have her money back. I want all the victims to get their money back. But some of it is mine." She tipped her head toward the house. "Ten thousand of it was money I inherited from my parents. Of course I turned it over to John, and it vanished along with the rest. But I must recover that. That's why I hired Mr. Wakefield, to help me find it."

I asked, "Do you mind if I smoke?"

"Not at all. Please, let me get an ashtray." Before I could stop her she'd risen from the chair and darted into the family room. I used the business of lighting my cigar to avoid looking at Wakefield. She returned, slid a clean beaten-copper ashtray in front of me, then replenished her coffee mug and mine—Wakefield hadn't touched his—and sat down again.

I puffed, exhaled, and said, "I'd appreciate it if you'd fill me in. Vince and I haven't had much of a chance to talk."

"About John? Oh." She folded her hands in her lap and looked down at them, then said, "Seven years ago I was single. I had never married. I worked at the Royal Bank of Canada's main office on Ouellette. I was a cash management clerk. We offered cash management services to small businesses, mainly sole practitioners, professionals, doctors, lawyers, accountants, and so forth.

"One of our clients was named John Masters." She said the name smoothly, without inflection. I watched her from behind my curtain of cigar smoke and saw that she was uncomfortable telling the story, but she went on. "He was an accountant. He'd just moved to Windsor and was setting up practice. He wanted help with the financial management of his business." She made a small smile. "Imagine that, him an accountant, really, wanting to hire the Bank to help manage his money. But often we're better at tending other people's affairs than we are our own, isn't that true?"

No argument from me. If it weren't for that, guys in my line of work wouldn't have a line of work.

Her smile turned rueful as she looked at each of us. She picked up her coffee mug but just held it as she went on. "He asked me out. He was such a quiet man, so businesslike, I was surprised. But I went out with him for several months. Then we married. In my parents' church in Amherstburg. Beth Anne came along less than a year later. Robbie a couple of years after that."

Now she drank some coffee; getting dry, I supposed. Aside from smoking my cigar and taking sips from my own coffee, I remained as still as possible, and didn't say a damned word. While proficiency with your gun and your fists is important in this line of work, the ability to listen can help, too.

Vince Wakefield stared impassively back toward the woods as Mary Masters went on. "It was a fine marriage. John was such a fine man in so many ways. He provided well for us. He was a good father to his children and he was attentive to me even though he traveled. His business took him elsewhere quite frequently. But all marriages have troubles and one thing troubled me. He had no faith."

Her eyes found me, very direct, penetrating. I focused on the bricks of the house behind her. She said, "I never made demands upon him. I didn't pressure him to attend services with me. I prayed for him and, when he'd allow it, with him. It was something he didn't discuss much. But even as I have faith in God, I also had faith in John. I knew that he'd come around eventually. And he did. Early this summer."

My cigar singed my fingers. I stubbed it out. Mary Masters replenished my coffee as Wakefield cleared his throat and sat straighter, looking somewhere in between us.

She said: "He came to me one evening. Quite by surprise. And he told me everything, about his past, about the money, about his wife."

I drank some coffee. The older child, the girl, slid the patio door open and called something to her mother about a program. Mrs. Masters answered lightly, "Channel twenty, dear. Now leave us alone, please." When she turned back to us the smile she'd made for the child had changed into a tight, pained thing.

She said softly, "He found God that night. The Lord saved him. We got on our knees and prayed together the whole night through. We prayed for strength and for guidance. By sunup he knew what he had to do. He kissed the children as they slept and he kissed me at the door and he got in the car and he left. But before he left he gave me something. A map. A map of Detroit. And he told me that the money, the money he'd stolen, an awful lot of it, was hidden over there, and the map was a clue to where it was.

"But he added," she went on in a rush, "that the map wasn't the whole answer. Only he had the whole answer. He wanted me to have the map in case anything happened to him. That was exactly the way he put it, as if he *knew* something might happen to him. He wanted me to have the map so that—as he put it—anyone wanting to find the money would have to deal with me to get it and let me have my rightful share."

The hollowness in her voice had started before she began the last sentence, but she kept talking anyhow. "Then he died."

For the first time in many minutes I looked directly at Wakefield as she sobbed quietly. His face looked smooth and younger, stretched with tension. He cleared his throat several times and fidgeted with the cuffs of his denim shirt. I looked back at Mary Masters as she wiped her eyes brusquely with the back of a hand and stared glassily at Wakefield.

"For the first time," she said shakily, "for the first time I challenged the will of the Lord. I cursed Him and I condemned Him. He'd left me the widow of a man who lied, who entered into a marriage with me that was unlawful. He'd left me the widow of a common thief, an embezzler. He'd left me the mother of two small, fatherless children with no support and no income. He left me alone and disgraced in the eyes of God and man."

Her eyes gradually cleared, her voice steadied.

Her hands, which had been gripped together to dead whiteness, loosened. I noticed she wore a heavy gold wedding band. She said tonelessly, "I knew I would lose this house. I'll probably have it another month at most, then the bank will foreclose. When the facts of my illegal marriage become known, the Province will deny me benefits normally due to a woman in my situation, with dependents. I knew all of this, but there is an answer. The money. *My* money, the ten thousand. Included in what John hid away in Detroit. The money to which the map is part of the answer. The Lord means for me to have a share of it. The Lord provides, even in crisis."

I slid my chair back on the wood deck, stretched, propped one leg over the other. "I sympathize with you, Mrs. Masters. Hey, it's got to be tough, raising kids and that, all alone. But with all due respect, that ten grand is co-mingled with stolen money, and—"

She shook her head violently. "It still belongs to me and the children! I must have it! Mr. Perkins, with that ten thousand dollars perhaps I can keep the house a few months longer. It's on the market, times are bad but perhaps I can sell it. I can get an apartment and a job and start over. But I have to have the money. That's why I hired Mr. Wakefield."

She leaned toward me. "Will you work with Mr. Wakefield and get my money back for me? You'll be helping your client, too, and all those other people John stole from. It would...finish what John started, to atone for what he did, pay the victims back."

I glanced at Wakefield. His lips had scabbed in two places, upper and lower, and the rugged, hard-planed, sardonic lines were back. I wasn't sure, but I could have sworn there was the slightest twinkle in his good eye, as if to say, "Is there anybody in the whole wide world weirder than clients?"

"Sure, of course," I said to her. "I'd be stupid not to. Long as this fella and I can work together without problems, why—"

She whipped her glance toward Wakefield,

reached out around the coffee mugs, pistol, and tray, and put her hands on each of ours. "You *will* work together. You will help and protect each other. Is that clear? Otherwise, I shall be very cross."

Wakefield nodded solemnly. "Sure, Mary, no problem. How about getting the map?"

She gave me a penetrating look, then released our hands, got up, and went back into the house.

Vince Wakefield exhaled a sigh, puffing his cheeks, and said in a low voice, "Something else, huh?"

"Something else, all right."

"Whew. That's one determined lady."

I got out a fresh cigar and lighted it. "I was just sitting here thinking how this is the first time the Lord's ever been involved in a case of mine."

Wakefield smiled crookedly. "Boggles the mind, don't it?"

Mary Masters came back onto the deck with a large rolled paper tube. Wakefield and I cleared the mugs onto the tray and slid it aside as she unrolled the map out onto the table. I used the mugs to hold the corners down and the three of us scooted forward on our chairs and looked silently.

It was a large, colorful, extremely detailed map of the city of Detroit, including most of Wayne County and the southern halves of Oakland and Macomb Counties. Every highway, street, alley, and railroad right-of-way was clearly marked and named. Big dollops of green marked the major parks: Kensington and Lower Huron Metro on the north and south, and Dynamite Park in the far west end; neighborhood parks showed up like green dots sprinkled all over. The Detroit River gushed blue down the right-hand side, and the Huron River and the four Rivers Rouge meandered across in smaller ribbons. Detroit itself was laid out like a wheel with spokes of streets emanating from downtown, turning abruptly, toward the city limits, into the brutal crisscross grid of the Mile Roads going east-west, and

Van Dyke, Dequindre, Southfield, Telegraph, and their multitude of clones going north-south.

The usual cross-reference points, letters, and numbers, were printed on the sides of the map. In the white margins were meticulously hand-printed, extremely tiny sets of numbers, four to a group. So, you needed eight to triangulate, I realized. Oh, yeah. Extension 9. Heh, heh.

"Job of work he did here," I commented after a moment.

"Come on, Perkins, if you got the numbers let's zero in, okay, pal?"

Mary Masters gave Wakefield a reproving look. I squinted at the left-hand row of numbers and ran my finger down them till I reached 5586. Marking that with my finger, I buzzed along the top row till I reached 9809 and marked that.

Wakefield was pretty good with one eye. He did the triangulation and landed a long finger on the spot. "Bingo."

I let go of the coordinates. We stared silently for a moment. Then I said, "Okay, fine. Now, move your finger, so we can see where it is."

"Oh, yeah." He let go and the two of us nearly bumped heads leaning down for a better look.

"Where is it?" Mrs. Masters asked anxiously.

"West Lafayette," I answered. "Looks like the corner of Queens Street. Close to downtown."

"Nice neighborhood," Wakefield growled.

"*Real* nice neighborhood," I agreed.

"A hellhole," Wakefield grunted. "Pardon me, Mary."

"Would John have hidden money in a place like that?" she asked, staring pensively down at the map.

"Well," I said, "all we can do is go over there and take a look."

Wakefield was removing the coffee mugs and the map snapped together in a loose roll. He picked it up. "Let's go. We'll get back to you, Mary."

"Just a minute, gentlemen." She stepped between us, reached out and took my hand and Wakefield's in her cool, firm ones. "Hold hands, please."

"What?" Wakefield asked darkly.

"The circle of prayer," she answered. "You must hold hands."

Wakefield and I stared at each other. He shook his head quickly. "Ohh, no. Sorry, ma'am, not that, no way."

"Oh, for heaven's sake!" she sighed. "Let us pray."

We stood on the deck in the midmorning sunlight as she implored God to travel with us, to protect us, to give us His guidance, wisdom, and strength. I heartily endorsed the whole thing, especially the strength part.

CHAPTER 13

The U.S. Customs Service, like the Internal Revenue Service, thrives on a brilliantly promoted myth. Every now and then there's an article in the papers about a particularly lucrative bust at the border, like, some old innocent-looking granny in a sparkling-clean Olds sedan with a JESUS SAVES sticker on the rear bumper who's caught at Customs with fifteen hundred pounds of pure cocaine where the seat stuffing used to be. The Customs inspector who makes the bust comments, "I don't know why I ordered her over...just an instinct...something didn't feel right...you get a feel for these things."

When, probably, what got the smuggler inspected was the last digit of her license plate number, or the color of her car, or something. But Customs will never own up to that. They'd rather everyone believed in some mystical, psychic ability on their part to divine lawbreakers. I'm all in favor of it, actually. There will always be crime, so let there be good, clean crime, executed by professionals, without rookies and the faint of heart cluttering up the scenery.

The Customs inspector on the Detroit side of the Ambassador Bridge apparently didn't have his "instinct" turned on that day, nor was the color of my Chrysler or its license number on any hit list. He ran through the litany of questions: citizenship, time in Canada, anything to declare, any firearms or controlled substances, blah blah blah, and he never once got curious about how come an American citizen was driving a car with Ontario plates and carrying a bruised-faced Canadian in the passenger seat.

As we rolled away from the shed, Vince Wakefield unbent in his seat, extending his too-long legs so that his knees bumped the dashboard. "Makes me nervous, those Customs guys."

I shrugged. "Good thing you had your passport. That's not required to get across here, is it?"

"Nah, but it don't hurt to carry it with you. Guess you got nerves of steel or something, huh, Perkins?"

"We got nothing to hide."

"Right now, anyway. But what if we find the dough? How're we going to get it back across?"

So now it was "we," even though that very morning Wakefield had attempted to cut me out of the action violently. It warmed my heart all to hell. As for the money, I guess at that point I still wasn't a believer. Hundreds of thousands in small, untraceable bills, come on! Plus the map and the "coordinates" and the rest. Jeez.

"We'll jump off that bridge when we get to it," I replied.

"Heh, heh. Ha-ha-ha." I felt Wakefield's narrow-eyed gaze on me. "You don't think the money's there, do you."

I finagled a cigar from out of my pocket and into my lips and mashed the lighter button on the dashboard as I one-handed the car onto Porter Street headed west. "You know, I learned something a long time ago. What I think hardly ever matters. What I do, does. So, we'll go, and we'll look, and we'll see. See?"

"Hey, I'm with you on *that*." He yawned, and then winced. "I never met John Masters, but from what I've heard, what a character. Look at this. Salted the money away. Couldn't just keep a simple list somewhere of where the money was. Had to make a map and leave a trail of codes in his phone book. Seems a little too elaborate."

I beat the yellow and swung south on West Grand Boulevard. "Look at it this way. Masters or Barton or whoever, he was a finance man. Numbers guy. Crooked, besides. Guys like that, they're incapable of doing anything simple. They gotta make a big fuckin' puzzle out of stuff. Probably got his jollies thinking about what anyone would go through trying to figure it out."

The dashboard lighter finally clacked out. I jerked it free, tamped it against the end of my cigar, got it going, and replaced the lighter. If I'd ever entertained notions about acquiring a Chrysler product—and, with my family's heritage with Ford's, it was doubtful to begin with—this experience killed them once and for all. Don't tell me about fit-and-finish and fifty-thousand-mile rust-through warranty; give me a decent radio, a muscular motor, and a lighter that heats up quick. Easy to Please Perkins, they call me. "Main thing is, he was a numbers guy. Numbers are central to all this.

"Well," Wakefield rasped, "*I'm* no numbers guy. I can't hardly keep track of my checking account. Only numbers mean anything to me are, like: ten, twenty, fifty, hundred, and like that."

"Not to mention twenty-two, thirty-two, thirty-eight, and forty-five."

Wakefield laughed. I threw the car around the corner onto West Lafayette. Queens Street was just a couple of blocks farther on. Wakefield paused just a bit longer than usual, then said, quite casually, "So we find the dough, we split it fifty-fifty, right?"

I slowed for a mob of middle-aged Hispanic women crossing the street at a snail's pace. "My client gets one fifty, yours gets ten. We get extra, we split it between them."

"That's not what I mean." I felt his stare on my face as I gunned the accelerator. "*We* split it. You and me, pal. You in?"

"No."

"No, huh?"

"Not just no. More on the order of, no fucking way."

I didn't look at him and he said nothing.

"Don't even think about it," I added.

West Lafayette is a pretty important street downtown. Out where we were, it doesn't amount to a hell of a lot. Like most Detroit arteries, it's very wide, running three lanes in each direction. This anticipated traffic volume that just wasn't there anymore. Big flat-bottom trucks hauling coils of steel brayed and lurched in each direction. Old clunker cars tooled slowly along. Shiny new cars moved faster, looking for somewhere better to be.

The street was lined with sooty, one- and two-story brick buildings. Of these, a third were burned out. Another third were vacant and had been up for sale, if the condition of their signs was any clue, since 1960. The rest were occupied by pawn shops, bars, used-furniture stores, liquor stores, bars, salvage operations, welfare agencies, fifth-hand clothing emporiums, and bars. A theater at the corner of West Lafayette and Queens advertised on its riddled marquee that classic triple feature: BED SPREAD / AMAZING GRACE / LOTTERY TICKETS.

The block we wanted was between Queens and McKinstry. The south side of West Lafayette had been devastated, its buildings reduced to mountains of rubble. The north side's row buildings were dark and shuttered except for a couple of saloons whose dusty neon signs advertised Miller and Stroh's on tap. Young men clustered and strolled in the hot summer morning, engaged in unknown but guessable brands of commerce. Right in the center of the block, set off by vacant, rubble-strewn lots on either side, stood a five-story, grimy brick building whose dirty, dead-bulbed sign advertised it as the Empress Hotel, sprinkler-protected.

I U-ed at the corner and doubled back. Vince Wakefield leaned forward, elbows propped on knees, chin clamped down on folded fists, scanning the row. As we cruised past the Empress he said, "What do you think?"

"I think if Masters hid the dough around here it had to be at that hot-sheet palace there."

"Hey, I think it's our only option," Wakefield answered. "We'll just have to work it, huh?"

I made an illegal U-turn in mid block, kicked the accelerator, and skated the Chrysler into a parking space a couple of doors down from the Empress. "Yeah," I said, turning off the motor. "You be the heavy, I'll be the nice one. Okay?"

"Okay." We got out of the Chrysler and headed up the cracked, frost-heaved sidewalk to the entrance of the Empress.

It must have been built back in the days when the idea of having a hotel this far out on West Lafayette wasn't considered total insanity. It was tall, square, impressive, and foreboding, and even featured a porch that ran the width of the building and about fifteen feet deep. The only occupant of the porch, when Wakefield and I crossed it to the big glass double front doors, was a blond long-haired kid in blue jeans and a T-shirt. He slept in an old stuffed chair, his white thin feet slung over the porch rail, glowing in the sunshine. We ignored him as we went through the doors into the lobby.

I guess "lobby" is overstating the case a bit. It was really a small room with a big desk, two chairs for "visitors," and not much else. The Empress was obviously an apartment hotel now, and what had once been a large, imposing lobby had been reduced to miniscule size to make room for more apartments on the ground floor.

The desk was still big, though. It wrapped around the room in solid white-oak splendor, speaking of a more lucrative past. A couple of guys with booze and unemployment stamped on their faces pushed past Wakefield and me for the door as we went up to the desk.

Signs tacked to the desk said NO DRINKIN. FREE TRIP TO JAIL FOR TROUBLEMAKERS! NOT RESPONSIBLE FOR PERSONEL BELONGINGS. Behind the desk leaned a dead-eyed, balding old white man with a cold stump of cigar clamped in his teeth. He wore a limp, wrinkled white shirt buttoned loosely around his malnourished body, and was silent except for a squeak which he emitted with each breath. As Wakefield and I leaned on our side of the desk, the clerk asked, "Help you boys?"

"Perkins," I said and, nodding at my companion, said, "Wakefield. We're trying to locate one John Masters."

"Never heard of him." Squeak.

"We were given this address," Wakefield growled.

Squeak. "Nobody named that here."

Vince Wakefield went under the denim jacket to his shirt pocket and came out with a three-by-five black-and-white picture. "Him?"

The old man made a show of looking at the picture, then looked back up at us. He looked different now, but was covering it well. "Maybe," he said guardedly. Squeak. "Not lately, though."

The lobby smelled of old wallpaper and sweat and dirty wood and peeling linoleum flooring. There was no sound for fully ten seconds, then I went for the big enchilada. "He left something here for safekeeping," I said offhandedly, "and we want it."

"Can't do that," he said too quickly. Squeak. "Against the rules."

Vince Wakefield's hand came out of his pocket and had the badge in the man's face with blinding speed. He leaned forward till he was almost cheek-to-cheek with the clerk and shouted, "Can you read *that*, old timer?"

The old man's eyes widened and his jaw dropped open, showing badly fitting dentures and giving us a glimpse of what he'd look like as a corpse. "Well, hell!" he said, his voice a high, breathless whistle. "You boys should have said so!"

"My partner asked you a question," Wakefield said coldly, returning the badge to his pocket. "Give us the poop, why, we'll sort of forget all about reporting this fire-trap to the building board people, and stuff. Right, Ben?"

"For sure," I chimed in.

The old man's eyes had gone fearful and suppli-cating as they flicked back and forth between our faces. "We got lock boxes here," he squeaked. "This feller here, he rented one. Years and years ago. Come in every so often to pay up the rent on it. Paid cash money, good cash money. Name wasn't nothing like Masters, though."

I rolled an even bigger pair of dice. "Withrow, then," I said flatly.

His dead eyes brightened by a couple of watts. "Yeah, that was it."

Wakefield, secure in his role as the heavy, growled, "Cut the bullshit and go fetch for us what he left here, right now, old-timer."

"Yessir! Just wait right here!" He darted away through a door behind him, leaving us in the aro-matic silence.

Vince Wakefield and I glanced at each other. We stayed professionally calm, but I saw his eyes glitter, and I knew mine glittered, too. Here it comes, I thought. What would it be? A suitcase? A brief-case? A carton? A duffel bag?

The door opened and the clerk came through it with a small cardboard envelope clutched in his hand. He handed it to me like an offering. I felt it, glanced at it. Something heavy was inside, but it sure as hell wasn't cash. "Come on!" I snarled.

The clerk squeaked twice. "That's all there is! I swear! I wouldn't lie to you boys. I done survived here like I have 'cause I don't lie to you boys. *You* know that."

I looked at Wakefield to get his opinion. His glare stayed on the clerk. He didn't move a muscle, but he suddenly emanated an aura of menace that even I could feel. "You better not be crossing us up, old man," he said calmly, "'cause if you are, we'll be back. C'mon, pard."

We went back through the door, across the porch and down the heaved, poorly fitted cement steps. The long-haired kid was still sprawled in the chair. I hoped someone was checking his pulse periodically. Vince Wakefield and I didn't talk till we were back in the Chrysler; then he turned to me with a hard stare as I tore the envelope open.

It was a big heavy brass key. Lots of notches. Nothing else in the envelope. Stamped in the envelope: DMB MAIN 801.

"Safe deposit box," I said. Made sense. No one would leave big cash money in a dump like the Empress.

Wakefield's face spread in a wolfish grin. He held out a hard-calloused hand for the key, and I gave it to him. I fished out the plastic-tagged keys to the Chrysler, jammed the right one into the ignition, fired it up, and wheeled away from the Empress toward downtown.

CHAPTER 14

"DMB" stands for Detroit Merchants Bank. The name is obsolete. Thanks to the Byzantine banking laws of the state of Michigan, and the untiring efforts of legions of lawyers and accountants to circumvent them, Detroit Merchants Bank has been gobbled up by a bank holding company called, with some marketing mind's unerring sense of the right, patriotic-sounding name, AmericaWay. Its main office, as was that of DMB, is at Fort and Congress downtown, and I drove us there with an energy hyped by the sight of the brass key clutched in Wakefield's hand and the vision of the bundles of loose cash that the key hopefully represented.

We didn't talk till I began rounding the blocks near the bank, looking for a parking place. "What was the badge?" I asked Wakefield indifferently.

"Wayne County deputy sheriff. Comes in handy," he rasped.

"How'd you get it?"

"Wasn't easy."

"You gonna level with me, Vince?"

"Guess not, come to think of it."

I let it go. Hell, he'd done okay at the Empress, let him have his little secrets if he wanted.

The parking situation was terrible, it being the noon hour by now. Nothing on the streets, nothing in the parking lots or structures. I wheeled the Chrysler through a series of alleys and finally found a spot, marked with vicious-looking LOADING ZONE ONLY signs, in a canyon surrounded by the dirty backsides of skyscrapers. The shiny, clean, brand-new Chrysler looked out of place among the dumpsters and litter. We disembarked, I grabbed my briefcase from the back, and we began hoofing toward the bank building.

We burst out onto Fort Street, crossed it with a mob of lunch-hour pedestrians, and swung right toward the massive doors of the AmericaWay Bank Building, of which the bank itself occupied the ground floor. I held out my hand to Wakefield. "Key."

"Nah," he said casually. "I'll handle this."

"Ain't gonna be easy."

"Child's play, lad." We pushed through the revolving doors, walked across the building foyer, and entered the bank lobby.

"I'll be watching you," I said as Wakefield sauntered away from me across the crowded floor.

The bank's open lobby was massive, with small marble counters in the center for people to fill out their transactions. A row of open offices cluttered with huge desks ran along the right; on the left was a marble counter with teller windows, faced with marble and trimmed in gold and brass. Plush dark purple carpet ran the entire length of the floor, and poles with velvet ropes made a crooked maze to keep the customers in order.

Vince Wakefield sauntered along the velvet ropes toward the end of the teller windows. I strolled at a parallel course along the row of alcoves on the right. Wakefield didn't look like he belonged here. The customers fell pretty neatly in two groups: business people dressed to the teeth, and street folks in their best grungies. In his solid denim outfit, shiny boots, and tight curly hair, the hard-eyed, plane-faced Wakefield looked like the straw boss on a construction site, a guy who'd quit swinging a hammer several years ago.

The last teller window on the right said SAFE DEPOSIT. It was manned by a tall, thin, extremely young man with a blond crewcut, cold conservative eyes, black-framed glasses, disapproving, self-impressed mouth, and a deep blue tailored suit over a white shirt and black tie. Though I'd never seen him before, I made him right away. This was a kid who'd started working at the bank part-time while getting his M.B.A., had tellered forever, and had just recently been promoted to assistant junior manager trainee or some such, and thought he was number one with a bullet. Wakefield sauntered up to him and began talking, and I knew from the minute the clerk laid eyes on him that it was going to go all wrong.

Wakefield's back was to me, but I could see the

clerk's face and nameplate: MR. SIMPSON. Wakefield talked, the clerk squinted. Wakefield showed the key, the clerk examined it, shuffled some invisible papers, then asked Wakefield a question. Wakefield answered. The clerk's face darkened with suspicion. Wakefield pressed on. Though in the din I couldn't understand the words, I heard his rasping voice as he made big gestures with his hands. The clerk started to look alarmed. He glanced around, probably looking for a security guard. My feet wanted to move me in that direction, but I hung back.

Then, after a silence, Wakefield reached out and plucked the key out of Simpson's hand. He turned and made for the door, not sauntering now but dodging customers as he went. The clerk ducked from behind his window, called, "Sir, wait!" and went to the waist-high door that opens to the lobby. It was, of course, locked, and no one hit the buzzer for him, so he stood there helplessly, waving at Wakefield as I fell in behind the big man about ten paces back, followed him through the revolving door, and caught up with him a few paces later on the crowded sidewalk.

A city bus stood at the curb, huffing and puffing oily diesel stink as Wakefield faced me. His face was set solid as cement except for his cheeks, which puffed spastically. A reddish-purple flush built in his face, making the veins in his forehead stand out. "Little wimpy-ass swish bastard!" he growled, glaring over my shoulder back at the bank door.

"What happened?" I asked in a low voice.

Wakefield spun on his heel and stomped along the sidewalk. When I caught up with him again, he said, "I gave the key and Masters's name. He looked it up on a little file card and said the key number didn't match the name. I said, well, records must be confused or something. He gimme that fuckin' little prissy-faced look and said, 'Sir, the bank's records are never confused. I demand an explanation as to how you acquired this key.'" Wakefield puffed air through his clenched teeth. "There's nothing worse than a prissy little rule-book fairy. I'm gonna kill the prick. You hear me, Perkins? The little cocksucker is dead meat! I'm gonna—"

"Pipe *down*, for Chrissake." I had to restrain Wakefield physically from crossing Fort Street against a red light. He angrily shook off my grip and jammed his fists into his jeans pockets. The light changed and we started across. I said, "Let's grab a couple of brews in that saloon there and figure out what we do next."

"It better be good," Wakefield answered darkly.

"Hee-hee. I *like* it," Wakefield chortled, draining his beer.

I fanned a couple of dollar bills out on the bar, slid off the stool, and replied, "It'll work, but the timing has to be right."

The juke box was playing the Marshall Tucker Band's mighty fine version of "Can't You See." Wakefield stood and we pushed through the late lunch-hour crowd toward the saloon door. The big man said, "I still like the missing-kid thing better."

"This'll work just as good," I answered shortly as we hit the stifling heat of the sidewalk.

"I owe the little bastard," Wakefield insisted. "You don't want to do the kid bit, how about, 'Mr. Simpson, bad news; your wife's been kidnapped.' I know he's married, I saw his ring. How 'bout it?"

The light changed and we crossed Fort. "Look, will you just *lose* that? We don't have to overengineer this thing. All we want is him out of the picture; we can get that without scaring him purely shitless."

"Never had you pegged for a pussy, Perkins."

Enough, already. I grabbed the lapel of his denim jacket and spun him straight to face me. He smacked my hand away and stepped toward me, glowering down. Pedestrians split around us, paying no attention. I said, "You got a real short memory, Wakefield. Your lip and your nose and your face ain't even healed and you're back to giving me pure wise-ass."

"You sucker-punched me that time," Wakefield said, barely moving his lips. "You won't get away with it again."

"Stay tuned. Meantime, I'm calling the shots on this gag and you'll play it my way."

"We're working together, remember?"

"Vince, old buddy, you fucked it up on your try. Now it's my turn, and I suggest that we go and get it done and save beating the shit out of each other for later. 'Kay?"

We stood stock-still for a second, glaring. Then Wakefield grinned crookedly. "You got it. Let's do her to her."

The AmericaWay Bank Building's foyer had a row of pay phones. As the lunch hour was ending, more people were leaving the bank than entering. I flopped open a phone book, got the bank's number, dropped a quarter and dialed as Wakefield stood by me edgily, his hands jammed in the back pockets of his jeans.

"Mr. Simpson, please," I said when the phone was answered.

Buzz, whir, click. "James Simpson." Tenor, sober, and very young voice.

"Mr. Simpson, this is Ben over at the lot. You better get over here, there's been a little accident."

"An accident? What happened?"

"Well, sir, this fella in a pickup truck sort of hit your car."

"My *car*? Are you sure?"

"Oh, yeah, no question. We got it registered right here."

"Oh, Lord. Blue Mazda?"

"Yep, that's it. I'm awful sorry. But you got to come over and talk to the cops when they get here. We'll arrange for a tow to wherever you want—"

"A *tow*? Can't I drive it?"

"Oh, I tend to doubt it, sir. The front end took a real good lick. I don't think the radiator's—"

"You morons! You'll pay for this!"

"Hey, now, calm down! You know we got big signs here, not responsible for damage, et cetera. Your insurance will—"

"We'll see about that! You just wait there! Your name's Ben, you said?"

"Yes, sir. Ben. I'll be right here. Bye now." I hung up and said, "Have a *real* nice day."

Wakefield was grinning. "Slicko, lad."

"Pretty convincing, huh?" I grinned, edging to the inner doors. Through the glass I saw Simpson leave the teller area and, in an anxious trot, head toward us. "Whoa. Grab a phone, Vince, quick."

We grabbed phones and, with our backs to the foyer, carried on one-way conversations as Simpson bustled past us and thump-thumped through the revolving doors. I hung up my phone and said, "Let's roll." Wakefield handed me the key without comment and we entered the bank lobby.

I split off from him and strolled past the few bank patrons to the safe deposit window. It was now manned—or personed—by a young, wisp-thin brunette in a white one-piece sleeveless dress. From the looks of it, she was handling business at the foreign exchange window as well as at safe deposit. I stood and waited for a moment till she took care of a customer at foreign exchange and darted over to me. "Uh-huh?"

I set the key down on the smooth marble counter. "Like to get into my box, please," I said, bored.

"Okay. Your name?"

"Withrow. Wilbur Withrow." Wakefield could have figured that out for himself. Now my only worry was that Simpson had posted some kind of warning on Withrow's box card. The woman's fingers flipped efficiently through the small drawer to the right and came out with a six-by-nine index card. "Okay, Mr. Withrow. I need your driver's license."

I looked into her expectant eyes and said, with just the right touch of surprise, "I don't have it with me."

A couple more customers had lined up at the currency exchange window. She flicked them a glance and then looked back at me. "All right. Look, just sign on the next line there, okay? We're short-handed right now."

Oh, God, a signature match. It hadn't occurred to me. She set the card down on the counter in front of me. I looked down at it. There were three Withrow signatures, the most recent from several years ago. Fairly straightforward signatures, but forgery is not among my more advanced skills.

"Got a pen?" I asked her. She slid one across and I picked it up with my right hand, then dropped it. With my left I picked it up again and made a show of inserting it clumsily into the stiff fingers of my right hand. I got hold of it, lowered it to the card, and dropped it again.

"Something wrong?" she asked impatiently.

"Oh." I smiled bravely. "I've got nerve problems in this hand."

"Nerve problems," she echoed, staring at me.

"That's right. See, I work for Ford's? The Rawsonville Road parts distribution center. Well, about two years ago—or maybe it was three—"

"Sir—"

"I don't know, it was before the strike. Anyhow, I had a little accident. A fifteen-inch mag wheel fell off a pallet and landed right on my hand. Busted a couple of—whatchacallum—metacarpals. Or maybe it was metatarsals. I don't remember which. One's the foot, one's the hand. We're talking hand, this one here. Nothing wrong with my feet. Anyway—"

"Sir," she said with some desperation, "can't you just sign with your other hand?"

"—couple of nerves in here shot to hell. What's that?"

"Sign with your other hand," she repeated, as if to a child.

"My *other* hand? Well, sure I can. It's not so legible, but then, heh, signin' with my *right* hand's never been nothin' to write home about, either."

She shoved the pen toward me impatiently. I picked it up with my left hand and made Withrow's name in a jagged, childish scrawl. She grabbed the card, barely glanced at it, and refiled it. "This way. Push the door when you hear the buzzer."

With a barely disguised sigh of relief I went to the low, smooth Dutch door and pushed it open when the buzzer sounded. The woman met me and led me down a quiet, narrow hall, around two corners, and into the vault. She found the box, inserted my key into one lock and a key of her own into the other, twisted both, opened the small, thick steel door, and withdrew the long, narrow steel box with the sliding hiss of well-engineered metal.

I was reassured to see that the box seemed heavy in her hands. "Need a few minutes with it?" she asked, uninterested.

"Please."

"That's fine. We're awful busy." She led me to a small, dimly lighted alcove and set the box down on a clean, wooden built-in table. "Take your time. Just let me know when you're done." She walked away quickly, leaving me alone in the silence.

No one was around. I set my briefcase on the table and stared at the box for a long moment. This was the end—or *an* end, since all of Barton's money certainly wasn't here—of a trail that had begun in Joann Sturtevant's plush Bloomfield Hills mansion. The box could have anything, including a couple of bricks, in it. I only had the deceased Arthur Barton's word, third- and fourth-hand at that, that there was money there. Nothing to do now but open it, I thought, and did.

CHAPTER 15

Vince Wakefield's hard gray eyes pierced me as I crossed the lobby. He stood against the wall beneath a row of framed, colored bank promo posters and rubbed his hands, the manicured and buffed fingernails glinting in the light. I made a quick jerking shake of my head as I reached him, and he fell in beside me as we went through the doors.

"Well?" he asked as we crossed the foyer.

"Hoo boy." I ducked into the revolving door and shoved it, cutting off whatever he was going to say. He bounded up beside me as I walked quickly across the sidewalk, hopped down the curb, and crossed Fort Street on the yellow. "C'mon," he said tensely, "let me look."

"Shut up and walk, Vince. This means you." We pressed on into the dark alleys, heading toward the car.

The urban canyon where we'd left the Chrysler was unchanged. The car sat alone by a stinking, overflowing dumpster. Piles of pallets and rotting shipping cartons leaned against the grimy walls on both sides. The ground beneath us was uneven with dirty old cobblestones and it crackled with busted glass under our shoes. Aside from the steady, almost imperceptible big-city din, the courtyard was silent.

Except, suddenly, for a rustling from somewhere.

I had my car keys out, and I stopped. I felt Wakefield's puzzled eyes on me. I turned suddenly and faced the men.

There were two. A short young bearded tub in a dirty, stretched white T-shirt, and the long-haired

blond kid who'd been sacked out, seemingly coma-
tose, on the porch of the Empress.

The blond kid—actually, now that he was awake
I could see he was more like thirty—carried a sawed-
off Louisville Slugger ball bat with two sixteen-penny
spikes driven through the end. The heads and points
of the spikes would have glinted, had there been any
sun. Tub carried a knife casually against his thigh,
stretching five or six inches to his jeaned knee.

Wakefield had turned, also. He released a sigh
that hissed through his teeth, gave me a sidelong
glance, and said, "Now, see there?"

"What."

"Mary had to take the gun away from me. That's
religion for you."

The two men slowly closed some of the distance
between us, their weapons held casually. Blond said
to me, "Gimme the briefcase, man."

"Now come on, fellas. This thing cost me eighty
bucks. Have a heart."

Blond grinned, showing dirty teeth and overlarge
pinkish gums. "It's not the case we want."

"Nothing inside but business papers."

Vince Wakefield's jaw was clenched again, cheeks
puffing, face purpling, veins standing out. He said in
a husky, menacing whisper, "I'll tell you just one
time. Do one-eighty and disappear, or I'm going to
hurt you real, real bad."

It sounded to me like he meant it, but Blond's
smile didn't change. He was of average build but
spare and wiry. Tub was just that, a round mound,
but there was power in those massive arms and
shoulders, and no doubt of his intent on his implaca-
ble, glistening face.

Wakefield went on with a sudden burst of anger,
"You're white boys. Why're you down here doing
nigger work?"

"This ain't nigger work," Blond answered, jerking
his dirty hair off his forehead. "I been around the
Empress a long time. I seen Withrow come 'n' go a

few times. Grossman told me about the envelope. That skinflint little Jew bastard wouldn't never let me see it, though. Then today you guys show up and get it. I'm thinking, time to see what that envelope is." He gave the briefcase a benevolent smile. "Something from the bank, hey?" he whispered.

He swung the bat up and bounced the shaft in his other hand, giving us a good look at those nails. As if cued, Tub raised his knife hand and rubbed the blade on his dirty T-shirt as if to sanitize it, or hone its edge. I was getting pretty bored with the theatrics, but the men stood between us and the alley.

Blond and Tub spread apart a few more feet. "Give it over," Blond said.

I did, but not the way he expected. I swung the briefcase back and then whipped it forward by the handle, the way you'd toss a horseshoe, as hard as I could, giving it lots of wrist so it spun, whirling end over end right at him like a propeller run amuck. He dodged and the briefcase sailed past, singing in the stale air. I didn't see where it went because I'd turned to jump Tub, who was closer to me. Wakefield went after Blond.

It generally pays to assume that a man wielding a knife knows what he's doing. Anyone can point a gun and bang away till he puts a hole into somebody, but knife-work requires a particularly lethal kind of personality. Tub seemed to have the personality plus some experience; for one thing he held the knife underhand and, for another, he waded right at me like a barge moving into a slip.

But, swaddled with lard as he was, he wouldn't be very fast. He'd have won his fights by overwhelming his opponents with sheer ruthlessness and bulk. I hoped so, anyway, as I tore right at him, baiting him into taking a jab.

He did so, and he was slow, but not as slow as I expected. I got inside the swing, got a glimpse of his leer, sidestepped, caught his upper arm, chipped him a good hearty *smack* in the neck with the hard flat edge of my hand, and dodged back unexpectedly to avoid his follow-up slash. To my left, Vince Wakefield danced, long arms spread, weaving back and forth and side to side on surprisingly light feet, avoiding the slashing swings of the ball bat wielded by Blond. Their grunts and pants echoed in the courtyard.

Tub came implacably for me now, his teeth clenched, face drenched, wheezing from the blow to his throat. I faked him out by backing off toward the side of the courtyard where huge piles of rotting wood pallets and moldy cardboard shipping cartons leaned. I did not attack, but waited for Tub's next clumsy knife swing, and he obliged with a scythelike slash that was surprisingly fast and damn close.

When his swing reached its apogee, I caught his knife arm with both hands, stepped in, anchored a leg behind his right knee, and gave him a shove that, combined with his bulk, momentum, and lack of balance, plunged us with a crash into the cardboard cartons. Fortunately, I ended up on top of him, the stench of molding cardboard and sweat and rat shit all around us. I pressed my left hand down hard on his nose, as if to crush it, and arm-wrestled his knife hand with the other, as he ineffectually thumped at my ribs with his other fist. Strain, and panting, and sweat, and then I finally won the battle as our interlocked fists thumped down against his belly. We froze for a second, and then the heel of my hand turned wet.

The Louisville Slugger clonked to the cobblestones somewhere behind me. Blond's voice: "Shit!" I got a glance with my peripheral vision and saw Vince Wakefield execute a high kick that got Blond up side of the head and tore him off his feet. Then I looked back down at Tub. The knife was buried in him to the hilt, a flood of red soaking his dirty T-shirt.

I involuntarily lurched back from him onto my haunches. Tub was alert and conscious. He looked curiously at the knife, then took it in his hand and extracted it slowly. His face showed no pain. He carefully wrapped his fingers around the hilt, gave me a mean look, and tried to push himself up. The blood ran harder. I stood, stumbling back out of the slippery wet mess. Twisting cramps wrenched my gut so I couldn't stand fully straight for a minute. "Vince?" I said.

Blond lay groaning on the cobblestones, and Wakefield had stepped back, fixing to high-kick his head again. He stopped when I called him, gave Blond a surly, challenging look, then sauntered over to me, hitching his jeans a bit higher, shooting bony wrists from the cuffs of his jacket.

Tub got himself up as far as a sitting position, then went pasty gray and collapsed back down. The flow of blood slowed and stopped. His mouth slacked. His pupils rolled up away somewhere, leaving only the whites showing under the open eyelids. Wakefield reached out the polished toe of his boot and gave the mound of dead flesh an indifferent prod. "One less asshole to screw with, huh, Ben?"

The cramping had eased off in my gut, but my mouth was dry, my nerve ends charged with adrenaline. "Just shut the fuck *up*, Wakefield."

The tall man was about to reply when Blond stirred behind us, moaned, and clambered to his knees, head shaking as he tried to clear it. Wakefield looked at me bleakly. "Sorry, Ben. Guess I left some unfinished business." He strolled to the middle of the courtyard, picked up the Louisville Slugger, and started for Blond, who'd made it to his feet. I said with all the force I had left in me, "Hold it."

Wakefield stopped and gave me a sidelong glance. Blond, without looking at his partner, turned and lurched in a crippled gallop down the alley and out of sight.

Wakefield looked resigned. He tossed the ball bat away over one of the rusted dumpsters and retrieved the briefcase, which, miraculously enough, had not burst open. I got in the car and fired it up;

Wakefield jumped in the passenger seat and we got out of there.

We drove.

Vince Wakefield slouched in the seat, one knee propped up on the dashboard, the bill of his cap pulled down low on his forehead. "That was great, huh, Ben?"

"Yeah, swell."

He made an open-mouthed sigh. "Nothing like a little grabass to fire a man up."

"I'm fired up, all right."

I felt his stare on me. "What the hell's wrong with you?"

"I don't like killing people."

"Shit!" Wakefield snorted. "It *was* by accident. And even if it wasn't an accident, it was at the very least self-defense. And even if you iced him on purpose, what's the big deal? This is Detroit, one less blade-toting lardass isn't going to make the Mayor call for a day of mourning."

Of course, the man was absolutely correct, but it didn't make me feel any better.

Wakefield asked, "You ever kill anybody before?"

"Yeah."

"How many?"

"Two."

"How'd they happen?"

"Fella tried to strangle me with a garrote; I backed a riding mower over him."

Wakefield whistled.

"Got into a firefight with another guy in a garage; I blew him away."

"Part of the trade," Wakefield replied, staring out his window.

"Yours, maybe."

"Sometimes, sure. I should of followed my better instincts and taken care of that blond bat-swinging bastard while we were at it. His kind of loose end we don't need scurrying around." He turned his head to face me and asked calmly, "We going anywhere in particular?"

It was only then that I realized we weren't. I got hold of myself and surveyed the landmarks. Somehow I'd gotten on Gratiot, and we were almost to I-94 already. Amazing how quick you can get someplace in Detroit when you're not in a hurry, which is hardly ever. I said, "Where do you want to go?"

"Huh. Back to Windsor, you know that. But if this briefcase holds what I think it holds..." He picked it up and tried to open it, but I'd taken the precaution of securing the three-tumbler combination lock. He grimaced and set the case back down on the floor. "If it holds what I think it holds, we probably ought not to try to run Customs with it."

"I think you're right."

"You got any more coordinates?"

He asked the question casually, but I went on full alert. Kenny Slingluff was, hopefully, checking out more phone numbers for phonies, and would relay the information to me as I called for it. But I could take no chance of letting Wakefield know where they were coming from.

I answered, "More coming. Tonight or tomorrow latest. Just hold your horses." I whipped into a liquor store parking lot and jumped on Gratiot headed back downtown. "Let's find somewhere to hole up for the night, what do you say?"

"Hey, pal, it's your town." Wakefield said expansively. "Got any ideas?"

"Maybe." I kicked the accelerator, and the mighty Chrysler engine responded with a tinny whir.

The Detroit Plaza Hotel is part of the Renaissance Center, the multitowered, massive, cylindrical, steel-and-glass riverfront development built for the express purpose of "luring business and up-scale people back to downtown Detroit." What it has succeeded in doing is losing massive amounts of money while becoming a new focal point for con men, hookers, and street people.

But I picked it because it was handy to just about anywhere the map and the numbers were likely to take us next. And besides, to be honest, I'd never stayed there before and here was the opportunity to do so, thanks to Mrs. Sturtevant's Gold Card.

I turned the Chrysler over to a porter under the portico, and Wakefield and I went into the huge, modern lobby. We weren't overwhelmed with luggage; I had my briefcase, Wakefield had his map tube, and that was all. We waded through a mob of salesmen just ending a day of sales calls, and well-dressed women beginning an evening of theirs, and cruised up to the reception desk.

The clerk was short, bull-shouldered, immaculate in a dark blue blazer, crisp white shirt, and black tie, and was smoothly, shinily bald back past the midpoint of his head. His face was lined, weary, knowing; hotel desk clerks are right up there with police officers, hospital orderlies, cabbies, bartenders and—you betcha—private detectives, when it comes to seeing it all. "Yes, gentlemen?" he asked, sounding doubtful.

I slid the thick gleaming Gold Card across the counter. His countenance went from burned-out bulb to three-hundred-watt spot. "Yes, sir! Mr. Perkins! Good to see you again, sir."

"Good to *be* seen," I answered.

He whipped out a registration card and a pen and positioned both before me, palming the Gold Card as he did so. "What'll it be, Mr. Perkins? Nice double for you?" he asked, giving Wakefield a glance.

I filled out the card, lying about everything except my name, as Wakefield growled, "Two singles, bud."

"Yes, *sir*." The clerk gave Wakefield a registration card and pen, and the tall man popped his cap to the back of his bushy head and filled the card out, head cocked, tip of his tongue trapped in his teeth.

The clerk took both registration cards when we were done and skimmed them proprietarily. "Method of payment, Mr. Wakefield?"

"My buddy here'll cover it."

The clerk eyed me. I nodded. He ran the Gold Card through a stamping machine, gave the card back to me, and handed us each a heavy broad-billed key. "Eight-oh-one for Mr. Perkins. Six-twenty for you, Mr. Wakefield. Enjoy your stay, gentlemen." He banged his bell. "Front!"

We turned and stepped aside as other registrants crowded the desk. A tall, skinny, very young black bellhop glided up to us and reached out for my briefcase. "This way, sirs!"

I held onto the handle. "That's okay, I'll keep it."

He smiled jauntily. "Please, sir, happy to oblige!"

"I'll hang on to it," I said a bit more testily. The bellhop dropped his hands and his mouth went sullen. I understood; carry no bags, get no tip, he was thinking. I fished a five out of my slacks pocket and held it up. "Don't worry, we got you covered."

He snatched the bill and said seriously, "Thank you, sir. Elevators are right over there." He pointed to the other side of the crowded lobby, sang, "Later, gentlemen," and wheeled away on fluid legs.

We stared after him for a long minute, then Wakefield muttered, "Let's go stomp the little prick!"

I was very, very tired. On my expense account, what was five bucks? "Forget it. Let's go look at the loot." We headed up to my room.

CHAPTER 16

Vince Wakefield shut the door of my room as I walked to the enormous double bed and lay the briefcase down on the thick purple spread. As he flicked on a couple of lamps on the nightstand and the dresser, he said, barely containing his excitement, "Wait a minute, wait a minute! I gotta see this."

When he was beside me, tall and blue, his hard-planed face flushed red, I adjusted the tumblers on the combination lock and stepped back. "Help yourself."

Wakefield pounced on it like a teen-age boy going at his first willing girl. "Come to Papa!" he said. He swung back the lid of the briefcase. It caught on its hinges, open like an *L*.

"Oh, Lordy, Lordy," Wakefield breathed, eyes feasting.

There were ten medium-sized bricks of used U.S. bills, mostly fifties and hundreds, neatly rubber-banded together. Under each rubber band was a yellowed adding-machine tape. Arthur Barton, like most accountants, had been a painfully meticulous man; though I didn't check, I wouldn't have been surprised to find the bills all facing the same way.

"How much, you figure?" Wakefield whispered in the cool, antiseptic hotel room silence.

"Eyeballing the numbers on those tapes, I'd say a hundred G's or so." I sat on the edge of the bed and lighted a cigar. I didn't want to handle the money, it wasn't mine.

Wakefield reacted differently. He ran his big hard hands over the bricks, then picked one up and riffled it under an ear, a dreamy smile on his face. Then he carefully replaced it in the briefcase. "Well!" he said, looking down at me jubilantly. "We fired the first volvo, pal!"

After a second I got it. Wakefield had coined his very own brand-new word from *volley* and *salvo*. I forced a grin. "Yeah, and that ain't all. We'll go get us some more in the morning."

Wakefield hooked his fists on his hips. "In the morning? Why not today? It's not even six o'clock yet."

I blew out a stream of smoke. "It's way past five o'clock. I don't have the next set of coordinates yet. And if the pattern holds up, we'll be raiding a safe deposit box again, and the banks closed hours ago. I've got some things to do. You go settle in. See you in the dining room later."

Wakefield stared impenetrably down at me for a long minute, then said, "Hell, screw the room, I'm going to the saloon. Maybe meet up with some friendly ladies. Do some celebrating."

"Go on. Enjoy. See you in the dining room later."

Wakefield shrugged. "Your loss, pal." He turned and sauntered away, rolling his shoulders under his denim shirt. He'd just reached the door, around the corner and out of sight, when there was a long pause and then his voice: "Just. One. Fucking. Minute."

I stood as he walked slowly back in, his face flushed red, his jaw clenched, his cheeks puffed, his eyes turned into fiery little slits. "You must think I'm real stupid, huh, asshole?"

I shook my head. "What's the problem?"

"The problem?" he rasped, grinning poisonously. "The *problem*?" A long arm tipped with a bony index finger shot out toward the bed. "You mean, *that* problem?" He shook his head jerkily. "I'll tell you what the *problem* is. The *problem* is, you think I'm soooo goddamned *dumb*, you could trick me into walking out of here and just leave you footloose and fancy-free with *a hundred thousand fucking dollars!*"

The briefcase with its bundled green contents yawned at me. I looked back at Wakefield, whose color was purple by now and getting darker. How a man could sustain and build such a high degree of vitriol without blowing a valve was beyond me. I mean, he was *pissed*.

I'd had enough roughhouse for one day. I sighed cigar smoke. "Where the hell am *I* going to go with the money?"

"*I* don't know! I don't even know where you fucking *live!*"

"Okay." I spread my hands. "So what's your suggestion?"

His anger-stiffened stance loosened a bit. "That's easy," he growled. "I'll take it." He made for the case.

I took a step closer. "Ohhh, no."

He straightened, eyes wide. "You gonna stop me?"

"You want to *finish* the day the way we *started* it, Vince?"

He pressed his lips and stared down at me. "I'm not leaving the money with you," he warned.

"Same here."

"So, we stay together, right?"

That was out, too. I wanted to be alone when I made the call to get the next coordinates from Slingluff. I'd spent a long day with Wakefield and wanted to be rid of him for a bit. And I was tired. I don't normally get tired that early, except on days when I kill people.

I snapped my fingers. "Got it." I bent, snapped the lid shut on the case, picked it up, and said, "Come with me."

"Damn straight," Wakefield grunted as we left the room.

Our bull-shouldered bald clerk was still working the desk and, no doubt remembering the Gold Card, he rolled over to us as if on a skateboard. "How can I help you, Mr. Perkins?"

I laid the briefcase on the desk. "I have a peculiar request."

His eyes were knowing; his smile stayed fixed. "Yes, sir?"

"I want you to put this briefcase in a secure place, like your vault. And we require that you release it only to the *two* of us. Not just one, but *both*. Is that clear?"

The clerk replied readily, "Gentlemen, I'm only on duty in the evenings. And there are three clerks

on duty most of the time. I'd like to suggest something that will help." He bent, reached under the
desk, and came up with a sheet of hotel letterhead
and some tape. "Both of you put your signatures on
this sheet. I'll tape it to the briefcase, along with a
note informing the other clerks that this briefcase
can only be claimed by two men together. They must
sign for it in the presence of the clerk, and their
signatures must match those on the briefcase. Is that
satisfactory?"

I looked at Wakefield. He nodded. We signed,
and the clerk taped the letterhead to the case, scooped
up the ten-spot I dealt onto the desk, thanked us,
and rolled away.

Wakefield's complexion was back to its normal
darkish self. He said grudgingly, "Not a bad idea."

"Don't gush, it embarrasses me."

Wakefield barked a laugh. "Drink?"

"See you in the dining room in about an hour." I
split away from him toward the elevators.

I felt immeasurably better when I got back into
my room. Being shut of Wakefield was like losing an
abscessed tooth—something's missing, but you don't
hurt anymore.

Odd part was, in many ways he was the kind of
guy I normally become pals with: hard-edged, coarse,
street-smart, a player, a guy who makes things happen instead of going with the flow. But if there's
such a thing as a recipe for a likeable guy, a couple
essential ingredients were missing in Wakefield. His
temper wasn't the problem; hell, that could have
been theatrics for all I know. The problem stemmed
from that incident in the alley after we got the
money. He really, truly intended to kill that pathetic
little bat-swinging punk, for no good reason, and I
think he would have enjoyed it.

Further, Wakefield was in business for himself.
As long as he was around, I didn't dare turn my back
or I might find a knife growing out of it.

The hotel room—my third this week—was relatively small, but clean, decorated in various shades of blue and purple. Its hotel-room anonymity was intensified by the fact that, aside from the clothes I wore, I had absolutely no personal belongings with me. I pulled the drapes on the big fake patio door wall and looked across the darkening Detroit River toward Windsor. The setting sun behind the hotel glowed reddish-yellow on the rushing water and illuminated Windsor and the Holiday Inn, almost directly across the river from me.

I went to the bed, flopped down on it, shucked my LeHighs to let my feet breathe, picked up the phone and mashed out the number for my apartment. As it rang, I fished the small, cylindrical remote triggering device out of my pocket.

Click, then my own voice, flat, slightly impatient: "Perkins here. You've got just thirty seconds to tell me who you are, what you want, when you called, where I can reach you, and why I should bother. Be convincing." *Beep*.

I held the little triggering device against the mouthpiece of the telephone and pushed the button. In my ear, the answering machine squeaked and whirred, then, with a faint hiss in the background, began to play back my messages.

"Dick Dennehy. In case I never mentioned it, that is, without a doubt, the stupidest answering spiel I've ever heard on one of those miserable machines in my entire life. Anyhow, if you don't have my number, tough titty. I don't give a flying fart if you call me back or not. My life doesn't revolve around the mellow sound of your voice, pal. I just called to tell you that I'm walking your detective license application through the bureaucrazy up here, and I think it'll fly. Just think, before too long I'll be able to threaten you with loss of your license if you don't behave. Ha, ha, ha." *Click*.

Another *Click*; someone had called, left no message.

Click. "This is Mrs. Weingarten? I'm with Michigan National Bank? I called at, um, three-ten in the afternoon? You can reach me at 861-0909? I'm calling with regard to your account? The payment you promised us seems not to have arrived?" Probably because I never mailed it?

Click. "Hey, Ben. This is Kenny. Kenny Slingluff." He sounded tense, like a lot of people do when talking to a recorder. Kids screamed in the background; Kenny had pulled zookeeper duty again. "I been through part of those cards. Found you another bogus number. There's two of them on this card, one digit apart. 220-4611, 220-4612. Name of Dennis Kearney. That's all that's on here. I'll do some more checking for you tomorrow. Soon as you're done fooling around with whatever you're doing, how 'bout checking up on Mona? This keeps up much longer I'm gonna hafta do something myself. Seriously," he added softly. *Click.*

Through the phone line static I heard my answering machine whir and click again, then there was silence. All done. I hung up the phone, repeating the phone numbers to myself. 220-4611, 220-4612. In other words, 2204-6112. Cute.

I went into the bathroom, filled the sink with cold water, dunked my head into it, and splashed and gurgled for a minute. Toweled dry fast, combed hair flat, jumped back into shoes, and left the room. Right about then I'd have cheerfully traded the briefcase full of cash for a pair of clean socks.

As I emerged from the elevator on the ground floor, I saw that the lobby had thinned out considerably. Music thumped from a dark cocktail lounge to my right, and a group of well-dressed people stood at the maître d' stand by the dining room, waiting for a table. I made for there, and was halfway across when an idea occurred to me. I abruptly changed course and went to the registration desk.

Our bald, big-shouldered clerk wasn't around.

Replacing him was a young, red-haired, freckled kid who was shmoozing with a young, shapely, well-dressed blonde, both leaning toward each other across the desk. I stood and tapped my fingernails on the hard glossy wood till he finally broke loose from her and headed down to see what the hell I wanted.

"Name's Perkins. I checked a briefcase into the vault awhile ago. Please get it for me."

"Right." He spun on his heel and galloped through the door. I leaned my back against the desk, looking sightlessly across the ornate lobby. I felt the blonde's eyes on me but didn't look at her.

Behind me, the clerk piped, "Someone else with you, sir?" I turned. He held the briefcase in both freckled hands and squinted at the note taped to it. "A Mr. Wakefield?"

"Who the hell cares?" I asked roughly. "Just give me the case, son."

He slipped the case under his arm and gripped it to him. "Can't do it, sir. Instructions say specifically to release it only to the two of you, and both of you have to sign for it in my presence. And the signatures have to match. Sorry, sir."

I balled my fists and slid them across the desk toward him, leaning on my forearms. "Sonny, you hand over that case this second, or you're going to get a brand-new idea of what sorry is all about."

The kid had one of those round, all-American, open faces, cheerful and friendly except at times like this. "Mr. Perkins, I won't hesitate to call security if you start any trouble."

I got my wallet out, peeled off a couple of C-notes, folded them into thirds, waved them enticingly, and leered, "How about some walking-around money? You could show the cutie down there a hell of a good time. Whaddya say?"

His eyes fixed on the bills for a second, then went soberly back to me. "No way, sir. Absolutely no way."

I kept my eyes hard on him, then grinned and stood straight. "Terrific, kid. You pass."

"Pass what?" he asked suspiciously.

"The test. You pass. You done good. Guard the case with your life. Catch up with you later." I turned and winked at the blonde, who was staring open-mouthed at me, and walked jauntily across the lobby to the dining room.

No Wakefield.

I checked the time. It had been well over an hour since we'd agreed to meet here. I scouted the dining room just to make sure he wasn't there, and then lounged around the maître d' stand for a while, smoking and fidgeting. He didn't show.

On the off-chance, I strolled over into the smoke-heavy lounge. The die-hard early-evening boozing crowd packed the darkness on stools and at tables and in stand-up clumps. The place was a classic meat market, women outnumbering men by three to one. The juke box blasted Queen: "This thing called love, I just can't handle it." I brushed against countless hard elbows and soft buttocks as I worked the place from front to rear and then back again, looking for the tall man. No sign of him.

I burst back out into the lobby and took several deep breaths of clean air. I wondered where the son of a bitching bastard was. I spotted a bank of house phones by the news-and-sundry shop, went over, and dialed six-two-oh. It rang and rang and was still ringing when I hung the phone up.

Back up in my room, I ordered a club sandwich and a six-pack of Stroh's from room service, then took an excruciatingly hot shower. By the time I emerged from the bathroom, steaming clean with a big white towel wrapped around my waist, the food and beer had arrived. I signed off on the check, sat down in front of network news, and ate the food with an indifferent appetite, washing each bite down with cold beer.

I let the TV run on, drank beer industriously, sat through the prime-time soaps and called Wakefield's room every commercial break to no avail.

The late-night news had just started when I fuzzily pulled the remote triggering device out of my slacks pocket, dialed my apartment phone, and triggered the machine to give me my messages.

There was only one.

"Hi," came Terry's voice, unusually soft and defensive. "I said I'd be calling you, remember? What I called to say was, I think we're washed up. Why screw with this anymore. And believe me, I know it's all my fault. I fell in love with you, and it was my doing, not yours. What you want and what I want just aren't the same. If I can't have you, I'd might as well not see you, 'cause it hurts. Oh." A pause, a fluttering sound as if she'd switched the receiver from one hand to the other. Her voice sounded clearer, more assertive. "You know, on that case of yours, I might just do some poking around down here. That all right? Good." Another long pause, and she sounded gentler again. "Listen, forget what I said before. Wait to hear. And stay well, dear. Bye."

CHAPTER 17

My hands were slick with grease and sweat as I feverishly tinkered with the carburetor feed on the Spad engine. Far away, across the flat trampled wheat field, was a small, tree-shrouded village, and I could hear the bell's clanging in the church steeple. No doubt the civilians had seen my emergency landing and were raising the alarm. Here in eastern France, well behind German lines, as many citizens sympathized with the Boche as with the Allies. The civilians wouldn't try to capture me themselves, but they'd finger me for the Germans, and then, assuming I was taken alive, delight in taunting me and throwing rocks and rotten fruit and anything else they could get their hands on. That was by far the most pleasant thing I could look forward to if I didn't get airborne and westbound.

I only had ten minutes, fifteen at most, to fix the Hispano-Suiza motor and get the hell out of here.

Damn frustrating thing was that up till then it had been a splendid patrol. I went up alone that morning, right after breakfast, and just behind the Jerry lines encountered a lone German Halberstadt scout. We went after each other with eagerness in the bright, clean French sky. Inside five minutes I knew I was fighting no rookie. I tried all my tricks, but he knew them all. He tried a few stunts on me, and I countered them. Round and round we swooped and dived and fired and, with the prevailing winds, drifted farther and farther east, behind German lines.

Then I ran out of ammunition.

The Halberstadt had fallen back a quarter mile from me. I didn't dare let him know I'd run out of ammo. I decided to dive low and skim the ground westbound, hoping to get a good jump on him and take advantage of the Spad's superior speed to get away. But before I could turn, the German flew toward me at an unusually slow speed, and, with a start, I recognized the pilot.

Oswald Boelcke. Germany's ace of aces. Head of Jagdstaffel No. 2. Said to be unbeatable. He was laughing.

He reached forward and slapped his dual machine guns with his gloved hand and made an exaggerated shrug. Out of ammo!

I mimicked his gesture. For a couple of minutes we circled each other lazily, laughing, the incredible tension released. Then I kicked the Spad over and headed west, and would have made it home fine except that the carburetor seized up, forcing me to land. Damn the luck! Fought Oswald Boelcke to a draw, and downed by a busted motor!

The superheated engine tinked ominously. The summer sun made me sweat rivers under my uniform. The church bell clanged on, as if tolling for a funeral, and I thought I could hear loud male voices shouting in some harsh language.

There, damn you. A bit of linkage on the carb had seized up, but I had it working smooth now. At least I hoped I did, because if I didn't, the motor would cut out on me like it had before, forcing me to glide to a landing again, and next time there might not be such a convenient wheat field to land in.

I jumped onto the Spad's canvas-wrapped wing, leaned into the cockpit, and hit the magneto and ignition switches. She was still hot, ought to kick over real good. As I jumped to the ground again and ran forward to grab the big wooden propeller, I heard a new sound, a sound like heavy gunfire. *Thumpa-thumpa-thumpa. Thumpa-thumpa-thumpa.* I whirled to face the village and saw—

The hotel room blazed with sun from the east windows. The pounding came again—*thumpa-thumpa-thumpa*—from the door. I hoisted myself up and untangled my sweaty legs from the sheets. "Who is it?" I shouted hoarsely.

"Wakefield," came his muffled, rasping voice. "Rise and shine. Start your day with a smile."

What I felt like starting my day with was a brand-new freshly killed Canadian. Little gnomes wearing spiked sneakers tap-danced in my head. My mouth tasted like I'd spent the night sucking a Vaseline lollipop. I checked the clock: past eight-thirty. Ohhh, shit. Hail Mary full of grace, get this day out of my face. I swiveled, planted my feet on the floor, hoofed heavily to the door, and opened it.

Vince Wakefield had acquired a change of clothes somewhere. He wore pale blue beltless slacks and a dark blue, short-sleeved, open-necked pullover sport shirt with some kind of little, tiny animal embroidered in red on the breast. A very thin gold chain glinted on his brown neck. In one hand he carried the map tube.

He made a hard-planed, hawkish grin. "What'd you do, Perkins, go twelve rounds with a six-pack? Or six rounds with a twelve?"

"Get your ass in here." I stepped back and slammed the door after him. He sauntered across the room, surveyed the dead soldiers and the dirty clothes, and whistled. Like the sadist he was, he opened the curtains the rest of the way, blinding me momentarily with the sunlight. I said, "You'd look awful, too, if you'd fought Boelcke to a draw and then spent half the night trying to repair a Spad engine before the Germans arrived."

"Huh?"

"Never mind." I picked up my well-seasoned sport shirt, gave it a shake, and put it on. As I climbed into my pants, I asked, "So where the hell were *you*?"

"Me?" Wakefield snorted. "I was around. Didn't see you, though."

"Around where?"

"Here. The hotel." Wakefield turned to the window and squinted into the sun, seemingly absorbed in the view.

I sat on the edge of the bed, pulled my socks on, and stomped my feet into the LeHighs. "That's funny. I looked for you. I called your room fifteen, twenty times. No answer."

I let the silence drag on as I looked for a cigar. Out of 'em. Have to pick up some more at the hotel's sundry shop. In the meantime, to alleviate my nicotine fit, I retrieved a butt from the ashtray, unscrunched it, got a lighted match to the end, and inhaled. The smoke twisted down my throat like a coil of barbed wire, but it was still wonderful.

Wakefield turned to me casually. "Fact is, I met a

lady in the bar. Nice girl. Here in town for some
convention or something. We hung out together.
Sorta lost track of the time."

"Lost track of your room, too?"

"Slept in hers. Well, I mean, we *stayed* in hers,
didn't get much sleep though. God*damn*, that cigar
stinks. You always recycle 'em?"

"Stay upwind if it bugs you."

"Even fresh, your smokes could gag a corpse.
What are they, El Rauncho, three for a quarter?"

"Even cheaper at K-Mart." I stood. "I've got the
next coordinates."

"Ah!" Wakefield grinned. "Shall I do the honors?"

"By all means."

With a lusty smack of his palm, Wakefield shunted
the map out of the tube, uncoiled it on the bed, and
flattened two diagonally opposing corners with his
big hands. I found 2204 and 6112, then made the
triangulation.

"What's that town?" Wakefield muttered, peering.
"Berkley?"

"Yeah. Northern suburb." I eyeballed the triangulation more carefully and got a fix. "Sandra Street,
between Eleven Mile Road and Princeton. East side."

"Huh." Wakefield let the map curl shut with a
snap that sounded like a window shade. "Know the
place?"

"The town, anyhow." I knew Berkley all right;
Carole's home is just a couple of miles from Sandra
Street.

"Whaddya say we hit it?" He watched me load
my pockets with keys, coins, and wallet. "Just do me
a favor and leave that rolled ratshit in the ashtray,
okay?"

Before we headed for Berkley, I cruised the
Renaissance Center shops and gave the Gold Card a
workout: fresh slacks, a couple of shirts, and socks;
cigars and matches; and a new hand-rubbed brown
leather briefcase, five inches deep, trimmed in brass

with a combination lock. Theoretically, I spent a couple hundred bucks. But no money changed hands. I just handed over the card, signed the slip, and whee, new duds. Beats washing 'em. Beats paying, too.

I changed clothes in a stall in a public rest room while Vince Wakefield whizzed loudly in the urinal. On the way out we stopped off at the front desk, where I dropped off my dirty clothes to be laundered, and what was left of the new ones to be delivered up to my room. The clerk—yet another one—called down to the garage to have the Chrysler brought around front. As Wakefield and I went through the doors into the hot overcast morning, he said casually, "You try 'em out?"

"Who's that?"

"The desk people. The money. You try to get it?"

"Naturally. You?"

"Twice." Wakefield grinned. "Tried strongarm, tried money, tried sneak. Foiled every time."

"Same here." I couldn't get annoyed with Wakefield for trying to get the money, when that's exactly what I tried to do myself.

"Honest people here," Wakefield mused. "That's something, ain't it?"

"Yeah, it's something, all right," I answered, as the Chrysler screeched up to the curb in front of us.

I jumped on the Chrysler Freeway and took I-75 all the way out. Though we were going the right direction for that time of day—away from the inbound rush-hour traffic—there were the inevitable slow spots. Welcome to Detroit, home of the world's best cars and the world's worst highway system. It was typical big city, yet uniquely Detroit, big and blocky and stained and old, a place of sweat and steel and time clocks, a town of working men and those who fed on them.

Vince Wakefield didn't talk much on the way

out, except to complain once about the heat. Maybe it was a hint to turn on the air conditioning, but I didn't bite; the Chrysler motor was weak enough as it was. The day was turning into an ugly, damp, hot old bitch, all right. My brand-new shirt scraped at me as I perspired. The thumping hangover in my head backed off as we drove, and I thought through my plan, such as it was.

I mean, as far as I was concerned, the case was about through. We had a hundred grand now; another haul like that and Mrs. Sturtevant would have her investment back, plus cash to cover my expenses, my fee, and Mary Masters's share. Seth Flint in Cincinnati had said there was close to a million dollars lying around. Maybe it was true, and maybe it wasn't, but I didn't particularly care. I do my job, certainly no less, but no more, either.

Besides, with the dawning of this new, hot, humid morning, I was getting real edgy. There was that business in the alley in Cincinnati, when Terry Lowe swore we were being followed. There was the trashing of my motel room in Windsor while I talked to Wakefield—and, though I'd suspected Wakefield of being involved at the time, the fact that he thoroughly turned over my room the next morning seemed to rule that out. I mean, why do it twice? And, if he didn't arrange the first toss, who did? Not a pleasant thought.

Then there was our tangle with Blond and Tub. Wakefield and I had prevailed, and maybe they were just a random element in this case, but I didn't need any more random elements like them.

Then, finally, there was Wakefield himself.

I became very conscious of him with one part of my mind as the other part—the automatic pilot trained by several decades on Detroit streets—drove the car.

As opposed to the previous few days, Wakefield was quiet and calm as we drove. He rode in his usual position, half-slouched in the seat, one long, bony knee hiked up and propped on the edge of the dashboard, a long arm draped across the back. But he was almost perfectly still. Face set and vacant, fingers motionless, eyes barely blinking as he stared out the passenger window at the factories and the dirty gutter walls of the expressway.

I went through the bill of particulars.

Wakefield had jumped me once and tried to take me out of the play.

Wakefield had suggested—hell, urged—that we keep the money for ourselves.

Wakefield had gloated over the death of Tub, and had made a serious attempt to kill Blond for no good reason.

Wakefield had gotten irrationally furious when it occurred to him that I might abscond with the money. In my experience, people intensely suspicious of others are that way because they know they are totally untrustworthy themselves.

Wakefield—for what this was worth—quite seriously suggested "stomping" a bellhop who'd swiped five bucks from me.

Wakefield, the self-styled labor relations specialist and employee motivation advisor, was in business for himself.

Given half a chance—and maybe not even that—he'd make another try at me.

I knew that.

And it scared me.

CHAPTER 18

Berkley is a half-forgotten little suburb dropped down among a clump of others: Royal Oak, Huntington Woods, Oak Park, Southfield, and Birmingham. The furious storm of white flight overtook Berkley and left it behind many years ago, churning north and west to the more sublime climes of West Bloomfield, Pontiac, Rochester, and Clarkston. What's left is a quiet little enclave of squarely plotted streets, squarely built snug little homes, strips of national-brand shopping, and not much else.

Except Carole, of course. I'd spent many many hours at Carole's home somewhat north and east of where we were heading: hours in the garage under her car, hours in her bedroom under her. I forced the memories away as we entered Berkley from the east on 12 Mile Road: She's gone, Benjy old son.

Sensing imminent arrival, Vince Wakefield straightened in his seat as we jumped down to 11 Mile and then made the right on Sandra Street. It was a narrow, curbless two-and-a-half lane, densely parked on both sides, heavily treed, and lined with low brick professional buildings and shops. We rolled slowly up to Princeton, made a three-way turn, and headed back.

Wakefield peered intently past me as we passed the block's halfway point. "How 'bout that?" he rasped.

I slowed and got a quick look. It was a renovated old three-story frame house on a little spit of bristly lawn, shoulders jutting high above the buildings around it. A leaning sign on the lawn said ROOMS. A thirty-nine-cent placard in a window said APTS FOR RENT.

I glanced at Wakefield. "Rooming house?"

"Yeah," he answered, eyes staying on the house as we passed it. "I mean, it's the closest thing to the Empress that's along here. Maybe he used the same routine?"

"Accountants are creatures of habit," I said. "Let's go for it." I wedged the Chrysler into a three-quarter parking space along the side of a depressing-looking medical building. We bounced out of the car into the heat and crossed the narrow street and the dried-out weedy lawn up to the front door of the rooming house.

There was no sign of life around. I rattled the knob, but it was locked. A small discolored button next to the knob said MGR. I pressed it. After a moment, a speaker mounted by the light fixture above the door rattled, "Yeah?"

I said, "Kearney. You're holding something for me."

"Kearney who?" fluttered the distant male voice.

"Dennis Kearney."

A pause. A long one. Wakefield and I looked at each other. Then the voice: "Wait a minute."

The minute stretched into five or six. I wanted a smoke, but I also wanted my hands free. Wakefield jammed his balled hands into his slacks pockets and paced the narrow stoop, flat-planed stare looking up the street and down, up and down.

Finally the big front door squeaked heavily back and a man appeared. To Wakefield he said, "You Kearney?"

Wakefield jerked a thumb. "Him."

The man looked at me dimly. He was middle-aged and skull-faced and wore his long, limp brown hair dumped down the back of his head onto his bony shoulders. His off-white T-shirt and faded jeans showed his skeletal system clearly. He looked like he'd been used by a lot of people, particularly himself. He had the smell of a whipped dog who crawls into the bushes and looks out through anxious, milky eyes at the approach of small noisy boys. He said to me, "What do you mean, I got something for you?"

"I left an envelope here a few years ago for safekeeping. I want it," I answered quietly.

His gap-toothed grin was crooked and ingratiating. "I only worked here six months now."

Wakefield said harshly, "Look, chief, it's too hot to frig around. You got lock boxes here or something, go check, see what you got in the name of Dennis Kearney and bring it out here, tout suite. Capische?"

The man stared blankly at Wakefield, then turned

and shuffled into the house. I wiped my damp hands on my slacks, fished out a cigar and lighted it, and commented, "You got a real international flair there, Vince."

"Jawohl," Wakefield grunted.

The man shuffled back to the door. In his right hand he held a small brown cardboard envelope, virtually identical to the one we'd gotten at the Empress. I reached out for it, but he hung back. "Better have some ID," he said nervously. "Maybe something with a picture on it?"

I felt Wakefield coiling next to me, and I gave his arm a cautioning tap. "Why sure," I said easily. I went into my wallet, then held out my hand and slapped something into his. He stared down into the face of Benjamin Franklin, a former ambassador to whom I bear no resemblance whatsoever. "That picture good enough, friend?" I asked.

He squinted intently into it, then looked at me. "Sure," he said, his tone implying that he'd really had to make a decision. "You fellows have a nice day." He shuffled back quickly and swung the door shut, no doubt relieved to be rid of us.

Back in the Chrysler, I handed Wakefield the envelope as I fished out my keys and fired up the engine. He ripped it open, tipped a big heavy key into his palm, and squinted at it. "B.O.C. BR09 NO. 202," he read, then looked up at me. "Whafuck?"

"Bank of the Commonwealth," I translated. "The BR09, a branch number, I guess." I wheeled the car down Sandra Street, heading for 11 Mile.

"Well, where the hell *is* it?"

"What do I look like, a banking expert?"

"You got to be good for *something*. What do we do now?"

I swung west on 11 Mile. "We play it smart."

Bradley Printing is a small sheet-fed job shop located in an industrial park at Telegraph Road and the Jeffries Freeway. It's owned by Jane and Frank

Lewandowski, who started the business in their garage on Bradley Street (hence their company name; they decided that "Lewandowski Printing" was too much of a mouthful) in Detroit back in the sixties, and since then have built it up into a thriving operation specializing in audio and videocassette labels as well as general-run printing.

I got to know them while I was a security consultant for one of their printing clients back in the early seventies, and over the years we've palled around a lot, doing the ponies and the bowling alleys and the bars.

The shop occupies part of a fairly new row building. I parked in front and, as we got out, Wakefield muttered, "This don't look like a bank to me."

"Bear with me, okay?"

We pushed through the glass door into the front office. The hot, sweet, piercing smell of ink permeated the place, and from the back we could hear the clatter-boom and fluttering roar of offset presses and folders and trimmers going full tilt. Several ladies sat at desks arranged around the walls. One of the ladies was Jane Lewandowski herself, a thirtiesish, short-haired brunette, wearing a floppy blue lab coat. She stood and smiled when she saw me.

"Ben! How are you? Frank and I were just talking about you the other night."

"Doin' great, Jane." I gestured toward Wakefield, who stood awkwardly in the unfamiliar surroundings under the half-interested eyes of Jane's employees, hands hooked in the back pockets of his slacks. "Vince Wakefield, Jane Lewandowski."

She rushed at her normal frenzied pace around the desk, hand extended, and Wakefield shook it and muttered some vague pleasantry with a half-smile. Jane released his hand and looked at me again, smile still fixed on her face but eyes wary. She'd made him, all right. When you build your business from zip to a living, you either develop a good instinct for people or you don't stay in business very long.

She called over to a young woman seated at the desk by the door. "Louise, run out back and tell Frank that Ben's here, will you?" She turned back to us, still smiling. "Can I get you fellas some coffee? Mr. Wakefield?"

"No, thanks," Wakefield answered. He turned indifferently and busied himself looking at the framed prints of antique automobiles mounted on the walls.

I said to Jane, "Not for me, either. We're kind of in a rush. Need some business cards."

"Sure." Jane nodded. "What'll it be this time? Lawyer? Accountant? Professor? V-P of something?"

I considered. "Make it the lawyer, usual address. Different name this time, though."

"Better write it down for me." She grabbed a pad with their company name and logo on it and handed it to me with a pen. As I wrote the name in big and—for me—legible letters, the door to the back pushed open and Frank Lewandowski ambled through with Louise trailing him. "Ben," he greeted amiably, making a shy smile.

We shook hands. Where Jane is an adrenaline-charged ball of fire, Frank is, like most craftsmen, easy, relaxed, meticulous. They're a perfect team: Jane bitches, Frank fixes. Frank's in his fifties, short and stocky, and he was wearing a heavy ink-stained canvas apron. "How's tricks?" he asked.

"Goin' good, Frank," I answered, handing Jane the pad.

She gave it to her husband. "Business cards. Louise can set this on the Compugraphic. Get Mark to strip it in on Ben's lawyer keyline." She eyed me. "Quantity?"

"Fifty'll be plenty."

She turned back to Frank. "Burn a paper plate, then, and run it on the small press. The engine company job's off there now, isn't it?"

"Being trimmed," he answered.

"Put it on heavy white index. There's an extra package back there. It'll lay good and dry fast on that; Ben needs these quick." As Jane turned to me again, I noticed that Wakefield had drifted over and was listening to us. "Half an hour okay?"

"Sure, fine."

Frank said, "Got it. Nice seeing ya, Ben. Gotta have you over to supper sometime soon, okay?"

"Anytime." Frank turned and went into the press-room. I asked Jane, "Use your phone?"

"Sure. Help yourself to Paula's desk. She's off today. You fellas just make yourselves comfortable."

I pulled up a chair at the desk at the corner, and Wakefield seated himself on the straight chair across from me. I picked up the receiver, flipped the phone book open, and looked up Bank of the Commonwealth.

Frank strolled into the office and handed me the small gray box of business cards. "Here you go, Ben."

"Thanks." I turned to Jane and got out my wallet. "What's the damage?"

"Don't worry about it. We'll bill you," she said cheerfully.

"No, listen." I got out a hundred and handed it to her. Big Shot Perkins, they call me, sprinkling C-notes all over Detroit. "Apply this to the account. I may need some more on pretty short notice."

She handed the bill over to one of the ladies. "Okay. I never object to taking cash. You just let us know." As Frank waved and went back into the shop, Jane put herself between me and Wakefield, lowered her voice and said, "You on a case?"

"Yeah, working on a deal."

"Must be pretty good," she said, eyes shining. "You're *flush*."

I grinned. "For me, yeah. Strictly temporary, though."

She glanced at Wakefield, who was getting to his feet, and said, voice even lower, "What about him?"

"Co-conspirator."

"You just *watch* yourself."

"Right. See you later." I gestured to Wakefield and he followed me out of the shop.

The midday heat was in full force now, held smothering to the ground by intense cloud cover. The sun would not break through that day, nor, with our luck, would it rain, either. I'd just showered the night before, but felt like I hadn't for months. I fired up the engine and, against my better judgment, turned on the air conditioning as Wakefield slammed the door on his side. "Lemme see 'em."

I handed him the box. He opened it, took out a card and read, "Dennis Kearney, Attorney at Law, eighteen-ten Book Building, Detroit." His small narrow eyes found me. "Think this'll fly?"

"Hell, it's better than nothing, Vince," I said, pulling away from the print shop.

"What about the bank?"

I swung onto Telegraph and floored it. The small motor, strength sapped by the air conditioning, picked up speed with agonizing slowness. "Bank of the Commonwealth, Franklin Road at Northwestern Highway."

Wakefield laid the box of cards on the seat between us and stared straight ahead. "How'd you find that out?"

"Called the main branch, said I had a UPS delivery to Branch Nine, needed the street address. Simple."

Wakefield sighed and grinned as the interior of the car slowly cooled off. "'Nother hundred grand, here we come!"

It didn't quite work out that way.

We found the bank all right. It was a tiny place, almost like a sub-branch, with, even though it was lunch hour, just a couple of customers on hand. Wakefield, perhaps sensitive about his failure at AmericaWay Bank yesterday, insisted on handling this one, and strode up to the counter as I lurked browsing nervously behind the brochure stand. He did pretty well, considering.

The clerk bought the business card without question but, upon checking their records, found that the box rent hadn't been paid for a couple of years. Wakefield coughed up the cash, disappeared into the vault, and came back out with my new briefcase in hand a few minutes later, looking like thunder.

He was smart enough not to say anything till we were in the car and rolling away. "Goddamn bastard!" he sputtered finally, tossing the briefcase angrily into the back seat.

"Nada, huh?"

"Naw, there was *dough* there, but only about ten grand. Shit, this keeps up, it'll take us forever to put it all together."

A sobering thought. "Maybe this was his last hidey-hole," I suggested. "Maybe that was the end of the money. But there's more, somewhere."

Wakefield grumbled unintelligibly and propped a boot on the dashboard, his knee practically rubbing his chin. "Well, we better keep moving. Got any more coordinates?"

"Naw. Maybe later today," I said casually. Soon as I can shake *you* for a couple minutes, I thought.

"Tell you what," he said as I lighted a cigar and heel-handed the car onto Telegraph. "Let's go back to the hotel, you make your arrangements, and maybe we can score another one today."

"Sounds good to me." I jumped onto the John Lodge Freeway, headed for downtown Detroit.

Back at the Detroit Plaza, we temporarily retrieved our original briefcase from the vault, put the new cash in with it, and returned it to the clerk. Wakefield decided to grab a drink in the bar while I made arrangements for the new coordinates. I left him with a wave, took the elevator upstairs, and stuck my key in the lock.

Behind me, a young, unfamiliar male voice said calmly, "Just hold it right there."

I froze in the silence. A hand probed my armpits, spine, and crotch. Then nothing, till the voice again: "Now you can open it."

I said to the door, "Can I look at you first?"

"*Slowly.*"

I looked over my right shoulder into the brown eyes of a very young, uniformed Detroit police officer. He held a service .38 in both hands, regulation style, aimed at my heart. He didn't even bother to smile. "Now open the door."

I finished turning the key with slick fingers and pushed the door open. Across my hotel room, half leaning on the dresser, was a short, broad-shouldered, scalp-haired black man wearing a deep green polyester three-piece suit. It was Capt. Elvin Dance, chief of detectives, Detroit Police homicide section.

"Howdy, Ben," he said lazily. "Why'ncha come along with me. Let's boogie, baby!"

CHAPTER 19

Respectful knuckles tapped twice on the interrogation room's door, and it opened in to reveal a young uniform. "Perkins's lawyer's here, Captain."

Elvin Dance unpropped himself from the bored position he'd assumed, cheek on palm, elbow on table. He gave me a resigned look and said, "Yeah, right, send him in."

"It's a her, Captain," the uniform said as he left.

"A *she?*"

"Oh, shit," I said, wincing as Carole Somers came into the room, carrying a razor-thin leather attaché case.

Elvin Dance made a wolfish smile. "Well, all

right! I'll just leave you to consult with your, heh, counsel, Ben. Later." He stood, swung past Carole, and left the room.

Carole closed the door and faced me expressionlessly. She wore a tan pleated skirt, white-on-white long-sleeved blouse, and tan vest. Despite the climate, she wore nylons on her long, elegant legs. She'd have looked wonderful anywhere, but in that tiny, windowless, pungent interrogation room with its heavy, scarred conference table and battered, unmatched wood chairs, she was a shining jewel.

I was raised by people who required their children to extend all common courtesies—nothing could earn me the hard back of my Daddy's hand faster than failing to rise at the entrance of a lady—but I was so surprised to see Carole Somers there that I stayed seated. "What the hell are you doing here, Carole?"

She squinted and ambled toward the table. "Hm. Maybe I've got the wrong address. This *is* Detroit Police Headquarters, thirteen-hundred Beaubien, isn't it?"

"Wise ass ain't appropriate, Carole."

She set her attaché case down on the table and paced the floor, hands folded in front of her at the end of long arms. "And it *was* you who called my office awhile ago and requested the services of an attorney?"

"Yeah, but not you. I called your office and asked them to call *my* lawyer, Bob Curtin, and send him down here."

She stopped pacing and stared at me. "Now, why did you call my office? Why didn't you call Mr. Curtin directly?"

"I don't have his number. They only allow one call. Your office was the only number I knew by heart. Jesus, Carole, you can't represent me. This is business, not personal."

"I know that," she answered evenly. "As it happens, my office did call Mr. Curtin's office, and were informed that he's pleading an appeals case in Cincinnati all day today. Further, since I'm aware that you occasionally utilize the services—as misapplied as that term may be—of Freddie Flynn, we attempted to reach him as well, but he is also unavailable, since he's doing a year and a day for criminal misconduct." She made a bright cold smile. "So, here I am!"

"Swell."

"Enough chitchat, okay?" She pulled back the chair Dance had used, seated herself, and slipped a yellow legal pad and pen out of her attaché case. She scribbled something in the top margin, then looked up at me. "So," she said briskly, "what brand of sling is your ass in this time?"

"Murder or something."

"Oohkay." She wrote something else. "The victim?"

"Some kid they found knifed in an alley a couple blocks from here."

"Where were you apprehended?"

"Detroit Plaza."

"Were you read your rights?"

"I guess so."

She eyed me. "Were you or weren't you?"

I shrugged. "Elvin held up a little printed card and said, 'You know this shit, don'tcha?' and put it away."

She considered. "Maybe a hip judge would buy into it, I don't know." She studied her pad. "Were you placed under arrest?"

"I'm here, aren't I?"

She said patiently, "Did they say, 'You are under arrest'?"

"No. What he said was, 'Let's dance, baby.' "

She frowned. "Don't call me baby, please."

"I didn't call *you* baby, sweetie. That's what they called *me*."

She smiled faintly. "Did you, um, try to refuse the invitation?"

"Let's just say I didn't express any great eagerness to come down here."

She made some notes. "Did they book you?"

"Not as far as I know. They shook me down at the desk, put me in here and asked about the knifing. Then you showed."

She didn't look up. "Did you do it?"

Generally, I believe in leveling with your lawyer. Had it been Bob Curtin instead of Carole Somers sitting down the table from me, I'd have told the whole story. Instead, I kept it to the essence. "No. I don't even know the victim."

She stopped writing and looked at me. "So why'd they pick you up?"

"I don't know. They sorta haven't gotten around to telling me that yet." I was curious to know. Anxious, more like.

She dropped the pen, sat back in the chair, and folded her arms in front of her, staring above me. "They must have had *some* reason. No idea at all, huh?"

"No, I—" I drew up short as the interrogation room's door opened and Elvin Dance swaggered in, trailed by the young male uniform. Elvin had shucked his coat but retained his deep green vest and wore a burnt-orange tie over his crisp white shirt. Big, glittering chunks of gold glowed from his cuffs and from the ring fingers of each hand. As he rounded the table and lazily swung a chair around to sit on it backward, he said, "You all through billing and cooing now, so we can get down to bidness?"

The uniform leaned against the wall by the door and watched us through remote eyes. Carole said icily, "I'm Mr. Perkins's attorney, Captain."

Blazing white teeth showed as Dance grinned wickedly. "Now, counselor, I happen to know Ben here pretty well. He only uses but two lawyers: Bob Curtin and Freddie Flynn."

Carole gave me a meaningful look. "If you know Ben as well as you claim, Captain, you know that he generates enough business to keep three lawyers busy."

"Haw! Haw haw!" Dance laid his burly arms atop the back of the chair, linked his fingers, and rested his chin on his knuckles, grinning. His brown eyes went from me to Carole and back again. "Maybe we can get on with this here. Ben—"

Carole was putting her pad and pen back in her attaché case. She rose. "Ben," she said calmly, "I want you to walk out that door and leave the building with me."

I shoved the chair back and stood. The policemen didn't move. Elvin Dance asked, "Now, where you going?"

Carole looked down at him. "Inasmuch as my client hasn't been charged with a crime or even been formally placed under arrest, I've recommended to him that we leave."

Dance straightened. "He ain't under arrest," he said with a shrug.

"Very well. Let's go, Ben."

Dance straightened farther. The uniform let go of the wall. Dance said from way back in his throat, "You ain't goin' nowhere just yet."

Carole turned back to him and smiled. "Now we're getting somewhere." She looked at me. "Ben, you can consider yourself formally under arrest. Sit down, relax."

I sat down, but I didn't relax.

Dance's mouth was set hard in a frown as he glared at Carole. "You just have it any way you want, counselor. Arrest or no arrest, it don't matter to me."

She had her pad out and was writing industriously. "But it does to me, Captain," she said without looking up. "False arrest is a civil and criminal offense in this state. So, for your information, is malicious prosecution."

Steady steady steady, I thought, staring at Carole. You don't mess with these guys.

Dance retorted in an unimpressed voice. "Bo-shit. Criminal offense? Just who in the hell's gone arrest *me*? And that civil part, that's bo-shit, too." He jerked his head toward me. "Civil action takes real coin and ole Ben here, he's broke most of the time. Where's he gonna get the dough for a lawyer, even a cheap one like you?"

Carole favored him with dead eyes and a chilly smile. "Every now and then I do one just for sport, Captain."

She meant it, too. Every word. In that moment I saw something in her I'd sensed but never seen before, and Dance saw it, too. The killer instinct. The lethal competitiveness that is an essential quality of true trial lawyers, who thrive on the savage joy of the fight.

Elvin Dance is no shrinking violet, either, but he also has as keen a pragmatic nose as anyone. He let a long tense moment drag by, then squared his shoulders, stretched, yawned, and said, "There ain't no call for all this woofin', counselor. We been nothin' but real nice to this boy here. We asked him to come down here, and he said okay. We didn't cuff him, not his wrists, not his face. We gave him a nice ride in a air-conditioned city-owned car. Hell, we even read him his rights."

Carole said tonelessly, "I can't convince myself that showing my client a card and asking"—she consulted her pad—"'you know this shit, don'tcha?' fulfills the spirit, let alone the letter, of the *Miranda v. Arizona* decision. But, if he is in fact here voluntarily and not under arrest, we'll call it a moot point."

"He *ain't* under arrest," Dance said emphatically. "Hell, if he was under arrest, would he be in *this* room? Hell no, this-here's DPD's VIP lounge. If ole Ben here was under arrest, he'd be downstairs with Knucks or somebody, goin' through the routine. We just brought him in to ask a few questions, that's all."

Carole set her good shoulders back straight and asked pleasantly, "Is it all right, then, if Mr. Perkins leaves now?"

Elvin Dance extended a flat, black hand grandly toward the door. "Any time, counselor."

"Very well." She smiled. "Mr. Perkins is always eager to cooperate with the authorities, Captain." She nodded toward me. "Ask away."

Suddenly I was back on stage. Elvin Dance ran through his questions again. It didn't take long, because he didn't have much. A young white man, identified as Clinton Maddox, age twenty-three, last known residence an apartment on Second Boulevard, was found knifed to death in an alley downtown. The medical examiner set the time of death at sometime yesterday. The police had "reason"—that was all Dance would say—to believe that I was involved.

Carole watched us like a tennis observer as the question-and-answer session went on. I gave my standard line, hiding my nervousness as best I could. I didn't know, and had never even heard of, Clinton Maddox. I'd been all over the city yesterday. Sorry I couldn't be more help.

Elvin Dance listened to my answers placidly. When we'd burned up his script, he stared down at the scarred table top for a minute, then asked quietly, "What kinda game you working on right now, Perkins?"

I was about to answer, but Carole cleared her throat. "I don't think that's pertinent, Captain. From what I hear, you've got a stiff and that's all. No witnesses, no physical evidence, no nothing. The question that most immediately occurs to me is, what made you bring Mr. Perkins in?"

He looked at her. "He's been in trouble before, counselor."

"I'll concede that," she retorted. "Grand blasphemy, public smartmouth, promiscuity, and a weakness for Waylon Jennings music." Her voice hardened. "But nothing like this."

"Besides," I butted in, "you picked me up at the Detroit Plaza. You know very well that I live out in Belleville. What I'm wondering is, how did you know I was staying at the hotel?"

"Phone tip," he said so softly we barely heard it.

Carole straightened, her hand tightening on her pen. "*Phone* tip?"

"Yes, ma'am," he answered stolidly.

"Anonymous?" I asked.

"There any other kind?"

"Now wait a minute," Carole said.

"Hold it!" I glared at her. "This is important. What exactly did the phone tipster say?"

Elvin Dance looked depressed. He folded his fingers together and squeezed them, setting off his knuckles like a chain of firecrackers. "Said he saw a killing. Saw a guy get knifed. Gave us the location. Said that Perkins done it. Ben Perkins. Stayin' at the Detroit Plaza." He shrugged. "That's all."

I went tense and cold inside. Without willing it, my fists knotted. I thought about a certain tall, raw-boned, plane-faced Canadian gent. And I wondered what he was doing at this very moment. And I thought about my wrecked room in the Holiday Inn in Windsor, which Wakefield could *not* have perpetrated, and I wondered for the thousandth time who'd done that, who else was after me.

I became aware of Carole and Dance staring at me curiously. Elvin commented to her, "Maybe he didn't kill anybody, but if lookin' lethal were an offense, ole Ben'd be on his way down to visit with Knucks right now."

Carole asked me softly, "What is it, Ben?"

I addressed myself to Dance. "You sure the tipster gave my name?"

"Yup."

"What time did he call?"

"This morning. Nine or thereabouts."

At which time Vince Wakefield was with me.

When I didn't answer, Carole said to Dance, "You know, of course, you can't charge or even hold a person on the basis of just an anonymous tip. You don't even have any physical evidence."

"I know," Dance said glumly. "Prints on the murder weapon were the victim's own."

My mind flashed to Tub pulling the knife out of himself, staring at it curiously, and I shuddered inside.

Dance looked at me. His eyes were hard and skeptical and, yet, resigned. "Well, no harm in trying. G'wan, split, Ben. Keep your nose clean."

It wasn't going to be easy. Particularly now.

Carole and I walked down the broad stone steps of Detroit Police Headquarters. The gray sky was clamped down claustrophobically on the city, making me feel like I was wearing a suit made of rancid sponge. Though I felt elated at being out of jail, the elation was tempered by the presence of a woman whom I'd loved but who was no longer mine; and by being in the grip of a case that had turned into an octopus, two tentacles corkscrewing up my legs, sucking me down somewhere dark and unknown.

At the sidewalk we walked south on Beaubien. Construction work limited pedestrian space, forcing Carole to walk very near me. As I lighted a cigar and took a dreamy drag, I said to her, "What I'm trying to say is, thanks. You done good."

"A kid with moxie and a semester of pre-law could have done the same," she answered. "Maybe even Freddie Flynn, assuming it was before eleven A.M. on a day when he wasn't doing time."

"Freddie's okay."

"Freddie's a sleaze and you know it. If they don't lift his ticket to practice law, I'm going to sell my practice and go into a more respectable line of work. Like procuring, or dealing, or being a private detective."

We stopped for the light at Monroe Street. I looked into her sober, pretty face. "Why are you so angry with me, Carole? I don't take freebies. I expect you to bill me for today. The full tariff. You lost nothing here."

The light changed and we crossed the street. Drizzle misted down like steam in a sauna. She said,

"Of course I'm not going to bill you. There's a thing called the underground economy, you know."

I cupped my hand over my cigar to protect it from the rain, and took a deep drag. "Suits me. You're going to need brakes on that car before too long. Your water heater is going. Maybe you need some paint and trim work in your den. My professional services are yours for the asking, you know that."

"How about your friendship? Is that available?"

I gnawed on my cigar, took a drag, found it had drowned, and tossed it away into the street. In my mind I hemmed and hawed, looked for glib throwaway words, found them and discarded them, and decided to be honest. "I never seen it work out that way. Once you go all one way, you can't go anywhere else but all the way back the other. We can do business, sure, no problem, but beyond that I don't know."

Her hand got my arm, and she stopped me and faced me, her expression hard and cold and demanding, the face of a lawyer questioning a hostile witness. "That's it. *That's* it. That's what gripes me, Ben, what got me so riled in your apartment the other day—that goddamned all-or-nothing attitude of yours."

I winced. "Carole—"

She turned earnest. "Ben, I'm sorry I exploded the other day, but what I said was true! Sure, I know that love affairs end—but does a friendship always have to, too? Are you unable to be my friend unless you're sleeping with me?"

I made what I suspect was a crooked smile. "No. Hell no. Course not."

"Well, that's been your attitude toward me. Now, I'm not going to beg, Ben. But I've thought about it and I know I'm not so overrun with friends that I can afford to lose any. And if you think about yourself you'll probably feel the same way."

I looked down, in a quandary. "Yeah, well."

She said, "I hope you'll try. If not for my sake, for Will's. He loves you."

"The kid's special," I said through a tightening throat.

She nodded and smiled and swept her dampening bangs off her forehead with her unencumbered hand. I felt she was tempted to move toward me, but she didn't. She said, "We just passed Greektown. Want to go get some late lunch?"

I hadn't eaten all day. I hadn't even thought about my stomach. I didn't think about it now. "No, thanks."

"I'm buying," she said with strained humor.

Impulsively I grabbed her upper arms with my hands, but held her where she was. "'Preciate it. Wish I could. Honest to God do. But I got business."

I turned and continued alone, headed for the Renaissance Center and the Detroit Plaza Hotel.

CHAPTER 20

The Detroit Plaza desk clerk—a middle-aged woman this time—steamed over to me. "You here about eight-oh-one?"

I had little trouble disliking her because, just a half hour out of jail and soaked through from the walk and having seen what I just saw in my room, I wouldn't have had trouble hating Mother Theresa. "Yeah," I said extra loudly, tapping my room key on the desk. "I want to know what the hell is going on around here."

The clerk had a registration card in her hand. "The couple you barged in on," she said as if to a child, "are registered at this hotel and belong in that room. You had *no right* to keep that key. You had *no right* to go barging in like that. They were very upset when they called down here just now."

"I'm not surprised, considering what they were doing when I went in there. Used to be laws against that kind of thing."

"Shhhhh!" she said, eyes mean. She glanced back and forth to make sure no one had heard me, then fixed me with a poisonous look. "Now, hand over the key."

I kept it. "What I want to know is, what gave *you* the right to put other people in my room? My credit's good. And I was only gone for—"

"Because," she hissed, "you *checked out*, Mr. Perkins. Or don't you remember?"

My new room wasn't nearly as nice. It was only on the fifth floor, it was smaller, and it faced downtown. But, all things considered, I was lucky to have it at all.

The clerk had gotten the duty manager, who, all the while shooting me annoyed little looks, showed me the records.

Shortly before noon, just after I left the hotel with Elvin Dance, someone—no one on duty had a description, "they all look alike," I guess you'd say—came to the desk, said he was Ben Perkins, and wanted to check out. He didn't have his key, but said he'd left it in the room. He signed the credit-card slip and left. The housekeepers did their checking-out routine on the room, and then a couple checked in about an hour later.

Ironic. You have to have ID and a credit card to check *into* most hotels. But you don't have to prove who you are to check out.

Question was, why would anyone want to check me out of my room?

I didn't need this, not on top of everything else.

It just didn't make sense.

When things quit making sense, there are two smart alternatives. You can go crawl into a hole and cry for a while, or you can make yourself do some things that will get you back on track.

As tempting as the idea to run and hide was, I decided to do some busy work. First thing: I called room service and ordered up some beer. Second thing: I lighted a cigar. Third thing: I called the desk and verified that Vince Wakefield was still registered at the hotel. Then I called his room. No answer.

Okay. Not encouraging, but it made sense.

Then I called my apartment in Belleville and triggered the phone-answering machine.

Click. Someone called, didn't leave a message.

Click. Someone called, didn't leave a message.

My hand on the phone receiver moistened and I stared without seeing over the Detroit skyline.

Click. "Ben? This is Marge at Norwegian Wood. I don't know where you are, but you'd better get back here. Arn's been shot, Ben. He's dead." A moment of breathing. A radio played tinnily somewhere in the room with her. "Someone tried to crash the gate. Arn tried to stop them. They shot him. The police are here. They want to talk to you. Hurry."

A City of Belleville black-and-white blocked the access road to Norwegian Wood. I stopped, gave my name to the cop, and he waved me past. As I drove the Chrysler on toward the security shack, I saw two black unmarked Plymouth Furies, plus another black-and-white, parked at odd angles around it. The wood gate was busted off and lying on the pavement. The Plexiglas window of the shack was gashed in three places, spidery cracks running away from the holes. Uniformed and plainclothes officers worked singly and in pairs, inside the shack and out. All their eyes seemed to rise toward me as I screeched the Chrysler to a halt by the shack.

As I got out, Jack Hatfield, Belleville P.D.'s chief of detectives, lumbered out of the shack and around it toward me.

I got out of the car and swung the door shut. "What the hell's going on, Hatfield?"

He stopped dead-still and stared at me in a pantomime of surprise. Hatfield's a well-seasoned sixty-two or thereabouts. He's lumpy, slow, drawling, yet has an unchallengeable air of command. Most of the time he dresses like he did that day: tight, shiny gray single-breasted suit, white shirt, thin tie, and a snap-brim hat mashed down on his burr-shaved head. A spitty stump of cigar grew out of his mouth. You wouldn't recognize him without it.

"Well," Hatfield said in his hoarse voice, "where'd *you* materialize from, Perkins?"

"Got a message on my phone box from Marge." I gestured at the bullet-riddled shack. "What about this?"

"What, this?" His surprise seemed genuine. "Oh, I wouldn't call it much, except this old geezer you called a security guard got hisself blown away some- how. *That's* all."

The other cops were watching me warily. I stared past the shack at the buildings of Norwegian Wood sitting peacefully a distance away. From some- where far away came the *thock* of a mis-hit golf ball. A double-bottom semi-truck brayed down Huron River Drive.

I walked past Hatfield to the shack. Its sliding door was open. Inside, a detective worked with tools, apparently trying to pry a slug out of the plain unpainted plywood wall. The tiny shack's desk lay cluttered with papers and a loose-leaf notebook and Arn's big AM radio—"eight transistor" as he'd proud- ly told me a million times—lovingly wrapped in friction tape from the time he'd knocked it off the table with his elbow.

The cement threshold of the shack was smeared reddish with drying blood, which ran down the step onto the sidewalk outside. It was already rust-colored, and there was a lot of it. Several emotions, none of them very nice, warred inside me. I felt sick at the thought of poor old Arn, who'd retired from thirty years on the line at Ford Motor Company and took this tame, boring, and supposedly safe job not because he needed the money, but just to keep busy, to feel important and needed, and to help me out. I felt bewildered at this latest turn in what had already not been one of my better days. I felt jumpy, stomach-itching anxiety at the thought that here, at last, my two "lives," Norwegian Wood and detective, had crossed—with lethal results.

And I felt cold, smoking fury, the worst kind, the kind that makes it tough to do business.

Jack Hatfield lumbered up beside me, rubbing the back of his clean-shaved neck. I asked dully, "Where's Arn now?"

"Meatwagon carried him off half hour ago." Hatfield's tongue waggled his cigar around to a permanent groove in the corner of his mouth. "What do you know about this, Perkins?"

"What do *I* know? I just got here."

"Well," Hatfield said, then interrupted himself as the detective inside got something loose from the wall and examined it. "What do we got there, Carl?"

The detective looked at his boss. "Big slug, Chief. No way to do ballistics; it's all misshapen. Too bad the old fart was in its way and slowed it down, otherwise we might have gotten something intact that we could work with."

Before I knew it, I was inside the shack, had the detective by the lapels, had spun him, and flung him back through the door. Hatfield, caught by surprise, fell back out of the detective's way as he skittered off balance onto the asphalt, tripped over a decorative curbstone, and fell on the fringe of the lawn. A running ten-foot leap landed me right on the detective as he groped under his jacket for his gun. I grabbed his greasy hair with one hand and pulled and twisted it viciously as I got to his gunhand with the other and bent two fingers backward, freeing the pistol as he screamed. I got the gun, a .38 snubnose, by the barrel, freed it from his coat, raised it high, and started it down hard with his nose as ground zero.

I never got there because something caught my arm and wrenched me back. It was Jack Hatfield, straddling us on his two massive legs. With surprising strength he pulled me off the detective and onto my back, and slammed my gun hand hard on a curbstone. "Leggo of it," he grunted, panting, and slammed my hand again. "Let *go* of it." I went limp as the pistol dropped from my aching hand. Hatfield rose, picked up the pistol, and released me.

The detective had gotten back to his feet. Hatfield's voice above me said, "What the hell's *wrong* with you, Perkins?" The detective hovered in my peripheral vision for a second, strode purposefully closer and kicked me a glancing blow in the head, then stalked cockily back. As stars and tears blurred my vision, Hatfield rose and yelled at his detective, "*Back* in the car now, Carl. Git!"

The detective stood panting, mouth sagging, staring at me as I struggled to my knees and onto my feet. "Too bad," I said hoarsely, "that Arn got in the way of that slug and messed up your ballistics. Too goddamn bad, asshole. I'll make sure his widow sends you a note apologizing for her husband's clumsiness."

The detective held out his good hand and waved fingers toward himself invitingly. "Come on, let's do it, right now, cocksucker, you and me." Hatfield seized my upper arm as two other detectives got to my opponent and started hustling him away. He broke himself loose from them and stomped off, hurling obscene noises back over his shoulder at me. Hatfield asked me, "You gonna stay put now, Perkins?"

I pulled myself loose, blinking hard, trying to get my vision back in order. My head bonged like it had upon awakening that morning. "I'm surprised at you, Hatfield," I said. "I thought you'd train your boys to keep a civil tongue in their heads."

"Yeah?" Hatfield lumbered around to face me. I noticed that his cigar was gone and wondered if, in the tussle, he'd spit it out or swallowed it. I doubted that even he knew. "I'm surprised at *you*, Perkins. Christ on a bicycle, *you* of all people know how cops talk. You talk that way yourself. Plus, you been on the street long enough to know that it don't pay to mess with the cops. It just *don't pay*. We can't afford for it to. You read me?"

"So run me in," I said with a sneer.

"Now don't get snotty with *me*, young fella. I was just making conversation, that's all." Hatfield hitched his trousers up around his broad-beamed belly. Off down the driveway, Carl stood by the hood of one of the Furies, talking loudly to a couple of his colleagues. Hatfield gave them an evil look, then said to me, "C'mon over here."

We went back toward the shack. From somewhere in a baggy coat pocket Hatfield pulled out a half-smoked stogie, stuck it in his face with a look of contentment, and lighted it with a cardboard match. I've known Jack Hatfield twelve years and tangled with him at least that many times, and I've never yet seen him light a fresh one. My smokes may stink, but at least I buy new ones every now and then.

A brown stick-legged bird flapped away from the blood stain where it had been exploring. It was cooler in the shade of the shack, but not much. The chief shoved his hat toward the back of his head and said, "So you don't know nothing about this?"

"Hell, no," I said, folding my arms and staring at the bullet-riddled shack. "How could I? I wasn't even here."

"Well," Hatfield said, gravitating the cigar around to its normal position in the corner of his mouth, "what we found out was, whoever shot the guard was here looking for you."

I stared at him. *"Me?"*

Hatfield stepped into the shack, picked up the loose-leaf notebook, and handed it to me. It was a notebook I'd seen many times. "It was open to that page when we got here."

The notebook contains a page for each tenant of Norwegian Wood. Each page lists the names of people whom the tenants have authorized to visit them without calling ahead first. The page the book was open to now had my name at the top and about as short a list of authorized visitors as you'd find. Carole Somers. Dick Dennehy. Chuck Haye. Bill Scozzafava. And Dan Perkins, my very elderly, totally disabled uncle whose name appears on the list for sentimental reasons.

I stared at the list, irrationally thinking about substituting Carole's name with Terry's, as Hatfield went on. "Some old bag name-a Shaw, Arlene Shaw, was just rolling in here. Pulled up behind what she called a little bitty car stopped at the booth here. Ford car. She thinks. Michigan plate. She thinks. Two men in it, least she figured they were men, they had short hair. She thinks. Only saw the back of their heads. They talked to the guard. She heard arguing. Then the guard came up with this and pointed it at the driver."

Hatfield went under his coat and came out with an ancient Colt Lawman .357 revolver. I felt sick inside as I looked at it. "I told Arn not to pack that thing. I told him and I told him."

"He never got off a shot," Hatfield went on, "least, according to Miz Shaw. Somebody in the car cut loose with a gun. She saw the guard go down. The little bitty Ford-she-thinks car took off forward, busted through the gate, made a U-turn, and tore ass out of here."

I closed the notebook and tossed it back onto Arn's cluttered desk. I said flatly, "Not much to go on, huh, Chief?"

"Not unless you got some insight. You got any enemies, Perkins?"

My lips curled into a smile. "They have to stand in line these days, Chief."

"Huh. Why am I not surprised." Hatfield's cigar had gone dead, but he still sucked on it like a lollipop. "How 'bout lately? What kinda game you into, Perkins?"

He was the second cop to ask me that question that hot, miserable day. I shrugged and didn't answer.

"I could get real curious," Hatfield prompted gently, "about how come an old Ford Motor man like you drove up here in a Chrysler. I could get real curious about how come an American citizen like you drove up here in a car with Ontario plates. I could get real curious about a lot of things."

I stared stonily at him and didn't answer.

"Oh, yeah, I forgot," Hatfield said with sudden harshness. "Old Tight-Lips He-Don't-Talk-To-Nobody Perkins. Only, if there's something you know I oughta know and you're not letting me in on it, that can be called obstruction of justice. Just thought I'd mention it."

"Chief Hatfield," I answered in a hard voice, "I said my enemies have to stand in line. These days, so do the cops."

"What the hell's that supposed to mean?" he grated.

"I'll see you around, Chief. My advice is to let me get to the bastards who did this first, and save you a lot of paperwork and expense. And one more thing." I grabbed the notebook back off Arn's desk.

"What?" Hatfield asked warily.

"What's Carl's last name?" I asked, leafing through the pages to the one with my name on it.

"Portman. Why?"

I wrote CARL PORTMAN at the end of my list after Carole's name, flipped the notebook shut, and tossed it back on the desk. "You tell him he's welcome to visit me. Any time."

CHAPTER 21

I unlocked my apartment door, went in, kicked the door shut behind me, tossed off my blazer, and looked around at the mess.

Nothing had changed, nothing in the apartment, that is. Newspapers and magazines were strewn and stacked. A couple of Stroh's empties from my meeting with Dennehy last week—last lifetime, it seemed like—sat on the coffee table. A crowded porcelain ashtray stunk up the air. A big flat white Domino's box sat open on the floor next to the couch, exposing a couple pieces of petrifying pizza. A sunbeam spotted on a framed poster on the wall above the couch, a poster that Carole gave me for Christmas, depicting an elegant, shapely, scantily dressed woman holding a bottle of champagne and leaning on the hood of a Rolls, the caption saying: POVERTY SUCKS. The air was chilled from the air conditioner. I ambled to the leather chair, flopped down, and propped my feet on the coffee table.

Ten lousy G's from the box this morning. Dance dragging me in on a tip about Tub's death. Someone checking me out of my room at the Plaza. Arn blown away out here.

Add to the mess Carole, ex-lover, new professional associate. And Terry, calling me on the phone half-drunk. Kenny Slingluff on the phone sounding strung-out about his precious Mona, indignant over her apparent infidelity. Elvin Dance and Jack Hatfield, both cops, one black Detroit, one white Belleville, both after a piece of me.

Plus, the Random Element. Whoever he, or she, was. The person who had tossed my room my first night in Windsor. The person who had reported me to the police in connection with Tub's killing. The person who had checked me out of the Detroit Plaza this morning. The person who had been involved in Arn's death. Whoever it was, he—or she—was ahead of me. And would stay there. Unless I got real smart, or real lucky, or real mean, or some of all three.

I reached down to my LeHighs, untied them, and shucked them one at a time with a toss of each foot. I checked my shirt pocket and found I was out of cigars, so I padded on cooling feet into the kitchen—clean, or reasonably so—and got a fresh pack out of the cupboard by the sink. Could I be so fortunate as to still have some beer in the fridge? I could. In fact, I had a whole six-pack of Stroh's. I snapped a can open, lighted a cigar, went back into the living room and sat down.

I took a long, gurgling slug of beer. The coldness of the liquid hit my stomach. The heat of the alcohol fanned out like a squad of infantry on patrol. I dragged on my cigar and puffed it hot, sending streams of smoke roiling up my face and wafting away from me in the room.

It all seemed so far away. My Mustang was out at Metro Airport. My suitbag and most of my clothes were still in Windsor. My briefcase with a hundred and ten G's was at the Detroit Plaza. Tub held down a slab in one morgue, Arn was in another, and Vince Wakefield was God knew where. It all seemed so far away, and there was no reason, really, not to keep it there.

I could keep my door locked. I could shower in my own stall and put on jeans and a clean shirt from my own drawer and order pizza from my neighborhood Domino's and go to sleep happily drunk in my own bed. No reason to deal with the shit till tomorrow. If then.

Sounded like a great agenda to me, so, draining the beer with a long swig, I got up to head for the bedroom, but stopped when I saw the red light glowing on my phone-answering machine.

I stared at the light, cigar smoldering in my teeth. I was tempted to ignore it. I mean, giving any kind of a shit took a real effort just then. But before I knew it I'd padded over there, rewound the tape, and hit PLAY.

Hiss. *Click.* Someone called, didn't leave a message.

Click. A pause. Then a youngish unfamiliar male voice said, "Mr. Perkins. This is Michael Maul. I want to reach my sister. I called at two-ten. You can reach me at 431-1100. But you shouldn't bother, because"—he laughed—"I called the wrong number! Sorry!" *Click.*

I covered my eyes for a moment and shook my head.

A youngish female voice. "Mr. Perkins? Hi. This is Jeannie Riley. I don't know if you remember me, but I work for Satellite Service in Ann Arbor, and you helped fix my car a few months back when it was broken down." She cleared her throat. "Cindy Jones gave me your name. I wanted to thank you again for what you did. Why don't you call me at work sometime. I'd like to buy you lunch." Pause. "Okay?" *Click.*

After a moment I remembered her, and smiled, as the tape wound on.

"Ben. Kenny." His voice sounded very subdued, very distant. "Two of them. 282-8116, extension two, Steven Bird. 309-9753, extension one, Dennis Kearney." He paused. "Weird. That was a name on one of the other ones, wasn't it? Well, anyway. I've been through most of the Detroit ones now, maybe two or three to go. But you know, you've got cards here from all around the country. Could be a lot of other fake ones, too. No way to tell without checking. You let me know. But first get going on Mona. Please, Ben." A pause. "Bad moon arising, man." Another pause. "I just don't know, Ben," he added softly. "I just don't know." *Click.*

Oh, goody. More money. Maybe there really *was* a million bucks or more out there somewhere. Seth Flint had thought so. Right then it didn't matter to me. "Bad moon arising," Kenny had muttered. He sure had that right.

A pause, a hiss of faraway static, and then: "Hi, it's me. You know what? It's hot down here. Job's slow, real slow. I've been thinking a lot. Guess what about." She laughed. "You know what? That back-door man thing you told me about. Friend of mine, Cathleen, she's into old jazz. I asked her about the song. She'd heard it. Told me that—get this"—she

giggled—"the song's about a married woman's lover.
Calls him her back-door man. I don't think that's
exactly what you had in mind. I like the idea, anyhow." Silence. "You know something, I've been playing
detective on this case of yours. It's getting interesting." She didn't elaborate. "You haven't called me
back. I hope you've gotten my messages." Pause. "I
hope you're all right." A very long pause, then,
faintly, "I feel like doing something outrageous."
Click.

I wished Terry would do *nothing* outrageous. I
wanted her to stay right where she was and out of
harm's way. I didn't like the sound of her "playing
detective" on the case. But worrying about her would
have to wait.

I rewound the tape, reset the machine to take all
calls, and wandered into the kitchen. A fresh Stroh's
came to hand, and I popped the top and swigged
thoughtfully. Out the window the setting sun was
sending streaks of red across the golf course. The
day was ending.

I could let it end. My agenda was set.

But it wasn't. Not really.

Not with the money sitting in Detroit. Not with
Vince Wakefield running around loose. And with
Joann Sturtevant in Bloomfield, Mary Masters in
Windsor, and Arn Vogel in the morgue—clients all.

I leaned on the table, staring sightlessly through
the window with the smoldering cigar in one hand
and the cold Stroh's in the other, and thought about
my daddy.

He was born and raised in the hills of north
Georgia. The one dream he ever had—of earning
riches on the Ford assembly line—collapsed, and he
moved on to the carpenter job at the Kerns Casket
Company and became a dour, humorless, bitter man.
He died in '63, and as far as I can remember, in his
whole life he only gave me four things. Love for, and
ability at, working with tools and with hands. Undy-
ing loyalty to Ford Motor Company—"Mr. Ford's,"

he always called it. A repertoire of Southern maxims, of which his favorite, ironically, was "The sun don't shine on the same dog's ass all the time"—ironic because it's a matter of record that the sun never shone on his. And he gave me one intense, burning commitment: to do my job.

To the extent that he had any patience at all, my daddy was patient with screwups, with immaturity, with inexperience. Just as long as you did your job.

God*damn* it.

I shook my head grimly, sighed, went into the living room, sat on the leather chair and picked up the phone.

Kenny Slingluff answered with the screams of preschoolers in the background. "Thanks for the info, Kenny," I said.

"It's okay," he answered listlessly.

I rushed on, "Just wanted to tell you, don't worry about the numbers anymore. Don't call here. Don't try to get in touch with me. Okay?"

He sniffed and made an odd chuckle. "Sure, Ben. What's happening?"

"Pretty complicated," I answered. "I just don't want you involved any further. People are starting to die, Kenny."

"Oh," he said airily.

I stared at the receiver in my hand. "*Die*, Kenny. People are starting to *die*, as in, cease to live, you follow?"

"Oh, I follow, all right," he hummed. "As in, the die is cast?"

Wonderful. Old Kenny must be dipping into the pharmaceuticals again, I thought sourly. "Just hang loose, Kenny. Later."

I made just one more call, to Bill Scozzafava, who was working nights at Under New Management. He agreed to come over and man the gate for a couple of days. He even agreed to bring the heavy artillery with him. Good old Bill, he always comes through for me and never asks for anything in

return. I told him he could reach me at the Detroit
Plaza if he needed anything, and hung up.

I shut off the lights in the apartment and had
the door open to leave when I froze. Leaving the
door standing open, I went back into my bedroom
and got my .45 automatic off the shelf. I jacked in a
clip, stuffed a couple extra ones in my pocket, stuck
the .45 in my waistband against my spine, put my
blazer back on, and left for Detroit.

CHAPTER 22

I spotted the housekeeper at the end of the hall and
trotted down to her. "Excuse me, ma'am?"

She was short, black, pushing sixty, and wore a
light blue dress. She looked up at me with bored
eyes. "Yes, sir?"

"I locked myself out of my room. Would you
mind?"

I don't think she bought my smile, but I also
don't think she cared. She reached to her side and
unsnapped a bundle of keys that was clipped to a
ring on her uniform dress. "Pretty late to be locked
out, ain't it?"

"Hey, you know how it is," I said with a grin.

"No, sir, I *don't* know how it is. Which room?"

"Six-twenty."

She trudged down there with me, jingling the
keys in her hand. As she went to unlock it, I said
casually, "Keep it real quiet, okay? My wife's sleeping
in there. I don't want to wake her up."

She gave me another dark look, then inserted
the key and turned the bolt very slowly. It unlocked
with just a faint snap. She withdrew the keys and
clipped them back to her dress. I slipped her a
five-spot. "Thanks. 'Night," I whispered, and stood

there till she'd trudged down the hall and around the corner.

No one was in sight. I listened at the door and heard nothing from inside. I reached under my blazer and came out with my .45 automatic. As quietly as I could, I worked the action once to jack a round into the chamber. Then, holding the weapon pointed up in my right hand, I soundlessly pushed open the door to six-twenty, slipped in, and let the door sigh shut behind me.

All was darkness except for the faintest of night lights shining through the window at the other end of the room. I stood in the blackness to let my eyes adjust a bit and listened to Vince Wakefield snore like Dagwood Bumstead: *Snkx-x-x-x.* When I could see sufficiently well to navigate, I slunk soundlessly on the deep carpet to the bureau and hit a switch which activated the lamps on the bureau, the night-stand between the beds, and the table by the window. Then I leaned on the bureau, held the .45 in both hands and pointed it toward the head of the bed.

Vince Wakefield charged awake with a roar, shoving himself upright under the sheet, eyes blinded to slits. The woman under the sheet beside him turned sleepily, mumbled something, then saw me and the gun and froze, eyes widening.

"Perkins!" Wakefield shouted.

"Evening, Vince," I said pleasantly. "Ma'am."

The woman had pale, doughy features and short, bright, permed blond hair. One soft breast flopped over the edge of the sheet. On the floor beside the bed were her clothes: pink polyester pants, a white-and-pink-striped tank top, high-heeled platform sandals. She didn't look much over eighteen, and gals in her line of work tend to age fast. "You card this young lady, Vince?" I asked pleasantly, training the .45 on his face.

"Hell, no!" she retorted shrilly. "I don't go for kinky stuff. And you listen here, Dave"—she turned to

Wakefield—"I don't go for threesomes or hardware either, so either he goes or I go."

"What she said, Dave," I added.

Wakefield's face was numb. The sheet had slid down him a bit, showing that he wore nothing but heavy brown chest hair and the narrow gold chain around his neck. He glanced at the woman. "G'wan. Split," he said roughly.

"You promised me all night," she whined. "You promised me a bonus in the morning, you bastard. I did what you wanted, all of it."

"I'm no lawyer, Dave," I said judiciously, "but it sounds to me like you got an oral contract there. In a manner of speaking."

Wakefield's eyes were poisonous. "There's another fifty on the dresser," he said to her, staring at me. "Take it and get out."

She rose to a sitting position and covered her breasts with a long, white, freckled arm. Her eyes looked dull and hateful at me. "I wanna get dressed. Go in the bathroom or somewhere."

"Such modesty!" I sighed. "But as it happens, the urge to blow your friend Dave's head off could overcome me at any moment, so I think I'll stay here, if it's all the same to you."

She muttered obscenities as she flung the sheet back and sat on the edge of the bed. I kept my eyes on Wakefield and watched her out of the corner of my eye as she pulled a pair of white bikini underwear up her long white legs, slithered the tank top over her head and breasts, yanked on the pink pants and thrust her feet into the sandals. When she rose and stomped toward the dresser, I saw that she was nearly my height and close to a quarter century younger. She flicked a bill expertly off the junk on Wakefield's dresser, stuffed it in her pocket, stomped to the door with the trained, exaggerated butt-waggle of the professional, and left, slamming the door behind her.

I turned back to Wakefield. The .45 was getting

heavy in my hands and I lowered it to my side. Wakefield looked defenseless under the sheet, and he plainly did not like it. Before he could talk, I said mildly, "That kid's probably a Seven-Eleven of social diseases, Vince."

"So, I'll soak it in gasoline tomorrow," he growled. "And thanks a bunch. Hundred bucks gone and I didn't have but a couple shots at her." He straightened to a full sitting position in the bed. "I want to get dressed. Put the friggin' iron away. Makes me nervous."

"I like you nervous. And I'll keep the iron where I damn well please. But you're welcome to get dressed."

He glowered, then tossed the sheet back, swung his long, muscled, hairy legs over the edge of the bed, and reached down for his slacks which were telescoped on the floor. As he bent over, I quickly stepped over and socked him hard on the side of his head with the flat barrel of the automatic. The sound was like a ball bat hitting an unripe pumpkin. He spun back and cracked the other side of his head on the solid wood headboard. He groaned and his hands went to his head blearily. I grabbed an ear, twisted it, pulled him to within range, and smacked him again with the automatic, straight down into the bed. He went limp. Stunned, not unconscious.

I stared down at him, feeling a light, giddy trembling all over that was hard to control. Easy, guy, I thought, take it easy. It's been a long day with too little nourishment and too much violence. Don't end it by killing this miserable bastard, too. You don't have any evidence on him anyway.

I walked into the bathroom and turned on the light. Sure enough, a big Styrofoam bucket, full nearly to the top with half-melted ice, sat next to the sink. Beside it stood a quarter-full fifth of Canadian Club and several of those cheap-ass plastic hotel-room glasses with cigarette butts floating in dregs of drinks, and lipstick stains on the rims. Looked like Wakefield and his lady fair had had a gay old time up here, for a while, anyway. I picked up the ice bucket and went back into the room to Wakefield. With my gun hand I picked up a stray pillow and held it under my gun arm, then dumped the bucket of ice over Wakefield's head, distributing the pellet-sized cubes and ice water down his chest to his genitals. I tossed the empty ice bucket down at his face and it bounced away onto the floor. As he stirred, moaned, and started up, I bundled the pillow around the .45 automatic and stood back by the dresser and pointed the weapon his way.

He rose in thick semifunctional chunks and stared at me. He had identical welts on both temples and his lip bled where he'd apparently bit it. He had that jaw-clenched, cheek-puffing, face-reddening look about him again. He said, "You son of a bitch."

"Vince! I'm surprised at you! I ring your head like a gong and that's the worst thing you can think of to call me?"

I was maybe eight feet back from him with a clear field of fire, but he tensed and coiled himself as if he were actually going to jump at me. I extended the pillow-shielded .45. "Ah-ah," I warned.

He froze. "You shoot that thing," he said in a low, rusty voice, "pillow or not, and you'll have cops around your ears in two seconds."

"Gunfire in the night doesn't raise alarms in Detroit as perhaps it once did. I shoot this thing, and you'll get a real fast trip home to Windsor, pal."

He untensed, eased back into a sitting position, reached up one hand and wiped away a streak of blood that had run down his sideburn from the cut in his scalp.

I lowered the .45. "Somehow, I've always gotten the impression that you think I don't mean business. Well, now you know how I feel. I'm gonna ask you some questions, and I want some answers. You make a move, or give an answer I don't like, and we'll play us another exciting round of tetherball with your head. Dig it?"

"I want to get dressed," he said sullenly.

I went to the side of the bed and used my foot to prod his pants and underwear and shirt. I detected nothing more lethal than keys, change, and a wallet. I gestured to them with the .45, then went to the bathroom. The ice was gone, of course, but I mixed some Canadian Club with a splash of water in one of the filthy glasses, picked up the bottle, and went back into the room.

Vince Wakefield had his pants on and was buttoning his shirt. I set my .45 within easy reach on the dresser and gave him the glass. He took half the drink and winced. He looked ashen and his hand trembled. The welts on his head were bulging into bruises, and one of them—where he'd hit on the headboard—was still oozing blood. I took a swig out of the bottle, set it on the dresser next to the .45, then got out a cigar and lighted it. I noticed that my hands were no steadier than his. The whiskey, which was the first nourishment aside from cigars that I'd had in over twenty-four hours, burst to life in my stomach and glowed steadily.

Outside, on the Detroit River, an ore carrier made a long moan like a car-struck dog. The two A.M. silence hugged the hotel like a fur coat. Wakefield got off the bed and lurched away from the wet, icy mess on his bed into a stuffed chair that sat by the window wall. His bare toes curled into the thick carpet as he bent over and propped his elbows on his knees, holding his drink in both hands just below his chin. His eyes were tired. "So what are the questions?"

Against my better judgment, I took another swig of whiskey. "Just one question, really. Where were you today?"

"Where was *I*? Where were *you*?"

"I know it's late," I said carefully, "but your memory is better than that: *I'm* asking the questions. *You're* giving the answers. I won't tell you again."

He cleared his throat. "I was in the bar. I saw the police take you out. I found out where police headquarters is and walked up there. I didn't see you around. I didn't see anybody I knew. There was no way I could ask about you or find out what was going on. If you were in a mess, I didn't want to get dragged into it, too." He paused, then his small eyes gleamed and he said with sudden harshness, "We're working together, but that doesn't mean going to jail together."

I nodded. "Go on."

"I came back down here." Wakefield yawned, shaking his head with a snap. "I went to the desk to check on the briefcase. I thought maybe you had some con going. But the money was still there. Yet they told me you'd checked out." He stared at me. "How did you check out if you were in jail?"

"Good question."

Wakefield fidgeted with his drink. "There isn't much else to tell. I decided to hang around till morning, in case you came back. I went to a movie in one of the Renaissance theaters, something with Shirley MacLaine in it, I don't know the name of it. I got something to eat. I picked up Rona, and we had some drinks and then came back here." He shrugged. "That's it."

I puffed on my cork-tipped cigar. It tasted like burned cardboard. I washed away the taste with a swig of whiskey. Wakefield downed his drink, tossed the plastic cup over in the corner, then asked quietly, "What did the police pull you in for, pal?"

"Murder. Some fat guy name of Maddox. Knifed in an alley a couple of blocks from here."

Vince Wakefield rose in his chair to stiff-backed posture, the dullness in his eyes gone. "How'd they *know*?"

"Phone tip, they said."

"But nobody saw us!"

"Nobody but you," I retorted mildly.

"*Me?*" Wakefield's mouth went into a straight-lipped angry frown. "Hey, how could I call anybody? I was with you all day. And why the hell would I bother?"

"Maybe to get me off the street for a while, so you could do a little operating. You know where Belleville is, Vince?"

Wakefield eyed me, looking for a trick. "West of town, right? Why? What's in Belleville?"

If it was a performance, it was a damned good one. I could spend all night grilling him and not get anywhere, not this late, not after the kind of day I'd had. I raised the whiskey bottle again, then thought better of it and set it down. "Dead guy," I said dully. "No matter."

"Friend of yours?"

"Yeah." I looked back at him. "Listen to me, Vince. Tomorrow's the end, you understand? We'll get what we can, split it up and be done with it."

"I don't know why," Wakefield retorted. "We're just getting rolling."

"Someone else is in the act, you follow? Somebody called in that phone tip. Somebody checked me out of this place, why, I don't know. And somebody—somebody caused a ruckus out in Belleville and got a friend of mine killed. We've got a hundred and ten grand now. Another score like that and we've got all we need. We're getting out."

Wakefield bowed his head and stared into his lap for a second, then put his hands on his knees and stood slowly. "Look," he said gently, "let's talk about that in the morning. You're not thinking too clear, pal. You've had a rotten day. I understand that. That's why you beat on me tonight. You know something, Ben? I'm not pissed off about that." He smiled toothily. "I'm really not! I understand!"

I picked up my .45 and bounced it in my palm, inspecting it. "Big of you, Vince," I said casually.

He stayed where he was. "You just go on, get some rest. We'll meet up in the morning and press on with it."

I nodded and left the room.

The night-silent hall yawned empty what seemed to be an incredible distance as I hoofed down toward the elevators. The whiskey had hit my empty stomach hard, producing not euphoria but a feeling of suspended animation.

What I'd done to Wakefield tonight was something I hadn't done in years, not since the union days. My job with Emilio Mascara had no official title. The newspapers called me a "top aide." Other union honchos called me Mascara's "gofer." Various friendlies referred to me respectfully as an "enforcer." One federal prosecutor characterized me as "nothing more than a thug." To the extent that I had a job description, it was simply this: straightening people out. While there was plenty of room for creativity, there were several standard methods. One was the dark hallway and the soap in the sock: *Whop!* Stairways were always good, and events there generally looked like accidents. Contrived bar fights were good settings for seemingly spontaneous disciplinary action. All that was many years ago, back in the days when, to me, violence was simply an officially sanctioned way of doing business.

That was the basis on which I whipped Wakefield's head that night. At the time, I thought I did it simply to make sure I had his complete attention. But now, as I pressed the down button at the elevators, I realized that I'd done it for a couple other reasons as well. I did it to punish him for what had happened to me that day. If he was innocent, then shame on me. If he was guilty—*if* . . .

An elevator rang and the chrome doors hissed open. I realized I still held my .45 in my hand. I tucked it away under my jacket against my spine and got on the elevator. It was very late and I was very tired, but in my heart I knew that Vince Wakefield was the enemy—or at least one of them.

But I was going to finish the job. In the end, that was all that mattered. And I knew that to do it

I'd have to be very smart, very lucky, and—most likely—very ruthless.

CHAPTER 23

Door latches clicked, keys jingled, and leather creaked as suited, shiny-faced businessmen smelling of Brut and Old Spice and Skin Bracer locked their room doors and toted briefcases, suit bags, and sample cases down the hall toward me. They were on their way to enormous breakfasts, too much coffee, and exciting hours of sales calls, presentations, airport lounges, and the friendly skies. Each one that passed me gave me a big, hearty, hail-fellow grin—"smile at everyone you meet; he may be your next customer"— but I didn't smile back. Something told me my day was going to be somewhat different from theirs.

I pounded on Vince Wakefield's door with the bottom of my fist. The door opened almost at once and the tall Canadian stood there, ruddy from shaving, dressed in a white T-shirt and light blue brushed-denim slacks. He had almost identical purplish bumps high up on his temples, but he seemed to be feeling no pain. "Morning, Ben!"

"Get out here."

"Huh?"

"In the hallway, and wait."

He laughed as if I'd made a joke. "Hey, Ben, I don't even have any shoes on, pal!"

"They don't enforce the indecent exposure laws." I unbuttoned my blazer meaningfully. "Just do it."

He shrugged."Okay." As he came out, I pushed the room door to its locked-open position, went in, and quickly checked the place out. Nothing had changed from the night before—earlier that morning, to be more precise—except that a cart with the remains of a big breakfast stood by the table at the window wall, and the map of Detroit lay uncurled on the unused bed, corners held down by cheap glass ashtrays. I turned back to the door. "Okay, come on back in."

Wakefield came in and chuckled as he closed the door. "What'd you figure, I had some kind of trouble in here waiting for you?"

"Nothing would surprise me," I answered.

"Maybe," he said, grinning slyly, "a big beefy hit man all primed to blow away good ole Ben Perkins?"

"Nothing would surprise me," I repeated.

"Now, come on, Ben, cut the crap. We're partners. Besides, you're the man with the numbers."

"Right." I went to the map. "Let's go to work."

"Hey, what's the big rush? You had any breakfast?"

"No," I said absently, staring down at the map. "Breakfast makes me want to puke. Has since I was twelve."

"Come on. Order up some coffee or something. Let's relax a bit. Charge it to my room here."

I looked up into his hawkish face. He looked solicitous, except for his narrow small eyes, which gleamed hard as ever. "Nice of you to offer," I said, "particularly since the room is billed to my own credit card."

"I'm just trying to shake loose that wild hair you've got up your ass," Wakefield said pointedly.

I stared steadily at him, then leaned down over the map. "I've got the coordinates," I said softly. "Let's rack 'em up and roll, Vince."

Only the weather outside had Vince Wakefield beat in the bright and cheerful department. It was a typical Michigan Fast One: from yesterday's gray skies and grungy, humid air so thick you could chop it into chunks, to today's deep, rich blue sky, brilliant sunshine, 25 percent humidity, low seventies temp, and just enough breeze to keep the pollution moving. There should be a state law making days like this a paid holiday, particularly in light of the winters we live through in Michigan. Days like this make me wish I had a nice nine-to-five job that I could play hooky from. Guys in my line of work are clearly discriminated against. The job can be unhealthy, but you can't call in sick.

We kept the windows rolled down and headed north on the John Lodge, swung west on the Edsel Ford Freeway, got off at Michigan Avenue, took that through the two Dearborns, and entered Inkster. All the while, Wakefield regaled me with anecdotes, jokes, and puns, and when I didn't respond to that he shut up finally, turned on the radio, and found himself a talk show to talk back to. I drove and smoked silently and kept thinking: just two more. Two more scores and we're home free.

I'd already thought about the end, which could come as soon as tonight. We'd take all the money back down to the Detroit Plaza. We'd retrieve our briefcase at the desk and go up to my room. There I'd sap Wakefield one more time, but good and hard, enough to knock him out for a while. I'd take my share of the cash, tear ass out to Metro Airport, return the rental car to the counter there, pick up my Mustang from long-term parking where I'd left it before leaving for Cincinnati, and drive sedately home. Wakefield didn't know where I lived and had no way of finding me. And he'd have no grounds to because I'd leave him his money. 'Course, he might have a slight problem getting it across the river. Tough titty.

It was beautiful, and it would work. All I needed was two more scores—maybe, if we were lucky on this brilliant summer day, only one—and I'd be home free.

The coordinates had aimed us to a site on Michigan Avenue just west of Merriman Road, on the fringe of the city of Wayne. Michigan Avenue is a heavily traveled eight-lane highway there with a me-

dian down the middle. On the north side of the road
is a huge cemetery; east looms the spooky brick
complex of the old Wayne County General Hospital;
on the south side of the road is a dark bar that looks
closed but, to my knowledge, never is; west of that is
a long, long plain of absolutely nothing except a
field of dying weeds, an old cracked asphalt driveway, and, at its end, the half-destroyed shell of a pink
brick one-story building surrounded by yellow Cat
tractors, dirty black dump trucks, a couple of front-
loaders, and a gang of men in yellow hard hats.

I passed the place going west and made the loop
to head back east. Wakefield stared at it as we
approached. "You sure that's it?"

"That's where the coordinates said."

"Jesus. They're knocking the place down."

"Let's go have a look," I said as I wheeled into
the lumpy, worn asphalt driveway.

A rusting green custom-made marquee heaved
up from the weeds and swept over the driveway in
an arch. All the neon stuff had been busted off (or,
more likely, shot away) long ago, but you could still
make out what it had said: MIRACLE MILE MOTEL. Below
it, in smaller letters, WE ARE NOT HI-WAY ROBBERS. Still
lower, in lieu of the traditional VACANCY/NO VACANCY
designation, there had been: Y'ALL COME or SORRY
COME BACK. "Charming," I said over the noise. "It's a
wonder they didn't make it."

We stopped, parked in what had been the motel's parking lot, and got out. The lot was half full of
vehicles, most of them dirty, middle-aged, half-rusted
cars and pickup trucks that were probably owned by
the workers. Off to the side, parked together and
away from the rest, were two others—a Cadillac
Seville and a Mercedes—that were, together, worth
more than the rest of the Detroit iron in the lot.
Three semitractors dragging long flat trailers stood
on the yellow grass around the sides of the lot, their
drive-down ramps extended, the ribbed tracks of

bulldozers chewed in parallel grooves away from them.

The noise of unmuffled, industrial-strength diesel engines was incredible. One 'dozer pushed against the long pink wall at the far end of the building; another chomped through inside, knocking down walls with its blade and crushing with its tracks. Its driver, a tall thin black man wearing a Detroit Tigers cap, a dirty white T-shirt, and sunglasses, flipped the levers expertly as the machine ground and tore, backward and forward. Behind him, a front-loader played clean-up man, the bucket shoving up a load of bricks and wood and debris, hoisting it high in the air, twisting, and dumping the mess with a hideous crash into a dump truck that stood on the dead lawn beyond what had been the motel's eastern wall. Another 'dozer/front-loader/dump truck team worked from the other end. At the rate they were going, they'd have the place leveled, loaded, and out of there in a day, and by next spring you'd never know anything had ever been built here.

Wakefield looked at me, squinting from the sun in his eyes. "What do you think?"

"If I had to guess," I shouted over the noise, "I'd say our chances of finding anything here are pretty slim."

Wakefield mouthed, "Shit." He gave me a grimace, then straightened alertly, looking at something behind me. I turned and saw two men walk around the corner of the building, giving the dump truck wide berth. When they saw us they hesitated, glanced at each other, and then strolled over.

One was portly, totally bald, wearing an outlandish white suit, navy blue shirt, and white tie. The other was in his forties, short and slim, with longish black hair modishly shaped in a blown style just to collar length. He wore an open-necked, floppy-collared green silk shirt, designer jeans, and a hand-tooled leather belt. Both men wore patent-leather white shoes.

They both wore the phony smiles of sales guys zeroing in on live meat. The big guy in white said loudly, "Morning, gentlemen. You looking for property?"

I ignored the question. "You the owner?"

"No. That's Mr. Silver, here." Silver was one of these middle-aged types who thinks growing a mustache, even the wispy, straggly thing he had, helps him pass for thirty. His smile glinted gold from three or four places. The big guy pulled a wad of business cards out of his coat pocket and dealt a handful to Wakefield and me. "I'm Floyd Vanson. Our House Realty, commercial and business property division. We're listing the place for Mr. Silver." His voice and tone assumed that we'd be impressed.

"Yeah?" Wakefield yawned, squinting at the card.

"Yes, sir," Vanson said heartily. "Twelve-acre parcel here. Available as raw land for investment, or we'll build to suit for sale or lease. I must tell you fellas, we haven't even officially put it on the market yet, and already I've had a lot of inquiries, so if you're interested—"

"Skip it," I cut him off, and looked at Silver. "We're here to ask you about a fella named Bird. Steven Bird."

Silver looked blank, then pulled his mouth closed. "Who are you guys?" he asked curiously. He showed no nervousness, no stress, no anything.

"Just two fellas standing here," I answered, "waiting for an answer."

"You can leave," Wakefield informed Vanson.

Silver looked from Wakefield to me, as if memorizing our faces, then nodded at his agent. He made effusive farewells, cautioned us to keep his card and to call him when we were ready to make an offer, and waddled away toward the Seville.

One of the front-loaders dumped a bucket of debris so clumsily into the truck that a hail of busted brick, splintered wood, and pulverized dry wall splattered on the ground around us. The three of us danced a couple of yards, then in silent agreement walked onto the parking lot near the Chrysler. Though it was not much quieter there, it was certainly safer.

Silver stuffed his hands in his back pockets and looked at us. "I asked you guys who you were," he said mildly.

"Just a couple of grunts checking up on stuff," I answered. "Our information is that Steven Bird left an envelope for safekeeping here at the motel a few years ago. We're here to retrieve it."

Silver seemed to make up his mind. "I don't know any Steven Bird. I've got no idea what you're talking about. There's no way I can help you. Now," he went on in the very same mild voice, "get the hell off my property."

He turned and started toward the Mercedes. I felt totally at a loss; one more lead down the drain. A glance at Wakefield told me he felt the same. He grinned crookedly and shrugged. Just then Silver stopped walking.

Even in the din of the demolition, I heard him mutter to himself, "What's the difference?" He turned and walked back to us, looking at the ground and nodding. When he got to us, he raised his head and looked into our faces. His mild, vapid expression was gone, replaced with a grin that had a snarl behind it, eyes grimly jubilant. "I don't have to tell you this," he said. "I got the key."

"What key, pal?" Wakefield said, bored.

"Don't give me that!" He chuckled. "I knew there was something fishy about that Bird fellow. Fat little guy in dark suit and thick glasses. He left the envelope here and paid a year's rent on the box at a time. I didn't look inside, I couldn't have cared less. Then it hit the papers. Arthur Barton. Big-time embezzler. Hundreds of thousands of bucks hid away around Detroit somewhere. I recognized his picture. I opened his envelope, and there it was. A safe deposit box key. I knew it was risky, but I thought about it, and looked around at what I got here." He waved a tan hand, taking in all of Michigan Avenue. "This strip here, it's all going to hell, has been for years, actually."

He stepped closer to us, unafraid even though we were much bigger men. I wondered if he was going to kick dirt on our shoes, or reach up and bite my knee. "I found the bank. I made up some fake ID. I got the box and I took the cash." He looked at each of us for a long moment, making sure he had our full attention. "Two hundred grand, boys. Two hundred! Untraceable cash money."

He stared past us at what was left of his motel. "All these years I been scraping by on nickels and dimes from whores and con men and bums and no-counts, doing God-knows-what in their rooms. But no more. I'm having the place razed. I put the land on the market. Could be it'll sell, prob'ly it won't, but I don't care. It can sit here and rot till the state takes it for taxes, 'cause Michigan ain't squeezin' one more nickel or one more drop of blood outta me. I got a beachfront condo down in Pompano, now. I'm gonna fish and swim and sit on the beach and keep a personal, running inventory of young, ripe titties and buns."

He gestured around him with a brown hand. "I mean, who needs *this* shit? Who needs the single-business tax, and the unions, and twenty below, and ice storms? *Fuck* it. Fuck Detroit, and fuck Michigan. If you boys are the last ones to leave, be sure to turn off the lights, okay?"

Silver had worked himself up to a first-class lather, strutting and gesturing like a miniature Billy Martin. We just stared into his hot, happy face. There was plenty to say, but nothing that would make any difference. I said, "C'mon, Vince," and we silently turned and walked toward the Chrysler.

Silver hollered from behind us, "Better luck next time!"

Vince Wakefield growled, "No honest people

left in the world, huh, Ben?" We got in the Chrysler
and tore away.

One set of coordinates left.

CHAPTER 24

Odd, what happened to me as we rolled east on
Michigan Avenue: I became ravenously hungry. I
guess it wasn't so odd, considering I hadn't eaten in
thirty-six hours, but when I'm busy and preoccupied
I can go practically forever without eating anything.
I guess this time it had caught up with me. It also
might have had something to do with seeing a Burger Barn at the corner of Michigan Avenue and John
Daly Road.

We got us a big sackful of thirty-five-cent cheese-
burgers, another sack of soggy fries, a couple of
ice-packed Cokes in half-quart paper cups, and then
gobbled and smacked and guzzled and slurped in
the front seat of the Chrysler. Burger Barn makes
the ultimate convenience food. You don't have to
chew it; it kind of slides down your throat on its own
grease slick. The tinny AM radio blasted some good
Rod Stewart out the dash: "Love is the bitch." I
finished my meal with enormous contentment, wiped
my mouth with a wad of napkin, jammed the trash
into an overflowing barrel by the curb, and got back
into the car.

Vince Wakefield made a long, rattling belch,
grinned, and said, "Hell of a note, that little slob
Silver, huh?"

"Yeah." I stuck a cork-tip in my mouth and
lighted it with a match. "But I've got another set of
coordinates."

"Oh, yeah?" Wakefield pulled his leg up, boot
on the seat, elbow wrapped around his knee, and

rubbed his jaw. "Lemme ask you something. How many coordinates do you have?"

"Right now, one more set."

"Yeah, but I mean," Wakefield prodded carefully, "total."

I shrugged and blew a long cone of smoke. "Many as we need to get the job done." In other words, I fervently hoped, one more set.

Wakefield let go of his knee, twisted himself around, reached into the back seat, and got the map tube.

East Detroit is not the same thing as east Detroit. East Detroit is a city in its own right, as much north of Detroit proper as east of it, in Macomb rather than Wayne County. My last set of coordinates, 3099-7531, with Dennis Kearney's name attached, landed us in East Detroit on Newman Street, just north of 9 Mile Road. It was past one o'clock before we got there, having gone east on Michigan back to I-94, then through the city to 9 Mile and west into East Detroit.

By now, having tracked down three of Arthur Barton's coordinates, I'd come to expect a motel or a rooming house. But Newman Street, for its entire length between 9 Mile and Norton, had nothing but little two-bedroom bungalows on treeless, carefully plotted 60 by 120 tracts of sod-covered dirt.

I drove the block up and down a couple of times, both Wakefield and I scanning the houses. Nothing.

It was finally getting hot, pushing past eighty-five. I pulled over to the curb behind a big gray pickup truck, and shut off the engine. Wakefield wiped wetness off his neck and said to me, "So what now, pal?"

"You call it."

"Shit, don't give me that. This is your town."

"I'm from the near west side of Detroit. This here's the east side. It's a foreign country to me."

Wakefield gave the quiet block a long look from over his shoulder to straight ahead. "You sure your numbers are good?"

I shrugged, thinking about Kenny Slingluff, realizing for the first time how much I'd depended upon him to do right. "Numbers is numbers and they say here."

Wakefield had been counting. "There's thirty-five houses on this block. No hotels or rooming houses. How're we supposed to know which is the right one?"

I bit my lip and thought, staring at the sun-drenched street which, as in many Detroit neighborhoods, was lined with shiny Ford and General Motors and Chrysler automobiles. Kenny Slingluff was a skinny, blond, mustached fella who'd screwed up his marriage, screwed up his kids, screwed up his finances, and screwed up his friends. One thing he'd never screwed up was the phone company. If there was a thing in his life that he knew and loved, it was the phone company. If there was one thing I could depend on Kenny for, it was information involving the phone company. If he said the number 3099-7531 was bad, then it was bad.

I retrieved the small gray box from under the front seat, got out a handful of Kearney's "attorney" business cards, and handed them to Wakefield. To his expectant face I said, "You start at that end of the block, on the other side of the street yonder. I'll start at the other end and work this side. All we do is show the business card. First one that gets a glimmer hollers. You follow?"

Wakefield pressed his lips, then nodded. We opened our doors in unison and dived into the early afternoon heat, headed in opposite directions.

It was a hot, slow, uncomfortable business. This was an older, more established neighborhood; judging from the meticulous lawns, lush gardens, top condition of the homes and the large numbers of cars per house, I gathered that most of the residences were still occupied by the original owners, now in their forties and fifties with their youngest kids in high school.

Fortunately, that generation of people still believed in housewives, which meant that someone was home at just about every house I visited. Mostly they were wives: busy, bustling, wearing aprons and smocks and cutoff shorts, hair dampish and faces glistening from the heat, smoking cigarettes and drinking Diet Pepsis as they plunged through their well-established housekeeping schedules.

The pattern never changed. Ring the bell or knock. Wait. Pounding inside. The woman would come up to the screen, half-hesitantly. I'd see the look of disappointment and then resignation: another damn salesman. I flashed my card. Said I was Dennis Kearney. My client's car had been sideswiped while parked on this street last week. Hit-and-run. His insurance company was balking. My client wanted to find the hit-and-run driver and sue him. Had anyone seen anything? I got more inventive with the car, the accident, and my client as I went along. I don't know what approach Wakefield used, but mine played well; while none of the ladies, of course, knew anything about an accident, most listened—some downright eagerly—and two of them suggested I zero in on a Mr. Peltier down at the corner, a man who, apparently, lived alone, had questionable sexual proclivities, let his dogs run loose, drank a lot, let his lawn burn dry in the summer, never shoveled his snow in the winter, held loud parties attended by burly, much younger men who arrived on Harley-Davidsons, and in general was not well thought of on Newman Street.

But none of the ladies showed the slightest interest in the name Dennis Kearney.

As I approached the ninth house—or tenth; I'd lost track by then—I saw that there was no car in the driveway and all the curtains were pulled down tight.

Like most of the others, this house was rectangular brick, but it lacked most of the adornments that others had added over the years. It wasn't a pigpen by any means, it just didn't get the hours and hours of loving attention its neighbors did.

I walked up the sidewalk to the small porch and knocked on the door. While waiting, I glanced across the street to check on Wakefield's progress. I didn't see him. Maybe he had to walk around to the back of a house to find someone; I'd had to do that once myself.

The big inner door pulled open and a short, young, heavy-hipped woman with limp black hair cut just to the shoulders, dark eyes, prominent lips, and a big wedge of a nose, stepped into sight, half leaned on the door frame, and looked at me. She wore a baggy black T-shirt over cutoff jeans, and nothing else. Printed in light blue over her prominent left breast was, IT'S NOT PRETTY BEING EASY. The room behind her was dark, and a breeze sucked my way from somewhere reeked of stale cigarette smoke and bourbon. I made my nicest smile and said, "Afternoon. Sorry to disturb you. Are you the, uh, lady of the house?"

She looked me up and down and answered throatily, "The man, too."

"Heh heh." I got out a business card. "I'm Dennis Kearney. Could I ask you a few questions?"

"You're who?"

I held the card up. She squinted at it. I answered, "Dennis Kearney."

"No, you're not." Her voice had an odd, innocent wonder. Her posture had lost its cocky, come-hither stance.

Bingo, damn it, I thought.

She began to sob, turned suddenly, and lurched away from the door, bare arm clutching her stomach, half stooped as if she'd gotten food poisoning. "No, you're *not*! No, you're *not*!" she chanted tonelessly in a thick voice.

I opened the door and went in after her.

                           *   *   *

The junior-high kids were out and groups of
them lollygagged and skylarked up Newman Street
from where big yellow buses had disgorged them at
9 Mile Road. I walked up Wakefield's side of the
street, heading back toward the Chrysler, looking for
the tall man. Finally, at the third house up from the
car, I heard his hard, braying laughter. I looked up
at the house and saw him pop out the screen door.
As he trotted down the steps, he called over his
shoulder, "See ya, Kathy!" and sauntered toward
me.

I made an abrupt gesture with my hand, pointing
him toward the car. He was smart enough to keep
quiet. We got in the car and rolled down the windows to flush out the heat. Wakefield was chipper
and ebullient. "So, you find something?"

"Yeah," I said deliberately, starting the engine.
"And so, apparently, did you."

"Who, me?" He grinned. "I was just asking
around like you said."

"You only covered four houses," I said acidly. "I
managed to cover ten."

Wakefield's grin broadened. "Can I help it if
certain ladies, like Karen, like to get their hands on
me?"

I gunned the engine, then turned on the air
conditioning, got out a cigar, and lighted it with the
flare of a kitchen match. "You damn well better help
it when you're on the job, Vince."

He struck his relaxed pose, half slouched, one
knee propped up on the dash, long arm flung over
the back of the seat. But his voice was anything but
relaxed. "Lighten up, Perkins. You ain't my mother
or my boss. Be a faggoty tight-ass all day long for all
I care, just stay outta my face."

I rolled up my window and pulled away from
the curb. "Let me just say that this experience con-
firms my feeling that working with people sucks. You

dogged it back there, Vince. You didn't hold up your end."

"You just turn around and ask Carrie how well I held up my end, asshole."

"Kathy? Karen? Carrie? How many women were *in* there, Vince?"

He ignored me. "Besides, you didn't work but half the block yourself."

"But. *I* found the key."

He charged on. "Well, see there? Didn't make any difference. I would've been wasting my time hitting the rest of them houses." He drew up short as I coasted to a stop at 9 Mile Road. "Where was it?"

I stuck my cork-tip in my teeth so I could keep both hands on the wheel. "Woman, ninth or tenth house up. She and Masters had a thing going."

"You got to be kidding."

"No. For the past, I don't know, seven years, practically."

"Jesus," Wakefield said with wonder. "That fat little four-eyes? I never figured him man enough for Mary, let alone side action, too."

I kicked the accelerator and half willed the Chrysler onto the east-bound 9 Mile demolition derby. "Well, whatever, he left the key with her. Take a look, right hand pocket of my coat."

He fished it out. With my peripheral vision I saw him inspect it closely. It was chrome, conical, with a big flat handle like a duck bill. He said, "This isn't a safe deposit key."

"No, it sure isn't. Not like any I've ever seen."

He brought the bill close to his face and read aloud, "S—S—C—O—period. Twenty-one. Do not duplicate." He looked at me. "Any ideas?"

"Just a vague one," I said casually.

After a silence, he said, "Well, you going to tell me about it?"

"Not yet. Need to find a phone book."

"Not *that*. About the broad."

I stayed in the center of 9 Mile's three east-bound lanes, checking the shopping strips on both sides for a phone booth. "Oh, her. Well, Masters gave her the key a couple months ago. Said to keep it hid till he came for it. Told her, if anyone else came looking for it, she should give it to 'em, but it would mean he was dead."

"Huh." He said, staring at the key. "This one feels different, Ben."

"What do you mean?" I asked, veering into the center turn lane when I spotted the phone booth.

"It just does, that's all," he answered vaguely and closed his fist tightly around the key.

CHAPTER 25

"State Security Company," I said as I climbed back into the Chrysler and slammed the door behind me. "Four thousand Bonham, St. Clair Shores."

"Sounds like a Commie *apparat*," Wakefield growled.

"Not exactly." I ripped open the new pack of cigars I'd picked up in the nearby convenience store, shook one free, popped it into my mouth and lighted it. "It's a private vault company. You know, like those apartment storage places, only they specialize in real tight security. People rent boxes or even lockers there and keep their real valuable stuff in them."

"Uh-huh." Wakefield tried to sound bored but was not successful. "So that's what the key's to, huh?"

"Yup. Guess Barton or Masters or Kearney or whoever—shit, man had more names than Liz Taylor— looks like he stashed some of the cash there." I checked the dashboard clock, which actually worked. "It ain't but a tad past three. Want to roll over there?"

"You *kidding*?" As I fired up the engine, Wakefield gave me a crooked grin. "How'd you figure it out from the initials?"

I backed up the Chrysler, jumped over to 9 Mile, stopped, and scanned the traffic. "As it happens, I do security consulting for a couple of those outfits. One in Ann Arbor, one in Canton. It's turned into a big business the past few years. B&E's are so bad, people don't keep their valuable stuff at home anymore. They rent these lockers somewhere else. Places are built like Fort Knox." I didn't add how ironic I thought this was. People work their whole lives to acquire some material possessions, then, because they're terrified of the criminal element, they pay additional money to secure those valuables where even they can't see and use and enjoy them.

"Anyway," I went on, "I recognized the type of key; they all pretty much use the same kind. Can't be duplicated. I checked the Yellow Pages under security, and there it was."

I found a niche and pedaled the car out onto 9 Mile. St. Clair Shores was due east on East Detroit and, if I remembered my geography, Bonham was a secondary street that branched off Harper and ran fairly close to the shore of Lake St. Clair. We'd be there in less than twenty minutes.

It was getting to be a long day already, but Vince Wakefield showed no signs of flagging. Maybe it was because of his unscheduled sexual interlude, but, if anything, he was more relaxed, buoyant, and cheerful than I'd ever seen him. We crossed the line on 9 Mile from East Detroit into St. Clair Shores, then in a couple of minutes made the left onto Harper. Wakefield faced me and said, "Know something, Ben?"

"Huh."

"I think this is the big one."

"The big what?"

"The big stash." He pulled his knee down from the dash and turned sideways on the seat and faced me. He was so charged up, I thought he might physically grab me to make sure he had my attention. "Think about it. Key held by a friend, not at a hotel. Key's to this fancy-schmancy security joint, built like Fort Knox, you said. Shit! Maybe this is where he hid most of the dough!"

I answered agreeably, "There's certainly that possibility."

"Man!" Wakefield clapped his hands once, sharply, and faced forward again, giving the traffic and the stores and the crowds around us a patrician look. "I think we got it now, pal. I really think we *got* it."

I hoped so. I fervently hoped so. Not only because I was working under the self-imposed deadline to have the job done today—but also because, back at the phone, I'd tried to reach Kenny Slingluff to get him going on more coordinates, and had been unsuccessful.

Kenny hadn't come to work, and hadn't called in. Didn't answer the page at Detroit Race Course or Northville Downs. His girl friend told me she hadn't heard from him in two-three days. And, at his house, no one answered—not Kenny, not Mona, not the kids—nobody at all.

Bonham would probably be a truly popular street if it ran along the lake shore. Only problem is, Jefferson Avenue got there first. But Bonham's nice in its own way. It is a narrow, asphalt two-lane, lined with trees, quiet and lightly traveled, and, for the most part, populated with widely spaced stone-and-glass mansions, set apart from each other with long rolling lawns and groves of trees. Grosse Pointe and Bloomfield Hills aren't the only burbs in Detroit where the big bucks are tied up.

At about the four thousand block, where State Security is located, the bucks start to dry up. On the east side of the street there's some estate-sized places, but on the west side, south of the security company, a row of duplexes and apartment houses begins. State

Security Company itself is a low, one-story, windowless white brick building, surrounded by a very high chain-link fence topped with quadruple strands of barbed wire. Its security is enhanced by groves of thick trees that surround the place on three sides. On the street side, facing Bonham, there's a deep, thick grass lawn between the fence and the street—to give a clear field of fire, maybe?—and then the fence juts up high, barbed tips glinting in the light. A gravel lane leads from Bonham past a big steel gate, which apparently stands open during business hours, to the parking lot in front of the building.

They had all the cosmetics of security. I was sure they had many of the realities of security, as well. But places like that remind me of the Maginot Line. It was too tough to attack directly, so the Germans just went around and nailed the sucker from behind. There's always a way.

As we swung left into State Security's driveway, I was distracted by the high-pitched whine of a small engine. I looked out to my left and saw a tiny, red-and-yellow ultralight aircraft zoom down on its landing approach over Bonham. The pilot sat open and exposed to the elements, bent forward, intent on his landing. The aircraft dropped precipitously and touched its tricycle wheels down perfectly on the driveway of one of the estates, then taxied up the hill past the big stone house and out of sight.

Without realizing it, I'd stopped the car. "Isn't she beautiful?" I said. Wakefield grunted impatiently, and I returned my attention to driving the Chrysler into the parking lot of the State Security Company.

A couple of other cars sat in the lot; that was all. I eyed the featureless front of the building as I parked and shut the motor off. Wakefield had his door open before the car even stopped. I said, "Hold it."

"Come on, let's go," he said impatiently.

"Steady on." I rescued myself a few more of Dennis Kearney's business cards. "I'm Kearney. You are a Wayne County deputy sheriff. You still got that badge?"

Wakefield nodded.

"You're here under court order, retrieving what I have in the locker or whatever. You're very officious and insistent. Got it?"

"This is Macomb County, not Wayne," Wakefield pointed out.

"So, we got special dispensation from the Pope or something. Work with it, huh? Use your imagination. Come on, let's get it over with."

The front door was deceptively benign, wood and glass, the kind of thing you'd see on the front of your average four-bedroom colonial. I had no doubt that the "wood" was really steel, and that the "glass" was three-quarters of an inch thick. I turned the knob and the door opened, admitting us to a tiny paneled foyer.

A video camera was mounted in the corner. Below, next to a more businesslike steel door with no knob on our side, was a speaker. From it issued a metallic, male voice, not blatantly unfriendly: "Name, please?"

I looked into the camera lens. "Dennis Kearney."

"Are you a keyholder?"

"Yes," Wakefield growled.

"Key number?"

I fished it out. "Twenty-one."

A pause. Wakefield fidgeted. I stared at the camera. Finally the voice came again. "Push the door and enter, please."

I heard a soft *burr* sound behind the door. I pushed it and it clicked open easily. Wakefield followed me through and we entered a dimly lighted lobby which was small, had undecorated walls of polished stone, and a gray steel door leading off it. To our right was a wall with what looked like a teller's window in it, only this window had no opening; it was a three-by-three-foot section of bulletproof glass.

Behind it was a man in a khaki uniform with no insignia except for gold leafs on his collar.

Uniform and rank insignia aside, he had "retired military" written all over him. He had that burned-thin, whipcord build that spoke of a lifetime of intense physical fitness activities. At any distance, he looked completely bald, but in fact his full head of grayish-blond hair was shaved to about a quarter-inch length. His only concession to age, which I figured to have been middle fifties and maybe even older, was a pair of gold-framed aviator-style glasses. Behind their crystal-clear lenses, his pale gray eyes were small and skeptical. His lips were bloodless and thin around perfectly straight, white teeth. A small black plaque pinned to the exquisitely pressed breast pocket of his khaki shirt said BAYMER. In my mind I could picture him, or a younger version anyway, slink into a Japanese command hut on Guadalcanal in the middle of the night, silently strangle and cut the throats of twenty sleeping men, and then slink out again.

When he spoke, it was into a hand-held microphone that lay on the desk in front of him. His voice issued from an invisible speaker above us: "State your business."

I held up a Kearney business card and the key. "Want to retrieve my belongings."

Col. Baymer did not change expression. "Please show positive ID and be recognized."

Positive ID, as opposed, I suppose, to negative ID. I glanced at Wakefield. He had his badge out. "This man is in my custody," he said, his voice a staccato rap. "I'm under orders to pick up what Kearney's got stored here. Police investigation."

Baymer asked flatly, his voice metallic and robotoid from the speaker, "He has no identification, Deputy?"

"No, Colonel. He's being held for questioning. Naturally, we confiscated his personal effects back at the station house."

It was beautiful, and it came close to working. So close. So very damned close.

Col. Baymer looked impassive. "You're out of your jurisdiction, Deputy," he pointed out mildly. "*And* out of uniform."

Wakefield was smart enough not to get ingratiating with this man. "I'm a field operative, Colonel. I work in civilian clothes. And we have a reciprocal agreement with Macomb County, as I'm sure you know."

Baymer replied, "I'm sure that's true, Deputy, but let's follow procedure, shall we?" He reached for a black telephone set and pulled it to him.

I almost swallowed my tongue to keep from talking.

Wakefield asked in a bored voice, "What are you doing, Colonel?"

Baymer picked up the phone and started dialing. "I'm calling the sheriff's department in Warren, just to touch base. Routine."

It was all I could do to keep still. All I could think about was the automatically locking door behind us. Unless Baymer chose to release us, we were caught.

Wakefield said, with just the slightest edge in his voice, "Hold it, please."

Baymer quit dialing and looked at us impassively through the bulletproof glass, the phone receiver gripped to his ear by his shoulder. "Yes?"

Wakefield exhaled a breath. "I apologize for not doing my homework." The words, totally out of character for him, sounded forced and wrenched. "I wasn't aware of the procedures you have here. Very commendable, by the way." He slipped his badge back into his pants pocket. "I got a chain of command to deal with myself. How 'bout I have my commanding officer call through to the Macomb County people, and have them clear it with you?"

I'll never know, but I think the term "chain of command" clinched it. We wouldn't get to the locker, but at least we might get out of here unscathed. Col. Baymer scratched his forehead and set the receiver back down on the phone, replacing the set precisely in its former spot. "I approve, Deputy. You'll have to make your call from off-post, however. There are no phones here authorized for public use."

Wakefield nodded. "Thank you, Colonel. We'll be back." He grinned. "I promise." He took my arm and marched me back to the door. "Come on, you."

The door buzzed, Wakefield opened it, and frog-marched me out into the sun-drenched, late-afternoon heat.

My upper arm hurt from where Wakefield had gripped me. I fired up the Chrysler and, for no particular reason, headed south on Bonham. "Okay, wise guy, just how are we going to get some kind of call through authorizing us?"

"Shit if I know." Vince Wakefield was slouched totally down, his bushy head propped on the seat back, one ankle propped on the opposing knee. His long lean fingers were pressed together in front of his hawklike face. "Best I could think of at the time. If he'd made that call, we would've been trapped."

"Too right," I muttered.

"Fuckin' Nazi."

"Everybody's not dumb, Vince."

"I'm surprised he didn't strip-search us in there. Probably one of those ass-fuckin' little military-type homos."

We drew up and waited at a light. The sun was in my eyes, and I closed them and rubbed my temples with my palms. I was acutely conscious of the day slipping away. Between Silver and Baymer, we'd drawn a big fat zero, and I had no more coordinates to work on. Dandy, Perkins, I thought. Real dandy.

"'Show positive ID and be recognized,'" Wakefield mimicked angrily as the light changed and I kicked the car forward. "Yes, sir, Colonel! No, sir, Colonel!

Bite my big one, Colonel!" He focused his hard-
planed stare on me. "You got any tame cops you can
get to grease this for us?"

"I got friends in the cops," I answered, "but
none of 'em will do this for us, no way."

Wakefield turned his stare straight ahead. "Even
for a piece of the action?"

"We can't do that, Vince," I said patiently. "The
money's not ours to share."

"Yes, *sir*, Mr. Rogers, *sir*."

I ignored the slander. "Besides, paying cops sets
a bad precedent. If they take money to help you,
they'll take money to screw you, too. It's bad for
business."

Wakefield stared grimly ahead for a minute,
then said, "I think we oughtta just go *in* there and
take it."

We were approaching the I-94 interchange. The
traffic coming against us was getting thicker, signal-
ing the beginning of the afternoon rush hour. I
swung onto the entrance ramp and punched the gas,
hoping to get the car up to thirty-five or even forty
before I got onto the freeway. "Oh, yeah?" I asked
Wakefield. "That place is only built like the Federal
Reserve Bank. Maybe we can hire the A-Team to help
us crack it, right?"

Wakefield pushed himself up straight in his seat
and leaned toward me. "Listen. It's a night deal. We
knock out the power, blow the doors, go in and grab
the dough, and split. Neat, clean surgical operation."

"Neat and clean, all right," I said sarcastically.
"Number one, how do you find the power source at
that place?"

"No need to. We find the transformer for the
neighborhood and disable that. Simple."

We passed the Detroit city limits. "Look, I'm
pretty good wiring light switches and plugs and
two-twenty outlets for dryers. Doin' transformers is a
little beyond my level of expertise."

"Well, it ain't beyond mine," Wakefield said smugly,

looking straight ahead at the hordes of cars running fast and thick with us. "I used to be a lineman up in Chatham. I know just how those suckers work." He looked back at me. "I'll get my hands on the tools. You line up some explosives so we can blow them outer doors. We do it at three A.M. tonight, grab the money, and we're through with it. Agreed?"

"I don't like it," I said definitely.

"We may not have any choice," Wakefield retorted.

"We'll see about that. We may have some other options, Vince."

"Like what, pal?"

"Like, maybe I can get us some more coordinates."

"I can get the tools to disable the juice," he pressed. "What about explosives?"

I thought. "No problem. If we need to. But only if."

CHAPTER 26

Wakefield objected to going all the way back downtown to the Detroit Plaza Hotel. He argued that we could make arrangements for cracking the State Security Company a lot closer. Of course, he was right. But I was hoping that we wouldn't have to go back up there. I was hoping I could track down Slingluff and get some more coordinates, even if it meant carrying the operation over into yet another day. Wakefield finally saw it my way when I told him I wanted to check on our stash, hidden away in the hotel vault.

We got to the Detroit Plaza just after five o'clock, where Wakefield and I commended the car to the care of a porter, went silently into the crowded lobby, and checked in at the desk. The briefcase was still safely in custody, and we left it there.

Wakefield hitched his hands in his back pants pockets and hiked his shoulders up as we strolled away from the desk. "So you can work out the explosives?"

"Yeah," I said, offhandedly. "Give me a minute to make some calls."

Wakefield nodded toward the jammed lounge. "I'll be in there. You get that squared away, then I'll go out and pick us up some tools for the electrical end. Division of labor. Okay, pal?"

"Okay, Vince." I watched him saunter across the lobby toward the bar, then turned and went to a set of pay phones at the end of the hall by the elevators.

It goes without saying that I had no intention of arranging for any explosives. Not that I'd lied to Wakefield; of course explosives were available, and of course I knew who to call and what to ask for. But this whole idea of a nighttime raid on State Security sounded foolish at best, and bloody dangerous at worst. I didn't have any particular qualms about the illegality of breaking the place. Legalities are fine when they work in your interest, negotiable when they don't. But I have definite qualms about getting killed. Particularly if the job can be finished without risking same.

I dumped a handful of change on the pay phone shelf, sorted the Canadian toy money away, picked up the receiver, fed some coins into the slot, and dialed Slingluff's number. Heart pounding. Hoping someone would answer. Which he did.

Male voice, unfamiliar: "Hello?"

"Yeah," I said. "Ben Perkins. Kenny around?"

"This is Ben who?" came the voice.

"Perkins. I want to talk to Kenny."

"Um." A muffled sound as if a palm had been glued over the mouthpiece at that end. Then a different voice came back on. "Yeah, what do you want?"

I switched the phone from right to left ear, and turned and stared at the elevator doors as they hissed shut. "Who is this?"

"Sgt. Zunk. Garden City Police Department. You're Ben Perkins, you said?"

Police? "Yeah, I'm Perkins," I said impatiently. "What the hell's going on out there, Sergeant?"

"Ben Perkins, huh?" he asked absently.

"Yeah. You don't have to keep asking me. I'll be Ben Perkins till I die, or whenever this conversation ends, whichever comes first. Now, I'd appreciate it if—"

"Ken Slingluff is dead," he said, much more briskly.

I didn't say: "What?" I didn't say: "Oh, no." I didn't say anything at all. I just listened.

"Friend of Mrs. Slingluff's got worried; he hadn't been able to reach her since yesterday. Came over here to check up. Found her dead. Him, *too. And* the kids."

I became conscious of my breathing, or rather my recent lack of it. I pressed the receiver against my ear till it hurt and leaned on the phone box.

Sgt. Zunk was saying something about a .22 caliber rifle. "...the kids in the back of their heads. Her in the face. Then he did Deep Throat with the barrel and blew the back of his head out. Hell of a mess, pretty bad for a .22, musta used holla points, won't know till they slab 'em and see. Anyway, Perkins, if you know something about these people, we'd like to get a statement."

"Yeah," I said tonelessly.

"What did you want him for, anyway?"

"He's got something of mine, I wanted to get it back."

"Yeah? Well. Guess you'll have to deal with the relatives. A sister of hers from up in Charlotte'll be down tomorrow or next day. You might want to check in with her. 'Course, there'll probably be a inquest. They'll probably freeze the possessions till then."

"That so."

"I'm no lawyer, Perkins. You can't go by my

word on that. It's just my best guess. You just check in with the kinfolk, and maybe you can work out something kinda off to the side."

"I'll do that."

"Only, give 'em a few days, willya? This kind of thing, it can be unsettling, you know? I've been a cop twenty years, I know what I'm talking about."

"I hear you."

"And if you get a chance, stop on by the station house and give us a statement. No big deal, just a formality, this is pretty cut and dried, you know?"

"Sounds like it." I had my head bent, eyes closed.

"Listen, the M.E. just got here. I got to run. Have a nice day." *Click.*

I hung the receiver back up. So there it was. Kenny Slingluff had tried it all, and nothing had worked well or for long. Finally, the only thing left to try was death.

I remembered my last conversation with him, on the phone from my apartment at Norwegian Wood the previous afternoon. When I told him to back off from the case, that people were starting to die, he'd answered puckishly, "Die, as in, 'the die is cast'?" He had it on his mind even then. Only I was too preoccupied to notice.

I exhaled a long, long breath, staring at the coins winking up at me from the pay phone shelf. I told myself not to play the what-if game. "If I'd gotten off this case sooner . . . if I'd helped Slingluff when he asked for it . . ." There was no point now. And it probably wouldn't have made any difference anyway. Kenny was a tragedy looking for a place to happen, and I'd known it, and helped him when I could, and taken his money cheerfully. But I felt sick and rotten about his kids. I wished I could have done something to save them, anyway.

I didn't have time to play what-if, only what-now. I could probably get the Rolodex cards back sooner or later. But what then? Even if I could weed out the bogus ones and turn them into coordinates, did I really want to press on with this case, and with Wakefield, for days and days more?

Especially when there was an alternative.

When a decision gets made in your mind and your heart, your body immediately begins to act on it. I found myself with receiver in hand, feeding in money into the Ma Bell one-armed bandit, and punching a number. Then the man with the Louisiana twang was drawling in my ear, rattling off price and delivery on certain very specifically designed items of explosive.

CHAPTER 27

The crystal-bright, warm day had given way to a crystal-bright, cool night. Outside the wide-open drapes of my hotel room window, the skyscrapers of downtown Detroit stood shoulder to shoulder, black against the lighter night sky, lights glowing through many windows. Washington Street, Woodward, East Jefferson, and the John Lodge Freeway flowed with rivers of headlights; a fat-faced moon hung high and peaceful, glowing its spooky, second-hand light down over the whole scene. All looked sweet and peaceful from up here. You couldn't see the muggers and the hit men, the bag ladies and the pimps, the dope dealers and the flimflam men. It was a scene that would have made Norman Rockwell lunge for his paint set.

I turned from the window. With a couple of jabbing gestures I crushed out my half-smoked cigar in the ashtray on the table, then sat down in the chair and stared sightlessly at the TV. Over on the dresser sat a tray with a plate and a half-eaten club sandwich. Next to it stood an ice bucket with the capped neck of a single Stroh's jutting crookedly out the top. Folded neatly on the dresser was a brand-new pair of Levis and a heavy-denim jacket-shirt. On the floor below was a very old, very worn brown corduroy duffel bag, both handles wrapped together with friction tape.

Inside, I knew from having checked, were fifteen globs of very heavy, darkish clay, each about half the size of my fist. They were securely wrapped in aluminum foil. A short, heavy plastic fuse jutted from each. Five seconds' worth, as ordered.

The man with the Louisiana accent—Ole Lou, as his friends call him—is indisputably Detroit's premier illicit weapons merchant. Anything you want, from a zip gun to a Kalashnikov, he can get for you. Not only can he get it for you, he offers weapons in various conditions: new, unused, reconditioned, used, working, or as-is; something to fit every budget. He offers special pricing for case lots. He occasionally runs close-out sales. No order is too small, or too big. His big claim has always been that he could get a tank for you, if you wanted one. Everyone always thought that was just salesman bullshit. Then a couple of years ago some joker took him up on it and placed an order, and, sure enough, Ole Lou delivered a working General Grant tank. The thrilled customer tooled around his Melvindale neighborhood in the thing for a couple of weeks till the cops finally took him down. There being no laws on the books specifically outlawing tanks on the public streets yet, the cops nailed him for damaging public property, since the treads on the thirty-ton tank did a pretty good job tearing up the asphalt. So the tank's for the memories. Must have been great on icy roads, though.

But Ole Lou's personal specialty is explosives. I heard he fell in love with them as a child, helping his daddy blow stumps on their farm in Louisiana. He conducts his hardware business at arm's length, dropshipping direct from supplier to customer; but the explosives end he handles personally, whipping up custom-made products in his own kitchen. It's a labor of love for him. Tell him your needs and he designs a *ker-boom* just for you. For a price, of course.

I'd never done business with Ole Lou; as my daddy would say, we'd howdied but never shook. But he'd come across for me tonight. On the phone, I told him I was up against heavy steel doors flush-mounted in steel frames anchored in cement, with top-grade, case-hardened hardware all the way around. I needed to take them out fast with as little noise as possible. No time for drilling, and the available crevices were extremely small. Ole Lou whipped up these babies for me—Whiz-Bangs, he'd called them. The price was one thousand dollars cash. I'd originally ordered ten, but Ole Lou threw in five extra ones free, not because he's particularly generous, but because, in his enthusiasm, he'd gotten carried away mixing the ingredients and would have had to toss the rest of the batch anyway.

Ole Lou never made deliveries personally, and tonight had been no exception. I had followed his instructions for payment and pickup, to the letter. Just after seven o'clock, while Vince Wakefield was out lining up what he needed to take care of the electrical end, I strolled over to the Cobo Hall parking structure and took the elevator to the third level. Toward the corner facing the Detroit River, there was, sure enough, a rusted, sagging Earl Scheib–purple 1969 Plymouth Challenger. The newest thing on the car was a bumper sticker that said THIS CAR IS NOT ABANDONED. The trunk lock was gone. I reached in the hole with my index finger, fiddled with the mechanism, and raised the lid with a horrendous squeak. There was the duffel bag with the goods. I dropped the plain envelope full of crisp, new hundreds—which I'd just gotten at the hotel cashier's office as an advance against my Gold Card—in the trunk, hoisted the duffel out, slammed the lid down once, twice, three times till it latched, and strolled back to the Detroit Plaza.

Don't get the idea that Ole Lou is a trusting soul.

No one has ever cheated him. With his weapons and his friends, no one would dream of it.

I'd picked up the new jeans and denim jacket on the way back. Let's face it, dress slacks, sport shirt, and blazer aren't exactly suitable for commando operations. I'd ordered up a sandwich and a couple of beers from room service. Now I sat and smoked and stared at the TV, waiting for Vince Wakefield to return with what he needed to knock out the power in the neighborhood of State Security Company.

By this time, my reservations about taking down the place were gone. Sure, it was risky and dangerous, but that is what I'm paid for. Sure, it was illegal, but so was what had happened to Joann Sturtevant and the other victims. Sometimes you have to commit a crime to set right the effect of a previous one. If you're not willing to do that, you don't belong in this work. That was the line of thinking I'd sold myself, anyhow.

Besides—I have to confess it—I was getting excited. I'm an action junkie. The cerebral end of this work gets to be a drag after a while, and I was ready to kick some ass. Thus far, the action in this case had been generated by someone else. Now, I was going to generate it. I felt the way I did as a kid on the streets of Detroit in the dead of winter, making a mound of snowballs and taking a bead on the first car to come along, with my escape route all planned out. Fired up, in high gear, ready to roll.

I bounded from my chair, walked over to the dresser, popped the top on the last Stroh's, and swigged half of it. It was past eight-thirty. Come on, Vince!

He returned just before nine. I let him into the room and he swaggered past me. He wore new dark work pants, a light blue chambray shirt, and high-topped, lace-up black boots. He carried a white hard hat in one hand and a big gray tool box in the other.

He grinned at me and spread his arms, modeling. "Look legit?"

I shut the door. "Looks great. You could pass for Detroit Edison anytime, at least at a distance."

"You get the stuff?" he asked, tossing his hard hat on one of the beds.

"Down there."

Wakefield squatted and peered into the duffel bag. "Looks like baked potatoes," he grunted, "with long stems."

"Wait till we light 'em. This guy knows what he's doing." I finished my beer, set the empty on the dresser, and lighted a cigar as Wakefield set his tool box on the floor next to the duffel bag, paced over to the window with hands on hips, and stared out over the Detroit skyline. I waved my match out, puffed, and said, "You look the part. Problem is, isn't it going to look suspicious, a guy crawling up a light pole at three in the morning?"

Wakefield faced me, his hard-planed face hawkish, his jaw set in a smug grin. "Not with a Detroit Edison pickup truck parked at the curb next to me."

I blinked. "A truck?"

If anything, Wakefield's grin broadened. "Gotta admit something to you, Perkins, you've showed a lot of resource on this case. Made me feel a little stupid sometimes. I have to show you I can operate, too."

"Where'd you get a truck?"

Wakefield answered airily, "Got these duds first. Bought a clipboard and some paper and a pen. Found out where Edison's maintenance dispatch center is. It's out on West Fort, by the way. Took a cab over there and strolled through the gate. The day-shift guys were bringing their units back. I flagged down one of them as he rolled in. Checked the clipboard, told the driver his unit was due for overhaul, I'd take it from there. Them guys don't care, 'specially when they're talking to a fella dressed like this with a clipboard and an officious manner." He smiled wolfishly at the phrase. "I took it with the engine running and drove right out. It's parked at the curb downstairs."

"Not bad, Vince," I said, more impressed than I sounded. "Got the tools, too?"

"Right there in the box."

I stared past him at the window, thinking. "Guess we're all set. Now we wait."

"Yeah. Well," Wakefield said, dropping his hands, "you can wait, but I'm going back to my room to catch a quick nap."

I grinned. "You can sleep before we go out on something like this? Nobody's that cool."

He winked and sauntered past me to the door, grinning. "*I* am, lad," he said quietly, opening the door. "Be back around two or two-thirty. Enjoy."

He left and the door shut behind him.

To fill some time, I stripped and took a steaming shower, then got into my new, crisp denims. I wore a T-shirt under the denim jacket and verified that the jacket's tail hung low enough to conceal my .45 automatic, which I would carry, as I always did, under the waistband against my spine. I was flipping channels on the big TV, looking for something to fill the time, when there came a soft, diplomatic knock at the door.

I started for the door, then stopped. "Yeah?"

"Room service?" came a reedy voice through the door.

I moved toward the door, then stopped again. "I didn't order anything."

"Says right here, sir."

Jesus. I went to the door and opened it. A thin, elderly black man in a white waiter's uniform stood there holding an ice bucket, just like the one sitting on my dresser, with three capped Stroh's in it. He was looking down at a check. He asked, "You Mr. Perkins?"

"That's me, pal. Lemme see that."

He handed the check to me. Sure enough, Ben

Perkins, Room 552, three Stroh's. I looked into the thin man's indifferent eyes. "Must be some mistake."

"I don't know," he whined. "I'm sorry." He turned and started down the hall. I didn't really need more beer. It was going to be a long night, and I'd need an absolutely sharp head. But there's a part of me that's always thirsty. Nothing's sadder than cold beer moving away. I said impulsively, "Hold it, pal. What the hell, long as you're here."

He came into the room and set the bucket on the dresser. I offered him the other one with the empties in it, but he informed me sourly that clean-up wasn't his job. I begged his forgiveness, signed the check, tipped him a buck, and he left.

Back at the TV, half-empty Stroh's in hand, I found Channel 62 showing *Day of the Evil Gun*, a pretty bad old western. But I couldn't complain; it was the best of a bad lot. I lay down on the bed with the beer bucket on one side and the ashtray on the other, and smoked and half watched the movie. And opened another beer. Then jumped and blinked when a loud commercial came on. Then propped the pillow behind my head and—

Loud hissing noise from the set. Hideous pounding from the door. Beer spilled around my right leg, soaking my pants. Feet and hands numb. I was *late for school!* What the hell happened to the TV? I lurched up in the bed as the pounding continued from the door. Damn beer, made me look like I pissed myself. I wobbled my feet over to the floor. Oh, shit, what time is it? The cold, clinical numbers on the digital clock said 2:45. You gotta be kidding. I hollered in a rusty voice toward the door, "Yeah, who is it?"

The pounding stopped. "Rise and shine," came Wakefield's quiet voice. "It's showtime, pal."

I rubbed my forehead and got to my feet, which had started to tingle, and walked over to the door. I couldn't believe I'd slept. I hadn't felt the least bit sleepy before. I opened the door, spotted Vince Wakefield in his Edison-like uniform looming in the hallway, said "Gimme a minute," and turned back to the room, looking for my shoes.

He didn't answer. I half heard footsteps behind me. Then the back of my head exploded and the blue carpet rushed up and smashed me in the face.

Head shots don't necessarily knock you out, as I'd demonstrated on Wakefield the night before. I sucked carpet and blinked blurrily as pain screamed in a high-tenor barbershop quartet from the back of my head. I heard Wakefield mutter something, and one pair of legs stepped over me, then another. An unfamiliar male voice said, "Where's the explosives? Quick."

"Over there in the duffel." Wakefield talking.

With tremendous effort I braced myself on my arms and winched my head up. Wakefield wavered like a mermaid in water as he picked up the duffel bag and set it on the bed. "In here," he said, his voice issuing from a tunnel. Beside him stood a shorter man, plumpish, wispy blond hair, horn-rimmed glasses, petulant mama's-boy mouth. He wore white slacks and a dark sport shirt. I knew him from somewhere. Damned if I knew where. I croaked something that sounded like a question.

The men glanced at me. Then I placed the plumpish blond: Cincinnati, Yeatman's, the old IRS ploy, Arthur Barton's personal accountant and best friend.

"Good evening, Agent O'Gannon," Kevin Kohls said pleasantly.

CHAPTER 28

"Bglzrb smf," I answered Kohls. He smiled at me benignly. Vince Wakefield, who had the duffel bag open on the bed, suddenly let it go and stomped toward me, face darkened, cheeks puffed, jaw clenched, small eyes hard and bright. The duffel toppled over onto the floor, scattering Whiz-Bangs everywhere, and Wakefield kicked me very hard in the head.

Through the blackness and stars I heard his staccato rasp: "That's for the first time, in your room."

Kevin Kohls muttered something about clumsy bastard, we gotta pick these up now. I thought deliriously about the number of head shots I'd taken on this case; must be turning into a real live detective. Have to find out how come Dick Dennehy's stupid form didn't make head shots a requirement. It was unfair somehow: All this punishment, and I wasn't even licensed yet.

Wakefield growled, "And this is for the second time, in *my* room," and kicked me again, sending me away.

I came to only halfway, if that. I was naked, and my pants were being tugged off my feet. I was on my back and the off-white fake-plaster ceiling did a roulette-wheel routine above me. My head felt like it had been used for a basketball. At first I couldn't hear, then a voice from above and behind me— Wakefield—said, "Hey, Kohls, screw this. Let's just blow him away and get the hell out of here."

I became conscious of the sound of water crashing into the tub in the bathroom. Kevin Kohls came into sight as he rose and tossed my pants across the room. "Don't be stupid, Wakefield. You're registered downstairs, you've been seen with this guy. Let's play it safe."

"Hell, by the time anybody finds him, we'll be out of the country." The voices were blurry, disjointed like an old, oft-spliced movie. I told myself to concentrate. I told myself to move, to do something.

Let's take it one step at a time, Ben, old son. First, find your body.

Kohls sucked in his lips, eyes flinty behind his glasses. "You do like I say. Come here, help me drag this son of a bitch."

Wakefield stepped over me. The two men bent and each seized one of my bare ankles. I saw, but could not feel, my feet rise in their grip, and then they turned and dragged me like a skid-barrow across the floor, around the corner, and into the bathroom. My head bounced as it crossed the threshold, and I slid much easier on the tile floor. The sound of the gushing water was much louder. It was crowded in there with me helpless on my back and the two men on each side of the toilet.

Kevin Kohls said: "Up and over the tub."

They got me by the ankles and the wrists and lifted me. The steaming bathroom turned upside-down and revolved. The edge of the tub passed my vision, then I was staring at the back of it, the clean, clear water boiling higher and higher.

The four grips on my wrists and ankles felt like steel. The pounding of my heart hurt more than my head, but I was curiously unafraid. Sorry, yes—sorry about leaving Uncle Dan and Terry and Dick Dennehy and especially little Will and even Carole—and plenty angry, too, at least in an abstract way. But I was not afraid.

Kevin Kohls said: "Bash him."

They swung me a couple of times. The wall of the tub went farther and came closer, farther and closer. It was like the initial seconds of a roller-coaster ride, the first few deceptively easy slopes. Then the coaster went into its first hideous gut-wrenching drop; the tub wall rushed at my face and hit me, and my consciousness exploded like a light bulb struck by a bullet, bright sharp fragments flying away from a center which went utterly black.

*   *   *

Familiar lips pressed mine, urgent with passion, pulling and sucking. A tiny pinprick of light appeared in the center of nowhere, then spiraled out to a dull panorama of colors and shapes, like looking through rippled glass bricks. I floated, absolutely painless, a feeling with all the properties of a Demerol high except giddiness. I was bemused. So Ma, the Bible-thumping southern Baptist, was right, there *is* something on this side, after all.

The lips left mine. I said huskily, "Well, hi there, Carole. You get dead, too?"

One of the blobs of light tightened and focused into something that looked like a face. A shaky voice said, with some amusement, "I'm Terry, not Carole. I'm not dead, and, for the moment, neither are you."

The pain didn't begin anywhere in particular, just made a surprise attack as a flat-planed, atonal basso profundo in a totally unexplored part of my mind. I coughed and gagged and abruptly realized that I was on a bed, twisting, retching. I felt warm comforting hands on my shoulders, and through the agony was aware of a voice in my ear, a voice husky and weeping: "Thank God. Oh, thank God."

The spasm passed, leaving my mouth feeling like I'd been chewing rusty carpet tacks and oily gravel. The shrill din of pain in my mind jacked up a couple of notches, and I moaned and twisted onto my back away from the mess. Terry Lowe leaned over me, eyes brimming, staring at me like she was seeing me for the first time. She wore a snug white short-sleeved shirt and soft blue pre-washed jeans. In the light of the bedside lamp the streaks in her brunette hair glowed. My tongue felt like it was the size of a hotel room pillow. "Water," I said thickly.

She got off the bed and, eyes still on me, went around and into the bathroom. I was naked, soaking wet, and starting to shiver. I tried to sit up, but the pain held me down with giant hands. Terry came back with a glass, sat next to me with a soft round hip pressed against my leg, and, one hand cupped gently behind my head, fed me some water. It tasted good and cool, and it stayed down. She opened her palm and showed me three white pills. "Think you can do these?"

"No harm in trying." Though it was like swallowing bullets, I got them down. Terry gave me some more water. I asked rustily, "What are they?"

"Aspirin with codeine. Your head must be feeling fierce."

"It's been better." I stared at her, wondering for the first time how the hell she'd gotten here.

"What happened to you?"

I counted: back of the head, a kick on each side, bashed in the tub on my forehead. At least the damage was evened out. "I had a disagreement with some guys."

She studied my face. "Your forehead looks like mush. I think your nose is broken, too. How's your vision?"

I checked. "It's all right. No blurring or anything."

"Still feel nauseous?" I shook my head. Her eyes narrowed. "Was Kevin Kohls one of them?"

I squinted at her. "How'd you know?"

She ignored me. "Who's the other guy?"

"Wakefield," I answered faintly. She helped me as I struggled, successfully this time, into a sitting position. My mind, my conscious thoughts, were vague and spotty, like a brick wall with some of the stones missing. "From up here, from Windsor. How'd you know Kohls was here?"

Without the slightest hint of sensuality, she began to probe about my head and face with her strong gentle fingers. "You'd told me about Kohls and the old IRS ploy, so I did a little investigating. I decided to interview Kohls. Formally, as a Cincinnati police officer. But he wasn't available. Out of town, they told me. His people were very close-mouthed, but I ran the check on the airlines, and I found out he'd come to Detroit on the same flight you were on."

I rubbed my bruised forehead gingerly, staring

down at my big knobby knees. I remembered that I'd been jumpy and nervous on that flight. I'd sensed something was not right. Kohls had been on the plane, too. Somehow I'd missed him.

"I assumed he was on your trail," she went on, "that he was in the thick of the case. I hadn't been able to reach you on the phone, so I got up here as fast as I could."

I felt foolish. So Kohls, the dirty little bastard, was the one all along, the Invisible Man, the one I'd sensed but never seen. Tossed my room in Windsor. Probably was the tail Terry had spotted in the alley in Cincinnati, too.

I said to her, "Not that I'm complaining or anything, but how did you end up here tonight?"

She stood and paced like a caged lioness, her muscles flowing smoothly beneath her soft jeans. "Hell, *that* wasn't much. I left town after dinner and drove straight up here to your place. You gave me your address once, remember, you impetuous fool? The man at the gate said you weren't there and, besides, I wasn't on your 'list,' whatever the hell *that* is. So I dropped my badge on him and gave him my name. And he smiled at me and introduced himself. Bill somebody."

"Scozzafava," I said faintly, thinking about the big ex–Chicago Bear who knits and fixes cars and tends bar and helps me out sometimes.

"That's right. What a nice man," she said with a smile. "He said you'd told him all about me. He must be a good friend of yours."

"He's all right."

She stopped pacing and faced me, thumbs hooked in her jeans pockets. "He told me you were at the Detroit Plaza. He gave me directions. I came down and went to the desk and showed my badge again. Fortunately, hotelkeepers never look closely at badges. I made them give me your room number and a passkey. I came up hoping to sneak in and surprise you." She looked away from me and shuddered. "Christ!"

"Good thing I'd chased that other broad out a few minutes before," I joked lamely.

She stared stonily at me and did not rejoin. Instead she asked curtly, "So what's the scoop? Aside from trying with near total success to bash your brains out, what'd Kohls do?"

"He got in with Wakefield somehow," I mumbled. "Turned him. They set this up. They're going for the money."

"Where is it?" she asked.

I inhaled and squinted. "Some of it downstairs, checked in at the vault. A hundred and ten grand. A lot more up in St. Clair Shores. A security storage place. We were going to break into it tonight. Guess they're on their way to do it now."

Her narrow, skeptical cop-look smoothed out; she had made a decision. "Let's get you dressed. I'm dropping you off at a hospital. Then I'm going to go nail those bastards."

"Hold it," I answered easily. I took her arm. She misread me, smiled, leaned to me, and we kissed for a long, long time. I pulled back and said blurrily, "I'm not going to any hospital. I'm going with you. I owe these guys."

She shook herself loose from my grip, got to her feet, and glared down at me. "Ben, look at you! You're a wreck. You've had the absolute *shit* kicked out of you. You're in shock and very probably concussed as well. I don't want you dying on me. You can't die on me. It was close enough as it was, me barging in here and finding you hanging over the edge of the tub with water pouring out all over the place. You were *blue*, Ben. I wasn't sure you'd ever come around. I'm not going through that again."

"I'm all right," I lied stubbornly. To prove it to myself as well as to her, I got to my feet. The room swayed crazily for a second, then righted itself. Beyond the pain and the shock, I also felt *stoned*, somehow.

Damn codeine must be strong stuff. As Terry glared at me, I located my jeans against the wall where Kohls had thrown them, picked them up and pulled them on. Balancing on each foot took tremendous effort, but I pulled it off without falling on my face. I looked defiantly at Terry. "See?"

She was anything but impressed. "You need a doctor."

"Listen, Dirty Terry," I said distinctly, "what I need is the chance to cut me some prime asshole. I done paid for the chance and I'm cashing in. You with me?"

She grinned despite herself. "With you?" she breathed. "I wouldn't miss it."

"Dynamite." I spotted my denim jacket at her feet by the bed, reached down and grabbed it. As I picked it up, it dragged something out from under the bed with it. Something about half the size of my fist, wrapped in tinfoil, with a fuse jutting out the end. I picked it up and giggled. "Well, well. Ole Vince doesn't know how to count, looks like."

"Look at me!" Terry commanded. When I did so, she grabbed my jaw in her hand and leaned close, staring into my eyes. "What are you babbling about?"

"I wasn't babbling. I'm not delirious. I was just commenting. This here's an item our friends didn't mean to leave, that's all." I told her what it was. She let go of my jaw. I asked, "My pupils still the same size?"

"Looks like it." I put my shirt on, stuffed my bare, wrinkled feet into my shoes, and presented myself to her for comment. She said, "I still think you'll end up in the hospital. If not the morgue."

I ignored her. "You carrying?"

She reached a hand down and tapped her calf. "Yep."

I got my .45 automatic from the nightstand drawer, stuffed it under the denim jacket against my spine, and ushered her out.

*   *   *

Our friend, the bald, bull-shouldered clerk, was on duty at the desk. If he was at all curious at that hour of the morning about the appearance of a wild-haired, broken-nosed man in denim and a neat, trim young woman, he gave no sign. He said to me, "Your briefcase was picked up half an hour ago."

I leaned toward him. The pain didn't command my mind anymore, but it was still there, off over the horizon like distant cannonfire. Another part of my mind was dreamy cotton candy. I felt stronger by the minute, propelled by adrenaline and the fierce desire to smash something. "How could that be, friend? The rules were it could only be taken by me and the other guy together, and our signatures had to match."

The clerk was prepared. He laid the sheet of hotel stationery on the desk in front of me like an offering. "There were two men," he said softly, "and the signatures did match. See?"

I looked, and the signatures were there, and they did match. I looked back at him, temporarily without words, and then it came out of nowhere. The unordered beer that had arrived at my room earlier, just after Wakefield had left. I'd had to sign for it. Simple matter for someone—like Kohls, for instance—to bribe a waiter to deliver the beer to me and the signed receipt to him. Then, no doubt, he practiced my signature a few times, and, having finished me off, came down here with Wakefield, and the two of them posed as—

I said, "Did you see the two guys?"

"No, sir," he assured me. "One of the other clerks handled it."

"Figures." Then I thought of something else: the fact that I'd fallen asleep after drinking one of the beers. Maybe Kohls had drugged it somehow to give them just one additional edge when it came time to take me.

Yeah. It just could be. Dirty bastard. He'd been ahead of me practically from the first, and was getting farther ahead by the minute.

I took Terry's arm, and we walked toward the lobby doors of the hotel, past a black man in a maintenance uniform who operated a noisy Hoover upright. Outside the quiet, dry, late-night air had just a snap of cool in it; the Detroit Plaza gets breezes from off the river, which pushes the city stink back a bit. Terry slipped her hand through mine and guided me left on the sidewalk, walking around the oval, parked-full driveway of the hotel.

I still felt cloudy but better, ready and anxious for action, and glad to have the lady along, walking Detroit ground with me for the first time. I looked down at her and said, "I know you came here only for the case and for the action, but I'm damn glad you're here."

She snorted. "I didn't come here expecting to do physical work, though. God, you're heavy, Ben. Big bones, I guess. It was hell getting you out of that tub, and I had a hell of a time carrying you to the bed."

"Ought to be used to it. You've carried me before, lady. To some mighty fine places." She glanced up at me without humor. I added, "That's my first attempt to thank you."

She looked at me sardonically. "Don't thank me. You probably wouldn't have died. The water had floated you up over the edge of the tub. Those guys didn't hit you hard enough to kill you. Must have been in an awful rush."

I picked up the pace as we walked. Up ahead I saw her brown Honda Civic, with its Ohio plate, parked behind a cab. I unstuck my dry bruised tongue from the roof of my mouth and said, "This case, this the outrageous thing you were talking about on my recording box?"

She looked down, puffed, looked up at me searchingly, then looked straight ahead. "No." I felt the urge to press her, but couldn't find the words. She continued, "This is hard. I've never done it before." She looked at me and we stopped. "No, Ben, I'm here because I want to give us a try."

I cleared my throat. "Oh. Well, great. I mean—"

"I'm taking thirty days' leave," she rushed on. "The department owes it to me. I'm staying here for thirty days. If you want me."

"Goddamn dummy." I took her shoulders in my hands and squeezed them, then let go and pulled her hard and wrapped her tight. "What do *you* think, babe? What do you think?"

"Mm." She pushed me back gently and looked into my eyes seriously. "But listen now. There are rules. Just three of them, but you have to agree."

"Shoot."

"Number one: After the thirty days you come to Cincinnati for thirty. Fair's fair."

The folks at Norwegian Wood might not care for it, but I'd deal with that when the time came. "Roger."

"Number two: No marriage. Don't even think about it."

"Okay, but—"

"No buts. I'll accept the okay, though. And number three: No other women. Not even Carole."

I stared at her.

She smiled. "Yeah, I knew. Didn't have a name till tonight. But I knew."

"Out of the picture, babe."

"Of course." She grinned with total poise and assurance. "So that's the package. Agreed?"

"I just have one question."

"Yes?"

"When does the thirty days start?"

She stood up to me gently, and we kissed briefly. "After we're done with this business tonight," she said softly.

"Well, hey, let's get it done then!" I took her arm and we trotted down to the Civic. She handed me her keys, I opened the door for her (another habit, courtesy of my parents), and shut it when she'd gotten seated. As I walked jauntily around the front of the car, jingling the keys in my hand, I felt something eating at me. A sobering thought.

Inside, as I fired up the little Honda engine, I said to Terry, "You realize, of course, that your badge has no authority here."

"So what? You're not licensed yourself."

"But I live here."

"And I'm with you."

I banged the car into gear and screeched away from the curb. The little Civic steering wheel felt like a toy in my hands. Her last words registered a second time and I glanced at her. She was smiling.

Okay. So let's do it and be done with it.

I wheeled the car out onto East Jefferson headed for the Chrysler Freeway, goosing the small car into fifth gear as we gained speed. I mashed the gas pedal to the floor and held it there. We had to haul. Even going at top speed, there was no way we'd catch Kohls and Wakefield going into the State Security Company.

But we had a good clean shot at catching them coming out.

I said casually, "Thirty days, huh? Piece o'cake. Plenty of time to talk you into staying on in Detroit."

"Or," she shot back, "plenty of time for me to talk you into moving to Cincinnati."

"Anything's possible. I guess. But bet on me, kid. Detroit's *my* town. If I don't succeed at selling it to you, I'll personally eat it, brick by grimy brick."

I ran two stoplights and swerved left onto the down-ramp entrance to the Chrysler. Terry looked around at the skyline of Detroit, as peaceful at this hour as it ever gets. "Doesn't seem like such a bad place. Maybe you *will* succeed, at that."

CHAPTER 29

The streetlights were cold and dead about halfway up Bonham toward the State Security Company.

Terry asked, "How far now?"

"Just past the dogleg here." A long grassy slope ran uphill to our right, ending at a row of majestic estates surrounded by trees. On our right were the closely grouped duplexes and apartment houses, lots parked full of cars and more parked at the curb. The deadened streetlights left the neighborhood spooky. Only the moon gave light, and not much of that; clouds had rolled in during the night. We cut left at the hinge of the dogleg and there was the low, white, fenced State Security Company.

"Looks like a bunker," Terry said softly.

"That's what it is, kid."

The steel gate across the gravel driveway hung open. A white Chevy pickup truck sporting a Detroit Edison logo stood in the empty parking lot by the front door. I geared down to second, slowing the Civic, and said, "They're still inside. Must've just got here."

Terry Lowe said with great relish, "Then we've got them."

The Civic engine was bogging in low revs. I hit the clutch, coasted to the curb, and stopped, idling. I looked at Terry's eyes, which were the brightest things in the dark car, and said, "Oh, sure, we just march in the front door and say 'hands up,' right?"

"Sounds like a good idea to me," she said equably. She reached down to her calf, came back out with her .38 Police Special, and spun the cylinder, checking the loads.

"I got a better idea. Let's roll around the block and see if we can get in the place from behind. I've got that Whiz-Bang with me, we can blow anything we come to. Maybe take them by surprise."

"Yeah," she retorted, "and they'll just sashay out the front and drive away. Doesn't sound like a good idea to me, Ben."

"I just want to get the drop on them, that's all."

"There's not enough time." She snapped the cylinder back in her .38 and restored it to her ankle holster. "All we have to do is go in and take the bastards. Why do you want to overfancy the thing?"

"Because," I said, grinning, "I'm the back-door man."

"Ben," she said soberly, "I love you and I respect you. But that back-door shtick just isn't going to make it. When you're dealing with assholes, you go in fast, and you go in hard, and you whack 'em. Take it from me."

I didn't like it. I didn't like it one, stinking bit. The best strategy would have been to box them in, attack from the back way and post someone out front to cut off the escape. Even better, I wish she'd stayed back at the Detroit Plaza and waited for me.

But I knew there was no talking her out of the action. All I could do was my best to keep her from harm, and to do that I had to stay with her. I had thirty days coming, and I would take no more chances than I had to.

We left the Civic at the curb and walked silently up to the State Security Company. The gate had, I saw, been blown, its heavy steel lock scorched and melted. Ditto for the front door of the building. Ole Lou's Whiz-Bangs had sure done the job.

We paused at the front door. I pushed it back gingerly. The inner door stood open as well. The stench of pyrotechnics hung in the air. There wasn't a sound and the place was pitch-black. I saw that Terry held her .38; I hadn't seen her get it out. I groped behind me under my denim jacket and came out with the heavy, reassuring Colt .45 automatic in my hand. As silently as I could, I cocked it. There was no need to work the action; I'm one of these daredevils who keeps a round in the chamber at all times.

I looked at Terry in the darkness, and she nodded. I pushed the inner door open. The small lobby area yawned at us. The moonlight from the heavily barred window in the wall to our left reflected on the swirled, heavily waxed vinyl floor. The bullet-proof window to our right was dark. The door across the way stood open. The air in here was still and heavy, uncirculated since the power had gone off.

Suddenly, a loud, piercing, hissing sound from behind the far door. A voice, a husky, echoing whisper, Vince Wakefield: "Son of a bitching bastard!" Then silence.

The butt of the .45 was warm and damp in my hand. I glanced at Terry. She turned, revolver extended, covering our rear, as I went through the door with her following.

Three long halls ran off from the door, faint light glowing from each of them. I paused at the intersection, Terry warm and very close to me. I heard a *scree* of twisting metal: It was from the center hall. I reached out and took Terry gently by the neck, bent to her ear, and whispered instructions urgently. She nodded and, without a sound, turned and walked around the corner down the right-hand hall. I waited a second to give her a head start, then spun around the corner of the hall from which the shriek of metal had come, .45 extended.

The inner halls of the State Security Company were equipped with emergency lights, battery-powered sealed beams mounted high on the wall by the ceiling. In this hall, the light focused away from me down the long, very narrow corridor lined with heavy steel lockers. About halfway down, Vince Wakefield—and only Vince Wakefield—stood illuminated in the pale light, smoke from a Whiz-Bang swirling around him, in the act of hoisting a heavy, massive gray American Tourister suitcase out of a locker on my right. His head spun to me, and he stared at me with the grim pale inhuman fury of a cornered snake. The suitcase slipped out of his hands and fell to the floor with an encouragingly heavy thud.

I felt a moment of giddy satisfaction. "Hi, Vinny," I said over the barrel of my .45.

At the end of the hall beyond Wakefield, Terry Lowe appeared dimly, training her .38 on him. "Hi, Vinny," she echoed.

He stood frozen, staring at me, big hard hands spread. "Who's the cunt, Perkins?"

I stepped toward him. Terry asked urgently, "Where's Kohls, Ben?"

"Does she suck cock?" Wakefield snarled.

Before I could answer her, a voice came from behind me. Amiable and bemused. "Good evening, Agent O'Gannon. Once again."

Vince Wakefield was the first to move. He jumped the suitcase and ran past me toward Kohls. I didn't turn, didn't move, just stared at Terry, a dim form at the end of the hall, her .38 glinting.

I heard Kohls's voice behind me, gently chiding: "You left the suitcase, Vince."

"So what?" Wakefield snarled. "Let's burn 'em right now!"

I remained frozen and asked as steadily as I could, "So where were you, Kohls?"

"Wait! First, the rules. You can die right now. Or you can turn extremely slowly without making one single move to make me nervous, and live longer. Perhaps much longer."

I took my eyes off Terry and turned very slowly. The light from the battery-powered sealed beam, mounted on the wall to my right, was in my eyes, making Kohls and Wakefield, who stood at the end of the corridor from where I'd come, almost impossible to see.

Kohls said, "Thank you. Now, Agent O'Gannon, or Detective Perkins, or whoever you are today: Please lower yourself very slowly and place your weapon on the floor."

I did a deep knee bend and set the .45 down soundlessly.

"Excellent. Now you can stand."

I did so. I said, as steadily as I could, "So you been on me since Cincinnati, right?"

"That's correct," he said equably. "You, miss. Please do as Mr. Perkins did."

"This second, cunt," snarled Wakefield.

"No," echoed Terry's voice from behind me, as if declining sugar in her coffee.

I said, "You were the one who called in the tip about the fat guy's knifing."

"Certainly," came Kohls's voice. "Of course, by then Mr. Wakefield was working with me. We had to get you off the street so we could go out to your house to try to find out how you were getting the coordinates. Wakefield had found your phone-machine triggering device when he frisked you; we knew you were calling home on a frequent basis, so it was only logical to assume that the coordinates were being fed to you by way of your answering machine. And we had to get access to the coordinates before we could cut you out of the action, naturally. . . . Please, young lady, do as I asked."

"No," Terry said tonelessly.

"You killed Arn?" I asked, dumbfounded, squinting at the men through the bright light in my eyes.

"The old security guard? Actually, no, Mr. Wakefield did that. In my short acquaintance with him, I've found him to be remarkably quick-tempered. . . . Listen, lady," he said, impatience in his voice, "in case you don't think I'm serious, consider this. I just finished strangling a man in the front office. A man who came here after Mr. Wakefield and I broke in. Apparently there was a battery-operated alarm that went off in his home and he came to investigate. That *should* impress upon you how serious I am about my request. Put the gun down, now."

Terry answered in a cold, deadly, toneless voice: "No." I heard footsteps and thought, my God, she's walking toward us.

I blurted, "But how'd you know where I lived? How'd you know what my home number was?"

"Simple," Kohls answered. "I checked you out of your room. Your bill had charges for local phone calls on it. Being a prudent accountant, I demanded a transcript of the numbers for verification. They were more than happy to provide it. Computers are amazing, aren't they? . . . One more chance, chick."

"Freeze," Wakefield added. "There are two guns on you, and your boyfriend, too."

Behind me, Terry's footsteps continued without a break. "You already tried to kill Ben once tonight," she answered. "I won't let you do it, you hear me?"

"Shut up, Terry!" I squinted into the light, trying to make out Kohls's expression. "Let's back up one more step. All the way back. To the plane crash."

There was a smile in his voice. "You figured *that* out?"

"What?"

"That I caused it."

Jesus. "Naturally."

"I'm impressed. Actually, it started when Arthur turned himself in in Cincinnati. I visited him in jail and he told me about the money." His voice softened. "All that money . . . anyway, time was of the essence. If Arthur were allowed to return to Detroit with the FBI, the money would be gone forever. Step one was to get him out of the picture. As it happens, I know Lunken Airport. I'm a shareholder in a general aviation company there. I have the run of the place. The plane the FBI was using was leased. It was no problem finding out which one was scheduled and, since I was an ADR1 in the Navy—aircraft mechanic specializing in reciprocating engines—gimmicking the motors was no problem either."

"Some friends Arthur had, pal."

"But," he said, ignoring me, "when I went through the late Arthur's personal effects, I found no clue or lead to the money. I'd about given up on it. Till you, Mr. Perkins, entered the picture. Fortunately for me."

He was rolling now. Behind me, Terry's footsteps drew closer, but Kohls didn't seem to care. "Despite your clumsiness in Cincinnati, I sensed that you would be difficult to persuade. You are one of those tiresome turtles who slide along on their bellies, ignoring opportunity on each side. Fortunately, I found that Mr. Wakefield was cut of a sterner bolt of cloth. He wanted money. You would not share with him, so he was quite receptive to my proposal." There was a silence, then he said gently, "Miss?"

She reached me then. Through my peripheral vision I saw her stand next to me, her .38 pointed harmlessly up and off to my right. "What?" she asked acidly.

"Miss," he sighed, "all I want is for you to put your weapon down. Then both of you will lie on your faces. I'll step over you and retrieve that suitcase that Mr. Wakefield so thoughtlessly left behind you, and we'll leave. I have no wish to kill anyone who cooperates."

"For Chrissake, Terry," I said tightly, "do what the bastard wants." I was scared. Despite the bright light shining in my eyes, it felt very dark and close in there, with two guns trained on us from dead ahead.

"Mister," she answered Kohls, mimicking his world-weariness, "I am thirty years of age. I quit buying that brand of bullshit an awful long time ago. Besides, I am a police officer. You don't really think I'd just let you walk out of here with that money, do you? I mean, seriously?"

She fired without moving her hand, and her shot was excellent. It caught the sealed beam dead in the center and blew it all to hell, throwing the hallway into total, numbing darkness. For an endless split second, nothing happened. Then the world exploded.

I don't know who fired first. Shots exploded simultaneously from both directions, twin flames from Kohls and Wakefield, deafening answering fire from my left. I was in horizontal freefall to the floor to get my gun when something crashed into me with the force of a Mack truck, knocking me onto my back, then holding me down with leaden weight.

Then, silence.

I'd been shot before, once. I knew that you generally don't feel much at first. The fact that I was conscious meant I wasn't dead. Not yet, anyhow. But there was a terrific weight on my chest, and a terrible ringing in my ears, and, for all I knew, my intestines could have been hanging out. I decided to lie still, and then realized I probably couldn't move even if I wanted to.

I heard no sign of Terry. I listened hard, and heard footsteps from the end of the hall. They stepped close and brushed against me, then I heard the clatter of the suitcase bumping the lockers behind us, then a foot stepped on my arm. I bit my tongue to keep from screaming. The foot kicked my arm aside impatiently, and the footsteps clicked down the linoleum away from us and disappeared.

But before they did, I heard Wakefield's voice mutter: "Dumb stupid bitch."

Then, in the terrible silence, I heard her trying to breathe, very close to me.

It was a wet, sick, awful sound, that breathing. It was like she was trying to inhale through a bullet-riddled wet suit. I thought it was close to me, then I realized that it was very, very close to me. I experimentally raised my hands and found that she was atop me, pressing down with that awful weight. My hands went slick with blood, and I felt the warmth of it soaking through my denim jacket.

I didn't know if Wakefield was gone, and now I didn't care. I groped my hands over her body and found her head lying limp on the floor at my right side. I grabbed her hair and pulled her gently to me and whispered anxiously, "Terry?"

Nothing. Nothing but that rasping: in and out. In . . . and out.

"Oh, Jesus!" I muttered. I called her name again,

several times, in full voice now. No answer, just the breathing.

I felt down her front, over her breasts to her belly. Judging from the rents and the wetness, she'd been gut-shot, probably more than once.

I carefully edged myself out from under her. Blood soaked my jacket and my left sleeve, but I didn't appear to be hit. I bent over her in the pitch-blackness, desperate to do something, helpless to do anything at all except listen to her try to breathe.

I lurched to my feet. I was totally disoriented and my first attempt to move bought me a head-on collision with the wall. I reeled away from that and staggered laterally, hoping like hell I was going the right way and wouldn't end up at the wrong end of the hall. I stumbled along and my foot hit something that clattered against the wall with a familiar sound. I bent and groped and found my automatic, picked it up, shoved it into my waistband in front, and kept groping blindly on down the hall.

In just seconds I knew I had guessed right, because I saw a glow of light from the adjacent hallways, and I tripped over a body.

I bent clumsily down over it. It was, as I figured, Kevin Kohls. He'd been hit twice: one an inconsequential shot in the left arm, and the other mortal, right through the left eye. Amazingly, his glasses were still entrenched on his face, despite the blasted-out left lens.

I stared for a moment into Kohls's face, then lurched to my feet, stepped clumsily over his body, and spun through a door into the foyer of the State Security Company.

Here the moonlight provided some illumination. The door to Colonel Baymer's office stood open. I stomped into there, looking around for the phone. It was right where I'd seen it before, on Baymer's little table by the bulletproof window, but before I could grab it I saw, sticking out of the closet on the other side of the room, a highly polished shoe at the end of a khaki-clad leg that ran back into the darkness.

I bit hard on my lower lip, turned to the desk, and grabbed the receiver. It stuck viscously to my bloody hand as I pressed it to my ear and dialed 911. When the woman answered, I said the only words I knew that would bring help fast. "Police officer down. Police officer down. Four thousand Bonham, St. Clair Shores. Police officer down."

I hung up on her babbling, urgent questions, went through the door into the foyer, turned toward the darkness in which Terry lay, and froze.

The last thing in the world I wanted to do was to leave her. But to stay here would mean letting Vincent Wakefield get away. With the money—all of it—a winner.

I'm no doctor, I thought.

People with the skills to help Terry will be here very soon, I thought.

If anyone's going to catch Wakefield, it'll have to be me, I thought.

"We'll be out of the country," Wakefield had said back in the hotel room. That had to mean the airport.

I turned and walked out of the building to go do my job.

CHAPTER 30

The faintest hint of false dawn lighted the low eastern horizon as I half-trotted down the driveway of State Security Company past the blasted gate to the street. Aside from that, and the setting moon, there was no light at all; the power still had not been restored. I listened for sirens as I lurched toward the Civic, half hoping for Terry's sake to hear them, and half hoping for my own I wouldn't; I had to be out of there before the cops came or I'd never catch Wakefield. I heard nothing. My luck was in, and Terry's wasn't.

The Civic was locked tight. I groped my pockets for keys and found nothing except the set for the Chrysler and the Whiz-Bang we'd found in the hotel room. I remembered handing the keys back to Terry before we'd approached the building. They were still with her. Inside, in the dark.

The effect of the codeine-laced aspirin was wearing off rapidly, and twin dissonant tympani pounded and growled in my head, the pain reaching a new plateau with virtually every heartbeat, making me feel shuddery and weak. I had the sudden insane notion of using the Whiz-Bang to blow open the Civic door and then hot-wire the sucker. But I was an old Ford Motor man; I'd never hot-wired a Jap car before, and I giggled at the thought of sitting there stripping and grounding wires, trying to find the right combination, as the police closed in on me and, thirty miles away, Vincent Wakefield boarded a DC-10 to Rio or someplace.

I left the Civic and trotted south along Bonham toward the row of cars parked at the curb by the duplexes and apartment houses. I glanced in the window of each one as I jogged, looking for keys; you never know. No luck. Damn it to hell, I thought furiously, nobody trusts anybody anymore. I'd reached the dogleg and run out of parked cars before I slowed down to a walk, panting, my head doing an all-out flamenco throb.

The false dawn was heightening to my left. I stopped and breathed hard, trying to fight back the pain that spiraled in my head. Nothing to do now, I thought, except go back and try to find the keys to the Civic. Maybe I could still get out of here before the cops came, and then nail Vincent Wakefield at the airport.

I did an about-face and hoofed back up Bonham.

To my right was the long, grassy hill with the long multistory stone estates at the top. They were silent and dark and the only sound on the street was that of my hard-soled LeHighs pounding the pavement. Then it occurred to me: maybe there was a car available, up at one of the estates.

I stopped to scan them, my hands on my hips. Each estate had a long driveway, most of them asphalt, running up the hill. Each had at least a three-car garage attached at the back. No cars were visible, but just then the new light from the east caught something colorful by the garage at the estate to my right. Something sticking out from the corner at the back. Multi-colored, long and trim, like a wing.

My mind rewound sluggishly back to that morning. No—the previous morning. The ultralight coming in for a perfect landing on the driveway of the estate. Yeah, man, yeah.

My feet were moving me before I'd given the matter any conscious thought. I ran to the right and then up the asphalt driveway, up the hill toward the big, two-story stone house with a tile roof. There were no lights on inside. No sound. I ran past it to the closed garage and around the neatly trimmed lawn to the side. And then I skidded to a stop and saw her.

She was an ultralight airplane. A Volmer VJ-25 Sunfun. Her single wing stretched better than thirty-five feet, aluminum framed with yellow and red Dacron. She was an older ultralight, really a hangglider with a seat added plus a motor, which couldn't have put out more than eleven horse. But she sat there, fully assembled, ready to fly, except—

Except for the big heavy chain wrapped around the down tube of the aircraft and through a ringbolt in the stone wall of the garage, secured by a heavy Master lock.

I stared at her numbly. Compared with my Maxair Hummer, this was a slow, unstable pig. But, gotten loose, she would fly, and she would get me to

Metro airport, thirty miles away, faster than any car, since, for one thing, I could fly direct, and for another, I had no car available to me.

Besides—I have to confess it—I suddenly wanted to fly. More desperately than I'd wanted anything in a long time.

I went over to the aircraft, giving her the quick preflight inspection. I did it in the same sequence that I preflighted my own aircraft. Nuts, bolts, rivets, cables: all fine. Struts and landing gear: all secure. So far, she was ready to fly, except for that chain.

I squirmed the Whiz-Bang out of my pocket, went to the chain, stripped the tinfoil from the explosive, and wedged its puttylike substance into one of the links. When it was ready, I took out a box of my kitchen matches, flared one, and set fire to the fuse. It flamed with an unseeable blue-white glare, then, when the charge was reached, it hissed hideously, making a shearing, tearing sound that was almost deafening. When I could look at it again, the chain smoked limp in two halves in the dewy grass.

I grabbed the chain, freed it from the aircraft's down tube, and tossed it like a jangling metallic snake across the grass. Then I bent under the wing and did a final, extremely hasty preflight inspection in the darkness. The transparent fuel tank showed that it was full—a whole couple of gallons, enough to get me to Metro at top speed, maybe. A couple of tugs of the stick told me that everything was free and unbinding. I'd have spent more time preflighting my own aircraft in the leisure of a Sunday afternoon, but under the circumstances I'd wasted enough time here. I adjusted the throttle to idle position, squeezed the primer pump a couple of times, turned on the ignition and gave the handle on the starter a hard jerk, praying.

The tiny two-cycle engine caught with a couple of big coughs and then made a steady flatulent purr, smoke gushing out the exhaust. I grabbed the root tube in one hand and one of the flying wires in the other and, leaning the aircraft off its tail skid, wheeled her back on her tricycle gear from the shed and pointed her roughly toward the driveway and the slope leading down to Bonham Street.

Even the rankest novice knows that you must take off into the wind. In Michigan, for the most part, toward-the-wind is west, and that meant, from where I was, toward Bonham Street. It was ideal, actually. If there's any kind of breeze at all, you don't need more than a hundred feet or so to take an ultralight off, and here, with the downslope, I probably needed less.

That's what I hoped, anyhow.

I dived into the tiny narrow seat. Ordinarily, you're supposed to warm the engine for at least five minutes, but a couple of lights had just gone on in the big stone house, and I decided it was time to haul ass. I jacked the throttle up and down a couple of times, felt its smooth response, then mashed her up to high throttle and felt the aircraft roll through the grass toward the driveway.

The Volmer, like my Maxair, has a pusher engine—in other words, the prop is behind the wing and pushes the aircraft along. The advantage of this is that the aircraft is easy to taxi since the prop wash runs straight back past the rudder, elevator, and stabilizer. By the time I hit the driveway and started over the downslope, I was making good speed, and the aircraft was responding well to the stick. To my left I heard, over the engine's hideously high whine, a shout. I looked over to the porch of the house and saw a man, dressed in white pajamas, run across it toward me, yelling something. I gave him the thumb's up—by which I meant, don't worry, I'll take care of her, you'll get her back—and then looked straight ahead at the downslope, building speed, readying my takeoff.

The street rushed toward me, the high-power wires facing me on the other side, the three-story apartment houses on the other side, and trees beyond.

I knew there was a bit of wind coming at me, maybe ten knots, and I kept a steady hand on the stick and a hard hand on the throttle, depending on the wind, the wing's dihedral angle, and the aircraft's all-out downhill speed to get me away. Sure enough, well before reaching the street, she lifted off.

The power lines, buildings and trees rushed at me, so I went straight into climb-out, keeping the maximum angle of attack on the aircraft, increasing throttle to full, and pulling back hard on the stick. The aircraft rose almost magically—with the right angle of attack, the right engine power, and the right head-wind, they can go up almost like a helicopter— and I kept the juice on, thrilling to the whir of the wind in the flying wires as I rose.

The street and the trees dropped below me and became unimportant. I winced in the force of the unprotected windstream and glanced automatically left and right and over my shoulders, checking the wires and the gear and the trim of the ship, and was satisfied. I tapered off on the throttle and, looking down, saw that I was well above a thousand feet by now and still climbing. I laid off the throttle just a bit more and heard the engine calm back down to cruising speed.

My extreme peripheral vision showed brightness behind me: False dawn had, with my altitude, become the real thing. It threw brown shadowy light across the green landscape below me. Down there, people were rolling over in the blurring scream of alarm clocks, getting ready to, in Ian Anderson's immortal words, skate away on the thin ice of a new day. Meanwhile, I was up there, with my objective already logged in.

Metropolitan Airport was roughly west-southwest of St. Clair Shores. Detroit City Airport was almost directly in my flight path, and I had to avoid it. I decided to proceed just south of west till I reached the Southfield Freeway, then bend south of southwest till I neared I-94, and then take her in from there.

The land below me steadily brightened. The engine hummed sturdily above and behind me. The stick in my hand and the hum of the flying wires told me I was in good trim, doing fifty plus change, probably top end for this beast. From the looks of the ground I was between four and five thousand feet and I came off the throttle just a tad more and kept her in trim with the rising sun resolutely behind me. Then—and only then—did I back off from the immediacy of getting her aloft and come back to myself, sitting on a tricycle seat with the nearest floor nearly a mile below me, and think about what I had left behind.

Terry.

Dumb stupid bitch. Wakefield had been right about that.

I'd been a hair-span from death twice within the past twelve hours, but only now did my life pass before me. I thought about how rare the moments of beauty had been. The slow, welcoming smile of a woman who liked me. The brute slap on the rump by a teammate after a particularly good play. The sweat-drenched smile of a buddy after we'd finished a grueling physical job of work....

Dumb stupid bitch. Nobody had asked her to come up to Detroit, particularly now.

...Eric Clapton doing "Bell Bottom Blues," John Lennon crafting a classic with "Stand By Me," and Elvis struck by lightning with "Suspicious Minds"...

Dumb stupid bitch. She could have put her gun down like Kohls had demanded. Maybe he'd have turned us loose.

...Little kids giggling and singing and swinging in the sun. A bright cool/hot Michigan Sunday morning with no obligations but the deck, fresh coffee, and the *Free Press*...

Dumb stupid bitch. Had to be Dirty Terry. Blowing out the light had been a good move. But then, after taking her shots at Kohls, she'd jumped between me and him. To protect me, when I was already diving.

. . . But just past the midpoint of my life I discovered the ultimate moment of beauty. Flying. Uncontrolled, unlicensed, in the clouds, with my faith in a tiny engine and the laws of physics and my own sense of luck and indestructibility.

I lost all sense of the aircraft. My eyes blurred with tears and I wiped them roughly with the back of my throttle hand. The horizon sat like the edge of the world in the distance, a clear brown and green line etched against the lightening blue of the sky. This was flying, but it wasn't beautiful. Not with that woman back there. Badly hurt, and in the dark, and all alone.

CHAPTER 31

I approached Metropolitan Airport from due north with Merriman Road, already crowded with morning rush-hour traffic, about eight hundred feet below me. Landing is the toughest part of any flight, particularly when you're in an unfamiliar aircraft on an improvised "runway."

Air/Park Company sprawled off to my left. This is one of several airport parking facilities, flat pavement stretching out for many acres with a tall control tower and flat administration building just off Merriman Road. You can park there for a small daily fee and the company provides free van service to and from the terminal of your choice.

But, I thought grimly, this would probably be the first time they'd ever had anyone park an aircraft there.

Judging from the trees, the prevailing wind was

still from due west—my right. I picked my landing strip, a long unparked stretch of gravel at the very rear of Air/Park, and thought through my traffic pattern.

I'd been slowly but steadily descending and now, as I banked left to enter the downwind leg, I was maybe two hundred feet up and doing close to fifty. Too high, and too fast. I steadied back on the throttle just a bit more and adjusted the stick till I felt the aircraft begin to mush. Then I adjusted the throttle upward again and banked left ninety degrees onto the base leg. One more turn and I'd set her down.

When I made my turn to final, conditions were damn near perfect. The long empty parking lot was fifty feet below me and approaching slowly, and I was doing a flat thirty. I leveled off, keeping plenty of gas in the motor—it's better to land too fast than to pussyfoot, stall, and crash—and came down to just a foot or two above the pavement. Now ground effect grabbed the aircraft, making her want to float, but I was too experienced a hand for that. I kept back pressure on the stick, teasing the aircraft down, down, working in inches now, till the tricycle gear touched down perfectly. We bounced and rolled and I kept control, guiding her straight and true, till she glided to a stop.

I cut the ignition and the sharp whine of the McCulloch engine stopped. Stiffly, I got out of the seat. A jet screamed by overhead, and traffic noise from Merriman Road, a quarter mile away, filled the air. I stood and faced the new morning sun and gave the wing's leading edge a pat. Good old gal.

From behind me came the squeal of brakes and the hiss of tires. I turned to see a nine-passenger Air/Park shuttle bus pull off the driving lane into the empty lot on which I stood. It was unoccupied except for the driver. He pulled up near me and hollered through his open window, "Hey, pal! Airport's over thataway. Heh heh!"

"Good, thanks," I said, strolling on stiff legs to the van. "Mind giving me a lift over there?"

"Listen, mister, you—" He stopped as I reached the van door and opened it. He was middle-aged with receding short reddish hair, grizzled face, thin lips, and prominent Adam's apple. From beneath the bill of his ball cap he gaped at me and, without even having to look, I knew why.

My denim jacket hung open to my navel, showing my bare chest. Over my heart was a big, dark-reddish bloodstain. Another discolored the front of my jeans. My hands were stained with dried blood as well. The blood-stained grip of my .45 automatic jutted out from the waistband of my jeans. I hadn't seen myself in a mirror, but I knew that my forehead and nose must have been a sight, as well. I probably looked like I'd been cleaning up after the Texas Chainsaw Massacre.

The driver said in a cracking voice, "Jesus, mister, what in the world happened to you?"

I ignored the question and pulled out my .45. His lips went white. I grinned humorlessly, stuck the automatic under my denim jacket in my waistband against my spine, and climbed into the van and sat in the shotgun position. "Just run me over to the airport," I said calmly.

He made no move to put the idling van motor into gear. "I don't want no trouble."

"I got all the trouble they're handing out this morning. You just do like I say and keep your big yap shut, and I won't share it with you. Okay, partner?"

"Yes*sir*." He slapped the shift into drive as I slammed my door. I added, "There's a twenty in it if you make this a solo run."

"Yes*sir*," he said emptily. He punched the gas, wheeled the van around, and headed down the main driveway toward the exit. He picked up the microphone of his CB radio and said, "Number eight, going in carrying one."

"Number eight," crackled the dispatcher, "we've

got two waiting, one in Two B North and the other at the Delco section."

"Number eight," the driver answered tonelessly. "This here run's special, you read me?"

"Ten four," came the reply, sounding just a tad impatient. The driver snapped his mike back on the dash and, as he turned south on Merriman headed for the airport, asked automatically, "What airline, sir?"

"International terminal," I answered.

I gave the driver his twenty as he idled at the busy curb at the international terminal. "Do me a favor. Call the cops and tell them where the airplane is. They'll notify the owner." At his gaping expression, I smiled, shoved the door open, dropped to the pavement, and headed for the automatic doors of the terminal.

The area was jammed with uniformed skycaps and well-dressed passengers streaming noisily in and out. If you like to be ignored, go to the airport. I don't think I got more than a second glance from anyone as I walked inside into the air conditioning. I looked dirty and tired, sure, and I had those blood stains, but hell, dried blood looks like maroon paint, and nobody wants to believe he's seeing a blood-stained man, anyway.

I wandered toward the ticket counters. I'd like to claim that I had a plan, but, of course, I didn't. My only thought was to lay eyes on Wakefield. At the moment, all I wanted was that. I'd figure out what to do from there.

The ticket counters were crowded with customers forced by velvet ropes into zigzag lines. I started at the end and, staying back from the crowds toward the big windows, walked them: Pan Am, TWA, BOAC, Lufthansa, Air Canada, and the rest. I walked the length of the madhouse, scanning the passengers. No Wakefield.

Maybe he beat me here. Maybe he knew the way,

hit good traffic, got here just in time to catch a flight, and even now was 41,000 feet up, the gray chop of the Atlantic Ocean far, far below him.

Maybe he hadn't arrived yet. Maybe he got lost trying to drive through Detroit, hit a traffic jam, and was out on the Edsel Ford Freeway somewhere with his engine boiling over.

Maybe—worst yet—he wasn't headed here at all. Maybe he decided to cross the Ambassador Bridge, bluff his way through Customs, then leisurely drive the 401 highway up to Toronto and go on from there.

After all, I only had Wakefield's word for it that they planned to leave the country. Maybe it was all bullshit. Maybe, with Kohls's death, Wakefield had decided on another escape route, while I stood, bleary, blood-stained and furious, among the well-heeled businesspeople and jet setters populating the international terminal this fine late-summer morning.

I started along the row of ticket counters again, and hadn't taken more than two steps, when I spotted the son of a bitch.

He leaned at the Pan Am counter, talking with the short, pert, blue-uniformed ticket agent. He wore a blue corduroy jacket over his slacks, and looked every inch the affluent world traveler. The ticket agent smiled, and I saw Wakefield's brown bushy head tilt back as he laughed heartily. She handed him a ticket folder, nodded and smiled, and reached down to the cavity next to her ticket station. When she rose, she had my briefcase and the big gray American Tourister suitcase in her hands. She turned and put them on the moving conveyor belt behind her. Wakefield called an unintelligible farewell to her, and she smiled and waved as he turned and pushed through the shuffling line of passengers and sauntered for the concourse on his long legs.

For the moment, my elation at finding him was gone. I stood where I was and watched the conveyor belt carry my briefcase and Arthur Barton's suitcase to the end of the ticket counter, around the turn, and through a rubber-flapped hole into oblivion.

Oh, hell. Oh, bloody *hell*.

I rubbed my forehead, then started at a fast trot after Wakefield. I lost him for a minute when he rounded the corner into the concourse, then picked him up again just as he got to the crowded security checkpoint with its guards and metal detectors. I skidded to a halt again.

Shit!

Digging into my pocket for some coins, I veered off to a small service hallway by a pair of rest rooms. Built into the wall was a row of steel public storage lockers. Fortunately, one of them—just one—sported a key. I inserted a quarter, extracted the key, opened the locker, then, backing my butt against it, I reached behind me under my jacket, slipped out my .45, and laid it on the floor of the locker. I slammed the metal door, verified that it was tight, put the plastic-capped key into my pocket, and barreled around the corner toward the security checkpoint, slowing down to a stroll that exuded innocence as I approached it.

I waited my turn, then walked through the metal detector. No sirens screamed, no bells gonged. I drew a bead with my eyes on the back of Wakefield, now a tiny figure halfway down the packed concourse, and was picking up speed to overtake him when a tall, husky, flat-faced Wayne County deputy sheriff stepped in front of me and invited me to the side with the steel grip of his hand on my upper arm. He couldn't have made dragging me look easier if I'd been wearing roller skates.

"What gives, bud?" he asked laconically in a Tennessee twang, staring down into my eyes.

I faked a thick eastern European accent of unspecified parentage. "I don't understand, officer."

"Whatcha up to? You don't got no luggage. You got mess all over you. What's the story?"

"My sister," I continued in the thick accent,

gesturing expressively. "She coming in down there. I meet her, okay?"

He gestured at my stained clothes. "What's all this?"

"Painter!" I grinned inanely. "I painter. *Good* painter. Trim, walls, ceilinks, even floors sometime. I take break today. I"—I groped for slang—"goof off today, Captain."

"Look like a rat clumsy painter," he grunted. "Mashed up your nose real good, pardner."

I made an embarrassed grin. "My sister, she coming in—"

"Down there, I know," he sighed. "Brang us your tard and your pore to suck up our ADC money. G'wan, keep moving." He let me go.

"Good painter!" I called to him over my shoulder, still grinning. "Zev Butovsky. River Rouge, Michigan. I'm in book. Work cheap." He dismissed me with a wave of his hand and I turned and continued at a half trot down the concourse.

Vincent Wakefield had disappeared.

I checked each gate quickly. The boards above the check-in desks had the names of exotic destinations: Mexico City, Montreal, Paris, Rio. Most were crowded, but there was no Wakefield.

The second gate from the end was Pan American Flight 102, and Wakefield was at the counter, checking in. The destination board said:

NEW YORK (JFK)
LONDON (HEATHROW)

I hung back in the corridor, watching Wakefield as he took his boarding pass and his ticket jacket, stuffed both into the inner pocket of his jacket, and strode over toward the rows of chairs, which were already half-full of waiting passengers. Something must have triggered in his peripheral vision, because he glanced over and fixed his hard, narrow eyes on me, and stopped.

I stared at him.

His thin-lipped mouth was expressionless under his blank stare.

Then he smiled, showing two full rows of perfectly even teeth, turned casually, went to a chair, sat, picked up a discarded copy of *USA Today* from the seat next to him, and snapped it open to read a story on one of the inside pages.

Though he was but twenty feet away from me, he sat with his back to me. It took me a little longer to reason it out than it did him.

Even if I'd been armed, blowing him away would have gotten me little more than emotional satisfaction. No one trades emotional satisfaction for life in Jackson Prison.

I could call the police in. But then I would never finish my job, because I'd have to kiss the money good-bye forever. If it didn't disappear via some airline cargo hold overseas, it would end up held by the authorities for evidence, possibly for years. Things have vanished from police property facilities before. Lots of things. I figured even Eliot Ness would have trouble resisting the temptation of a fortune in small, untraceable bills.

And even if I forswore my mission and got Wakefield arrested for personal satisfaction, I couldn't convince myself that much of anything would stick to him legally. The only person who actually saw him commit a capital crime—the shooting of Arn Vogel—was Arlene Shaw, a Norwegian Wood tenant who's older than God and thinks it's perfectly fine to drive as long as she can see her hood ornament. Her testimony would hold up about twenty seconds.

Nope. Wakefield would maybe take a fall for felony firearm and breaking and entering. But, then, so would I.

Besides, I don't like involving the authorities. I do for myself. As Mrs. Sturtevant had put it, "You use the rules when you can and break them when you have to.... You're the back-door man."

Couldn't shoot him, couldn't call the cops, and couldn't just leave. The job wasn't Wakefield, the job was the money, period. I had to get my hands on it. Somehow.

I needed muscle, but it couldn't be the police. A thought occurred to me that I didn't like one bit. But as I stood there, looking at the back of Wakefield's bushy brown head, I realized it was the only chance I had left, a chance that would cost me dearly, but one I had to take.

I broke for an island of pay phones in the center of the corridor a few paces down from Wakefield's gate as the ticket agent got on the public address system: "Good morning, ladies and gentlemen..."

Digging frantically through my pocket, I rescued a quarter, fed it into the machine, and punched out a number I hadn't used for years.

"...and welcome to Pan American Flight One-Oh-Two, nonstop DC-10 service to London's Heathrow Airport with an intermediate stop at Kennedy Airport, New York...."

The phone purred in my ear once, twice, three times. Then a raspy, cigar-eroded baritone voice answered: "All right."

"...At this time we'd like to board all passengers requiring special assistance: elderly and handicapped persons or small children accompanied by their parents...."

I said, "Blob! Perkins here."

"Hey-hey, Benjy!" he said hoarsely. "I just heard about you the other day. Guess The Man stopped to visit you, huh?"

"...Passengers holding first-class tickets are welcome to board at their convenience. Please extinguish all smoking materials before boarding. Thank you."

I saw Wakefield rise, toss his newspaper away, and walk over to the skyway. I answered, "Yeah, he did. Listen, I'm in a hurry. Is he there?"

"You kidding?" the Blob growled. "He ain't street

legal around the union, Benjy, *you* know that. But"
—he lowered his voice—"I might can reach him."

Vincent Wakefield handed his boarding pass to
a blue-uniformed male flight attendant, smiled as
the stub was handed back to him, then without a
glance my way turned and disappeared down the
skyway.

"Okay, how?" I asked the Blob. "Quick."

"Gimme your number." I did so. "Stand by for a
few." We hung up.

The ticket agent came back on the intercom as I
stood guard over the pay phone. "We'd now like to
commence general boarding of the aircraft. For your
safety and convenience, we'll do so by sections. First,
the smoking section, rows . . ."

I stood and waited by the silent phone, willing it
to ring.

CHAPTER 32

By the time the phone rang, the tourist and business
coach sections of the DC-10 had been boarded. I
grabbed the receiver in a flying tackle and pulled it
to my ear. "Yeah? Perkins."

"Ben," greeted the wheezing, familiar voice.

"Mr. Mascara. How are you, sir?"

"My granddaughter's here. She's five, just the
sweetest little blond thing you ever saw. We just
finished checking the tomatoes. Twenty-four today,
Ben. Nice, fat, ripe ones. Make for great spaghetti
sauce, and plenty to can besides. Where are you,
Ben? It sounds noisy."

"The airport. I'm in a jam."

"Oh," he answered coolly.

I gritted my teeth hard and said, "I need help.
Really big help."

I heard him mutter something to somebody near him. Then he came back on. "Tell me."

I talked for two, maybe three minutes. Behind me, amid the clamor, the ticket agent made the call for remaining first-class passengers to board Flight 102.

When I finished, Mascara said immediately, a disappointed tone in his voice, "That's impossible, Ben. Surely you understand that."

"It's important to me," I said, staring at the emptying gate, my hand moist on the receiver.

"I understand that," he said gently, "and of course I want to help. But putting a snatch on a guy...that's what you're asking, isn't it? It's impossible, Ben. There are many very delicate things going on. I can't involve myself in—"

I interrupted, "With respect, sir. With respect." He listened. "Another idea." I breathed deeply and explained quickly.

The ticket clerk came on the intercom again. "Final call for Pan American Flight One-Oh-Two, DC-10 service to New York's Kennedy Airport and continuing to Heathrow Airport, London. All passengers should be on board at this time. Final call."

A long silence on the phone. Then Emilio Mascara said briskly, "Stand fast. You'll be called." He hung up.

I slowly set the receiver down on the hook and faced the gate. The waiting area was empty. Behind the counter, the ticket agent gathered up some papers, then walked briskly from behind the desk and down the corridor away from me. Outside, a high hissing screaming sound began, the roar of jet engines. Through the windows I saw the Pan Am DC-10 pull forward, loop around the apron with tremendous slowness, and then crawl away for the runway.

The corridor was suddenly very silent. I waited by the phone and fidgeted, desperately wanting a smoke. I felt bitter and helpless and potentially foolish.

The phone rang.

I reached out slowly, picked up the receiver and pressed it to my ear without answering. A young, brassy male voice said, "Perkins?"

"Yeah."

"You're reserved on the eight o'clock American flight to LaGuardia. Be on it. You'll be met at the other end."

"LaGuardia? But One-Oh-Two's going to—"

"Perkins," interrupted the clipped voice, "you'd better shake some ass. The flight leaves in fifteen minutes and you're in the wrong terminal." *Click.*

I slammed the phone down and began to trot up the concourse toward the terminal, passing slow-walking arrivals going my way, and fast-trotting late-runners headed against me toward their gates. Terry—I slowed down, distracted by the thought and the unexpected stab of pain which accompanied it—Terry? In my mind I pictured State Security Company crawling with cops, plus medical people zipping body bags over the remains of Col. Baymer and Kevin Kohls, and urgent, efficient paramedics carefully but swiftly loading Terry onto a stretcher and then into the back of an ambulance, its lights revolving.

Yeah, I told myself. She'll be taken care of. You'll get the job done and get back here fast. In the meantime, as the man said, better shake some ass.

So I shook some ass.

The jam-packed DC-9 came to a final, shuddering halt at the gate. I unclipped my seatbelt, stepped into the aisle, and followed the slow, shuffling line of passengers off the plane, through the narrow umbilical skywalk, and emerged into the hot, crowded, windowless ground level of LaGuardia Airport.

It was midmorning. I was unbelievably tired, very hungry, and wired from the effect of three steaming cups of airplane coffee. I was in New York City without an earthly idea of what the hell I was doing there.

"You'll be met," the man had said. That assumed

the person meeting me knew what I looked like. I ambled along, going with the flow toward the terminal down the old, dim, tiled corridor. We approached a slight incline between two sets of steps that descended into darkness. As I reached the incline, a short, hatchet-faced man in a greasy dungaree uniform with the American Airlines logo on it hailed me from the steps. "Mr. Perkins?"

"That's me," I said, stopping.

"Right this way, sir." He turned and headed down the steps. I darted around and followed his brisk pace. We turned right, went through a pair of swinging steel doors, then walked side by side through a dimly lighted tunnel. I said to him, "So what gives?"

"Don't ask me," he said cheerfully. "I got my instructions, that's all. Right here." We made the turn into an area that was better lighted, better ventilated, and busier. There were three very small, cheaply decorated gates along this hallway. The man directed me to the second one. The heading on the destination board said COMMAND AIRWAYS and the destination was POUGHKEEPSIE/DUTCHESS COUNTY AIRPORT.

I looked down at my hatchet-faced escort. "Poughkeepsie?"

"Yeah, on the Hudson, upstate from here," he answered. "Next to Hyde Park. Rooz-evelt and all that." He gestured at the gate. "You're reserved. Flight leaves in five minutes. Be on it."

"I know," I said, "don't tell me. I'll be met."

My prescience didn't impress him. "You got it."

He turned to go back the way he came. I said, "Hold it. What happens there?"

His look back at me was very old and very cynical. "I don't know," he answered. "I just follow orders." He walked away.

I went to the ticket counter and got out my Gold Card yet another time.

*   *   *

The aircraft was a twin-engine prop job that seated about thirty people. We flew low up the Hudson River in brilliant sunshine. The scenery was truly spectacular, and I'd have been impressed as hell if I hadn't had other things on my mind. Like, worrying that my instructions to Mascara had gotten screwed up somehow. Believe me, Poughkeepsie was not part of the deal as I'd discussed it with him.

But I was in no position to file a complaint with the management.

And then that stab of pain again and—Terry. I closed my eyes and saw the hospital. Didn't matter which one, they all looked alike. The ambulance shrieking to a stop at the E/R entrance, the back door being ripped open, the stretcher lifted out by men in white and wheeled swiftly through automatic double doors as doctors shouted instructions . . . rolling in a blur down green halls as doctors scrubbed and donned masks and snapped on rubber gloves. . . .

We came straight into Dutchess County Airport and landed without any preliminaries. I was the first off the aircraft, clambered down the open ladderway, and stood there in the sun for a minute, waiting to be "met." Nothing happened, so I walked over into the terminal building.

It was brick, well windowed, and about the size of your average small-town post office. There was only one desk manned by two people who apparently took care of all airline activity and did a thriving business in car rentals on the side. The waiting area consisted of a row of five vinyl chairs sitting against the wall below an array of brilliantly colored airline posters specially designed to lure people away from Poughkeepsie, New York. Two old people sat in the chairs, one, a man, reading an old *People* magazine, and the other, a woman, sound asleep with her head cocked back on the chair and mouth sagging wide open.

I ambled up to the desk, trying to look expectant. A busty redhead in a tight gray two-piece suit worked the far end and was apparently trying to negotiate an intricate car rental transaction with a swarthy man who had a dark raincoat, a cigar the size of one of the guns on the *New Jersey*, and, judging from his eagerness to argue, a lot of time on his hands. At my end stood a beaming, round-faced, middle-aged man wearing a dizzying red-and-green-checked blazer over an open-necked white shirt and black pants. He looked so eager to serve me that I wanted to smack him. As I approached, he said, "Oh, Mr. Perkins!"

I slowed down suspiciously and said, "Yeah."

"Lord, I can't tell you how sorry I am." He beckoned me closer, apparently wanting to be able to talk out of the earshot of the others in the room. When I got to him he whispered, "Just one of those airline screwups, you know? Believe me, it happens a lot. I'm just sorry it had to happen to you."

I caught on. "Well," I said with considerable sternness, "I've made it clear the airline has to reimburse me for all this inconvenience."

"Oh, certainly, I'm sure," he gushed. "And I've had specific instructions in your case. The plane you came in on is being held till you reboard, and will take you right back to LaGuardia. Then there's an American flight all booked for you back to Detroit. Compliments of the airline."

"Thanks," I said grudgingly, taking the proffered ticket jacket from his hand.

"Least we can do. Again, so sorry about all this." He gestured to me. "Right this way. No sense in delaying things further, eh? Ha-ha."

Several passengers had come into the building and waited in an impatient line behind the swarthy man with the cigar. My agent came around from behind the counter, opened an unmarked closet door next to me, and stood back. "There."

I looked, then bent down and picked up my briefcase and the big gray American Tourister suitcase. "That's them, all right," I said, keeping my voice level.

"Good." His voice had a slight edge to it. He took my elbow and led me to the door facing the apron. Outside, the twin-engines of the commuter plane roared impatiently. "Just one thing," he said very softly, facing the window.

"Yeah, pal."

"I was told to give you a message."

"Yeah? What?"

"I don't know what it means," he murmured. "The message is, 'This will cost you.'"

I snorted, nothing more.

The friendly, round-faced agent said in a louder voice, "Well, again, sorry about this, Mr. Perkins. There's your plane, you're all set." He turned to go back to his counter.

I set the cases down. "Not so fast."

"Yes, sir?" He faced me, eyes cold.

"Cigars." I named my brand.

He stared at me. His face stayed friendly, but a chilly gray cast came over his features. He boomed, "Why, certainly!" went to the counter, and brought me a five-pack of my favorites.

I flipped him a half buck, turned my back on him, and stared out the window at the waiting plane. Very carefully, very deliberately I took a cigar out of the pack, stuck it in my teeth, and lighted it with my last wood match. I filled my lungs with exhilarating smoke and stared at the plane. I saw blurry faces behind the windows. Waiting for me.

And they could keep waiting till I finished my smoke.

Terry—the operating room. I saw the stainless steel table, the stools, the sideboys with glinting silver tools, the anesthesiology equipment, the light fixtures staring down like medieval steel eyes, the silent respirator and blinking monitors on the walls. I looked for the nurses, I looked for the doctors, I looked for Terry.

I searched the room thoroughly, in my mind's eye, and found no one.

CHAPTER 33

Joann Sturtevant threw back her head and laughed and laughed. "Oh, God, that's the most hilarious thing I've ever heard!"

I fidgeted with my unlighted cigar. "What's that, ma'am?"

On this late summer afternoon she wore a pure white strapless sundress and her blondish hair was loose around her shoulders. She'd improved her tan some since I last saw her; it made her face look less lined, and today she looked like she was in her early fifties. She got control of herself, folded her thin arms in front of her, and said, eyes twinkling, "I just wish I could have seen the look on Wakefield's face when he went to baggage claim at Heathrow . . . and waited . . . and waited."

"Oh, he got luggage all right," I answered dully. "Lookalikes, with old Sears catalogs in them."

Today we sat out back of her mansion, on a sweeping oval cement patio that looked bigger than the runway apron at Dutchess County Airport. Off in the distance, gaggles of well-dressed golfers roamed the course. Mrs. Sturtevant's Olympic-sized pool lapped lusciously next to us. We sat in well-upholstered patio chairs at a solid, glass-topped table that was bare except for my ashtray plus Mrs. Sturtevant's gold pen, blank legal pad, and battery-powered Sharp calculator. The briefcase and the suitcase stood unopened at Mrs. Sturtevant's sandaled feet like expectant dogs at the dinner table.

Joann Sturtevant kept her amused expression as her uniformed maid brought her a king-sized glass full of chipped ice and clear liquid. I lighted my cigar as the maid walked away, and when she was out of earshot Mrs. Sturtevant said, "I know Mascara's got a lot of clout, but I'm surprised he could swing switching the luggage like that."

"Guess you didn't know the union's got the baggage handlers organized," I replied, puffing. "Has for years, since when I worked for them, even."

"No, I didn't know that," she said indifferently, then grinned. "First time an airline luggage foul-up has ever worked to my advantage. Tell me; when you flew back from New York, did you check the cases in as baggage?"

"You kidding? I carried 'em on. Hell, I'd have locked 'em to my wrists if I'd had handcuffs with me."

She laughed briefly. "May I?" she asked politely, looking down at the cases.

"Be my guest."

I sat back in my chair and smoked and watched as Mrs. Sturtevant flopped both cases open, sighed, then began piling the bundles of cash onto the table. As she worked, she entered the total amount of each bundle in her little calculator. It whirred and purred and the paper tape lurched out longer and longer like a thin white tongue as the bundles of cash mounted in an irregular green rubber-banded wall around her. As she worked, I saw her eyes gleam, her skin darken under the influence of something quite apart from her tan.

When the cases were empty, she punched the total button on the calculator with a flourish similar to a concert pianist hitting a final note, peered down at the LCD, and said, "Four hundred, ten thousand and sixty dollars." Her respiration was advanced, she could hardly sit still, and she made a strange smile with open, moist lips. She looked like she'd just gone off a hundred-foot ski jump or enjoyed a vigorous romp in the sack, not that I've shared either experience with her.

She looked at me. "You exceeded your charter by some margin, Ben."

"Just an overachiever. What can I say." I went into my blazer pocket and got out a heavy clipped wad of flimsy papers, on top of which was the Gold Card, and handed the mess over to her. "Might as well do these, too, long as you've got your adding machine warmed up."

"Ah," she answered. "The cost side." She unclipped the papers and began adding. The maid strolled to us and replenished Mrs. Sturtevant's drink from a pitcher. Her employer said absently, "Bring Mr. Perkins whatever he'd like to drink, please, Claire."

Looked like I'd made the grade. "Beer," I said.

"Beer?" the maid echoed blankly.

Silly me. This was, after all, Bloomfield Hills. "Jack Daniel's Black," I amended, "straight up."

"Very good, sir." She went away and had my drink to me by the time Mrs. Sturtevant had finished adding up the expenses. She took one of the bundles, unsnapped the rubber band, expertly peeled off some bills, and set them on the pile of receipts.

As I sipped my drink, she eyed me. "Now for your fee." She rapidly riffled some more bills off, counted them again, then handed them to me.

I set down my drink and counted it. Four grand. "Not that I'm complaining," I said, "but this is more than we agreed."

"Double your usual rate," she answered. "You earned it. End of discussion. Now!" she went on, rubbing her thin hands together. "What about this, uh, excess income?"

Seemed like a silly question. "Well, aren't you going to send it to the other victims that Barton swindled?"

She snorted. "Are you kidding? Can you imagine the can of worms I'd fall into? Starting with, 'How did you recover the money, Mrs. Sturtevant?' If I've counted right, three people died violently, either directly or indirectly as a result of this inquiry. A story like that getting out with my name attached could make life very uncomfortable."

Yeah, probably mess up the party season and everything. "I've got another thought," I began.

"Yes?" she asked, voice neutral.

"What you do with the rest doesn't concern me, but I think you should send twenty-five thousand to Mary Masters in Windsor."

"Whatever for?" She leaned back and crossed one knee over the other.

"She said part of the money was hers, and I believe her."

"Then she should have kept better track of it. Forget it." When it comes to cash, the milk of human kindness is nowhere to be found in Joann no-e-at-the-end Sturtevant.

"It's important to me," I continued in a low voice. "She hired Wakefield to get the money for her. She hired him in good faith. He intended all along to screw her. It's not right and she should have her money."

Joann Sturtevant made a white smile. "It's not my fault she hired a crook. Anyway, don't be a sentimental fool, Ben." She stared at me defiantly from behind her wall of cash. Sort of symbolic, now that I think of it.

I drained half my drink, picked up my smoldering cigar and took a drag. "You looking for other suggestions?"

"Please," she said equably.

"Nice of you to double my daily rate." I made my voice rougher. "But I think I earned kind of a productivity bonus, see? Bein' as you got more than you figured, and everything."

She barely contained her satisfied smile. I was acting in accordance with her expectations—whether up to them, or down to them, was anybody's guess. "I certainly am open to a discussion. What figure do you have in mind?"

I squinted over my smoldering cigar. "Hm. Say, twenty-five thousand."

The satisfaction in her eyes faded, replaced by sarcasm. "Where have I heard that amount before? Seems to be some sort of echo out here."

"I don't know. It just came to me. Kind of a neat, round number, somehow."

Her face went stony. She picked up a brick of bills, split it, counted part of it, wrapped a stray rubberband around it, and tossed it across the table to me. As I caught and hefted it, she said, staring out toward the golf course, "I'll just consider your silence bought and paid for, now."

I pegged the brick of bills back, hard, right at her. It hit her wrist and fell in her lap. She jerked her face to me, eyes fiery. I said, voice husky with anger, "No one's ever bought my silence, Mrs. Sturtevant. If it was for sale, it would cost you a lot more than twenty-five grand."

Her face lengthened, her eyes clouded, and she suddenly looked much older. "It was tactless of me. I apologize."

"Tactless!" I snorted. I pointed my cigar at her, then down at the stacks of bundled, used bills. Suddenly I was filled with disgust at the whole affair, this business of going out at the behest of a pampered, rich bitch to track down money she didn't need. "You think you own the world! Let me tell you something, lady, your grip on things is no tighter than the rest of us. I mean, how do you know that's all the money there was?"

"I know," she answered grimly.

I laughed. "You *don't* know. For all *you* know, maybe I recovered eight hundred grand, and split off half of it for myself. You'd never be the wiser."

"*Don't* do this," she said harshly, yet with an undercurrent of pleading. After a pause, she asked levelly, "*Did* you keep part of it?"

"No." I grinned. "But if I did, I wouldn't tell you."

"Bastard," she said with feeling. She slowly picked up the bills, reached across the table and set them down in front of me. She looked very directly at me. "I don't understand why you're being so obnoxious and perverse. You act like you lost the case. You didn't lose, you won. In a fairly spectacular fashion, I might add."

I stared back at her. "Rah-rah-rah. Sis-boom-pah."

She didn't answer, just stared at me, looking troubled.

"I haven't won," I went on distinctly, gnawing on the end of my cigar, "till Wakefield is dead. And he will die, Mrs. Sturtevant. Sooner or later, he'll come back to Windsor, and I'll be watching out for him. If you ever read in the papers how they find this stiff in a car trunk somewhere, tell them to look up one B. Perkins, Belleville, Michigan."

She paled, opened her mouth to speak, paused, then said, "I don't think I like you quite as much, Ben."

"Who cares? What does liking have to do with anything? We both got what we wanted. Only difference is, it didn't cost you anything but money." I picked up the cash and shoved it into the side pocket of my blazer. I extracted the smoldering stub of cigar from my teeth and mashed it out in the ashtray, grinding the ashes into dust. I got to my feet, anxious for the wheel of my Mustang at seventy miles an hour with the top down and the wind in my hair.

She looked up at me, eyes sad. "But you see, I had a kind of ideal built up around you. The back-door man. But I was wrong."

"Oh, I'm the back-door man, all right," I answered. "I'm just not yours, that's all. Ciao, kid."

I'd walked halfway across the patio when she called, "Ben?"

I turned.

"Come here, please."

Despite myself, I walked back.

Joann Sturtevant sat at the table, eyes fixed on

the stacks of cash. When she talked, it was in an uncharacteristic monotone. "About the rest of this money. Michigan State University has a four-year program in police administration, I believe."

"I wouldn't know."

"Well, it does. How would you feel if I arranged an anonymous endowment for an annual four-year scholarship in the name of that policewoman friend of yours?"

"How would I feel?" I echoed. "I'd be surprised."

She picked up her gold pen. "Her name?"

"Lowe. Terry Lowe. Teresa Julianna Lowe."

She wrote it down carefully in script letters large enough for me to read. She set the pen down and looked up at me with a wan smile. "I'm not doing this anonymously out of false modesty or anything. It's just that a donation of this size could give me serious tax problems. You understand."

"Not really, but—"

She got to her feet and the sundress swept close around her slim body. "But it will be done," she promised.

"Thank you, ma'am."

She took my hand and squeezed it, then let go and stood back against the table suddenly as if recoiling. "So long, Ben."

"Later." I headed for the house.

As I walked, she called, "Don't forget. You won. You've got money in your pocket and a victory under your belt."

I turned, and kept walking, and looked back at her over my shoulder. I waved once and got out of there.

At the First of America Bank branch office on Telegraph at Maple Road, I purchased a money order in the Canadian equivalent of twenty-five thousand U.S. dollars, and paid the fee for it out of my own funds. The teller was delighted to give me an envelope and a stamp. I sealed the money order inside, addressed the envelope to Mrs. Mary Masters, 1090 Elvis Street, Windsor, Ontario, Canada, and dropped it without a second thought into the public mailbox outside the bank.

Marge, the ever-helpful, friendly, cooperative, and incurably nosy sales agent of Norwegian Wood, must have heard the rumble of my Mustang engine as I entered the complex's parking lot in the gloom of early evening, because she stood waiting at the entrance of my building as I walked up. She had a big bundle of envelopes and stuff in her hands.

"He returneth!" she said melodramatically.

"Back outta my life, Marge," I greeted.

"Oh," she cooed, "has he had a rough, tough vacation?"

"Let me put it this way. Arn gettin' blown away wasn't even the low point, you follow?"

She sobered and shifted her load clumsily in her hands. "Bill's still working the gate nights and I've got security temps doing the other shifts. You going to fill the spot?"

I tried to get past her to the door. "Tomorrow."

"Stop by and see me. There's a lot of catching up to do."

"Tomorrow." I reached for the door.

"Wait!" I turned. She extended the envelopes and stuff to me with a fake bow. "Your mail, sir."

"You'll never get a chance to find out, Marge." I smiled, taking the stuff out of her hands.

Inside my apartment, I dropped the pile of mail on the floor next to the big leather chair, went to the phone, and ordered Domino's biggest super-combination pizza for delivery. Then I called the party store on Huron River Drive and ordered a six-pack of Stroh's tall boys, for delivery also. What the hell, I was rich.

I switched on the stereo, laid on some good full-volume Bruce Springsteen, went back to my bedroom, stripped and dumped the blazer and slacks and dress shirt into a pile on the floor, and jumped into my best jeans—faded practically white with a seam torn twelve inches down my left thigh—and a blue T-shirt which said across the chest: HE WHO DIES WITH THE MOST TOYS WINS.

Back in the living room, I dragged a steel wastebasket over beside the big leather chair, sat down, stretched, and began sorting the mail. Following normal routine, any envelope addressed to OCCUPANT, or with a headline screaming YOU MAY ALREADY HAVE WON, or any bill that didn't say FINAL NOTICE on the outside, got the toss. A third of the way down I found an envelope addressed to me with the return address: STATE OF MICHIGAN. DEPARTMENT OF STATE POLICE. I didn't open it. I didn't have to. It was my brand-spanking-new detective license. I frowned at the unopened envelope for a long moment, then tossed it at the wastebasket. It teetered on the rim, then fell out onto the carpet.

The final item was a long narrow box, addressed to me by hand. I unwrapped it and found that it was a box stuffed full of the Rolodex cards I'd sent to Kenny Slingluff. There was no note with them.

I left the open box on my lap, reached out a bare foot, and kicked the wastebasket so that it skidded over against the couch. I took out a cigar, lighted it with a wood match, and stuck it in my teeth, leaving the box of matches in my lap. Then I took a wad of the Rolodex cards out of the box and began folding carefully. In minutes I had ten neatly folded paper gliders.

I took out a match, lighted it, then picked up the first baby glider and set its tail on fire. As it began to flare in my fingers, I thought, victory, huh? I threw the burning glider toward the wastebasket. It veered wildly to the left and crashed and smoldered on the carpet.

I now knew what they meant when they said that every victory has its price.

I lighted another glider, held it till it burned good, then tossed it toward the wastebasket. It left a trail of smoke, crashed beyond the wastebasket, and smoldered on the floor.

You can't win without giving something up. So there's no winners and no losers. No victory and no defeat. Only a shift in the puzzle pieces, a huge, almost imperceptible reorientation, while the world continues its trip down a slick slope paved with good intentions, spinning on its merry way to hell.

I had the third glider lighted and ready to toss when my door latch clonked and the door opened. I heard the happy, piping voice of a young boy: "Ben! Hi!"

I didn't look back. "Hi, Will. You bring your mom, or are you goin' stag tonight?"

I threw the glider and it made the wastebasket and smoked briefly from inside. Will Somers appeared beside my chair, eyes wide, staring at the trail of smoke. He was a big, stocky boy of four, dressed in jeans and a red T-shirt. His blond hair was cut in a bowl. He looked at me and asked in his high, guileless voice, "You playing with fire, Ben?"

"Exactly so, young fella." I lighted another glider and said in a louder voice, "You back there? Don't bother answering if you're not."

"I'm here," Carole said.

I tossed the glider. It mushroomed into flames and was hot ash before it fluttered to the floor at the end of the couch. I heard the door close behind me. I said, "How'd you know I was here?"

"Marge told me," she answered. "I asked her to call me when you got back. She even lent me a key."

Will reached out his big sturdy hand, picked up one of the gliders from my lap, and examined it intently. I said, "Nice of you but—why? Why're you here?"

I did not look back. I heard no noise, and assumed that Carole was still by the door, staring at me. She said, tonelessly, "Because I meant what I

said about being friends. After what happened to
you downtown, I thought maybe you could use one.
I'd like to know what happened, but only when
you're ready—"

"Okay."

"I feel real bad, Ben. About the whole thing.
About that woman, the one in Cincinnati—you were
right, it's none of my business."

"Doesn't matter anymore," I replied. "She's dead
now."

Will looked at me and echoed, "Dead?" Not a
sound came from behind me for a full minute. I
picked another match out of the box, struck it on the
edge, and lighted the tail of a glider. I let it burn till
it singed my fingers, then tossed it. It made about two
feet of headway, then dropped like a stone.

Carole said, "I'm sorry, Ben." She paused. "Please
believe how sorry I am." I stared vacantly at the
wastebasket. Carole said, "Come on, Will, we've got
to go."

Will obediently turned and walked toward his
mother. I heard the door open, then I heard him
stop walking. He said, "No, Mommy. I want to stay
with Ben."

"We can't, Will. Ben wants to be alone. Come
on."

"I want to stay!" he cried urgently. "Please! I
want to stay with Ben! Can't we, Mommy? Please?"

I couldn't turn around. I couldn't look at Carole
and say what I felt, not till I'd passed some time.
And I didn't want to pass the time alone. As Carole
had pointed out, I'm not so overrun with friends
that I can afford to squander any.

I said without looking back, "Listen to the boy,
Carole."

After a moment of silence I heard the door shut.
Then Will made a satisfied giggle, and I heard
Carole walk toward me.

ABOUT THE AUTHOR

ROB KANTNER is the author of *Hell's Only Half Full, The Harder They Hit, Dirty Work,* and *The Back-Door Man,* winner of the Private Eye Writers of America Shamus Award for Best Paperback of 1986. His Ben Perkins short story, "Fly Away Home," also won a Shamus Award for Best Short Story of 1986. His short stories, many of them featuring Ben Perkins, appear regularly in *Alfred Hitchcock's Mystery Magazine.* Kantner lives in Detroit with his wife and three children, where he is at work on the fifth Ben Perkins novel, *Made in Detroit.*